the
Last Dance
of the
Debutante

Also by Julia Kelly

The Last Garden in England

The Whispers of War

The Light Over London

the Last Dance of the Debutante

Julia Kelly

GALLERY BOOKS

NEW YORK   LONDON   TORONTO   SYDNEY   NEW DELHI

G

Gallery Books
An Imprint of Simon & Schuster, Inc.
1230 Avenue of the Americas
New York, NY 10020

This Gallery Books Canadian export edition November 2021

GALLERY BOOKS and colophon are registered trademarks of Simon & Schuster, Inc.

For information about special discounts for bulk purchases, please contact Simon & Schuster Special Sales at 1-866-506-1949 or business@simonandschuster.com.

The Simon & Schuster Speakers Bureau can bring authors to your live event. For more information or to book an event, contact the Simon & Schuster Speakers Bureau at 1-866-248-3049 or visit our website at www.simonspeakers.com.

Interior design by Jaime Putorti

Manufactured in the United States of America

10   9   8   7   6   5   4   3   2   1

The Library of Congress has cataloged the hardcover edition as follows:

Names: Kelly, Julia, 1986– author.
Title: The last dance of the debutante / Julia Kelly.
Description: First Gallery Books hardcover edition. | New York : Gallery Books, 2021.
Identifiers: LCCN 2021030501 (print) | LCCN 2021030502 (ebook) | ISBN 9781982171636 (hardcover) | ISBN 9781982171650 (ebook)
Classification: LCC PS3611.E449245 L36 2021 (print) | LCC PS3611.E449245 (ebook) | DDC 813/.6—dc23
LC record available at https://lccn.loc.gov/2021030501
LC ebook record available at https://lccn.loc.gov/2021030502

ISBN 978-1-9821-8833-7
ISBN 978-1-9821-7165-0 (ebook)

To Mum

the
Last Dance
of the
Debutante

Prologue

WINTER 1957

Lily felt the top book in the stack she carried slip slightly and hitched her arm to brace it so that it didn't fall to the pavement. It was misting rain as it always did when the crispness of autumn gave way to London's winter chill. She glanced down at the books. They should be in her worn leather satchel, but the copies of *The Way We Live Now* and *Hard Times* already stuffed in there next to her composition books made it too full.

A woman in a neat canary-yellow suit with her hair tied up in a scarf of blues and creams that gave the telltale shimmer of silk hurried by Lily. Across the road, a nanny stopped to fuss at her young charge, urging him to put his hat back on so he didn't catch a chill.

This was not a neighborhood of housewives making dinner for hardworking husbands or young bohemians who considered the late afternoon a perfectly suitable time for breakfast. Belgravia was a quiet sanctuary for the elite who, at this time of day, would be taking tea in china cups as they considered whatever entertainment of dinners, dancing, or theater their evenings would entail.

Lily turned off Pont Street and onto Cadogan Place, its row of white houses decorated with columns and balconies like an iced cake facing the gated oasis that was Cadogan Place Park. Halfway down the road, she stopped, tugged at the hem of her navy school jacket, and smoothed a hand over her light blond curls. It was silly to check. She'd combed them in the ladies' room of Mrs. Wodely's School for Girls before taking the bus to Hyde Park Corner, and they'd been perfect because she'd set them in pin curls only yesterday night before bed, taking care when brushing them out that morning. However, she knew not to leave perfection to chance when it came to Tuesday tea with Grandmama.

Lily rolled her shoulder back, lifted her chin, and twisted the large brass key of her grandmother's old-fashioned doorbell.

One . . . two . . . three . . . four . . . five . . .

The heavy black door creaked open, revealing Grandmama's tidy, wiry housekeeper, just as always.

"Good afternoon, Mrs. Parker," Lily said as the housekeeper stepped back to let her into the hall.

"Madam is in the drawing room," said Mrs. Parker, no expression crossing her always-composed features.

As usual.

Lily placed her spare books on the entryway's wide circular table that bore a crystal vase filled with flowers and handed her satchel to Mrs. Parker, impressed when the older woman did not flinch at the weight of the bag.

With one hand on the polished banister, Lily tried her best to float up the stairs as Grandmama had instructed her so many times before.

"A lady does not move with *effort*, Lillian," Grandmama had said, watching her from a chair Mrs. Parker had brought to the base of the stairs just for the occasion.

Lily could still remember the frustration rising in her like water trapped behind a dam as she "floated" again and again up and down the stairs. Finally, Grandmama had said, "That will have to be good enough, I suppose," letting Lily know that it would never be enough.

At the top of the stairs, Lily turned to her right, knocking softly on the drawing room door and waiting.

"Enter," came Grandmama's rich, measured voice.

Lily twisted the brass handle to push open the heavy door and—

Stopped.

Everything in the room was as it should be. Grandmama's pure white hair was swept into the prim chignon she always wore, and there wasn't a crease on her emerald dress with its long, slim sleeves that tapered to her wrists. As always, a silver tea tray sat next to Grandmama, the china cups painted with pale pink roses accented with turquoise ribbons and gold scalloped rims at the ready. But instead of just one seat angled to face Grandmama, there were two.

"Mummy?" Lily asked. It was Tuesday tea, not Friday dinner. Mummy never accompanied her to tea.

Mummy offered a weak smile, but Lily could see the way her hands shook in her lap.

"Good afternoon, Lillian. Your mother will be joining us today," said Grandmama. "Please sit down."

With careful steps, Lily crossed the room to her chair and lowered herself into it as she'd been taught. Ankles crossed and to the side. Back straight. Hands resting in her lap. After a full day at school, it took every inch of discipline not to slouch with exhaustion.

"Your mother is here because something has happened," said Grandmama as she placed the silver strainer on top of one of the china cups and poured the first cup of tea.

"Has something happened to Joanna?" Lily asked before she could stop herself.

Mummy stiffened, and the faint lines on Grandmama's forehead deepened.

"We do not speak of that woman in this house," Grandmama reminded her.

Mummy's hands twisted over and over themselves, and guilt flushed Lily's cheeks. She knew better than to ask about her older sister.

"I'm sorry," she said, directing the words mostly to Mummy. "Please tell me what's happened."

"Show her, Josephine," said Grandmama, giving her daughter-in-law a crisp nod.

Mummy reached for her handbag that sat on the table next to her chair and pulled out an ivory envelope. She moved to open it, but Grandmama said, "Let Lillian read it herself."

Lily took the envelope from Mummy and read the direction.

Mrs. Michael Nicholls
17 Harley Gardens
London
SW10

She slid her fingers through the slit made by Mummy's letter opener and pulled the card out.

Her eyes went wide.

"Read it aloud," said Grandmama, satisfaction playing at the corner of her lips.

She swallowed and began to read, "'The Lord Chamberlain is commanded by Her Majesty to summon Mrs. Michael Nicholls and Miss Lillian Nicholls to an Afternoon Presentation Party at Buckingham Palace on Wednesday, the 19th of March, from 3:30 to 5:30 o'clock p.m.'"

Mummy leaned forward in her seat. "You're going to be presented at court, Lily."

The breath left Lily's lungs in a great whoosh. "Presented?"

"Just as your mother and I were presented, as were all of the women on your father's side of the family," said Grandmama.

"Your aunt Angelica, too," said Mummy, her smile quivering with unshed tears.

"You're going to be a debutante, Lillian," said Grandmama. "One of the last."

"The Queen has decided that 1958 will be the final year of the court presentations," Mummy explained.

"A tradition of centuries, gone," said Grandmama, her tone arch. It was the closest to disapproval that Lily had ever heard her when speaking of the Queen.

Lily shook her head. "I remember that the final presentations are next year. It's all some of the girls at school talk about. But me? A debutante?"

"It's part of your lineage. This is what Nicholls women do," said Grandmama.

"And Bute women," Mummy reminded her mother-in-law. "Angelica telephoned to say that Georgina received her invitation today as well. You'll both be presented, and you'll both do the Season."

At least her cousin would be by her side, but still she hesitated. She hadn't expected to become a debutante, because everything from the court presentation party to the Season required the support of a willing family.

"Who will present me?" she asked.

Mummy swallowed, but straightened a fraction of an inch, the black silk of her best day dress rustling softly. "I will. You're my daughter. It's only right that I should."

A girl could be presented to the Queen only by a woman who had herself been presented, but Lily couldn't imagine Mummy standing in the queue outside the palace with all of the other mothers and debutantes. Not when the circle of people Mummy willingly associated with was so small.

"Your mother agrees that it is time she reenters society," said Grandmama, seeming to read Lily's mind. "It has been long enough since Michael died."

Mummy's hands went white at the knuckles at the mention of Lily's late father. It had been eighteen years since Mummy had retreated to this half-reclusive life. Since she'd last worn color outside of her bedroom. Lily had never known her mother to be anything except what she was now.

"She lost her bloom when she came back from America and Michael wasn't there to greet her at the port. I know it was her greatest regret that she wasn't there when he died," Aunt Angelica had once said before hurriedly adding, "Of course, none of that is your fault, dear. Or your sister's for that matter. Who could have known that when Joanna fell ill, Michael would, too?"

But Lily could still remember the sinking sensation that had tugged at her when she realized that it might have been Joanna's illness that had called Mummy to America, but it was the newborn Lily who had been the anchor that had kept her there.

"Your mother will accompany you through the Season, and I, of course, will guide you and lend my support at a few of the more important parties," said Grandmama, pulling Lily back to the drawing room, the tea, the invitation. "Do you have any questions?"

Lily looked between Grandmama and Mummy. "Do I have to be a debutante?"

Grandmama's cup rattled against its saucer. "*Have* to be? Do you know how many thousands of girls applied to the palace for an invitation? I wrote to the lord chamberlain myself to secure you a position."

"I'm sure Lily didn't mean to sound ungrateful," said Mummy, shooting Lily a worried look.

Grandmama fixed Lily with a hard stare. "I should hope not, especially when I am underwriting the cost of your Season."

Dread rose in Lily's throat.

Not another allowance.

She knew she should be grateful to Grandmama because, without her, she and Mummy wouldn't have the house on Harley Gardens, and Lily wouldn't be able to afford to attend Mrs. Wodely's. There would be no money for shoes and handbags—even if their housekeeper, Hannah, had taught her long ago how to cut a pattern and thread a sewing machine.

Lily could still remember a time before Grandmama had swept into their lives like a savior. Mummy had tried hard to hide it, but even at twelve Lily had known that her mother was desperate. So one Saturday afternoon, Mummy had put on her best dress and left Lily with Hannah, only to return some hours later. Mummy had called her into their little-used sitting room and told her that she would be going to a new school—one her Grandmama had selected.

Soon there was more money for little things like new hats and gloves for all seasons, and Hannah lit the coal fires in both the morning room and the sitting room morning and night—an extravagance that never would have been tolerated before. Yet there were other changes, too. Every Tuesday after school Lily would go to Grandmama's house for tea, and every Friday Mummy would join them afterward for dinner. Mummy had tried to make it sound fun—like an adventure—but Lily had heard the strain in her voice and knew. None of this generosity came without a cost.

"My apologies. I'm very grateful that I will have a Season, Grandmama," she murmured.

"Good. Josephine, the first thing you must do tomorrow is book an appointment at Worth for Lily's coming-out gown. She's tall, but I'm sure they can make up something flattering to cope with that," instructed Grandmama.

Mummy nodded, even as Lily's lips parted at the thought of the expense of a dress from the legendary fashion house.

"Surely I can make my own," she said.

"Make your own dresses for your debut? Who ever heard of such a thing," Grandmama scoffed. "We shall also have to consider your outfit for your presentation, Lillian. It's such a shame that trains and feathers are no longer worn at court. Day dresses and hats seem so shabby in comparison.

"And then there is your dress for Queen Charlotte's Ball. That will have to be white, of course. And you'll need at least three other gowns and a handful of cocktail dresses. Oh, it will be such a bother."

Lily's head began to spin.

"I thought that we could have Mrs. Mincel run up some of the simpler dresses," said Mummy, naming her own dressmaker. "And then there's Harrods."

Grandmama pursed her lips, no doubt thinking of grander times when she had come out. A deb would never have dreamed of showing up to a ball in a dress from a department store, even if it was one as distinguished as Harrods.

"Angelica says that all of the debs are going to Harrods these days," said Mummy.

Grandmama inclined her chin, silently conceding on this one point.

"We'll have to do something about your hair, Lillian," said Grandmama.

"I can take her to Mr. Antoine," said Mummy.

Lily touched her shoulder-length hair, horrified at the thought of trusting it to her mother's hairdresser, who seemed to specialize in the tight clouds of curls that graced the heads of so many of her schoolmates' mothers.

"She will go to Mr. Gerard. He has an uncommon eye for elegance, and I have been with him for years," said Grandmama, her tone conveying exactly what she thought of Mr. Antoine's work.

"For Lily's coming-out do, I was thinking a cocktail party hosted with Georgina. It can be done for two hundred pounds," said Mummy.

"She should have a ball," said Grandmama.

"Oh, no," said Lily quickly, drawing both generations of women's attention. "That is, I'd much rather have a cocktail party with Georgie. I don't know many girls outside of my school friends."

Grandmama's expression softened at her distress. "If that is what you wish, a cocktail party at an appropriate location would suit. The Dorchester or the Hyde Park Hotel, perhaps. And I have no objections to you joining with your cousin, Lillian. Georgina is a good girl."

At least that would be a relief. The thought of an entire party dedicated just to her seemed a daunting novelty. Some girls might enjoy the attention, but Lily had never had so much as a birthday party.

"These next few months will be critical, and we will all need to do our part. I shall begin to write to my friends and secure what invitations I can. While Lily is in Paris, Josephine, you will need to attend the mums' luncheons to do the same."

How could her reclusive mother be expected to launch herself back into society? And then—

"Paris?" she asked, the city just registering.

Grandmama tilted her head slightly. "Yes. Paris. You'll need to be finished."

"But I'll be in school," she said.

"I think we can agree that Mrs. Wodely's establishment has served its purpose," said Grandmama.

"What more can they really teach you, Lily?" Mummy asked, her voice softly imploring her not to disrupt the delicate balance of Grandmama's favor.

"But the school year isn't over yet," she protested weakly.

"Be serious, Lillian. This"—Grandmama gestured at the invitation Lily had placed on the table—"is what is important. You're rather unpolished, and you cannot possibly navigate the Season without attending finishing school."

Lily pressed a hand to her chest, trying to slow her rapidly beating heart. It felt important to finish the year. To say that she'd stuck with it through the end. That she'd done something completely on her own.

"You *must* have a successful presentation and Season, and the only way to do that is to prepare," said Grandmama.

"I thought the lessons that you gave me every Tuesday had done that," said Lily.

"Your manners are passable, but that is not good enough. They must be immaculate. A finishing school and lessons would be necessary for any girl, but for you even more so. You have the misfortune of family working against you."

Her family. Her mother, plunged into the depths of mourning so deep that she hadn't emerged in eighteen years. Her estranged sister, a wild girl sent off to America only to return to Britain after the war and leave her family behind without a word.

"You must be *perfect* this Season," said Grandmama. "You have one chance to show them that you are not your sister. One chance to charm the right sort of man, or you will be left with so few options for a husband."

"A husband?" she whispered, suddenly feeling a strange new sympathy for every heroine of every nineteenth-century novel she'd ever read.

"Or a nice boyfriend. You'd like that, wouldn't you?" Mummy offered her a little smile.

"This is what women of our class do, Lillian. This next year will determine the rest of your life," said Grandmama.

Lily bit her lip and nodded. In the space of an afternoon her world had changed completely. She let Grandmama speak about dancing and curtsy lessons with Madame Vacani, finishing school in Paris, debutante teas, when to meet the other girls she would come out with. There would be fittings and photography appointments—nothing too vulgar, of course, just a few shots that could go in *The Sketch* in March when all of the debutantes vied to have their photographs featured to help encourage the first flush of invitations to cocktail parties and balls.

By the time Grandmama dismissed Mummy and her, Lily could hardly think straight for all of the instructions.

Since she was with Mummy, Mrs. Parker had secured them a taxi to take them home to Chelsea rather than Lily's usual bus. They were just rounding Sloane Square when Mummy reached over and took Lily's hand, the softness of her leather gloves comforting against Lily's skin.

"I know that being a debutante must seem overwhelming," said Mummy, "but you will do this, won't you? It would make me so happy."

If Lily had had any doubts that the next year as a debutante was set for her, that one sentence banished them to the back of her mind. She couldn't say no to Mummy. Not when it had been only the two of them for so long. Not when, for the first time in years, Mummy seemed determined to venture outside of the boundaries of their house.

"What shall we do first?" Lily asked.

PART 1

Presentations

‖

"The Pride of a Family"

Each Season there comes a time after the first parties are firmly behind us that we must reassess. Some debutantes who seemed to hold such promise in the days before their presentations have already faded, while others surprise like a flower that struggles at first and then bursts forth into bloom. It is now that these girls come to the forefront and show what is truly extraordinary about the Season: that any deb may rise to our attention if only she has fortitude and fortune on her side. She may become the pride of her family, showing that she has all of the elegance, poise, and grace that becomes a successful debutante.

One

*L*ily shifted from foot to foot, trying to loosen the hard press
of new leather against the backs of her heels as she craned
her neck and squinted at the long queue of billowing silk skirts that
stretched out in front of her.

"Don't fidget," Mummy murmured, nudging Lily almost imperceptibly.

Automatically she straightened, the months of training in Paris and
London naturally taking over. "We're nearly to the front of the queue."

"Oh, this wind!" Mummy grabbed at the black felt and net hat perched
on her gracefully graying hair at the same moment that the other women
standing against the iron fence of Buckingham Palace let off a chorus of
gasps and giggles.

Lily watched as a half dozen girls away, the gust ripped a petal hat
from a debutante's head and sent it careening down Buckingham Gate.
She clamped a sympathetic hand on her own hat—a white silk band
with a pair of cream feathers curling up to meet over the crown of her
head. It had been an economical purchase, fitting every color of day dress
in Lily's wardrobe, not just the pale pink watered silk that was her presentation dress.

"Don't crush your hair, Lily," her mother chided, sending a glance at
the soft waves that Mr. Gerard had spent that morning sculpting into

place. "Now, remember, when you enter the Ball Supper Room, you'll be seated until you're called. Then you're to—"

"Present the beige card that says 'To Be Presented' to the lord chamberlain. I know, Mummy."

"Do you remember all that Madame Vacani taught you?"

How could she forget? The hours of lessons learning how to make a proper curtsy at Vacani's Academy of Dance in Knightsbridge would be ingrained in her for life.

Chest out. Float down. Steady, steady. Eyes to the ground. And rise. And for heaven's sake, don't *look at the Queen.*

The queue in front of them began to shift forward again, bringing the palace door into view. Mummy gripped Lily's arm just above her wrist. "Remember, this is *important*, Lily. To your grandmother and to me."

The last few months, all she'd heard about was how important this day was. How everything rested on her successful Season. And every time she sat quietly, she clenched her hands to her sides, willing herself not to scream.

"If one little thing goes wrong—one wobble or a misstep—everyone will know and no one will forget," warned Mummy.

Lily lifted her chin, trying to push down the mixture of nerves, excitement, and exhaustion. She *knew* that this mattered.

Just yesterday, Grandmama had held her hand in a rare show of something akin to affection and said, "You are not Joanna, but you will carry around the burden of her mistakes. You will have exactly one chance at your presentation. It is more than your pride that depends on a perfectly executed curtsy."

"I won't forget, Mummy." Lily touched Mummy's forearm and found Mummy was shaking. "Are you okay?"

"Don't say, 'Okay.' You sound like an actor in a Western film," said Mummy, her eyes flitting over the crowd like a trapped animal assessing every means of escape.

"Are you well, Mummy?" Lily corrected herself.

Mummy refused to look at her. "I'm perfectly well."

Lily wanted to press her mother, but finally they were through the palace gate. Attendants directed the stream of women through the doors, politely separating the debutantes from their chaperones. Each deb would run the gauntlet that was her presentation alone.

"Remember that you need to say hello to Fenella Melcrew and Claudia Lessing. It was kind of them to invite you to their deb's luncheons so you can meet other girls," said Mummy.

"I remember," she said.

Mummy gave her one last appraising look that melted into a quiet smile. "You look beautiful. I will see you at the reception after."

Lily watched her mother—distinctive in her somber widow's black with long white gloves that were a nod to their courtly surroundings—fade into the stream of chaperones destined for the Edwardian Ballroom. There her mother would wait, listening to the String Band of the Irish Guards with all of the other mothers, aunts, and grandmothers who'd themselves been presented as girls. There would be one or two professional chaperones, too—women who had the indisputable credentials of having been a debutante themselves and whose services could be purchased at great expense to bring out girls whose families lacked the necessary background to make a presentation. New money, new status—these girls and their families were trying their best to break their way into the rarified circle that women like Mummy and Grandmama had grown up and thrived in before completing their ultimate purpose.

For Mummy, that had been marrying Lieutenant Michael Nicholls and bearing first Joanna and then, later in life, Lily. Now, facing the same task that marked her mother's launch into society, Lily let herself be swept up into the steady stream of excited, chattering debutantes headed into the Ball Supper Room.

On her way in, she nodded hello to a few women she recognized from Mrs. Wodely's School for Girls as well as her Parisian finishing school, Madame Corbin's, as she cast glances around the ornate Ball Supper Room. The walls glowed in ivory and gilt, illuminated with enormous teardrop chandeliers. Gilt chairs set up with military precision filled the room, and half were already occupied. An attendant ushered her to a middle row. Careful to keep her full calf-length blush skirts free from catching on a stray nail or ill-placed heel, Lily shuffled her way down the row and took her seat next to a brunette girl who trembled so badly the two presentation cards she clutched flapped against each other.

Lily smiled at the girl, trying her best to look reassuring and friendly. "Hello."

The brunette looked up, eyes so wide that Lily couldn't help thinking of Bambi. Almost immediately, the girl's gaze dropped to her hands again.

With a small sigh, Lily set about straightening her skirts so they wouldn't wrinkle. The irony was, of course, that this girl next to her had probably assumed she would be a debutante her entire life.

Lily should have known it would be expected of her, but she never really thought Mummy would be able to present her. From time to time, she'd heard stories of the woman her mother had been before the war: a charming hostess who threw gracious though modest parties, danced a lively foxtrot, and could sing a duet when called upon. That version of Josephine Nicholls sounded so confident, so different from the sad, frightened woman who lingered at home, rarely venturing out and never in anything but black.

She hadn't realized how odd Mummy's behavior was until she'd overheard a group of girls at a birthday party for one of her schoolmates when she was eleven. It had been a garden party, and the hot sun had made Lily's limbs heavy and sleepy. She'd found a quiet spot on a bench tucked into the hedge and was letting her head loll back when the birthday girl and two friends' laughter reached her.

"I can't believe she came," said one girl.

"Mummy made me invite her. She said that Lily's mother was her friend before the war," said the birthday girl. "Mummy says that Mrs. Nicholls doesn't come out of her house anymore, and people call her the 'Old Vic,' like Queen Victoria."

As the other girls burst into laughter, Lily had sunk back against the bench in shame.

"Goodness, they let anyone in, didn't they?"

Lily turned to the owner of the smooth, assured voice. The chair to her left was now occupied by a beautiful raven-haired girl whose perfect curls floated down from underneath a small chic hat done in pale yellow to complement her pistachio dress with artful slashes of lemon at the hem and neckline. Her high cheekbones sloped down to a pair of peaked red lips and a sharply pointed chin, and her green eyes darted around the room, taking in everyone and everything in a flash and then dismissing them immediately.

"Hello," Lily tried, cautious after her failure with the nervous girl on her right.

The angular beauty sitting next to her stilled, her eyes narrowing as though assessing Lily for quality. Finally, the girl said, "Hello. I'm Leana Hartford."

Lily's lips twitched. She should have recognized Leana Hartford from the issues of the *Tatler* and *The Sketch* that Grandmama had insisted she study since she'd returned from Paris, replacing schoolbooks with gossip. The society journalists had declared only two weeks ago that Leana was one of two serious contenders for Deb of the Year—the other being a petite blonde named Juliet Milner, whom Lily hadn't met yet. Last Thursday, one of the papers had run an extensive article detailing Leana's wardrobe for the Season designed by favorite of the Queen, Norman Hartnell.

"How do you do? I'm Lily Nicholls," she said.

Leana took her proffered hand with a laugh. "The Old Vic's daughter?"

Lily yanked her hand back. "People are rarely so thoughtless as to call my mother that in front of me."

Leana's eyes widened, and Lily thought she might huff, but instead Leana did something completely unexpected. She smiled.

"That was unkind of me, wasn't it? I say the most unthinking things. You must forgive me," said Leana.

This time it was Lily's turn to be surprised. It wasn't a real apology, but Leana did sound contrite.

"Some of the dresses here are simply shocking, don't you think?" Leana continued, taking in their fellow debs.

"Shocking?"

Leana waved a gloved hand. "Surely we can all do better than a second-rate dressmaker."

"I think most of them are rather pretty," said Lily.

Leana shot her a look. "Which ones? I challenge you to name one other than you and me."

Lily craned her neck and spotted Philippa Groves, who'd been at school with her. "There. Look at Philippa's floral dress."

Leana turned to where Philippa laughed with a girl named Ivy, who'd been in Paris at Madame Corbin's, and a few others Lily vaguely knew. When Philippa looked up and caught Lily's eye, she lifted her hand in an effortlessly elegant wave. Lily waved back, feeling far more gangly than the sophisticated Philippa.

"You know her?" Leana asked.

"We used to compete for the same prizes in English at school."

"She's very pretty," said Leana, the way a horse trainer might size up the competition before a race.

"She is. And I know for a fact that her dress came from Troubadour." She knew that because she and Mummy had passed by Philippa and her mother on their way into the shop by Claridge's.

"But what about all of the girls who had to shop at Harrods? Imagine the risk of showing up to presentation day in the same dress as another girl." Leana shivered.

"Not everyone can afford a wardrobe from a couturier," Lily said pointedly.

Leana's mock horror dissolved into laughter. "Don't you believe me now? I really can be a beast sometimes. My brother, Geoffrey, says that it's because I'm spoiled, but I so rarely have my way that can't be true."

Somehow Lily doubted that very much.

"Who else do you recognize?" Leana asked.

Lily scanned the crowd. "There are two girls with their heads together three rows ahead of us, Claudia and Mary. We all went to Mrs. Wodely's School for Girls. And"—she squinted—"is that Katherine Norman just down the row from them?"

"The newspaper magnate's daughter?" said Leana with the faintest touch of a sneer in the direction of the dark blonde.

"Yes, that's right. She was two years ahead of me in school, but we crossed paths in the school play. It was a horrid production of *Twelfth*

Night with only girls to play all the roles, but she was good as Olivia. I made the costumes."

From their brief snippets of conversation over cups of tea during breaks in rehearsals, she remembered Katherine as a warm, kind girl who didn't mind talking to those in the years under her. But then, Katherine was also the sort of girl the others talked about incessantly because she was picked up and dropped off at school in a chauffeured Rolls-Royce, a fur blanket spread over her lap on particularly cold days.

"I've read about her," said Leana. "She refused to come out until finally the lord chamberlain announced that this was to be the last year of presentations. It would have been best if she'd stayed home."

Lily frowned. "Why do you say that?"

"Well, just look at her parents. They've done everything they can to buy their way into society, hiring Mrs. Kingsley to be her chaperone. And the ball that they're planning for her at that awful estate that they purchased. It sounds as though it's going to be a farce."

"And yet all anyone seems to be able to talk about it whether or not they'll receive an invitation," said Lily.

Leana waved a hand dismissively. "Wanting to see a spectacle is one thing. That doesn't mean that anyone actually *wants* the Normans around. It certainly won't change the fact that they're never really going to *fit*, will it?"

The girls in the rows ahead of them began to stand, and an excited bubble of noise rose up over the room, followed by stifled giggles and the shuffling of skirts and petticoats. For her part, Lily was happy for the distraction.

"Finally," Leana breathed next to her, shaking her curls back so they fell evenly across her long neck.

Lily stood and followed the stream of girls, her heart pounding as she reached the door of the Ball Supper Room. Just steps away, she knew Queen Elizabeth II and the Duke of Edinburgh sat, waiting patiently as every debutante that day made her curtsy. All at once, everything she'd been taught since she'd left school to prepare to come out fled from her mind. She might have been petrified if it had not been for a stronger, baser knowledge that to freeze now would be to show weakness. Weakness that a roomful of girls all jostling and striving would surely scent.

When she reached the door where Lieutenant Colonel Terence Nugent, the lord chamberlain, stood, she held her "To Be Presented" card out.

"Thank you, Miss Nicholls," the lord chamberlain said, reading her name from the card.

She dipped her head, preparing herself. A hand fell on her elbow. She looked behind her to find Leana, beautiful and glowing under the light of the thousands of crystals hanging from the chandeliers above.

"Good luck," said Leana.

"And to you," Lily whispered.

Turning back, Lily waited for the lord chamberlain's signal. Then she began to walk.

Her eyes fixed on the figure of the Queen and the Duke of Edinburgh, who sat high on a dais, their thrones topped by a brilliant red canopy. They looked every bit the handsome couple she'd seen in newspapers and on the television at Aunt Angelica's home: her dignified and regal, him handsome and perhaps a touch roguish. Slightly to the side sat Princess Margaret, impossibly glamorous as she looked on with a cool expression.

"Miss Lillian Nicholls," she heard her name announced.

Lily took a deep breath and stopped in front of the Queen on the little white dot on the carpet Madame Vacani had promised her would be there. Careful to keep her gloved hands to her sides and her heel out of her skirts as they pooled to the floor, she dropped into her curtsy. Down, down she sank, her eyes cast slightly low in obeisance. Her left knee locked behind her right and—miracle of miracles—she managed to make her sweeping curtsy without a wobble.

Delicately Lily rose, took three steps, and repeated her curtsy to the Duke of Edinburgh. This time she chanced a flicker of a glance up at the Queen and her husband. They sat, polite expressions frozen on royal faces.

Lily forced herself to walk with the same controlled grace that she'd exhibited when she entered the ballroom. But when she reached the open door and was at last out of the royal presence, she placed a steadying hand on her pounding heart. The ceremony had lasted only a moment, but it contained in it an eternity in which every possible thing could go wrong. Still, Lillian Nicholls had survived, and now she was out in the world.

Two

At the doors of the State Rooms, Lily gave over her card for the reception and entered to the music of the String Band of the Welsh Guards. All around her, groups of girls and their mothers, grandmothers, and aunts chattered, the relief of having navigated the gauntlet that was a presentation safely out of the way. Grandmama had warned her that by the end of the week, any gaffes or outright embarrassments would have made their way into veiled mentions in the latest issue of the *Tatler* or *The Sketch*, and more open versions of the stories would circulate around drawing rooms and through debs' luncheons.

Lily glanced around for Leana, who should have been right behind her, but already the crowd had closed around her and she nearly collided with another girl.

"Oh! I'm very sorry!" she cried, hoping the other girl hadn't been holding any sort of refreshment. When she looked up, she realized she'd almost upset Katherine Norman.

"Not at all. It's Lily Nicholls, isn't it?" asked Katherine with a wide, open smile that lit up her heart-shaped face.

"That's right."

Katherine laughed. "Of course. You did my dress in *Twelfth Night*. It was midnight blue with spangled net overlay and far more gorgeous than any school play costume had a right to be."

She smiled, pleased the other woman remembered something as simple as a costume for a school play.

"How was your curtsy?" Lily asked.

Katherine exhaled as she smoothed her hands over her simple but elegant white organza dress decorated with wide white stripes. "Solid and without wobble, I'm happy to say, although I'll admit my embarrassment over how nervous I was."

"I think we all were," she said.

"There you are, Lily!"

Lily gave a little jump to find Leana had glided up next to her.

"You were so quick you escaped from me. I've decided you're the most interesting person here, and I can't be without you. Now, come with me. We'll have a chat and compare notes," said Leana, looping her hand through Lily's arm and casting a tight smile back at Katherine. "You don't mind, do you?"

Katherine, watching with what Lily suspected was amusement, swept her hand out in front of her. "Please do."

Lily opened her mouth to introduce the two, when Leana spun on her heel, dragging Lily in a large circle along with her.

"I'm so glad I was there to save you," whispered Leana.

"Save me?"

"From Katherine Norman. Now, tell me all about it. Did you stumble? I'm sure you didn't. You look so calm and collected."

"Not even a wobble," she said, glancing back at Katherine, who was already speaking to a tall, redheaded girl who had stepped into Lily's spot.

"Neither did I, although the Duke of Edinburgh did wink at me," said Leana.

Lily glanced at the other girl. "Did he?"

Leana tossed her black hair back and grinned as though to say, "Of course he did." And why wouldn't he? Leana's was a breathtaking kind of beauty, and—while the other girls seemed to chatter and flitter around each other like nervous butterflies—she held herself with a worldly-wise sophistication.

"Now, we have something very serious to discuss. You must come to my deb's luncheon Friday," said Leana.

"That would be lovely, thank you. I'll just need to check my diary. I'm afraid to do anything without looking at it first," she said.

"I'm sure you're invited everywhere," said Leana.

"No, not at all, but I do have a few friends from school, and I've been to two luncheons with my cousin, Georgie Laningham, already."

"Georgie Laningham," Leana mused. "I shall send her an invitation as well, if you'd like."

"Oh, I couldn't ask you to do that," she said, even though Georgie, who was far better at keeping up with the debs in the *Tatler* and *The Sketch*, would be delighted.

"I'll tell my mother to send the invitations. She knows everyone who is worth knowing, so we've invited all of the girls you would want to meet during the Season. It means I can avoid all of the other ghastly teas and luncheons so far, except my own," said Leana.

Lily frowned. The luncheons were engineered to allow the girls to mix before the Season really started. Armed with address books, they would eat coronation chicken and then circulate around some drawing room or another, writing down each other's names and addresses in the hopes that an invitation would follow.

"Most of the girls who will be at my luncheon are being presented to the Queen tomorrow, and I thought I would have no one to talk to today, but then I met you.

"Anyway, you will come Friday, won't you?" Leana's brilliant smile transforming into a pretty pout as she asked.

"As long as I'm free," Lily said, a little overwhelmed at Leana's insistence. "I really do have to look. Oh, here's Mummy. She should have her diary with her. We can ask her."

"There you are," said Mummy as she rushed up. "I've been looking for you. How did it go?"

"Just as I hoped it would. The Queen was there, and so was the Duke of Edinburgh. Princess Margaret, too," she said.

Mummy gripped her hand. "Did the Queen nod at you? Smile? Your grandmother will ask."

"I don't know. I kept my eyes lowered," she said.

"Lily did *very* well," interjected Leana.

Her mother's shoulders bunched up, and Lily watched her recompose her face into something resembling a calm mask before turning to say, "I see you've made a friend."

"Oh, Mummy, this is Leana," said Lily.

Mummy's lips parted. "Leana . . . ?"

"We sat next to each other while we were waiting to be presented," she continued.

"Lily is going to come to my deb's luncheon on Friday," said Leana.

She laughed. "If I'm not due anywhere else that day."

"How could you want to go to any other party?" asked Leana, touching her hand to her chest in mock horror. "But I suppose you're bound to meet all sorts of people at luncheons and the first parties, and you'll be flooded with invitations. Then you won't have a free moment for me."

"I'm sorry, my dear. What did you say your surname was?" Mummy asked.

"Hartford." The new voice cut through the hum of the reception. "But I expect you knew that already. Hello, Josephine."

Lily peered over her mother's shoulder at the statuesque woman with rich dark hair swept up and back into a tight twist who had spoken. A strand of large, antique ivory pearls lay against her cream-white skin, set off by the rich cobalt and gold of her jacquard dress and matching jacket. The woman looked utterly at ease in the palace's State Rooms, as though she had no doubt about her right to be there.

"Ruth," Mummy murmured, her Elizabeth Arden lips standing out against skin paled by shock.

Lily didn't know what it was about this finely dressed woman, but instinct had her slipping her hand into Mummy's and squeezing it tight.

"I didn't know that Leana had made your daughter's acquaintance," said Mrs. Hartford.

Lily felt her mother's grip tense in hers, and for a moment, she thought Mummy might bolt. Instead, Mummy straightened and said, "It certainly wasn't with my encouragement."

Lily blinked. Although she may have almost entirely retreated from society after returning to England at the end of the war, Mummy was still very much a product of her upbringing. Who *was* this woman that her mother—governed always by manners and breeding—couldn't hold back such rudeness?

"Hello, Mother," said Leana, one hand on her hip and a hint of insolence in her smile. "My curtsy was a great success, if you wanted to know. Prince Philip winked at me."

If Mrs. Hartford heard her daughter, she did a good job of hiding it. Instead, her eyes narrowed.

"It really is for the best that they're ending the presentations this year. They really *do* let anyone in these days," said Mrs. Hartford before raking her gaze over Lily from the top of her ivory hat to the tip of her heeled shoe.

The insult—the mirror of the one her daughter had muttered not an hour before—smacked Lily square in the chest, but before she could say anything, Mummy tugged on Lily's hand. "We really must go."

"You won't forget about the luncheon?" asked Leana. "I'll send you a note with the direction."

"Lily," hissed Mummy.

"I'm sorry!" Lily managed as her mother began to pull her away.

They drew a few looks as Mummy surged forward through the wall of pastel-clad debs and their chaperones.

"Mummy," she protested, "there are so many girls I'm meant to say hello to. I haven't had a chance to speak to Philippa Groves, and she's already invited me to her drinks."

"You can say hello to your school friends another time," said Mummy, her voice harder than Lily had heard it in ages. Grandmama was the stern one. Mummy was . . . weaker, more prone to long bouts spent locked in her bedroom or holed up with Aunt Angelica, who seemed like the only one who could coax a laugh out of her mother some weeks.

Lily nodded and smiled tightly at whomever looked as though they might step into their path. At the door to the State Rooms, a liveried servant showed them the way down the hall, the opulence of the royal palace rushing by as Mummy hurried the two of them along. Lily wanted desperately to stop for just a moment and take it all in—she'd never have a chance at another presentation, after all—but it wasn't until they stood outside the palace with a page hurrying to hail them a cab that she was finally able to shake her mother's hand away.

"Mummy, what were you doing? The entire point of the reception is to meet the other girls," she said, rubbing at the bones in her hand that ached from her mother's grip.

"Not if you're going to associate with girls like Leana Hartford," said Mummy.

"I would have thought you would be thrilled that I'd met Leana. She's ever so popular. Everyone thinks she might be named Deb of the Year."

"That family is not worth knowing," said Mummy.

"Isn't Mr. Hartford a politician or a diplomat?"

Mummy whirled around, hands clenched as though trying to hold back a wave of rage. "I do not want you speaking with her. I don't know why you sat next to her in the first place."

Years of managing Mummy's moods told Lily that she shouldn't push, but she just couldn't understand what she'd done wrong. Not after all she'd been told these last months was that her connections would make her Season.

"I didn't choose to sit next to Leana," she said. "I took one chair, she took another. I tried to speak to the girl on my other side first, but she was shaking so badly I'm surprised she was able to walk at all. I know Leana seems rather grand, but I think she is more generous than she pretends to be," she said.

A taxi rolled to a stop in front of them. Mummy hardly waited until the attendant opened the door before diving into the back seat. Lily slid in, her skirts puffing up around her from the layers of net that made up her petticoats.

It was silent in the taxi until they had crossed Eaton Square. Then Mummy rolled up her black net veil and sighed. "I know that you are only trying to do what you think is right. Normally, I would agree with you: you should meet as many girls as you can. The handful of invitations you have is a good start, but it isn't enough. However, you need to be careful."

She wanted to ask why, when Leana's name was on the lips of every deb at the last luncheon she'd gone to, but the hardness in Mummy's eyes made her hold back.

"Now, your grandmother telephoned this morning insisting that we call on her as soon as we left the palace. You can tell her everything," said Mummy.

Lily settled back against the taxi's black leather seat. Mummy might hold old prejudices against the Hartfords, but Grandmama, despite her age, was a more social creature. Surely, Grandmama would understand the importance of accepting Leana's invitation.

"Were you a success?" It was the first question Grandmama asked as soon as they entered the drawing room at Cadogan Place.

Lily, exhausted from the tension of the taxi ride from Buckingham Palace and the stress of the presentation itself, wanted to throw herself down onto the sofa. Instead, she perched on the edge of it, as Grandmama had insisted she do since she was twelve.

"Lily performed very well by all accounts," said Mummy, tiredness edging her voice.

"Lily?" Grandmama prompted.

"I didn't fall over or put my heel through my dress or sneeze in the middle of my curtsy or any other disasters," she teased.

"Be serious, Lillian," chided Grandmama.

She fought the urge to grin at her grandmother's irritation. "It was all exactly as it should have been. Even Madame Vacani would have been proud of my curtsy."

"Very good." But then Grandmama looked between the two of them. "What is the matter?"

"Nothing is the matter," said Mummy automatically.

"I was not expecting you until at least an hour from now," said Grandmama, looking between the two of them with a raised brow.

A pause stretched to the point of awkwardness.

"The reception after presentations is an important part of the day. You shouldn't discount any opportunities you have to meet other debutantes, Lillian," Grandmama continued.

Lily hadn't though it was possible for Mummy to shrink down any further into her hunched shoulders.

"I wasn't feeling my best," said Lily quickly.

Grandmama narrowed her eyes but then nodded. "Have any further invitations come in?"

"One came this morning from Madeline Cargrew. Her cocktail party will be on the second of May," she said, rattling off the invitation's details from memory. That one was easy to remember because Mummy had gasped when she saw the invitation card was merely printed and not engraved.

"Perhaps Georgie can ask if you can come along to some of her luncheons," said Mummy.

The cheek of Mummy to suggest that she rely on her cousin's charity while she had a perfectly good promise of an invitation from Leana Hartford. Leana, who, by the very nature of her prominence as a possible Deb of the Year, was invited everywhere and was known by everyone.

"What about Leana Hartford's invitation?" Lily asked brightly.

"You met Leana Hartford?" asked Grandmama with interest.

"No. I do not want Lily associating with the Hartfords," said Mummy.

"But why?" Lily pressed. "Why shouldn't I go to Leana's luncheon, when you *know* that it is bound to have some of the most well-connected girls? You've both said that it's important who I meet this Season."

She knew that the argument would cut to her advantage.

"Lily, I do not want to speak about this any longer," said Mummy, her voice shaking.

"But why?" she pressed.

"Your mother and Michael were very good friends with the Hartfords before the war," said Grandmama.

"And they showed me just how little they cared for that friendship after my husband died," said Mummy.

"You're being unreasonable, Josephine," said Grandmama.

"What happened?" asked Lily.

Mummy clamped her lips shut, even as Grandmama made an exasperated noise. "You can at least tell the girl so she understands."

Mummy gave a tight nod. "Just after war was declared in 1939, Michael and I sent Joanna to Washington, DC, to keep her safe. Many people were evacuating their children then. But she fell ill, and I went over to nurse her. I knew that it was a risk because U-boats were already firing on passenger ships, but my daughter needed me."

"A foolish thing for a pregnant woman to do," said Grandmama with a sniff.

Mummy took a deep breath but pushed past the censure. "I gave birth to you, Joanna recovered, and we were ready to return. I had asked Ethan Hartford to use his diplomatic influence to secure me passage to America, but he refused to help me on the return journey. I learned later that he *knew* Michael was ill with stomach cancer. He kept that from me and did not help me in a time of need. I cannot forgive him for that."

"None of us knew about the cancer," said Grandmama, her voice losing some of its usual frost. "Michael never wanted any of us to worry."

Lily reached across the gap between their chairs and laid a soft hand on Mummy's arm. "I'm sorry. I didn't know."

Mummy lifted a hand as though to cover Lily's with her own, but then she hesitated before shifting out of Lily's grasp.

Silence stretched out in the room until Grandmama straightened and declared, "I shall ring for tea, and then I wish to hear every detail of your presentation, Lily."

Lily bit her lip and nodded, trying not to let the sting of her mother's rejection bury its way too deep into her heart.

Three

The silence among the Nicholls women over Leana Hartford seemed to hang heavy amid the quiet corridors of the house at 17 Harley Gardens, pressing down on Lily from the moment they'd stepped through the front door to the late hour when she'd closed her book and announced she was going to bed. She'd forsaken the warmth of the sitting room's coal fire for the electric fire in her bedroom earlier than usual because cold was better than disappointment any evening.

When Lily woke the following morning, she'd hoped that all would be forgotten. She came down to the morning room for breakfast and found a little pile of her post beside her place setting. On top was a small, buff-colored envelope with her address written in blue ink in an elegant hand.

"Good morning, Mummy," she said, picking up the top envelope.

"Is that what you're wearing to Georgie's luncheon?" her mother asked, sweeping her eye over Lily.

Lily looked down at the two-year-old robin's-egg-blue dress she'd cinched at the waist with a black leather belt. She was proud of this dress, having tailored it just so, but apparently it would not do for meeting other debs. She quickly ran through her wardrobe before saying, "I have a few errands to run, and then I thought I would change into my rose-colored wool dress with the dark pink piping."

"That is a pretty dress. Where will you go this morning?" asked

Mummy, neatening the cuffs of her ebony cardigan that she wore buttoned to the top with a large jade brooch pinned over her heart.

"Peter Jones," she said, naming the Sloane Square department store. "I need another two pairs of stockings and some fabric for a blouse I'm making."

Mummy looked at Lily, head tilted gently as she studied her. Finally, she said, "I was thinking, I know how much you enjoy making your own dresses. I don't see any harm in making some of your cocktail dresses."

"Grandmama was very specific that we should buy everything new," she said.

"Your grandmama has not been a debutante for decades, and neither has she brought one out. She's been generous with your allowance for the Season, but the expenses are higher than even she knows. Sending you to Paris cost more than we anticipated, and even sharing the expense of your coming-out party with your cousin . . ."

"I would be happy to make my dresses," said Lily.

Mummy breathed a sigh of what looked like relief. "Good. The ones for your party and Queen Charlotte's Ball are already ordered, so there's nothing to be done about that."

"I'll see if there's any pretty fabric at Peter Jones," said Lily.

Mummy gave her a rare smile.

"I thought I might also go to the library," Lily said, reaching for the toast that Hannah, their housekeeper, had slotted into its holder.

"You won't have much need for books with the Season underway," warned Mummy.

Lily laughed. "I can't only go to parties and teas for the next few months. I'm sure I'll find some time to read."

Mummy set down her silverware. "These are not merely parties, Lily. They are a chance to meet the right sort of people. *That* is what you must focus on."

But Lily was determined to find the time. She loved reading, and besides, she'd lost the balance of her final year at school when Grandmama and Mummy had declared she was going to be a deb. Saying goodbye to her teachers had been more painful than she ever would have imagined because of the expression on each of their faces: another bright girl whose talent would be wasted. She might not have the lessons any longer, but at least reading would bring her pleasure.

"Your grandmama is right, you should have more invitations by now," said Mummy.

They both glanced at the neat line of white cards propped against the mantel over the morning room's fireplace. They were the Season's currency. At this stage before the large balls, invitations meant meeting more girls. Girls who might have brothers or cousins or family friends and who could make an appropriate introduction at a cocktail party or a ball.

"I've been invited to a half dozen teas and luncheons. The girls from Mrs. Wodely's School have all sent invitations to their coming-out dos," she reminded her mother.

"You've known those girls for years, and half of them don't have un-married brothers. You should be working toward more drinks parties and balls. That is where you'll meet men," said Mummy.

It all felt so old-fashioned, this push to introduce girls to appro-priate young men they might marry. Yet it was still how things were "done." The chance to meet a man from a group of people whose families all knew one another through only a degree or two of sepa-ration and could vet each possible match meant that in theory there could be few mistakes—although they still happened. But things were changing. Debs could and did hold jobs after their Seasons were done, living together in little shared flats. A few girls even earned places at Oxford, Cambridge, Edinburgh University, or Trinity in Dublin—the path her English literature teacher, Miss Hester, had pushed on her at every opportunity before retiring. But all of that came *after* the Season.

The Season was still sacrosanct.

With a sigh, Lily picked up the envelope on the top of her pile of post and slipped under its flap the delicate silver paper knife that had been a gift from Aunt Angelica last year. With a neat tearing sound, she sliced it open and pulled out an invitation. A separate slip of paper fluttered to the table.

The invitation read:

Miss Lillian Nicholls,

Mrs. Ethan Hartford
At Home
Friday, 21st March
For luncheon
1 o'clock
Hartford House, 51 Manchester Square, Mayfair

"Who is it from?" asked Mummy.

Lily swallowed and handed Mummy the card. With Mummy distracted, she opened the note.

Dear Lily,

We had such fun at court. Do join us Friday and save me from what is sure to be a dull time without you.

> *Yours affectionately,*
> *Leana Hartford*

"I don't want you to go," said Mummy, dragging up yesterday's argument that had simmered below the surface, ready to explode again.

"Mummy, Leana is popular, and she didn't attend Mrs. Wodely's. I'm sure she knows so many girls." She paused. "And Grandmama seemed to think going is a good idea."

"Is my request that you obey my wishes not enough?" asked Mummy.

"I'm simply trying to understand—"

"Enough." The word came out of her mother's mouth clipped and firm.

"Yes, Mummy," she murmured, dipping her head. Then she reached for the rest of her post, but not before slipping Leana's note into her pocket.

Friday afternoon just after one o'clock, Lily flicked aside the full skirt of her coat to smooth down a crease in her winter day dress. It was sky-blue wool with a contrasting indigo belt and covered buttons in the same deep blue marching up the front of it, and it made her feel somehow more polished than usual. She'd checked the bow of her cherry lipstick and the angle of her cream-colored hat before she'd alighted from the bus because something told her that today everything needed to be perfect.

She lifted a gloved hand and rang the brass bell of Hartford House. She held her leather handbag in front of her, her grip on the straps hiding any tremble in her hands while she waited.

As soon as she was alone yesterday, she'd written Leana and told her that she would come on Friday, knowing that after breakfast that day Mummy would go to Aunt Angelica's home to discuss the details of Lily and Georgie's cocktail party and no doubt also to receive some support before Mummy's first real appearance in society in years. With Hannah out at the shops, all Lily had had to do was slip out the front door and walk to the bus stop on the King's Road without a soul noticing.

When she had been younger, Lily had rarely defied Mummy—she hadn't wanted to upset her delicate mother, whose moods could swing from fearful to firm in a flash—but that had started to change around the time Lily turned twelve. It had been Grandmama's dinners that had done it. Sitting across from Mummy with Grandmama at the head of the table instructing her mother about how she should manage some aspect of her life had suddenly started to feel . . . wrong.

One night, as they rode back home to Harley Gardens in a taxi just after her sixteenth birthday, Lily burst out, "Why do you let her speak to you in that way?"

Mummy had looked at her as though Lily had reached out and slapped her. "Your grandmama is generous enough to pay for our lives, Lily. Angering her would mean no more school, no more living in Harley Gardens. When Michael died, the death duties had to be paid. I only just managed to retain the house. Without your grandmother, I'd have to sell it just to support us.

"The world isn't black-and-white. Sometimes people do things they don't want to because they need to do them. You'd do well to remember that and not judge me so harshly."

Lily had sunk back into the seat of the taxi, ashamed of her outburst. That day had opened her eyes. Everything that was familiar about their house was bought and maintained thanks to the generosity of Grandmama. Her education, her finishing, her Season? All Grandmama. But there was a cost to everything. Grandmama exerted her quiet control over so much of their lives, it had been a relief when Grandmama had declared that Tuesday teas and Friday dinners would no longer be the norm after Lily returned from France in order to accommodate Lily's increasingly busy schedule.

And now, she was taking her first steps out into society on her own.

The great white door of Hartford House slowly swung open, revealing the housekeeper, a trim woman in a long black dress.

"I'm Lily Nicholls," she said.

The housekeeper inclined her head. "Good afternoon, Miss Nicholls. Miss Hartford is expecting you."

The housekeeper stepped back to let Lily in. She tried her best to keep from staring at the grand entryway as she paused to hand the housekeeper her coat. She'd been to birthday parties at some of the more grand houses of her school friends before, but this was on a different scale entirely. The building's Georgian exterior had hidden a sort of Venetian palace inside, with white columns stretching to a ceiling of gold leaf and frescoes. The white marble floor stretched out before her and up a curving staircase that was punctuated by portraits of long-dead family members who seemed to stare down at her as though they disapproved of her defiance of Mummy.

"This way, miss," said the housekeeper, pulling Lily's attention back.

She blushed and held her handbag a little tighter as she followed the older woman down a plush carpeted corridor. The hum of dozens of girls' voices grew until they stopped at a polished oak door. The housekeeper opened it, a wall of laughter reaching out to pull Lily in.

The room was filled with girls, all dressed in apricot, pistachio, blush, powder blue, and cream, their skirts poofed around them like cream puffs. They chatted excitedly in small groups, glasses of punch balanced carefully in their hands. At the center of it all, with a half dozen girls around her, sat Leana, holding court in a Louis XIV chair, wearing a white full-skirted dress of the finest silk.

Etiquette said that Lily should greet Leana first, but the press of girls around her hostess gave her pause. She spotted her cousin, Georgie, close to the windows framed in damask curtains, two of her friends from the stables where she took riding lessons by her side, when a girl with her short hair styled into a cloud of soft blond ringlets approached her.

"Hello. You're Lily Nicholls, aren't you?" the girl asked cheerfully.

"Yes, I am. I'm sorry, have we met?" Lily asked.

The girl shook her head. "Oh, no. I'm Cressie Blessingham. How do you do?"

"How do you do?" Lily replied.

"I've been sent to fetch you," said Cressie.

"I beg your pardon?" asked Lily.

Cressie tilted her head in the direction of where Leana was watching them. "She wanted to be sure to greet you, but she can hardly break away. She's been simply swarmed since the party started."

"Oh," said Lily.

Without waiting for another word, Cressie made for Leana. Bemused, Lily followed.

Leana rose to kiss Lily on each cheek, the scent of L'Air du Temps enveloping them both in a cloud.

"Just the guest I've been waiting for," said Leana before turning to the girl sitting on the sofa nearest her. "Rebecca, make room for Lily."

Lily opened her mouth to protest, but Rebecca rose without complaint and settled onto the other end of the sofa.

"There you are. There's plenty of room now," said Leana as she retook her own seat.

Gingerly, Lily took the spot Rebecca had just vacated.

"I'm sorry I'm late," she began.

"I know how maddening it can be to have to rely on taxis. I'm always put out whenever Papa takes our driver for the entire day. I don't think he understands how much a deb relies on a driver."

Lily tilted her head as though in agreement while secretly wondering whether Leana had ever taken a bus in her life.

"You must telephone me next time you need a driver. I'm sure we could lend you Smythe, since we're neighbors," said a brunette with a pretty boatneck watercolor silk dress.

"How kind" was Leana's only response, letting them all know what she thought of the idea of borrowing someone else's chauffeur.

"Now, Lily, you must meet everyone. You've already met Cressie," Leana said. "This is Lady Fiona Summerton, Miss Sophie Cartwright, Miss Deborah O'Malley, Miss Elizabeth Yarley, and Miss Charlotte Damrosch."

Lily's head swam with the names, but she said her quick hellos to each of the debs.

"All of you should know Lily Nicholls. She was the only person who was even the littlest bit entertaining at our presentation party," said Leana.

"What day were you presented?" asked Charlotte in a soft voice.

"Wednesday," said Lily.

"I was presented Wednesday," murmured Elizabeth.

"Yes, darling, but you were miles back in the queue. I could hardly wait for you, could I? I think it's absolutely beastly that they had us line up along the side of the road as though we were waiting to enter a music hall," said Leana.

"I loved it," breathed Sophie. "It felt like being an actress at a film premiere."

"Speaking of actresses, did you see the photographs of Princess Grace and Princess Caroline in *The Times*?" asked Cressie.

"She's a beautiful baby," said Lady Fiona to a chorus of agreement.

The conversation spun on until the housekeeper reappeared to let Leana know that luncheon was served.

"Ladies, if you'd like to make your way to the dining room," said Leana.

The volume in the room rose as the girls stood and set themselves to rights. Lily was just adjusting her handbag on her wrist when Leana grabbed her free hand and said in a low voice, "I've seated you next to me on my left. Mummy and I quarreled about it—she wanted Lady Fiona on my right because she's an earl's daughter and Sophie on my left because her father's a baronet—but I told her it was my party and I would have whomever I wanted next to me."

Leana looked at her expectantly, so Lily smiled. "Thank you. I'm sure I'll enjoy luncheon all the more because of it."

"When you were late, I was worried that Mummy had scared you off," said Leana, looping her hand through Lily's arm, just as she'd done in the State Rooms. "You must promise me that you won't let her keep you away."

"I wouldn't want to be the cause of strife between you," she said.

Leana waved a hand as they crossed into the dining room with a table set for thirty-six, vases of hothouse ranunculus spilling over onto the crisp linen tablecloth. "If Mummy wanted to have any say over whom I spend my time with, she should have started paying attention to me years ago. Now, shall we eat?"

Luncheon was three courses starting with salty Scottish smoked salmon, followed by lamb chops cooked just until they were tender as butter and a delicate lemon tart. It was a welcome departure from the endless dishes of coronation chicken for luncheon or cucumber and cress sandwiches for tea that Lily had already grown tired of at the other deb's luncheons she'd attended.

After the meal was over, the girls retreated to the drawing room, and out came their address books and their pens. If the conversation before had been focused on getting to know one another, this was business.

Lily opened her light blue leather-bound address book and dutifully copied down the names of each of the girls who had crowded around Leana when she'd first arrived.

"My drinks are on the tenth of April," said Charlotte as she wrote down her address and telephone number in Lily's book. "I'll send you an invitation as soon as I'm home, and of course I'll send you one to my ball as well."

"Thank you. My cousin, Georgina Laningham, and I are having our drinks on the twenty-third of April at the Hyde Park Hotel. We would be delighted if you would come," Lily said, handing back Charlotte's address book.

"I'll look for your invitation," said Charlotte.

Their transaction done, Lily moved on to the next girl and the next, working her way around the room until she ran into Georgie.

"Hello, darling," her cousin chirped, kissing Lily on the cheek. "This is quite the coup that you've pulled off."

"Coup?" Lily asked with a laugh.

Georgie grinned. "Friends with Leana Hartford, one of the year's top debs."

"Lower your voice," she hissed, glancing around to see if any of the other girls had turned around.

"You're no fun." Georgie pouted her pink lips. "Although, I suppose I should do as you say. I'm sure you're the only reason I was invited."

Lily frowned. "What do you mean?"

"Out of the blue, an invitation arrived by the second post yesterday afternoon. It practically sent Mummy into palpitations because I have three dresses that are at the dressmaker being altered, and of course those are the ones that she thinks are prettiest. She practically had to beg our hairdresser to give me a set this morning," said Georgie, touching her auburn hair that she wore in waves pulled back from her face with a set of tortoiseshell combs.

Lily smiled at the thought of Aunt Angelica running around in a flutter.

"Well, I like this dress of yours very much," she said.

Georgie flicked her skirts back and forth, admiring the way that the white fabric with tiny peach flowers swayed. "Thank you. I wish I had your eye or half your talent with a needle, though. Now stop distracting me. I want to know everything about how you know Leana."

Lily told her cousin about the presentation day meeting, the frosty reception between Mummy and Mrs. Hartford, and Grandmama's interest in Leana.

"How very intriguing," said Georgie, pushing one of her combs back into place. "Your grandmama is right, though, terrifying as she is. *The Sketch* will probably name Leana Deb of the Year unless Juliet Milner nips her at the post. Although, Leana has more articles than Juliet at the moment, so that's doubtful."

"I can't believe you know all of this," she said.

"How can you not?" asked Georgie with genuine surprise. "It's important information."

"How many dresses Leana Hartford has or what tea Juliet Milner was seen at last week?" she asked skeptically.

"There's power in those society pages, and you know that, whether you like it or not. Of course"—Georgie leaned in close—"it's only power if you aren't caught campaigning. No one would respect a deb who is actually *trying* to be named Deb of the Year."

"I hate the whole idea of Deb of the Year. It seems ridiculous to be pitting us against one another," said Lily.

"Well, we never have to worry about that. Neither of us ever stood a chance, although I wouldn't mind the attention. It is what the Season's meant to be about, isn't it?" Georgie asked.

"I don't know. I suppose I hope to meet some lovely people and—"

Georgie threw back her head and laughed. "Men, Lily. We're meant to meet men. To marry."

"You sound just like Mummy and Grandmama," said Lily with a laugh.

"It's a pity neither of us has a brother or any male cousins. They would be useful as escorts," said Georgie.

"I suppose we'll have to find our own," she said.

"Well, if you stay with Leana's crowd, I'm sure you'll meet some men along the way. Just have a thought for your favorite cousin when you do," said Georgie before marching over to a new cluster of girls, her address book in her hand.

Four

That evening, amid the hubbub of the crowded Waterloo Room at the Cavalry Club, Lily decided that Isabel Crawford's cocktail party would likely be declared a success and an auspicious start to the Season's many drinks dos.

Lily had seen the deb of the hour for only a brief few seconds in the reception line that led into the Waterloo Room. Isabel had stood between her father and mother, shaking hands and kissing the cheeks of everyone who filed in. Once they made it in, debs, their escorts, and the assorted family members who'd donned cocktail dresses and suits spread out, some taking up the chairs that had been scattered around the outskirts of the room and others mingling under the huge cut glass chandelier.

Being that this was the first cocktail party that many of the debs attended—Lily included—most people seemed to have accepted the invitation.

"I wish they would open the balcony doors," said Ginny Douglas, a delicate, pale blond girl whom Lily had met at Madame Vacani's when they were learning to curtsy.

"It is a bit of a crush, isn't it? But it does make it seem very jolly," said Lily, maneuvering to protect her gin and orange from splashing over the rim of her glass and onto her gloves as a pair of laughing debs barreled by.

Ginny, who didn't seem to share her optimism, touched a hand to her forehead. "I think I'll find a seat somewhere."

As she watched Ginny peel away, she caught a flash of vermillion satin over wide petticoats and braced herself as Aunt Angelica came barreling toward her.

"There you are, darling!" Aunt Angelica exclaimed, coming to a stop in front of Lily with a cocktail glass in either hand, her enormous skirt shuddering before settling around her. "I've been watching you and Georgie all night. You're doing very well speaking to the other girls."

"Thank you. Have you seen Mummy?" she asked, craning her neck.

Aunt Angelica lifted her brows and tilted her head to her left. "I left her in the corner with Richard Prichard. He always had a tender spot for her when she was a deb."

Lily craned her neck to see over her aunt's shoulder. The entire trip over in the taxi, Mummy had stared straight ahead, twisting her handkerchief in her hands. Her nervousness, Lily knew, was only to be expected. It was Mummy's first time properly out at a party outside of their small family circle since before the war, and Mummy never would have done it if it hadn't been for the sake of Lily's Season.

"You needn't worry about her. You just focus on meeting as many lovely people as you can," Aunt Angelica trilled.

"I will," Lily promised, even though she knew that Mummy would never be far from her mind.

"And if you need a helping hand, just look for Georgie. She has a positive gaggle around her. Delightful!" And with that, Aunt Angelica swanned off.

On her own again, Lily swallowed down another gulp of her drink. To those not acquainted with the Season, being a deb must seem simple—dress up, attend parties, make conversation—but that didn't account for the incredible pressure bearing down on the shoulders of every unmarried girl in the room. They were meant to circulate, spending just the right amount of time with each person. They would engage in light conversation—never anything controversial—leaving everyone with a bright, sparkling witticism that would make them memorable for all the right reasons. And somehow, through all of these snatched moments, they were meant to find a man who would be first dance partner, then escort before graduating to boyfriend, fiancé, and finally husband.

For Lily, things were made even more uncomfortable by the realization that she had more acquaintances than friends in this room—a fact that held true in her wider life. Even when invitations to teas or birthdays had come in, she'd never been able to properly reciprocate because of Mummy's reluctance to open their home up to anyone. Aunt Angelica stepped into the void as often as she could, but she had Georgie to worry about, and Grandmama wasn't interested in entertaining groups of teenage girls in her elegant home. Without proper cultivation, the parallel relationships that grew between generations of a family languished, leaving Lily without the ease of long-held female friendships built on shared memories.

Across the room, Lily spotted Ivy Wark. She began to make a beeline to her fellow Madame Corbin's girl, when Leana, dressed in a one-shoulder deep plum taffeta dress, stepped into her path.

"There you are," said Leana with a brilliant smile, nodding to the drink in her left hand. "This is for you."

Lily set her half-drunk glass down to accept this fresh one. "Thank you."

"I was just about to give up hope that you'd come," said Leana, lifting her own glass.

"I've been here since half past six," Lily said.

"What a bore. That's far too early for my tastes." Leana took her by her free hand. "Come on. There are some people I'd like you to meet."

Leana wove them between silk-clad mothers, stiff-collared fathers, and young men in suits of every shade of navy and gray. Lily couldn't help but feel that people made note as the two of them passed by, their eyes firmly on the possible Deb of the Year.

Finally, her new friend stopped in front of a trio of young men. "I've found her!"

The party turned at once to study Lily, and she had to stop herself from taking a step back from the force of all those eyes on her.

"I want you all to meet my darling friend, Lily Nicholls. Lily, this is Second Lieutenant Gideon Moore of the Grenadier Guards," said Leana.

"How do you do?" she said automatically to a tall man with wavy dark hair and piercing light blue eyes who wore an amused smile.

"Believe nothing he says. I've known him for years, and I've never heard him tell the truth once," said Leana.

Gideon's smile softened with easy charm. "Believe *everything* I say, and ignore her."

Leana rolled her eyes. "Gideon suffers from the misapprehension that because we grew up a village apart, I will somehow tolerate his sense of humor. More importantly, these handsome gentlemen"—Leana gestured around the circle—"are Second Lieutenant Cecil Towey and Rupert Harper-Bowman."

She said "how do you do" to Cecil, who cut a rather romantic figure with his dark brown hair swept back from his forehead and dark-framed glasses, and Rupert, who was all ginger curls and lanky height. Just as she examined them, she could sense them taking in her hair, face, dress, shoes, figure. She felt a little like a kitten in a pet shop window, peered at as potential owners decided whether or not she was suitable to bring home.

"Are you enjoying being a deb, Lily?" Cecil asked.

"I don't know yet. This is my first cocktail party," she said.

"It's mine, too," said Leana before taking a long drink.

"That was rather a subdued answer, Lily. Aren't all debs supposed to be blushing with excitement and in raptures over every party?" asked Gideon.

She lifted one shoulder. "I've been told that the Season is a marathon, and I'd do best to conserve my energy."

"And your judgment, it would seem."

"You won't go far with Lily, prattling on like you do, Gideon," said Leana, not seeming to note the attention of the other men. "She's far too sensible for that."

"Sensible?" He grinned wickedly. "I would have thought intelligent, accomplished, and beautiful would come to mind first."

"All of which make her far too good for you, Gideon," said Leana.

"I think I can be the judge of that. If I'm allowed into this conversation," said Lily.

Gideon threw his head back and laughed. "Quite right."

Cecil adjusted his glasses with a sigh. "It's no use coming between Leana and Gideon when they're sniping at one another."

"You enjoy it," said Gideon, nudging his friend.

"I find it tiresome," said Cecil. "Fancy another drink, Lily? You're nearly empty."

Before she could answer, Leana said, holding her nearly empty glass that had been full just moments before, "That's so kind of you, Cecil."

"I'll fetch one for you," said Rupert, blushing deep to the roots of his ginger hair.

Leana flicked her dark hair behind her one bare shoulder. "Cecil, you can bring me mine. Rupert, you can fetch Lily's."

Lily's stomach was already churning thanks to nerves, a lack of dinner, and the gin she'd just consumed, but it seemed to give Leana a sense of satisfaction to send these young men scrambling about.

As the two men hurried away, Gideon said, "Cecil and I are both in the Grenadier Guards, so we're tired of each other's stories."

"What about Rupert?" Lily asked.

"He's Cressie Blessingham's boyfriend," said Gideon.

"Although she could do a great deal better," said Leana with a sniff.

"You're not the one dating him, Leana, so I don't think your opinion really matters," said Gideon.

"What's the matter with Rupert?" asked Lily.

"He's just so . . . ordinary. Cressie could be so much more ambitious for herself. His family is hardly noteworthy, and what is he doing with his life?" asked Leana.

"He's a civil servant, and a good one I'm given to understand," said Gideon.

Leana turned to her. "Lily, am I being unkind?"

Lily looked up from her drink. "Perhaps a little."

Gideon looked smug, and for a moment, she thought Leana might turn on her. Instead, Leana laughed. "You're right. Of course you're right. I'm appointing you my moral compass this Season. You can be a good influence on me."

"What a miserable job. Leave Lily alone to have her own Season," said Gideon.

The crowd in front of them shifted enough for Rupert and Cecil to squeeze through with their drinks.

"That didn't take very long," said Lily, smiling her thanks.

"We fought bravely and were triumphant," said Cecil.

Rupert handed Leana her drink and then jerked his head to the right. "Isn't that the Millionaire Deb?"

Lily followed his eyes until she spotted Katherine Norman across the room. She sparkled in a white dress of shimmering material tied at the waist with a wide belt of indigo velvet. Although Katherine couldn't be more than a couple of years older than most of the girls in this room, standing alone near the doors, she seemed impossibly sophisticated. Perhaps it was in the tilt of her head and slight lift of the left side of her lips that seemed to say that she'd taken all of this in and found it somehow amusing—as though the Season was part of an elaborate joke only she knew the punch line to.

"I heard Walter Norman's planning on inviting nearly every officer in our regiment, the Coldstream Guards, and the Scots Guards to his daughter's ball," said Cecil.

"I knew her at school," said Lily.

"Who? The Millionaire Deb?" Cecil asked.

"Katherine. Yes," she said, refusing to use the nickname. She knew all too well how much they could hurt.

"Do you think you could make an introduction?" Cecil asked, straightening his tie.

"Really, Cecil. You sound as though you're a third-rate hero in a second-rate Victorian novel," Leana chided.

"I suppose I could. I don't really know her that well," said Lily, a little dubious.

"There you are, Towey. Maybe being a deb's delight will be the making of you after all," said Gideon, clapping his friend on the back.

"Well, that settles things nicely, then, doesn't it?" asked Leana. When everyone turned to her, expressions curious, she waved her hand in a casual gesture. "For dinner. Gideon, you said yourself that the table is booked for five people. With Lily, Gideon, Rupert, Cressie, and myself, that makes five."

Cecil was sputtering. "But dinner—"

"I'm sure you'll have a lovely time getting to know Katherine Norman, Cecil," said Leana, ice touching her tone.

Cecil's broad shoulders sank under his navy jacket like a boy who'd just been told he couldn't play with his friends any longer. He muttered an excuse about needing to say hello to someone and shuffled off.

"Leana, you can't give Cecil's spot away to me," said Lily.

"Why not?" asked Leana.

"First of all, you haven't even asked me to dinner yet, and I haven't said yes, either." When Leana began to protest, Lily pressed on, "And if I were to say yes, I'm certain that the restaurant would be able to add a sixth place for dinner."

"You will come, won't you?" asked Leana, sounding almost anxious.

"If I can go tell Cecil that he can come as well, I'll go," said Lily.

Leana seemed to wrestle with this proposal, but then relented. "Fine. It really was only a joke anyway."

Next to her, Gideon softly said, "Well done."

Lily gave him a small smile and went off in the direction of Cecil. When she caught up with him, she laid a light hand on his arm. "Would you mind showing me where I can find a glass of water?"

Cecil started, but then he offered her his arm. "Of course."

They took a few steps, and he said, "You don't really want a glass of water, do you?"

She glanced over at him. "No, not really, but I thought you might appreciate some company. Leana realizes that she was being unkind. She'd like you to come to dinner."

He huffed a laugh. "What did you say to her?"

"Why do you think I said anything?" asked Lily. When he shot her a look, she admitted, "I told her I wouldn't come unless you also did."

He nodded once. "Thank you."

"I would be happy to introduce you to Katherine Norman if you like, although I really don't know her very well," she said.

He scrubbed his free hand over his mouth. Away from his friends, there was a weariness about his eyes, and he seemed a little less puffed up. "Perhaps another night."

"As you like," she said.

"The truth is, there are certain expectations. That is, my family . . ."

"Hopes that you will marry well," she finished for him.

He huffed out a laugh and glanced about them before lowering his voice to say, "My grandfather died a few months ago, and the death duties on the house alone are staggering. And then there's the estate."

She understood immediately. He needed to marry well to fill the family coffers. It was a tale as old as time among his class, but at least he had the good graces to look sheepish.

"Will that make you happy?" she asked.

"Not living a life of genteel poverty would make me happy. Anyway, don't worry about affecting an introduction. If there's one benefit to being in the Guards, it's that there's rarely a shortage of invitations to dos like this," he said.

"Lily? I was wondering where you'd run off to."

At the sound of her grandmother's voice, Lily stood a little straighter and fixed a pleasant look on her face and turned.

"Grandmama, hello," she said.

Grandmama's eyes swept Cecil up and down with ruthless efficiency, taking in the cut of his suit, the rather dashing curl of his hair, and the way he stood attentively next to her daughter. Grandmama raised a brow to Lily.

"Grandmama, this is Second Lieutenant Cecil Towey. Cecil, my grandmother, Mrs. Gerald Nicholls," she said.

"How do you do, madam?" he asked with a neatly executed bow of his head as they shook hands.

"Towey of the Gloucestershire Toweys?" Grandmama asked.

"Yes."

Grandmama drew her hand back. "I see." The two words were a curt dismissal.

As though sensing her disapproval, Cecil turned to Lily. "If you will please excuse me, I see one of my mother's friends. I should say hello."

"Of course," Lily said.

He pressed her hand in his, but then, before he could turn, he said, "It would be a great honor if you would call upon me as an escort if you should ever need one."

She blushed. Her first escort? Georgie would be so proud.

"That is very kind of you. Thank you," she said.

"How did you meet him?" Grandmama asked the moment Cecil was out of earshot.

"Cecil? I was introduced to a few of his friends," she said.

"His grandfather died not too long ago. They're swimming in debt," said Grandmama.

"Death duties, actually," said Lily.

"For your purposes, those are the same thing."

"Don't worry. Cecil doesn't have one ounce of interest in me, but I did meet several of his friends tonight. They've invited me to dine with them later. Oh." Lily spotted her mother over Grandmama's shoulder.

Mummy moved slowly on the arm of a middle-aged man, his head nodding softly as she spoke. When they stopped in front of Lily and her grandmother, she was introduced to Mr. Prichard, who bowed neatly and then excused himself.

"Richard Prichard. What a ridiculous name for a man," said Grandmama.

"He's been very kind to me," said Mummy with a thin smile.

Lily knew that this evening wasn't easy for her mother—this whole Season was bound to be a trial—but she was glad to have both Mummy and Grandmama there. There was something comforting about knowing that someone familiar was in the crowd of partygoers.

"Lily was just telling me that she's received an invitation to dinner. Very good work for her first evening out," said Grandmama.

"Will there be gentlemen there?" Mummy asked quietly.

"Yes," said Lily, earning a round of approving nods.

"And who will be in the party?" asked Grandmama.

"Cecil, Second Lieutenant Gideon Moore of the Grenadier Guards, and Rupert Harper-Bowman," she said.

Something close to approval flickered across Grandmama's face. "I came out with Rupert's grandmother."

"And I came out with his mother," said Mummy.

"Who are the girls?" Grandmama asked.

"Rupert's girlfriend, Cressie."

"Sir Blessingham's daughter. That is very good," said Grandmama.

"And Leana Hartford will make it six," she said.

Immediately her mother stiffened. "Lily, I've told you my feelings about the Hartfords. They can't be trusted."

"But, Mummy, it was Leana who invited me to dinner. Why would she do that if she is being unkind?"

"She was the one who asked you to dinner? Even after you said no to her luncheon?" Mummy asked.

"You said no to Leana Hartford's deb's luncheon?" asked Grandmama.

No matter the truth or a lie, either her mother or her grandmother was going to be displeased with her.

Does it really matter?

The thought struck her with the blinding brilliance of lightning. This wasn't Mummy's or Grandmama's Season. They didn't need to get along with the girls that she met. *She* had to find her own way among this crowd. These were her friendships, just as it was her own life.

"I went this afternoon while you were with Aunt Angelica, Mummy," she said.

"Lily!" her mother cried.

"Josephine, be reasonable for once and do not make a scene," scolded Grandmama. "How was the luncheon?"

"I met about three dozen other girls. I found the majority of them very pleasant, and a few were even good company," she said.

"And addresses?"

"I have them all." She paused. "Including Lady Fiona's."

"The Earl of Summerton's daughter?" Grandmama asked.

"Yes," she said.

Even Mummy had to look impressed despite making a show of being miserable about Lily's betrayal.

"Leana seems to know so many people," Lily pushed.

"There is a difference between knowing people and being known. I suspect that Leana Hartford may be the latter," said Mummy.

"Please. I haven't had a dinner invitation yet," she said, her eyes sliding to Grandmama.

Her grandmother spread her hands before her. "This is your mother's decision. I wouldn't dream of interfering."

Lily fought a scowl, knowing that Grandmama reveled in interfering, but then she turned her attention to Mummy. Her mother seemed to waver a moment before saying, "No. I won't allow it, and that is final."

Lily took a deep breath. "No, Mummy, it's not."

"I beg your pardon?" asked Mummy.

Her heart hammered against her ribs, but she kept her gaze on her mother, ignoring the overheated room, Grandmama's keen look, the adrenaline of her first party.

"I've been presented," she said slowly. "I'm going to go to teas and luncheons and drinks and dances. I'll have the same conversations with the same people night after night. I'll do whatever you and Grandmama ask of me to help advance myself as a debutante, but I will not stop seeing Leana Hartford unless you give me a better reason than the fact that you no longer like Mr. and Mrs. Hartford, because I'm a woman now. I should be able to choose my friends."

Her mother's lips pursed a bloodless white, and Lily nearly lost her nerve, but then Mummy shook her head. "You will do what you want to do. You always have."

That wasn't true. If it had been, she would be surrounded by her books, decidedly less "finished" than she was now. However, this was the path that she'd been set on, tradition stretching before her. She might as well embrace it for all that it was.

"I'm sure I will be home by midnight," she said. That would give her a respectable amount of time before excusing herself and asking whatever restaurant they were destined for to find her a taxi home. It would also give her enough time to study a little bit more before she went to bed.

"Don't bother coming to say good night," sniffed Mummy. "I won't be awake."

As Mummy walked off, Grandmama patted Lily's hand. "Very well done, my dear. Very well done indeed."

Five

Lily pushed aside any guilt she felt at defying Mummy in the argument over dinner as she made her way back to Leana's circle.

Cressie, who had joined the group in Lily's absence, spotted her first and waved hello before kissing her on both cheeks. "Oh, don't you look divine. I love your dress. How clever of your dressmaker to have made the bodice ruched like that."

The dressmaker, who was also the owner of the dress with gathers of chiffon at the waist, couldn't help but smile. Cressie would likely be horrified if she realized Lily had had to sew her own clothes, given that she'd overheard Cressie proudly telling the girls at Leana's luncheon that her mother had taken her to Worth for six cocktail dresses and three ball gowns.

"Thank you. You look beautiful tonight," she said, meaning it. Cressie had the sort of peaches and cream complexion that copywriters gushed about in advertisements, and her soft curls had been pulled back on one side with a comb that picked up the silver thread of her midnight blue brocade tea-length dress.

"There you are, Lily. I thought we'd lost you forever," said Leana.

"I was just going to tell my mother and grandmother that I'll be joining you for dinner," said Lily.

"Then you're coming?" asked Leana, her eyes brightening.

"Yes," she said.

"Oh good. At least there will be one sensible person among us," said Gideon, earning him a round of jeers from the men.

Leana rolled her eyes. "Shall we go, then? I don't think I can stand another weak drink."

"Some real food is what I'm after," said Rupert, glaring at one of the endless trays of canapés with a meager scattering of salmon toasts and vol-au-vents passed by waiters in white gloves.

"Where are we going?" Lily asked.

"The Ritz," said Leana.

Lily swallowed. She'd never been in the Ritz, let alone could she dream of paying for such a thing. She had a small amount of money in her clutch, but only enough for a modest meal and the taxi home.

A gentle hand touched the small of her back, and she looked up to find Gideon smiling down at her. "Dinner is my treat."

"Oh, I couldn't," she said.

"And miss out on all of the fun? You will accept, and you will have fun. That's an order, Miss Nicholls," he said.

She felt the corners of her mouth turn up. "As a soldier, aren't you the one who is meant to take orders?"

His grin widened. "Only if I like the look of the woman issuing the order."

She ducked her head and took a last swallow of her drink before handing it off to Gideon when he reached for the empty glass.

"Thank you," she said.

"Will Cecil be coming with us?" he asked.

She shook her head. "I think he's still smarting."

He sighed. "She should be more careful with him. Not everyone has a house on Hanover Square. Thank you for trying, though. That was a kind thing you did."

"Oh, it was nothing."

"No. It most certainly wasn't nothing. I'll be driving over to dinner. I know it sounds ridiculous with the Ritz only just down Piccadilly, but I hate to leave the car. Would you fancy coming with me?" Gideon asked.

He smiled so brightly, his handsome face lit up with it, that she couldn't help but nod.

"That's settled, then," he said.

"What is?" asked Leana, who had worked her way closer to them.

"Lily will drive over with me. That will give you plenty of room in a taxi," said Gideon.

Leana looked between Lily and Gideon and then back again. "Is that right?"

"Leave it, Leana," Gideon said, his tone hardening.

Lily couldn't help but feel that she'd somehow done something wrong. She started to speak but then stopped herself. Why shouldn't Gideon drive her? There didn't seem to be any prior agreement between Leana and him, and Gideon had asked Lily. Not Leana.

"We should be going," said Rupert, looking at his watch.

"Will you be dears and collect our things?" Leana asked sweetly.

Gideon scowled. "We're not your footmen, Leana."

"No, but you do a very good imitation when you're pressed into it. Be a darling," Leana said, holding her metal cloakroom tab out.

Whatever he thought of that, he didn't say, only taking the tab and turning to Lily. When she hesitated, he seemed to soften. "It's fine."

She unclasped her handbag and pulled out her own tab. "Thank you."

Gideon smiled. "I'll see you in the lobby."

As the men walked off, Leana looped her arms through Cressie's and Lily's. "Now, we'll go freshen up, and I want to hear everything you learned tonight."

"Everything you learned" turned out to be a chance for Cressie, who was simply bursting to speak, to share every bit of gossip she'd acquired in doing the rounds at Isabel's party.

"Did you know that Mr. and Mrs. Balcon are only staying together after her affair so that Cynthia could be presented?" asked Cressie as soon as she'd done a check to make sure they were alone.

"If the lord chamberlain heard that, Cynthia never would have had an invitation to court," said Leana, pursing her lips as she applied a carmine-red lipstick.

Lily pulled out her own powder and gently patted the shine off her nose, trying to shake the odd feeling of being an outsider, watching two good friends.

"And the rumor is that Harriette Pont's ball is already running into the hundreds of pounds. This Season might be the thing that finally pushes Mr. Pont over the edge," said Cressie.

"Papa says that he nearly lost everything before the war, speculating in the stock market. They've only had anything to live on the last ten years because they sold that monstrosity of a house in Hans Court." Leana looked up in the mirror. "Isn't that in Chelsea, near where you are, Lily?"

Hans Court was on the opposite, more fashionable side of Chelsea, well away from Harley Gardens on the Fulham end, but Lily simply tilted her head. "It is, more or less."

"And what about you, Lily? Have you heard any good gossip?" asked Cressie as she used a tissue to dab at a bit of mascara that had settled under her eyes.

Lily snapped her compact closed. "Not particularly."

"She knows Katherine Norman, Cressie, although I'm not sure that I would advertise that fact too widely," said Leana with a laugh.

"Before our presentation party it had been a couple of years since we'd last spoke. She was ahead of me in school, but I liked her. I was hoping to say hello tonight, but it seems that we missed each other," Lily said.

"I've heard her ball is going to cost a fortune," said Cressie.

"No risk of running out of funds there," said Leana with a sniff, as though the mere idea of the Normans' vast fortune was enough to sully them.

"The invitations haven't gone out yet, but I'm hoping I'll receive one. I want to see what a newspaper magnate's daughter's coming-out looks like," said Cressie.

"It will be crass and tacky," said Leana.

"But you'll still be put out if you don't receive an invitation," Cressie teased.

Leana arched a carefully plucked brow. "I'm sure that an invitation will come, but I will need to speak with Mummy to see if we really think that it's the best thing for me to go."

"I'll go if I'm invited," said Lily. "I'm sure it will be fun."

"My, you *are* brave." A slow smile spread over Leana's lips. "Then again, maybe we should be careful about underestimating you. You seem to be getting along with Gideon *very* well."

Lily shrugged. "He's been very attentive tonight."

Leana huffed a laugh. "Gideon is 'attentive' to every pretty girl who comes within his orbit. He likes the attention."

"I think he's dreamy," Cressie said with a giggle. "He looks like Montgomery Clift in *A Place in the Sun*."

"Don't ever let him hear you say that. He's already vain enough," said Leana, tilting her head back and forth to check her lipstick.

"He said that you've known each other since you were children?" Lily asked.

"His family is from Wootley, which is one village over from Elkenhurst," said Leana.

"The Hartfords' estate, Asheville Hall, is beautiful," said Cressie.

"It's where my ball will be held in June." Leana rose from the pink tufted seat she'd been perched on, the taffeta of her dress rustling melodically. "I think that we've made them wait long enough, don't you?"

The other two girls followed Leana's lead, but at the door Leana stopped. "I'm glad Gideon is paying you attention today, Lily. But don't make the mistake so many girls make over him."

"What is that?" Lily asked.

"Never forget that Gideon's great love affair is with himself," Leana said.

"He's only driving me to dinner," she said, a little sharper than perhaps she should have. She simply didn't like the way Leana presumed how she might or might not feel about Gideon. They hardly knew one another, and Lily wasn't some silly girl in a story. She wasn't going to go careening into love with a man she knew nothing about.

Leana lifted her chin and studied Lily.

"We'll see," Leana said before yanking the door open.

Alone together in the powder room, Cressie said, "Gideon always drives Leana whenever they go somewhere together. She's been going to parties for a few months now because Mrs. Hartford is invited so many places, and Gideon and her brother are in the Grenadier Guards together." Cressie nudged her gently. "Leana doesn't like it when things change, but she'll forget all about this in an hour or two."

Lily nodded at the explanation and the advice, but when they reached the lobby and the waiting men, she couldn't have been more pleased to take Gideon by the arm and head for his car.

Hours later, Lily stood in the center of an elegant drawing room of Hartford House, her bare feet cool against the polished wood of the floor that had been exposed when the men had rolled up the rug. In one hand was a glass of champagne, half-drunk and half-forgotten. Somewhere to the side of her, Rupert and Cressie danced while barely shuffling their feet. Leana lay draped over a pale pink velvet sofa, a champagne bottle tucked between her waist and the tufted backrest, and Cecil, who had shown up to dinner to make six after Gideon had tracked him down on the telephone at his club, was concentrating on pouring himself a whisky from a crystal decanter as he swayed on his feet.

Lily's head swam pleasantly as she tilted her head back so that her blond hair tickled her shoulders. Slowly she spun, her eyes closed, while on the record player Paul Anka sang "Diana." She was drunk. Drunk for the first time on champagne and laughter and the voracious need for fun because that's what dinner at the Ritz with this group had been. *Fun.*

"You're going to make yourself sick."

She opened her eyes to find Gideon laughing as he watched her. His tie hung loose around his neck, and the top button of his shirt was undone. With his hair slightly askew, he looked roguish—dangerous, even.

"I'm having a grand time," she announced, continuing to spin. "A grand, grand time."

When she circled back, he neatly stepped to her, taking her arms as though they were dancing.

"Have you really had a good time tonight?" he asked.

"It's been jolly," she said, discovering she liked the way the word rolled around in her mouth. She giggled. "A jolly, jolly time."

He laughed. "I was wrong. You aren't the sensible one at all."

She shook her head and sagged against his arm a little. "Oh, I don't like that."

"No, I couldn't recommend it," he said.

"How would you know?" she asked.

"Because, Miss Nicholls, I believe you are drunk—a state of being with which I am intimately acquainted."

She pulled back, her movements feeling like wading through gelatin. "I beg your pardon? A lady does not drink to excess."

He laughed. "Says who?"

She waved a hand. "Oh everyone. Mummy. Grandmama."

"That certainly is everyone."

"You're teasing me," she said.

He pulled her close again, resting his cheek on her temple. "I am. It's been one of my favorite parts of this evening."

"Dinner was lovely. Divine," she said, remembering the duck terrine, lobster thermidor, and chocolate mousse she'd had with lashings of wine poured so frequently that it seemed her glass was never empty.

"I'm glad you enjoyed it," he said.

She looked at her hands in his, realizing that at some point she must have set her glass down.

"I don't have any champagne," she said.

"I took it away." She pouted, and he added, "You'll thank me in a few hours, trust me."

She sighed. "Fine. Even without champagne, I don't know that there will ever be a more perfect night."

"What's made it perfect?" he asked.

"The lightness."

"Lightness?"

She frowned, trying to push past the champagne to form the words to explain. Instead, she finally said, "The fun. I've never had this much fun. Ever, maybe."

But even weaving through her mind's drunken haze, she knew it was more than that. That evening she'd felt a part of something. The raucous meal, Leana's emphatic declaration when they finally spilled out onto the pavement outside the Ritz that none of them were allowed to go home, the decision that they would all decamp to Hartford House for more everything. Dancing, drinking, laughing. The evening had been a whirlwind of memories with people who were bonded in friendship by food and wine.

That was what she really wanted. Friends. Real friends who laughed and cried with her. People she could rely on and look forward to seeing. And perhaps she'd found that here, tonight, with Leana's group.

"She's very beautiful, isn't she?" Lily asked, gesturing a hand wildly in Leana's direction.

Gideon glanced at Leana on the sofa. "She is. She also knows it. Always has."

She smiled, remembering that Leana had said something to the same effect about Gideon just hours before.

"Is there anything wrong with a woman knowing that she's beautiful?" she asked.

He shook his head, even as his expression darkened. "No, but there are some women who wield that beauty as though it's power."

"Because it is," she said, and hiccuped. Her hand flew to her mouth. "Excuse me."

"No," Gideon said, seeming not to notice her hiccup. "All our lives Leana has known she is beautiful and that it can get her what she wants. That is part of her problem."

Lily snorted. "What problems could a girl like that ever have?"

But when she looked up and caught Gideon's eyes, there was such sadness there. "I think that you will be a very good friend to her, but be careful."

"Why should I need to be careful?" Lily asked.

He leaned in closer and, when his lips were nearly touching her ear, he whispered, "Because I'm not sure yet whether Leana will be the same to you. And you, Lily Nicholls, strike me as a thoroughly decent person."

She wondered at the sadness in his voice, when there was a loud thump. The champagne bottle had slipped from Leana's arms and was rolling on the floor, spilling the dregs of the wine onto the hardwood.

Gideon gently spun Lily to a stop and stepped away. In a loud voice he said, "I think it's time for all of us to leave our hostess to sleep."

"Spoilsport," Cressie called from across the room.

Gideon strode over to the record player and lifted the arm to cut the music short. "Come on, I'll ask one of the servants to hail us taxis. Cecil and I have to report tomorrow anyway."

The others shuffled out, but not before Lily took one last spin, desperate to memorize this evening.

Six

ily's detour to Hartford House meant she was not home to Harley Gardens by midnight. She wasn't even home by one o'clock. The first pale oranges and pinks of dawn were creeping up over the buildings of Chelsea when the taxi one of the exhausted Hartford servants had hailed for her pulled up in front of her childhood home. With no one around to see, Lily had walked careful as she could in her stockinged feet, high-heeled shoes dangling off her fingers. Even as the world spun, she'd let herself in with her key, careful to close the door so that the knocker didn't rattle against its plate. Then she'd taken her dress and makeup off and fallen into bed in her slip, dead asleep in minutes.

Now, in the sitting room of a converted flat in Marylebone that served as the photographer's studio where she and Mummy were due to meet Aunt Angelica and Georgie, she was trying desperately not to give in to the rolling waves of queasiness roiling her stomach or the incessant ache behind her eyes. All morning, she'd been nursing regrets about her late bedtime. Or perhaps it was the champagne. All that champagne.

Mummy turned the page of the magazine that she was reading with more aggression that was entirely necessary and hissed in a whisper, "I cannot believe that you were gallivanting across town, alone in a taxi, until all hours. What were you thinking?"

Lily was saved an answer when Aunt Angelica strode in wearing a teal suit, Georgie trailing behind her in more demure peach.

"Hello, darlings! I'm sorry we're late. It was a nightmare rounding Hyde Park today. The taxi didn't move for ten minutes," said Aunt Angelica as she kissed them both on the cheek before pausing.

"Oh, Lily, you look positively green," said Aunt Angelica.

"What is the point of having a session with the photographer if you show up to it looking as though you've been dragged under a bus," hissed Mummy.

"Now, Josephine," warned Aunt Angelica, "Lily looks nothing of the sort. She just needs a little more powder under the eyes, and she'll be right as rain."

There wasn't enough powder in Britain to save her this morning.

Georgie slid in next to Lily, pressing a glass of water from the pitcher on the silver tray across the room into her hand.

"She was *drunk*, Angelica," Mummy whispered.

"Oh, who of us hasn't been? It's not 1921 any longer, darling," said Aunt Angelica.

"Are you saying I shouldn't scold her? She is eighteen!" Mummy snapped.

"Precisely. She is eighteen, and she was just having a bit of fun. If the Season wasn't fun, girls wouldn't do it," said Aunt Angelica.

Lily took a small sip of water and fantasized about closing all of the curtains and lying down on the cool oak floorboards while the other women argued.

"Have you had anything to eat, Lily?" asked Aunt Angelica.

"No," Lily managed, her stomach rolling at the idea of food.

"Well, after your session with Jacques, we'll make sure you eat. You have Lydia Turow's drinks at the In and Out club tonight, and it won't do to faint in the middle of it," said her aunt.

Mercifully, the photographer's assistant chose that moment to reappear and show Lily and Georgie to the powder room with a strong suggestion to Lily that she might like to "fix" her makeup.

In front of the vanity surrounded by bulbs, Lily slumped down on a floral-patterned chair. "I can't do this."

"You're having your photograph taken, not going to war. Now lift your chin up so I can see what I can do to help," said Georgie.

After a quick assessment, Georgie unclasped the top of her handbag and began to pull out pancake, a sponge, a cake of mascara, blush, and an array of lipsticks.

"How large is that handbag?" Lily asked.

"Large enough. You're lucky we have the same coloring, even though my hair's red. Now, I want you to tell me everything," said Georgie.

And she did, right down to Leana's cutting of Cecil, the drive over—fast and daring—with Gideon in his Jaguar, dinner, drinks, more drinks, dancing to the record player.

"It sounds romantic and chaotic all at once," said Georgie, laying pancake on under Lily's eyes.

"It was," breathed Lily.

Georgie stopped to assess her work and then pulled out a pencil and began touching up Lily's brows. "Leana, though . . ."

"What about her?" she asked, wincing when her cousin poked her a bit too hard with the pencil.

"Sorry. I was just thinking, Leana sounds as though she might be a little . . ."

"Difficult?" she provided.

"Yes."

"Maybe she is, although she could just be impetuous. I have the impression that she's used to having her way in most things, and when I tell her no, it seems to surprise her."

"Are you sure that's something she's going to continue to welcome?" Georgie asked.

She shrugged. "So far she has been."

"I just hope you'll be careful. I've known girls like Leana before. They can be like kittens one moment, but then they remind you that kittens have claws."

Lily nodded, wincing as the movement made her head throb.

"I'll be careful," she said gingerly, remembering Gideon's similar warning the night—morning?—before.

"And what about this Gideon? I don't remember meeting him at Isabel's," said Georgie as she put away the pencil and began applying blush to Lily's cheeks.

"He's fun."

"And handsome, it sounds like," teased Georgie.

She laughed. "And handsome. But I hardly know him."

"Well, it sounds like the Season is the perfect reason to know him better." Georgie sat back and then nodded. "There. I've done my best, which is pretty good, if I must say so myself. Choose a lipstick and then you'll have to pull out the most incredible acting you've ever done to try to look serene and innocent."

"I've never acted before in my life," she said.

"Weren't you in your school's production of *The Tempest?*" Georgie asked, tidying the makeup into her handbag.

"It was *Twelfth Night*, and I made the costumes."

Georgie rolled her eyes in mock horror. "Heaven help us."

Lily managed to hold herself together as the photographer Jacques snapped away, stopping to direct her and Georgie to pose, first together and then apart. He told them they were beautiful, "the perfect debutantes," and that the photographs would be "the best I've shot all year."

"I bet he says that to all of the debs," Georgie leaned in to whisper to her while Jacques was occupied changing rolls of film.

By the time that the session was done and Lily, Mummy, Aunt Angelica, and Georgie were all in a cab heading back to Harley Gardens, Lily was beginning to feel more like her usual self, only exhausted. Her stomach even growled when Hannah hurried them into the morning room, clucking that luncheon was nearly ready.

However, if Lily and Georgie had hoped that this meal would be a welcome break from the preparations for the Season, they were sorely mistaken. As soon as the starter of salad Nicoise was cleared away, Mummy's and Aunt Angelica's diaries came out, and Lily and Georgie dutifully pulled out their own.

"Next week is looking rather thin for invitations, Lily," said Mummy. "Just one tea on Tuesday and cocktail parties on Thursday and Friday. You should have spent more time at Isabel's meeting other girls."

"I spoke to so many people," said Lily.

"But were they the right people?" asked Mummy.

"I have Victoria Donaldson's drinks on Wednesday. I could telephone her and hint that you're free that night," Georgie offered.

"That is sweet of you, Georgina, but I don't think things are dire enough for that quite yet," said Mummy, reaching for the bell next to her plate. She rang it, and a moment later Hannah appeared.

"Yes, Mrs. Nicholls?" the housekeeper asked with her hands folded behind her back.

"Could you please bring in the afternoon post?" asked Mummy.

"Yes, madam," said Hannah.

"We'll check to see if any appropriate invitations have come," said Mummy.

"It sounds as though I can't be too picky when it comes to what's appropriate," muttered Lily.

"You still need to be discriminating, and it's far more efficient with Angelica here. She can warn you so you don't have another repeat of Cecil Towey," said Mummy.

"Cecil Towey of the Gloucestershire Toweys?" Aunt Angelica asked.

"He's a very nice young man," said Lily, conjuring up a vague memory of Cecil winging across Leana's drawing room with her in a haphazard dance to an Elvis Presley song.

"Handsome, too, if you like glasses," said Georgie.

The door opened again, and Hannah carried in two stacks of letters on a silver tray, which she lay between Mummy and Lily. "It only just came through the letter slot."

"Thank you, Hannah," said Lily, picking up the first note.

"Wait a moment," said Hannah slyly, pulling another bundle of letters out of first her right apron pocket, then her left. "It looked like a mountain of paper in the entryway."

"This is all for me?" she asked in disbelief, shuffling through the letters. Nearly every single one of them was uniform in size. Invitations.

Across the table, Mummy asked, "Are you certain?"

"Well, well," said Aunt Angelica with delight.

"It looks as though you've become quite the thing, Miss Lily," said Hannah with a bright smile.

"I can't think why I would be," she murmured, but when she picked up her paper knife to slice open the first letter, she realized that Hannah was right. Inside was the telltale snow-white card of an invitation.

"That will be all, Hannah." Her mother waited until the door was closed before demanding, "Who is it from?"

"'Mrs. Patrick Sanders at home, Tuesday, the eighth of April, six o'clock,'" she read out, scrunching up her nose. "She's Beatrice Sanders's mother, isn't she?"

"There's a photograph of you with her at Claudia Lessing's tenth birthday. I remember sending you with Georgie," said Aunt Angelica.

"Beatrice is nice enough. We see each other riding sometimes," said Georgie.

"What does the next one say?" asked Mummy.

Setting the invitation aside, she opened another. "'Lady Anne Faulks at home, Monday, the fourteenth of April, half past six.' I don't think I know any Faulkses."

"Horsey girl. Good stock from Somerset. Her grandfather was an admiral," rattled off Lily's aunt before frowning. "Georgie hasn't had an invitation from the Faulkses yet."

"Don't worry, Mummy. If she's horsey, we're bound to be invited to the same luncheon sometime soon," said Georgie with a laugh.

"Here's one I do recognize," Lily said, pulling free the next invitation. "Geraldine Prichard has finally sent me an invitation to her ball. She spent all last autumn talking about it, and lorded it over all of us that she was going to be quite selective about who she invited from school."

"You should attend," said her mother.

"Mummy." She laughed. "You can't be serious. I know that Mr. Prichard is a friend of yours, but Geraldine is awful."

"Not only are Richard and Agatha Prichard well-connected, Geraldine has three older brothers, all bachelors," said Aunt Angelica.

She looked between her aunt and Mummy, waiting for Aunt Angelica to make a joke about how the girls should be buzzing bees dancing from flower to flower this Season or some such nonsense, but there was none. Not only were both her aunt and mother serious, both had their heads bent over their diaries, taking notes. Across the table, Georgie just shrugged.

She worked methodically, opening invitations and spreading them out over the empty spaces at the table where Papa and Joanna might have sat if their family had still been whole. In the end, nineteen invitations—all nearly identical in look—lay before them, along with twelve handwritten notes inviting her to less formal teas and deb's lunches to get to know the other girls she'd come out with.

"Goodness," said Georgie softly.

"There are so many," she murmured.

"It appears, Lily, that you've made quite a splash. I think you should be jealous, Georgie," said Aunt Angelica.

"I think I am," said Georgie.

"Oh, please don't be, Georgie," she said.

Georgie reached across the table to her. "Don't worry, darling. It's a healthy kind of jealousy. I've become rather complacent with my little group of school friends and horsey girls."

Despite her cousin's reassurances, Lily's stomach still turned, and it had nothing to do with her sorry state that morning.

"You'll have to start deciding which you should decline, which you can double up, and which you should attend the entire night," said Mummy, still studiously copying down dates and times. "And we'll have to look at your wardrobe. Perhaps we should have gone to Harrods for more of your things. Someone is going to ask where you had your dresses made."

"Mummy, you know why these have all come this morning, don't you?" she asked.

Mummy looked up from the diary. "You did very well at Isabel's drinks yesterday."

"It was Leana. She's popular."

Georgie nodded. "You were seen leaving Isabel's dinner with Leana. I was speaking to Ivy Wark, and she commented on it."

One dinner, and everyone knew that Leana was Lily's friend, and since Leana was invited everywhere, it looked as though London society had decided to extend Lily the same privilege.

"Josephine, there's no use in being stubborn. You know the girl is right," said Aunt Angelica.

"Fine," Mummy said. "Be friends with Leana Hartford, just promise me that you will stay as far away from Ethan and Ruth Hartford as you can."

Slowly Lily nodded.

"Well," said Aunt Angelica, clearly trying to break the tension in the room, "I do hope whatever Hannah has planned for the main course is as good as the first."

The following day, Lily found herself summoned to join Grandmama after Grandmama attended church at St. Paul's Knightsbridge. Mummy was pointedly left off the invitation.

Grandmama had declared that Lily's diary would be too full during the Season for regular visits, but Lily should have guessed that she would soon be summoned. She dressed carefully in a navy suit with white piping at the collar and took the bus to the corner of Pont and Sloane Streets.

Once the usual pleasantries were done and the tea was poured, Grandmama came right to business. "I've heard that you had a very successful evening Friday."

"It would seem so," she said.

"May I see?" Grandmama asked.

Lily handed over her diary and watched Grandmama peruse the names and dates of the invitations she intended to accept.

"This is very good, Lillian. I'm very pleased," Grandmama announced, handing her back the light blue diary.

Lily breathed a sigh of relief.

"However, it is imperative that you do not lose momentum now," said Grandmama.

"It's only the first official weekend of parties," Lily said.

"The Season is a long marathon, and not for the faint of heart. You may not realize how much of a disadvantage your sister's past has placed you in," said Grandmama.

Lily straightened. So few people ever spoke of Joanna when she was around, and she craved any scrap of information about the estranged sister who seemed to haunt Harley Gardens, the mere thought of her imbuing the place with sadness.

"What happened to her? Not the illness in America. I know about that. I mean why was she sent there in the first place? And why doesn't she speak to Mummy any longer?" she asked.

"Joanna was wild. Your mother was young when she had Joanna, and she didn't know how to control the child. Only your mother could tell you what happened when she went to nurse Joanna, but Joanna only spent one night under your mother's roof when they finally returned to London.

"Fortunately, Josephine seems to have learned her lesson with you. You're a good girl, Lillian," said Grandmama, something akin to warmth filling her eyes.

"Thank you," she said, grasping at the rare nugget of approval that her grandmother had thrown to her.

"Now, back to the matter at hand. How was your time with the photographer?" Grandmama asked.

"It went well, I think," she said, sending up a prayer of thanks for Georgie and her incredible, ever-expanding handbag of makeup.

"Good. That photograph will be important for the article that will be running about you in *The Sketch*," said Grandmama.

"An article?" she asked with surprise.

"A short piece mentioning your success at various upcoming parties. It would be helpful if you were to be photographed somewhere significant in the next week or so," said Grandmama.

"But, isn't that . . . ?"

Grandmama leveled an amused look at her. "Not the done thing? People may *say* that it isn't appropriate for a girl to court the press, but they are usually the ones who are lobbying so stridently in the background for Jennifer's attention," said Grandmama, invoking the name of the *Tatler's* society columnist who held such sway over the Season that mothers arrived at her office, their diaries in hand, to check the wished-for dates for their daughters' drinks and dances against Jennifer's own calendar.

"If you see a photographer, smile. If someone asks you for a remark about a party or a ball, give them something sweet and generous that they can use," said Grandmama.

"Do you really think that's necessary?" she asked, surprised at her grandmother's candid calculations.

Grandmama leaned forward in her chair. "I know this. Some debutantes are a success because they are beautiful, and some are a success because of their families and their wealth. But others are a success because they understand how to play the game that is the Season. They are charming at the right times, know the right people, dance with the right men. Those girls have an instinct for moving through society. Conscious or not, you have that, too, otherwise why would you have befriended Leana Hartford when your mother was so adamantly against it?"

Lily blinked, stunned, as Grandmama sat back, a satisfied smile on her lips.

Seven

A horn blared from the street as Lily slipped on her light blue high-heeled shoe and straightened the seam of her stocking.

"Lily, is there a gentleman honking in the street?" Mummy said, emerging from Papa's study, where she'd shuttered herself most of the afternoon.

"That's just Gideon being a fool," she said, opening her clutch to check that she had her lipstick, pressed powder, coin purse, and front door key.

"He should know not to honk in the road for a girl." Mummy frowned. "I should go with you tonight."

Mummy hadn't said as much, but the two weeks since Lily's presentation at court had taken a toll on her. She was sleeping later, and she hardly spoke except to ask Lily about whether any new invitations needed to be sent to Lily's coming-out drinks. Night after night, Mummy had gamely donned another black cocktail dress and gloves and climbed into a taxi, but it was easy to see how the Season's unrelenting schedule weighed on her.

It had been a relief when Mummy had announced to Lily that morning that she was thinking about sending her regrets for Vita Auster's party that evening.

"You should rest, Mummy. I'll be fine. Besides, Aunt Angelica will be there with Georgie," she said, snapping the clutch closed.

"In my day, a deb would never arrive at a party without her chaperone," said Mummy, pulling a finely knitted shawl around her shoulders wearily.

"The world's changed since you came out in 1921. Besides, Gideon is acting as my escort," Lily reminded her.

Despite Cecil's offer to accompany her whenever she should need him, it was Gideon who had played de facto escort to Lily at four of the many cocktail parties that had been held since Lily had met him. He seemed to have an instinct for finding her just after she entered a room and sliding up to her with a grin and a quip. Granted, that wasn't particularly hard, given that where she was, Leana was almost certain to follow, a string of men and debs in her wake.

"You'll remember to give my regrets to Mrs. Auster?" asked Mummy, tugging on the sleeve of her black cardigan.

"I will," she said.

"And no nightclubs," her mother reminded her.

"I wouldn't dream of it, Mummy," she said lightly, even though Gideon had promised to drive them to the Astor Club for dancing after dinner—a promise that had thrown Cressie into a flutter because Princess Margaret was sometimes spotted there.

"You'll put your shoes just inside my bedroom door when you return," said Mummy.

"Oh, Mummy," she said with an exasperated huff.

"I want to know that you're home."

"Fine." She'd learned in the last two weeks of late nights that Mummy slept like the dead, so there was little risk of this parental precaution ruining any of her fun.

The horn sounded again, and Mummy frowned. "Tell Second Lieutenant Moore that if he wants to collect you again, he must promise never to make that sort of noise in the street. I'll never hear the end of it from Mrs. Hall."

"Goodbye, Mummy!" Lily called, scrambling out the front door before Gideon honked a third time.

The moment she appeared on the front step, Cecil popped out the passenger's-side door of Gideon's sleek black Jag to open the back for her.

"Thank you," she said, sliding into the back seat.

Leana snatched her cobalt tulle skirts away as Lily's dress pooled around her on the back seat. "Look where you're sitting, Lily!"

"Oh, I'm sorry," she said, although she was certain she hadn't touched the delicate fabric of Leana's dress.

"What took you so long?" Leana demanded.

Lily studied Leana, assessing her friend's mood. Given that they'd known each other for so little time, she didn't know if this was a strop or whether something was actually the matter.

"Mummy's been fretting about not coming tonight," Lily finally said.

"The unchaperoned deb out in the wilds of society," said Gideon with a laugh. "Hello, Lily."

"Thank you for driving us," she said.

"I'm the lucky one ferrying two beautiful girls around London," said Gideon as he gunned the engine and roared away from the curb and into a wide right turn on Priory Walk and then another onto Drayton Gardens.

"If you spent less time being absurd, we would be halfway to the Savoy by now," said Leana.

Lily caught Gideon's eye in the rearview mirror as he said, "Our dearest Leana is upset because Juliet Milner had an entire page to herself in this week's *Tatler*."

"I'm certain she paid the magazine," grumbled Leana.

Lily, who had met Juliet at a luncheon that Monday, thought that highly unlikely. The truth was the other prospective Deb of the Year and Leana's rival was uncommonly beautiful and intelligent, if a little quiet. However, Lily had been delighted to find out that Juliet shared a passion for literature with her, and they'd spent nearly a half hour speaking about Gothic novels while the other girls at the luncheon gathered addresses around them.

"If you love literature so much, you should consider university," Juliet had said in her soft voice.

"Oh, I don't know," Lily had demurred.

"Really, do think about it. I earned my spot at Somerville in the autumn," said Juliet.

Lily's eyes widened at the thought of a fellow deb going to one of the Oxford University colleges, even if she knew theoretically that it happened. "Really?"

Juliet laughed. "It was hard work. I persuaded my parents to let me delay my presentation from last year so that I could study for the entrance exam, and they were in a flutter that I might not be invited to the last court presentations this year. You should at least try for a place."

Lily bit her lip. "I don't know."

"Just think about it," Juliet had said.

"How is it to be out and about without a chaperone?" Gideon asked, pulling Lily back to the conversation.

"Actually, Mummy's rather cross with you, Gideon," she said.

"Me?" he gasped in mock horror.

"She disapproves of you honking the horn," she said.

"Blame that on our darling Leana. She was so impatient for you to join us that she practically leaned over and pressed it herself," said Gideon.

"That's absurd," Leana huffed in the corner. Lily smiled knowing that it was likely true. She'd learned over the last two weeks of parties and late nights that her new friend did not like to be kept waiting.

"Traffic should be easier today. The marches for nuclear disarmament around Hyde Park yesterday were a nightmare," said Gideon.

"Gideon . . ." grumbled Cecil.

"There will be no politics in this car," said Leana.

"It's my car," Gideon pointed out.

"Lily, you're wearing your pearls again," Leana said, casting a shrewd eye over Lily's ensemble.

She touched her right hand to the warm beads at her neck. Lily's birthday last November had been rather unremarkable, with only a "Happy birthday" over the morning room table from Mummy and a swift squeeze from Hannah before Lily pulled her satchel up on her shoulder and scrambled out the door. However, when she'd gone to Grandmama's for tea that week, her grandmother had presented her with the strand.

She had loved them from the moment she set eyes on the delicate pearls and two perfect matching earrings sitting on cream silk in their box. She had felt like a woman rather than a schoolgirl the first time she'd put them on, and she'd worn them to court for her presentation and to every cocktail party she'd attended. Besides, they were her only bit of good jewelry, even if the way Leana looked at them made her wonder whether anyone else saw them that way.

"Your earrings are lovely," she said, nodding to the sparkling aquamarine drops at Leana's ears.

Her friend twisted her head back and forth, catching the light of the streetlamps along Piccadilly. "Do you think? They're just Mummy's castoffs. She hardly wore them after my father inherited the Hartford rubies.

"Oh, I've an idea! Why don't you come over one day and have a look around in my jewelry box? You should have something special for Queen Charlotte's Ball. It will be our first official dance."

"Don't you have Lady Ursula Rawlings's ball on the twenty-ninth?" asked Gideon.

"The day after the Berkeley Dress Show," Leana groaned.

"Have you heard yet whether you've been selected?" Lily asked. The Berkeley Debutante Dress Show was one of the perennial events of the Season. Already the couturier, Pierre Cardin, had selected his short list of forty-eight girls from all of the debs in London. Soon he would announce the twelve girls who would don his clothes and model at the Berkeley restaurant in aid of the National Society for the Prevention of Cruelty to Children. Only the prettiest, most promising debs made the final cut. Juliet was certainly in the mix, and so Leana would be.

"Oh, I don't know. I suppose I shall find out soon." Leana placed a hand on Lily's and squeezed it as though apologizing for the fact that Lily's name hadn't been on the short list. "I promise you it will be such a bore. Honoria Davis, one of Mummy's friends' daughters, did it two years ago, and she said that you spend most of the time being poked and prodded and told to walk this way and then that."

Everyone slid to the side of the car as Gideon whipped around the corner of Duncannon Street and onto the Strand.

"Gideon!" Leana cried.

Lily pushed off her friend, but not before she caught the scent of gin on Leana's breath.

"A few ruffled feathers never hurt anyone," Gideon teased, pulling the car up to a smooth stop in front of the Savoy.

Leana clicked her tongue, pulling out a compact to pat at her waves as the men jumped out to open their doors. "Look at my hair. You really should be more careful, Lily. You crushed me again."

"I am sorry," said Lily, trying her best to fluff her friend's skirts, although they seemed just fine to her.

The door opened, and Gideon poked his head in. "My ladies?"

Leana snapped her compact closed and slid it into her handbag. "Oh, leave that," she said, slapping Lily's hand away before letting Gideon help her out of the car.

Lily sucked in a breath, fighting the annoyance rising in her. She didn't know what was wrong with Leana, but she wasn't going to let it ruin her night.

She started to inch over on the back seat but stopped when Gideon dropped his head to peer in. "Don't let her bother you."

"She is being wretched tonight," she whispered.

Gideon grinned. "They say that beauty is a beast."

"I'm being serious. What is the matter with her? One article about Juliet Milner and she's acting as though it's my fault that someone else is popular," she said.

"I think you'll find that the article is only part of it. She won't admit it to anyone else, but when Cecil and I collected her, it was clear she'd been crying."

She looked up sharply. "Crying? I can't imagine Leana crying."

His jaw set, but he nodded shortly. "I've only ever seen one person make Leana cry in all the years I've known her."

"Who?" she asked.

"Her mother. I'm not excusing Leana, but I suspect Mrs. Hartford had something to do with her foul mood."

Leana shouldn't take her anger or disappointment out on anyone, least of all her friends, but Lily knew that nothing would come of trying to draw Leana aside tonight while they were on the threshold of a party. Better to give Leana space and speak about it privately.

Lily let Gideon help her out of the car and tuck her hand into the crook of his arm.

"Ready?" he asked.

"As I ever am." But when he started to move, she held fast. "Gideon, did Leana invite you in for drinks before you came to pick me up?"

"Sober as a judge," he said. "Why do you ask?"

Lily shook her head. "It's nothing."

He gave her arm a gentle tug. "Shall we?"

They were nearly to the front entrance of the Savoy with its iconic silver sign when Leana marched over and pulled her away from Gideon. But as Lily braced herself for Leana to lash out about favoring Gideon over her, she realized her friend was smiling.

"There are two very important things you should know about tonight," said Leana in a low voice.

"What are those?" she asked.

"First of all, my father's protégé, Ian, will be here."

"Oh, I haven't met him before," she said.

Leana pulled a face. "Consider yourself lucky. He's an utter bore. I swear he's been forty years old his entire life, and he's just the sort who will try to monopolize your entire evening talking about books or some other dull thing."

"I *like* books, remember?"

Leana waved a hand. "Not your sort of books, darling. History or something equally dreary."

"What was the second important thing you wanted to warn me about?" she asked.

Leana's grip on her arm tightened, and suddenly Lily felt herself being swung around on her heel. There was the bright burst of a flashbulb, and stars exploded across her vision.

"Another one, Miss Hartford?" a man shouted.

"If it's completely necessary." Leana nudged her with her elbow. "Pose this time, will you, darling?"

Although the light of the photographer's flash still blinded her, Lily instinctively canted her left foot a little, turned her hips, and dipped her chin down in the direction of the brilliant light. This time, when the flash burst, she was ready.

Grandmama would be so proud she remembered her lessons.

"Very nice, miss," called the photographer. "And what about one alone?"

"You don't mind do you, Lily?" asked Leana with a tight smile.

Lily dutifully stepped away.

Snap. Pose. Snap. Pose.

"Thanks, miss. And what about one of Miss Nicholls?" asked the photographer.

"Me?" Lily asked. How did he even know her name?

Leana's nose wrinkled. "Are you sure?"

"Got my assignments here, don't I?" he asked, holding up a sheet of paper. "Can't go home until they're done."

"Oh, all right then," said Lily. She posed.

Snap.

"One more, if you don't mind, miss," said the photographer.

This time she smiled full and bright, her head tilted back a bit, enjoying the absurdity of it all.

"Thanks, miss," shouted the photographer.

"What's your name?" asked Lily, stepping forward to extend a hand.

He adjusted his short-brimmed brown hat and gave her hand a good shake. "Colin, miss. Colin Higgins."

"Thank you very much for taking our photograph," she said.

"My pleasure, Miss Nicholls." Colin gave her a wink, and behind her, she heard Leana huff.

"Come *on*, Lily," said Leana.

When Lily turned, she saw Leana was already three steps ahead of her, while Gideon and Cecil held back. This time, both men offered her their arms, and she fell into stride between them.

"I thought that debutantes were supposed to shun the press," said Gideon.

"I'm learning that apparently not every debutante pays attention to those rules," Lily said.

"Smart woman," he said as they crossed the Savoy's threshold.

Lily couldn't help agreeing with him.

Eight

"Are you ready?" Gideon asked as they reached the River Room, with its cool white tones and softly shimmering lights that lent the partygoers they could see just inside an ethereal quality.

"As ready as I ever am for these parties," said Lily.

"You're the perfect deb," Cecil, who still had her other arm, said as they joined the receiving line.

"Oh, don't say that." For so long she'd tried to be perfect, not upsetting Mummy and doing everything Grandmama wanted her to do. But perfect was beginning to feel boring—restrictive, even.

"Leana is the perfect deb," she offered.

Gideon shook his head. "No, she's beautiful and popular, but she can be jealous and petty, too. I'll bet that half of the girls here are frightened of her."

"That's very wicked speaking about your friend that way," she said.

"Ah, but wickedness and a propensity for absurdity are two of my better qualities, along with my incredible modesty and my ability to say absolutely nothing for an entire conversation," he joked.

"I keep telling you not to encourage him," groaned Cecil. "He loves the sound of his own voice."

"I try not to give him anything, but somehow he manages to be ridiculous all the same. Are you ever serious?" she asked Gideon, but he was saved an answer because they'd reached the front of the queue. She shook hands with Vita's father, passed along her mother's regrets to Mrs. Auster, and waited until Vita was finally free.

"Lily!" Vita cried out, placing a gloved hand on Lily's arm and leaning in to barely brush her cheek with her own. "We're very happy to have you." Vita's eyes flicked over to Gideon. "All of you."

"Vita, you've met Second Lieutenants Gideon Moore and Cecil Towey?" she asked.

Gideon executed a bow as Vita laughed. "Cecil, it's a pleasure to meet you. Gideon, however, I know by reputation. You went to school with my brother, didn't you?"

"I did. I'm sorry Auster isn't here tonight," said Gideon, glancing around.

"I am as well, but he's gone off to make his fortune in America," said Vita with a laugh that made it clear the eldest Auster child didn't need to seek his fortune for anything but his own amusement.

"Lily, Edith and June were asking after you just a few minutes ago," said Vita, mentioning two debs Lily had met the previous week at a tea.

"I'll look for them," she said, and then stepped away to let the next well-wisher congratulate Vita.

"Making friends? Leana won't like that," said Gideon in a low voice as Cecil turned to greet a friend with a clap on the back.

"Quiet, you," she said affectionately.

"Now, would you prefer a drink of something warm or something sticky? Chances are both will contain something masquerading as orange juice?"

She sighed. "I don't supposed it's too much to hope that at the Savoy the drinks will be properly iced, is it?"

"I'll go find out," said Gideon. "You look for your friends."

Without Leana by her side, Lily had found herself happily free to choose who she spoke to. She was looking for Edith and June when she stumbled across Philippa Groves, a fellow former Mrs. Wodely's girl who wore a rather daring red-and-white abstract print, and her friend Ivy Wark, who was adorable in a white cream puff of a gown.

They exchanged hellos, and Ivy said, "We were just talking about Elizabeth Yarley's luncheon on Friday. Elizabeth's brother, Henry, showed at the house unexpectedly and walked straight into the drawing room where we were all gathered. It caused ever such an uproar," said Ivy.

"Did he?" asked Lily.

"He took one look at us, went white as a sheet, and practically ran out without saying a word," said Philippa with amusement. "It sounds as though we can cross him off dance cards for the balls. Of course, you don't have to worry about that, Lily."

"I think every girl is worried whether or not she'll be asked to dance when the balls start," Lily said.

"Oh," said Ivy, looking surprised. "I had assumed that Gideon would be your escort."

"Gideon? Well, I suppose he might be."

"Didn't you walk in with him?" Ivy asked.

"She walked in with two men," said Philippa with a sly grin.

"Both Gideon and Cecil are friends," Lily said with a laugh, even as her cheeks heated.

"If you say so but you do seem to be seeing quite a bit of each other," said Philippa before sipping on her drink.

"He's been very kind to me, but he's only a friend," she said.

"That's a shame. He's handsome," said Ivy.

"He's fun, too," Lily said.

Ivy frowned. "I'm not sure that my grandmother would approve of a man who's 'fun.'"

"There isn't much your grandmother does approve of, Ivy dearest," said Philippa.

Ivy's eyes flicked to something over Lily's shoulder, and immediately her face fell. "Oh no."

"What's the matter?" Lily asked.

Philippa brought her glass to her lips and murmured into the rim, "*She's* coming."

Lily looked over her shoulder and spotted Leana approaching. Behind her, three deb's delights trailed at her heels, their suit jackets flapping behind them in their eagerness. Lily vaguely remembered seeing them at another cocktail party.

"There you are!" Leana exclaimed as though all the tension of the car and the photographer had never happened. "I've been looking everywhere for you."

"I was just chatting with Ivy and Philippa. Have you met?" she asked.

Leana hardly spared the other girls a glance. "Somewhere or another, I'm sure. How do you do?"

The two women mirrored the greeting with as little enthusiasm as Leana had shown.

"There are some people I just have to introduce you to," said Leana, grabbing Lily's wrist.

"Leana!" Lily cried.

"I think I'm going to find another drink," announced Philippa loudly.

Lily shot her an apologetic look as Leana tugged her away, but Philippa smiled nonetheless

"Leana, I hadn't finished talking with them," she said.

"Oh, what can there have been to talk about really? All of the debs see each other so often, it's all the same as the previous night. But there are two men I want you to meet," said Leana, apparently unaware that they were still being trailed by the men who had crossed the room with her.

"Here," said Leana, stopping in front of a cluster of men. "I've found her."

Lily rubbed her wrist and gave a weak smile as she was introduced to Gregory and Benjamin, "my brother's friends from school," Leana explained. Gregory was tall and good-looking but clearly more interested in Leana than any interloper. The other man, Benjamin, was short and stout and had thick glasses that magnified his eyes so that he looked a little like a bug dressed up in a suit.

"Lily is the intellectual among us," Leana announced.

"Don't be silly, Leana," she said.

"You're the only one who reads. Benjamin is at university. I'm sure you'll have plenty to talk about," said Leana before turning away to laugh at something Gregory said and stranding her with Benjamin.

Lily gave Benjamin a tight smile and asked, "What are you reading at university?" As expected, Benjamin launched into a description of his politics course.

Certain her contribution would not be necessary to this conversation, Lily cast about for anyone else in the room she might speak to. Her eyes landed on a stranger near the door. He had clearly been watching her, and even now, he didn't look away. His charcoal suit covered his long frame, and his light brown hair parted deeply on the right and swept back off his forehead the way Cary Grant wore it.

She must have been staring for longer than she realized because the man's eyes crinkled at the corners as he smiled and lifted his drink slightly in acknowledgment. She looked away with a hasty blush.

"I beg your pardon?" she asked, forcing her attention back to Benjamin.

"I was asking where your interests lie," her companion asked.

"A bit of everything. I suppose if I were to go to university, I would read literature." She glanced back in the direction of the man in the charcoal suit, but he'd disappeared.

Benjamin sniffed. "Oh, I don't know about that."

"I beg your pardon?"

"Women at university. It's a mistake," he said.

"A mistake?"

"It's the distraction to the male scholars I can't abide. We have two women in my lecture on the political system of ancient Rome, and all they do is chatter with each other."

Lily laughed in disbelief. "You can't really mean that."

He frowned. "I do. It isn't natural having men and women educated together."

"If men find it distracting sitting in a lecture or tutorial with a woman, then it's their fault. Not the woman's," said Lily.

Benjamin frowned. "I don't see why you should be so offended. You're not going to university. You're a deb."

There was a muffled cough to her right. She glanced over to find the man in the charcoal suit had stepped into their conversation. Her mouth went dry, but the man in the charcoal suit didn't speak to her. Instead, he turned his attention to Benjamin.

"I don't think we're acquainted," he said. He did not extend his hand in greeting.

"Benjamin Makin," he said, smoothing a hand over the front of his jacket.

"Interesting," said the man in the charcoal suit, not offering his name in return.

"Why do you ask?"

Their new companion tilted his head to the side as though considering his answer. "I like to know who the fools are in the room so I can be sure to avoid them in future conversations."

Lily gasped out a laugh as Benjamin's jaw dropped open. "I'll say, there's no cause to be rude."

"I agree," said the man in the charcoal suit. "Which is why I wonder that you were being so rude to this young lady." He leaned over. "Forgive me for not knowing your name."

"Lily Nicholls," she said, a little in awe.

"How do you do, Miss Nicholls?" The man in the charcoal suit turned back to Benjamin. "I would suggest you run along and find someone else to bother."

Benjamin puffed up like an angry house cat, but if he was going to say anything, he thought better of it and beat a quick retreat to another group.

"What a horrid little man," said Lily, watching him go.

"I hope you don't mind my interceding. I did think you were doing an excellent job of putting him in his place, but I also thought to myself, 'What a shame that that woman should have to waste a perfectly enjoyable evening on someone so thick,'" said the man in the charcoal suit with a smile.

She shook her head. "Not at all. I'll confess, I was becoming so angry there was a risk I might have said something I shouldn't. Debs are supposed to be so careful."

"Well, we can't have that, Miss Nicholls." He leaned in with a soft smile. "Can I make a confession?"

"Of course," she said, her heart beating faster at the nearness of him. He had the usual accoutrement that came with a deb's delight: good suit, hair groomed just so, excellent carriage, and polished vowels. Yet there was something different about him, as though he held himself apart from the absurdity of the evening like an observer.

"I also came over here because I saw you and thought, 'There is a girl I'd like to get to know,'" he said.

"You've been doing quite a bit of thinking tonight," she said.

"It's a dangerous thing at a cocktail party, Miss Nicholls."

"Lily," she corrected him. "I'm afraid you have the advantage of me. I don't know your name."

"Ian Bingham, at your service," he said with a little bow of his head.

"Ian, I see you've found me, then," said Leana, sliding up behind her, drink in hand, and sounding less than enthused about his presence.

"Hello, Leana," he said, kissing her on the cheek when it was offered to him.

"You've met Lily already," said Leana.

"We were just in the middle of that actually," he said as Lily returned his smile.

Leana looked at Ian and then at Lily and back again. "Yes, I see. Well"—Leana grabbed at Ian's arm and tugged him across the gap between them—"you'll have to meet the others as well. Lily, why don't you see if you can find Cecil with the drinks? He is taking an age."

"Miss Nicholls shouldn't have to do that," he said.

"Really, Ian, Lily doesn't mind. Do you, Lily?" asked Leana with false brightness.

Lily looked from her friend to this newcomer, wondering at Leana's tone. It was all subtle—a complaint about a crushed skirt here, some sharpness when Gideon teased her there, and the usual fobbing Lily off on whomever Leana thought the least interesting of the group—but taken together, she couldn't help but think that it all felt rather sour.

Space. She needed space for the night to let this mood dissipate.

"I don't mind," said Lily.

"Thank you, darling!" Leana trilled, turning her back.

It was only when Lily was halfway across the room in search of Cecil that she realized that Leana had had a full drink in her hand the entire time.

After an hour and a half at Vita's party, Lily was beginning to flag. She'd made the rounds in the room twice, careful to speak to some of the other girls and the deb's delights that didn't seem so easily pulled into Leana's orbit.

Normally she liked the sense of being a part of the mad, rollicking group that was lucky enough to be invited to dinner and then dancing with Leana. Her friend had an undeniable talent for whipping people up into a frenzy so that it seemed as though there was no other option than to go dance to rock 'n' roll records or spend hours swinging wildly between partners on the dance floor of a nightclub. But tonight Leana's demanding nature felt different. It grated, and the thought of trying to crush her annoyance for an entire evening exhausted her.

However, Lily knew that if she left without saying goodbye, it would cause more unnecessary fuss. Steeling herself, she wove through the crowd until she found Leana and slid in between two men she hadn't met just as the man her friend seemed to be paying closest attention to brayed out a laugh that made Lily jump.

"Reprimanded? The colonel clapped me on the back and said, 'A fine job, Lieutenant,'" the man said, his voice carrying over the conversations around them.

Leana leaned in and laid a hand on his arm. "You really are too wicked."

"You don't know the half of it," said the man with a grin that looked as though he might eat Leana up—if only she let him.

He was a soldier, of that Lily had no doubt. It was in the way he held his body at the ready, shoulders spread wide and back straight. He wore a thin black Clark Gable mustache, and his dark hair was oiled to keep it off his brow.

"Lily!" Leana cried, catching sight of her. "You're back."

"I never really intended to leave," she said, remembering how she'd been sent away to check on drinks that she'd never chased.

"I don't know what took you so long. I've been wanting to introduce you to Raymond," said Leana, her eyes shining.

"Raymond" turned out to be Lieutenant Raymond Troy.

"Of the Coldstream Guards," added Raymond, although she hadn't asked.

"We only just met, but I suspect we're destined to become very good friends," said Leana slyly, placing a hand on his arm.

Lily frowned at her friend's flirtation. It was the first time she'd ever seen Leana be quite so . . . engaged. Normally Leana let the men around her adore her, hardly giving them the time of day until she needed something from them like poor Cecil and his endless drink fetching. But this time Leana seemed eager to hook the lieutenant's attention and keep it on her.

"How do you do?" she asked Raymond.

"I know I would be better if these drinks were stronger," he said, reaching into his jacket pocket for a silver flask. Without any remorse, he untwisted it and dumped a slug of whatever was in it into his glass. Then he leaned over and did the same for Leana.

"Leana," Lily half hissed, looking around from side to side. But if she expected Mrs. Hartford or any of the other mothers present to descend upon them, she was mistaken. No one cared.

"It's just a little drink, Lily," said Leana.

"A dram of encouragement," said Raymond. "Go to too many of these, and you need it just to make it through the evening."

"You could have one yourself," suggested Leana. Raymond nearly succeeded in covering his reaction at the thought of sharing whatever was in his flask with her.

"I don't think I will, but thank you all the same," she said.

Tucking his flask away, Raymond half turned to Leana, giving Lily a portion of his back. "This is a bore."

"I beg your pardon," said Leana with a laugh.

"Present company excluded, of course," Raymond amended.

"We have a dinner reservation at half past eight. You should join us," Leana said.

"Who will be there? Can't stand dinners with dull company," he said.

"We're a large party. Rupert and Cressie will be there, and then Anthony Douglas, Henry Jaffe, Angela Garrick, and Peter Wharton. And there's Lily, of course."

"Who?" Raymond asked.

That made Leana stop short. "Lily. My very dear friend who you just offered a drink to."

Lily's chest squeezed. *Very dear friend.* No one had ever called her that before. Oh, she had plenty of acquaintances and even a few friends, but she'd never been close to anyone. Even after the friction between them that evening, to hear Leana describe her as such now made her want to press hard on her heart to stop the ache there.

Raymond grunted—hardly an acknowledgment of his gaffe.

"And then there will be dancing at the Astor afterward. If we had dance cards, yours would already be filling up, Lily," said Leana.

"Would it?" she asked.

"Yes, I promised Archie and William that you would dance with them. They were asking after you earlier," said Leana.

She shook her head. "Oh, Leana, I wish you hadn't done that."

"Why not? They're both perfectly nice men, and they both mentioned how much they liked the look of you," said Leana.

The urge to scrub her hands over her arms choked her. "That's even worse. You should have asked me before handing out dances on my behalf."

"I don't understand why you're being so ungrateful," said Leana sharply.

"I'm not even certain that I'm coming to dinner tonight," Lily said, knowing she was being a touch petulant but not caring. It was true. No one had asked her if she wanted to come to dinner; it was just assumed. In two short weeks she'd become part of the architecture of their group. She liked being included, but she didn't appreciate being taken for granted.

"Don't be ridiculous. Of course you're coming to dinner tonight," said Leana.

Lily balled up her hands into fists pressed deep into her skirts. "What if another group of friends has asked me to do something after dinner?"

Leana blinked at her, as though taken aback at the very possibility. "Have they? Who are they?"

She's beautiful and popular, but she can be jealous and petty, too. I'll bet that half of the girls here are frightened of her.

It didn't matter what Gideon had said, Lily was not going to be one of those girls.

"I'm actually not feeling particularly well just now. I think I'll go home. Perhaps Raymond can take my place at dinner," she said.

"The numbers will be off." When Lily didn't respond, Leana's eyes narrowed. "Fine. Go home. We'll have a lovely time without you."

Somehow, Lily knew this was a moment of great importance—a line drawn in the sand of their still-new friendship. It would be easy to capitulate, go to dinner, and be swept up in the fun of the dancing that would follow. She might even have enjoyed it under other circumstances. However, Leana's high-handedness irked her. It felt as though she was being managed rather than befriended.

Sucking in a breath, Lily said, "Good night," and then slowly walked away from her friend.

She made it through the crowded room with her shoulders held back, grateful that the receiving queue was no longer assembled at the door. However, as soon as she was out of sight of the party, she felt her body relax with a deep exhale.

"Are you all right?"

Lily turned and saw Ian Bingham lingering off to the side.

"You're still here," she said without thinking.

A small smile touched his lips, as though he was charmed by the idea that she might be glad to see him. But as he studied her, his expression sobered.

"You look a little shaken," he continued.

"I think I'm leaving," she said.

"You think you are, or you are?" he asked.

She lifted her chin. "I am."

"I see." He pushed off the wall he'd been leaning against. "That is a shame. I'd hoped that I would have the chance to speak to you again."

She smiled. "We never really had a chance to begin with."

"Leana doesn't seem to want us to have a proper conversation," he said.

"Do you think so?"

He tipped his head a bit as though to question why she didn't see it, too.

"She mentioned that you're a family friend," she prompted.

He grinned. "I'm certain she didn't say it like that. My father is the village doctor in Elkenhurst and has been tending to the Hartfords for as long as I can remember. I was brought around to Asheville Hall for lessons with the Latin master who taught Leana's older brother. Mr. Hartford took an interest in my education. And that means Leana doesn't approve of me really."

"How could she not approve of you?" she asked, and then blushed at his widening grin, realizing just how eager she sounded. "You know what I mean."

"In some ways, I'm a poor relation, without the benefit of being related to the Hartfords. Mr. Hartford paid my school fees, and he gives me an allowance that makes it possible for me to attend Cambridge and live more comfortably than most students. It all sounds rather Victorian, doesn't it?" There was an edge to his words, as though it cost him to admit them.

"I'm sorry you've been made to feel that way," she said.

He laughed. "Don't worry too much. I manage very well. How did you meet?"

"We're very new friends," she hedged. "We sat next to one another during our presentation."

"Well, in that case, I'm very glad you did."

It was ridiculous—absurd, actually—but that simple compliment made her feel light in a way that none of the other deb's delights had.

"You weren't leaving, were you?" he asked.

She looked at him, a part of her wanting badly to say no. That she could stay and speak to him longer. That she wanted to get to know him.

"Shall I ask the doorman to fetch you a taxi?" he continued.

She bit her lip, but ultimately nodded. "If you wouldn't mind."

It was the sensible thing to do on this night when she was so agitated with Leana. There would be other parties. Other nights.

He placed a hand on his heart. "It would be my honor."

Her lips quirked. "I'll just collect my wrap."

He nodded, and she watched him stride down the hall and out to the lobby before following him partway to the ladies' cloakroom, where she'd left the soft mink stole Mummy had lent her. There was another woman ahead of her, in a diaphanous white strapless dress with a huge skirt. Lily was just admiring the way the fabric caught the light as the woman reached to take her short white fur jacket when the lady turned.

"Oh, hello," said Katherine Norman with an easy smile. "I didn't realize you were here."

"I was just leaving," she said as she handed over her ticket to the attendant.

"As was I." Katherine paused, slipping her jacket on to lean in. "I have to confess, I found the novelty of a cocktail party wearing off after the third one in a week."

"I understand," she said with a laugh. "They've already begun to run together. I have to check my diary before I leave the house to make sure I'm going to the right one."

"And that you know which deb you're meant to congratulate. I know the feeling. You aren't on your way to catch the end of Anne Horvath's by any chance, are you?" Katherine asked.

Lily shook her head. Anne Horvath, a glamorous blond girl, often appeared in the magazines. Although not a serious Deb of the Year contender like Leana or Juliet, after Leana had made a point of saying that she wouldn't be attending Anne's do, Lily had felt obligated to send her regrets out of a sense of loyalty. Now she wondered why.

"That is a shame. We could have shared a taxi," said Katherine.

"Are you going by yourself?" Lily asked.

"I'm with Doris Irving. She's another of Mrs. Kingsley's girls," Katherine said, mentioning the professional chaperone paid by families without connections to prepare and present their daughters with such a casual air that it almost shocked Lily. Being presented by a chaperone rather than a mother, grandmother, or aunt was the sort of thing that girls usually whispered about behind a debutante's back.

"We travel together in solitary sometimes," Katherine continued. "Doris is a scream, and intelligent, too. You might like her."

"I'm sure I would," said Lily, and she found that it was true.

"I'll tell you what," said Katherine as the attendant handed Lily her wrap, "why don't you and I have lunch one day this week? Maybe Thursday if you're free. Then, if you aren't tired of me by the end of it, you can meet Doris away from all of this distraction. It will be nice to have a conversation without knowing in the back of your mind that you only have a limited amount of time before your feet go numb in heels."

Lily was a little taken aback by the casual offer of lunch. She and Katherine had said hello a few times this Season, but they hardly knew each other beyond a few conversations at school. Still, she liked Katherine's unforced, carefree quality.

"Thursday would be lovely," she said as they began to walk together to the lobby.

"Oh, I have a dress fitting that morning." Katherine glanced at her. "I don't suppose you'd mind coming with, would you? I could use a second opinion, and everything I've seen you wear this Season has been lovely."

"Thank you," she said, flattered that the other woman had noticed her wardrobe.

"I'd ask you for your dressmaker's name, but Madame Benum would never speak to me again," said Katherine with a laugh.

"I'd be happy to help," she said.

"Wonderful. We'll have lunch afterward. My treat," said Katherine.

When they cleared the lobby, she spotted Ian standing by the door and waiting for her. He smiled when he saw her.

"You have an attendant. How fun," said Katherine with a low laugh.

"I don't know about that. We hardly know each other," she said.

"Well, I'm sure that's bound to change sooner rather than later."

"Katherine!" called a lanky auburn-headed girl in a deep green watered silk dress who'd already peeled off her gloves.

"That is my far less handsome party," said Katherine with a grin. "I'll look you up and ring around tomorrow with a time for Thursday."

"I'm looking forward to it," said Lily. And, as Ian helped her into the taxi and closed the door, she found that she really was.

Nine

Lily yawned deeply as she made her way out of her bedroom and down the stairs in her wine-colored rayon dressing gown. The sun shone brightly through the window at the top of the landing, reminding her that the rest of the world had started its day hours ago. She, however, had become practically nocturnal, coming alive during the six o'clock hour when the Season's cocktail parties traditionally began.

As though layering another bit of shame on the former schoolgirl who never missed a day of classes, the grandfather clock next to her father's closed study door began to chime eleven. Her stomach growled, unsure of whether it craved breakfast or luncheon. She would have to wander down to the kitchen to see if Hannah had saved her anything from that morning. Then she could retreat to her bedroom to search her over-stuffed bookshelves and settle on a new book. Perhaps *The Long View* by Elizabeth Jane Howard or *A Note in Music* by Rosamond Lehmann. Then again, she had picked up Olivia Manning's *School for Love* at the library earlier that week . . .

She would decide later. First, she made for the sideboard in the front hall where Hannah had laid out Lily's portion of the morning post on a silver tray. Mummy always opened her letters over breakfast, retiring to the desk in her bedroom to answer them as soon as she was done eating.

There was a modest stack of envelopes addressed to Lily that looked like invitations or personal notes, as well as the week's edition of *The Sketch* waiting for her. While some people might read *The Times*, awash with articles about the nuclear disarmament marches from Hyde Park to Aldermarston in Berkshire, this was where a deb received all of her news.

She tucked the letters into the pocket of her dressing gown and picked up *The Sketch*, thumbing through the magazine. A few pages in, she stopped.

Debs Dazzle at River Room: Miss Leana Hartford and Miss Lillian Nicholls exhibit elegance and grace before entering Miss Vita Auster's debutante ball at the Savoy.

The photograph accompanying the caption was from outside the Savoy a few days before. The photographer had managed to capture both Lily and Leana when they were slightly angled toward one another and smiling, their heads tilted as though they'd just shared a laugh or a secret. None of the tension that had snapped and sparked that night shone through. They looked like the perfect debs.

If only they knew.

Lily flipped a couple pages forward and back, but there seemed to be nothing else of the two of them. She folded the magazine in half, deciding she would take a closer look while she was eating. She was just turning when a flash of white under the sideboard caught her eye. A letter must have fallen off the tray and lodged itself below the sideboard.

Sliding it out, she frowned. It was addressed to "Mrs. Michael Nicholls" in a thin, looping hand. The return address was for a Dovecote Cottage in a place called Hawkshead Hill in Cumberland, but there was no name included.

Her heart lifted at the thought that perhaps Mummy's world had begun to open up again. Although Mummy still didn't seem particularly comfortable out in society, she was gamely attending the more important cocktail parties in a show of support for Lily, knowing that when Lily and Georgie's drinks party came around, the mothers who had invited Mummy to their daughters' parties would be compelled to return the gesture.

"It's important that you have enough people at your drinks that it looks jolly but not so many that it seems like we've invited all of London," said Aunt Angelica the last time the four of them had sat down with the lists of invitations.

But it seemed unlikely that someone in the North of England would be writing to thank Mummy for attending a London cocktail party.

Curious about the letter, Lily decided to forgo her hunt for food just a little bit longer and was about to mount the stairs when she heard a cough from her father's study. Softly she knocked on the door.

"Yes?" Mummy's voice came muffled through the heavy door.

"May I come in?" Lily asked. She could count on one hand the number of times she'd entered her father's study without her mother's express permission, and each time had earned her a reprimand. It was, she understood now, not just the place that Mummy did the business of running the house and paying their bills. It was a shrine of sorts to the husband Mummy had mourned for years.

There was a shuffling of papers, and then Lily heard her mother call out, "You may."

She twisted the intricately molded metal door handle and breathed deep at the faint scent of wood polish and leather within. Paneling gave way to a long bookshelf that lined one wall, and green curtains were drawn against the light to protect the oil paintings that she imagined her father must have selected when he first moved into this house. Mummy sat behind the massive oak desk covered with a green leather blotter, an account ledger and a stack of correspondence in front of her. A brass key that looked like it fit the desk drawer lay within reach.

"You're not dressed," said Mummy.

"No," she said, fighting to suppress another yawn.

Mummy's expression softened. "I remember my Season. Sometimes it felt as though it was only champagne and hope that kept me awake."

"I wasn't expecting it to be so tiring," Lily admitted, gratefully sinking down into one of the oxblood leather chairs across from the desk. "It seems ridiculous to think that going to parties is strenuous, but it is in its own way."

"You won't know exhaustion until you've attended four country balls in a week," said Mummy with a wry smile.

"Did you see *The Sketch* this morning?" Lily asked, opening the magazine to the page with her photograph and passing it across the desk to Mummy.

She watched her mother's expression carefully. Mummy's lips formed a thin line as she processed the photograph of Lily and Leana together, but then Lily could see her eyes flick over the caption.

Finally, Mummy said, "The writer is right. You do look elegant. The dress suits you."

"Thank you," she said, a smile tugging at her lips at the compliment. "I thought I would make another in the light blue floral fabric that I bought last week. The pattern will make it look different enough."

"It might have been better had you appeared alone, but your grandmama would no doubt remind us that there are distinct advantages to being photographed with a potential Deb of the Year," said Mummy.

Lily saw the olive branch for what it was and reached for it. "Do you know the funny thing about this photograph? I was irritated with Leana when it was taken, and it didn't improve much throughout the evening."

"Irritated?" asked Mummy.

Lily tried to think of the best way to articulate what had happened four days ago.

"I think Leana is spoiled," she said.

Mummy laughed. "Of course she's spoiled. I'm sure she's been given everything her entire life. It was that way with her brother, Geoffrey. I've never seen a child so coddled by his nanny. Ruth should have taken a stronger hand with him, but she wasn't interested in raising that boy."

"What do you mean?" Lily asked.

"Ruth Hartford put everything into being a hostess before the war. She was good at it, too—which Ethan should be more grateful for than I suspect he is, given how she helped his career—although she stepped back during the war. Everyone did. It wasn't the done thing to be throwing lavish celebrations.

"Ruth did her duty and had her children, but she never was a maternal woman. I remember, his nanny would march Geoffrey out for us to see before dinner sometimes, and he would throw himself on the floor and give this low, hollow scream if Ruth didn't pay him any mind. Otherwise, she would hardly look at him."

Lily sat back. Acting out for attention? Demanding that she be at the center of everything? It sounded as though Leana had learned some tricks from her older brother.

"Are you excited for your drinks? It's just three weeks away," Mummy said, maneuvering the conversation away from the Hartfords and onto safer ground.

"I am. It seems a little less overwhelming having seen the other debs go through it," she said.

"You'll have Georgie by your side, and Aunt Angelica and I will be there," said Mummy.

"I wanted to thank you for that," she said.

"For what?" asked Mummy.

"For presenting me. For being at the first parties of the Season. I know that Grandmama would have done it all, but I appreciate that you were there," she said. She knew it must have cost her mother to reenter society again. To know that people must be whispering about her behind her back. Mummy still didn't enjoy society—that much was clear—but she was trying, and that mattered.

Mummy's throat worked as though she was swallowing back emotion. Finally, she said, "We all have to do our duty."

All of the tenderness that Lily felt for her mother deflated. Duty. That's what she was. Merely another piece of the tradition that had driven their family forward for years.

She looked at Mummy sitting behind this great desk, a small woman swamped by the black that she insisted on wearing. She wanted so badly to love her mother and to feel that love returned with the same openness that Georgie and Aunt Angelica shared. She wanted affection easily given and approval that didn't feel hard-fought.

"Do you have a luncheon tomorrow?" Mummy asked. "Angelica and I thought that we would go over the invitations one last time."

"Actually, I'm lunching with one of the girls I saw at Vita Auster's party."

"Who is it?" Mummy asked.

Lily hesitated. "Katherine Norman."

Mummy sighed. "Why couldn't you make friends with some of Georgie's group? They might not be the most exciting girls, but at least no one gossips about them."

"Katherine was very kind inviting me to luncheon and—"

"Do not pretend that you don't know why Katherine Norman might not be a suitable friendship for you to cultivate. Your grandmother would agree with me," Mummy warned.

"But Katherine is invited everywhere," she insisted.

"That is because everyone wants an invitation to that absurd ball she's throwing, even if none of them would be so vulgar as to say it. They do not, however, truly want to associate with that family."

"Is there anything wrong with Mr. Norman other than the fact that he made his money in newspapers?" Lily asked.

"Yes, there is. There's his wife, Kitty. Angelica tells me she's one of those grasping Americans, trying to climb the social ladder by throwing ridiculous dinner parties and mimicking the way we do things here without really understanding a thing about them. Angelica said that she heard Mrs. Norman seated Lady Annan below Lady Inwood at her last dinner."

"What's so wrong about that?" asked Lily.

Mummy fixed her with a look that told her that she should know this. "Lady Annan is the wife of a baron. Lady Inwood's husband is only a knight. And then there's the daughter. Do you know what they call her? The Millionaire Deb. It's positively vulgar."

"I think it's rather unfair to judge someone on a nickname they didn't ask for."

Mummy stiffened at that, and Lily rushed to add, "Katherine isn't vulgar. She's actually quite elegant. I'm sure you would think so, too, if you met her."

Mummy pressed two fingers to her temple. "Lily, why have you suddenly become so obstinate? You've always been a good girl."

That's because I had to be. Her world had been the house, Mrs. Wodely's, and Grandmama's. Visits to Aunt Angelica and Uncle Elliot's home was a treat. A trip out or a party with Georgie was an event of the highest order. She wouldn't do anything to jeopardize those special moments, so she'd taught herself to be good and not to do anything that would disturb Mummy or Grandmama in case they decided she didn't deserve those treats any longer.

But when Grandmama and Mummy had announced she would become a deb, they'd widened her world. Paris, London. She knew from her trips on the bus and the Tube that she was only seeing a small part of her world and the people who occupied it, but even that little bit was so much more than she'd known before.

"I'm not trying to be difficult," she said slowly.

"You've already shown your willingness to disregard my advice as I try to guide you through this Season. However, even your grandmother would tell you that associating with Katherine Norman will do you no good."

"I *like* Katherine. I wish I'd come to know her better in school, but now I can fix that. I'm going out with her because I want to, not because I think she can introduce me to some man or another or help me with an invitation to a dance I likely won't enjoy."

Mummy crossed her arms and gave her a look. "If you throw your Season away on people like Katherine Norman, you're a bigger fool than I thought you to be."

Only the ticking of the desk clock between them pierced the uncomfortable silence. They were at an impasse. Once Lily might have backed down if only to keep Mummy happy, but she didn't want to do that anymore. She wanted her own life, her own friends.

Finally, Mummy said, "You have to understand, Lily, how quickly this life you've lived can disappear. When I went to Washington, DC, to care for Joanna during the war, I never thought that Michael would die, but he did. He died alone in London when I should have been right here with him."

Mummy so rarely spoke of Lily's father's death that Lily rose from her chair and rounded the desk to slide her arms around her mother's shoulders, a gesture so foreign to them both that it took Mummy a moment to relax, the tension seeming to drain from her body on a sigh.

"My life was going to be so many things," Mummy murmured, touching Lily's arm but then letting her hand drop back to her lap. "But then everything changed. I had you to think about. Every week I sit here and go over the accounts. I know what it takes to create this comfortable life that you have, but nothing lasts. Things will change, and you need to be prepared, Lily. The Season isn't really about parties. It's about the rest of your life."

What if I don't want the same kind of life that you had? The words threatened on her lips, but she bit them back as she watched the mask of composure that Mummy always wore slide back into place.

Mummy was trying to protect her the only way that she knew how. It was what mothers of their class had done for their daughters for centuries.

Lily shook her head. The world was changing. She could sense it from the marches in the streets of London and the brewing threat of strike action among London bus drivers to a deb like Juliet Milner who wouldn't be marrying in the autumn but instead going to Oxford. Lily was never going to be the deb that her mother wanted her to be because that deb didn't belong to this decade.

This would be the last year of the true debutantes. There would be no more court presentations and, although society columnists and some mothers were already speaking about coming-out balls and the major events continuing next year, they all knew it would not be the same. This was high society's swan song.

Lily rose from her chair, picking up the copy of *The Sketch* from the desk. "I should find something to eat."

She turned, but then remembered the note in her pocket. Pulling it out, she slid it across the desk. "This was lodged under the sideboard. It must have fallen there when Hannah was cleaning."

Mummy picked up the letter, her eyes going wide as soon as she saw the address.

"What's the matter?" Lily asked.

Mummy simply stared at the envelope, frozen.

"Mummy. What's wrong?" Lily asked.

Mummy shook her head as though coming out of a daze. "What?"

"Who is that letter from?" she asked.

"I don't know."

Her mother was lying, and very poorly at that.

"Mummy—"

"You do not need to concern yourself with things that have nothing to do with you," Mummy said sharply.

Lily felt the thin bonds that had formed between them that morning snap. Stiffly she nodded and left, but as she turned to close the door she saw her mother sweep the small brass key off the desk in front of her and unlock a drawer before throwing the letter inside and slamming the drawer shut with a violent bang.

Ten

The doorbell of Harley Gardens rang at eleven sharp the next day. Lily, her hat and gloves already in place, didn't bother waiting for Hannah to come up from the kitchen to answer it. She was desperate to escape the house that had felt even more stifling than usual after her spoiled conversation with Mummy in the study the day before.

"Hello!" sang out Katherine as she kissed Lily's cheek in greeting. "Don't you look lovely."

"Thank you. So do you," she said, taking in Katherine's kelly-green suit with its sophisticated slim skirt.

"To tell you the truth, I'd rather be in trousers, but where we're going, I wouldn't be let in," said Katherine with a laugh.

"Luncheon?" asked Lily, looking down at her own maroon dress and jacket and hoping it was smart enough.

"Madame's, and don't worry one bit. You look wonderful. Better than wonderful, actually. Madame is going to love that ensemble," said Katherine. "Shall we?"

Lily nodded, and Katherine led the way to her little silver Austin-Healey, its top down to welcome the spring sunshine. Lily waited while Katherine pulled her handbag and a newspaper off the front seat and threw them into the back.

As Lily settled in, Katherine pulled a pair of silk scarves out of the glove compartment. "You'll want this," Katherine said, smoothing the scarf over her hair before winding the tails of the fine fabric in front of her neck and tying it off in the back. Lily did the same as Katherine revved the engine.

"Thank you for agreeing to come with me to my dress fitting," said Katherine, roaring off from the curb and taking the corner onto the King's Road fast enough that even Gideon would have blanched.

"Oh," said Lily, her fingers digging into her leather seat. "I don't mind."

"I've been admiring what you've been wearing whenever I've seen you out this Season. Your tailoring is always impeccable," said Katherine, keeping up a steady chatter of conversation that seemed incongruous with the way she mashed the little car's clutch and whipped around a taxi that was straddling the middle of the road near Peter Jones on Sloane Square.

"Thank you. My housekeeper taught me. Her mother was a lady's maid," said Lily, deciding that, as she might be on the verge of death by car accident, the truth was the best way forward.

"Really?" Katherine asked, glancing at her. "I never would have guessed that your dresses were made at home."

"Where did you learn to drive like this?" Lily asked as soon as they slowed to a stop in traffic and she could catch her breath.

"I'm sorry," said Katherine. "I'll go a bit slower. Mum tells me that I should really warn people, but I forget. Our chauffeur used to race motorcars before the war, and he thought it would be a lark to teach me out on the roads at Balcombe Manor. I don't think Mum and Dad will ever forgive him."

"I wish I could drive. It looks like fun," Lily said.

"Oh, it is. It's the best feeling in the world. Come down one weekend to Balcombe, and I'll teach you," said Katherine as traffic eased and they began to move again.

"That's very kind of you," said Lily, knowing that was the sort of thing that debs said to each other all the time.

Drop by anytime.

We really should have dinner sometime.

"I do mean it, you know. It would be fun," said Katherine with a wicked grin.

Despite the level of adrenaline pumping through her veins, Lily managed to return the smile. That *would* be fun.

"Do you read the paper?" Katherine asked.

Lily started a bit at the sudden change in conversation. "Oh. A little bit. Mummy gets *The Times*, although I think the only thing she really looks at is the Court Circular. I saw you have a paper with you."

"One of Daddy's. When I was growing up, all I ever wanted to do was go into one of his newsrooms. I loved the smell of them: cigarettes and typewriter ink. They're such noisy places, too, all that clacking and shouting and telephones ringing." Katherine took another corner and said, "Here we are."

The car slowed considerably as Katherine turned a corner and waited patiently behind another car before sliding into a parking spot in front of a nondescript Marylebone storefront.

"Oh," said Lily with surprise.

Katherine shot her a look. "You were expecting something more like Worth or Hartnell, weren't you?"

Lily smiled. "Well, I had heard that your wardrobe was all Dior from Paris."

Katherine threw her head back and laughed. "It would have been if Mum had her way. Dad pushed for Dior, too, but I put my foot down. If I was going to do the Season, I was going to wear what I liked."

What she liked, it turned out, was a dressmaker named Madame Benum who, as soon as they were through the door, rushed forward, tape around her neck and pins already anchored to the little pincushion pillow she wore as a bracelet.

"You are late," Madame said, taking Katherine by the arm and urging her toward a dressing room.

"I'm not late. I'm perfectly on time," said Katherine.

"Which is late. Off with your things, and wash your hands. I do not want dirty fingerprints on your Queen Charlotte's gown before you even wear it," ordered Madame.

"I washed my hands before I came," said Katherine.

"Did you see her touch a newspaper?" Madame asked Lily.

"Fine!" Katherine threw up her hands before marching off to wash.

"She left prints all over one of my patterns last time," Madame informed Lily before stepping back to study her. It gave her ample opportunity to do the same. Madame wore a brilliant red dress that set off her light brown skin beautifully, and its simple cut showed off its owner's tailoring skills. She wore her rich, mahogany hair pulled back into a large knot at the back of her head, and a slick of crimson lipstick was the only makeup that Lily could discern.

"The cut of your jacket is beautiful," Madame announced.

"Oh." Lily touched the hem of the crepe wool jacket that she'd ripped out at least twice before getting it right. "Thank you."

"And your dress is too well made to be from a department store. Who is your dressmaker?" Madame asked, her soft voice accented with French drawing out the last word.

She blushed. "I am."

That elicited a raised brow. "Impressive. A hobby?"

"A necessity," she admitted. "My mother does not have the most imaginative sense of style, although my grandmother is very fashionable."

And it's what I can afford on the allowance Grandmama gives me, hung unsaid in the air between them.

Madame made a noise of approval. "You are a debutante as well?"

"Yes."

"And you've done your Queen Charlotte's gown?" Madame asked.

She shook her head. "Mummy and Grandmama insisted that I have that made."

Madame Benum sniffed. "A shame."

Lily repressed a smile as Katherine called out, "I need help with the back."

They turned as Katherine stepped out of the dressing room in a white gown held up to her chest. "And yes, before you ask, I washed my hands."

"Oh, Katherine, that is beautiful," said Lily.

The other deb laughed. "It's not even properly on yet."

"This is Miss Norman's Queen Charlotte's gown," said Madame as she bustled around to do up the back of the boned bodice.

"What do you think?" asked Katherine, holding her arms out slightly.

"It's stunning," she said.

The dress was simple, leaving Katherine's shoulders bare above a tight bodice of snow-white crepe that flowed from a diamanté clip down to a romantic skirt that would dance with Katherine as she walked. It was a long white dress, which fit the requirements for Queen Charlotte's Ball, where all of the debutantes would be "ladies-in-waiting" to an older woman who had been elected to play the role of the long-dead Queen Charlotte in honor of her birthday. However, that was where this dress deviated from the usual debutante fare. There was no satin, no embellishment other than the clip, no fuss. It was a woman's dress.

"After you are not a debutante, we will alter it for a slit as we discussed," said Madame, holding the fabric to show where the slit would climb up Katherine's leg.

"But not before," said Katherine with a sigh.

"That would be too much for a debutante," Madame chided. "Hold still, please."

"What a strange ritual," Katherine said as Madame stooped to pin up the hem. "For one night, we'll all play the role of handmaidens to a woman who has been dead for more than one hundred years, and then we'll all bow to a giant cake and cut it with a sword."

"I do not understand the English," said Madame.

"My aunt Angelica says that the party's hardly changed since she and Mummy were debs," Lily said.

"When was this?" Katherine asked.

"Mummy's was in 1921. She met my father during the Season, and they were married by the following spring," Lily said.

"How convenient for you to have a mother who was presented. Mrs. Kingsley's the best I could do," said Katherine with a laugh that sent Madame tutting for her to hold still.

Lily couldn't help being disarmed by the easy way that Katherine talked about the Season. After weeks spent around debs like Leana and Cressie who took it so seriously, it felt like a relief to meet someone who found some absurdity in it.

"Did you mind being brought out by a chaperone?" Lily asked.

"What else could I do? Mum is really just a glorified shopkeeper's daughter, even if grandpa did end up owning three Boston department stores, and she's American—two strikes against her. And, well, you know about Dad," said Katherine.

Everyone in London knew about Walter Norman, who'd saved and bought the struggling East London paper where he'd trained as a printer and grown it into an empire of fourteen publications, including two in America.

"If it had been up to me, I wouldn't have come out at all, but they finally wore me down," Katherine continued. "Dad's been after me to do the Season ever since I turned seventeen, but I couldn't bear the thought of being presented. All those people watching. The Queen? Even now it makes me feel faint."

"But you seem so confident," said Lily, thinking of the way Katherine seemed to effortlessly glide across crowded rooms, nodding to the people she knew.

"It is all a trick of smoke, mirrors, and Madame's gowns," said Katherine.

"It is mostly the gowns," said Madame around the pins held between her teeth.

"I don't understand. If you don't enjoy it, why did you agree to it at all?" Lily asked.

"Do you enjoy every aspect of the Season?" Katherine asked archly.

She paused. "Well, no." The thrill of being one of the people invited into this world was still seductive. She enjoyed the transformation of zipping up a dress and going from regular old Lily to Lily the Debutante with her perfectly coiffed hair and painted lips. And there was something in the way that people looked to see who she was when she walked into a room and singled her out to speak to amid a crowd of debutantes, especially when she was with Leana.

But then there were things she didn't like. The long nights spent with the same people that would only grow longer when the balls began. The building pressure of Grandmama's expectations and the knowledge that, if she didn't please Grandmama, there could be real consequences for Mummy and her. And then there were the moments where she sometimes found herself standing back from the crowd, looking around, and wondering what any of it was supposed to mean when the only conversations she could have were cocktail party chatter in the same places, night after night. In those moments, the Season felt stultifying.

"I love my parents, and this is something that is important to them," said Katherine.

The gift of a daughter who had been presented. Taken into the fold. It was a strange, intangible thing, this designation of being one of those who were "in" or "out." The truth was that the older Normans would never be fully accepted, even in this day and age. The stains of ink on his hands might be gone, but Walter Norman's money was too new for him not to be marked by it. But Katherine could rise above all of that like so many wealthy tradesmen's children did during the last century. She would always be in the sisterhood of debutantes, presented to the Queen in '58 just like Lily or Leana or any of the other girls of the year.

"This is done," said Madame, standing up and rolling her shoulders. "Now you will try on the dress for your dance."

Katherine gathered up her skirts. "Not even Mum knows what it looks like, Lily, although she made me promise not to order it in red."

"I would not have let you," Madame said proudly, then added, "although red would suit your hair."

Katherine grinned. "Back in a moment."

That left Lily and Madame eyeing each other up in the salon. It was Madame who broke the silence first. "Midnight-blue satin."

"I beg your pardon?" asked Lily.

"I would dress you in midnight-blue satin, slim to the knee before flaring out, with a slight bustled train. It is not the fashion, but fashion is not interesting if all of us follow it," said Madame, grabbing a sketch pad and committing a few pencil strokes to paper. Lily watched as a dress emerged in a matter of seconds.

"A boatneck?" she asked.

"To show this," said Madame, placing a hand on her own collarbone. "It is the most seductive part of a woman, I think."

Lily blushed. "I'm not sure that debutantes are meant to be seductive."

"You will not be a debutante forever, no?" asked Madame.

"Madame, it's wonderful," Katherine said as she threw back the dressing room curtain and stepped out in a long ivory dress. Heavy copper beads at the waist cascaded down the full skirts until they nearly disappeared at the bottom edges of the skirt. The effect made it look as though someone had spilled a box of the tiniest topazes all over Katherine's skirts.

"It's beautiful," Lily whispered, half-awed and half-grateful for the distraction from Madame's question about her future.

"It should be for all the time it has taken my assistant and me to bead it," said Madame.

"It is just as I hoped it would be," said Katherine, placating Madame with a smile as she let her fingers dance over the beadwork. "I don't think even the worst of the mothers can find fault with this."

Lily could hear the optimism in Katherine's voice, and her heart ached for her a little. She knew the things that the other women said about Katherine. Her wardrobe might be enviable, and her coming-out ball might be one of the most anticipated invitations of the Season because of the spectacle that it was sure to be, but there was nothing that would stop the rumors from stirring around her. Everything about Katherine's Season was too grand, too expensive, too much.

"Up, please," said Madame, indicating the dais. "I will cut the tulle for the hem now."

Katherine obediently stepped into place.

"If you weren't a debutante, what would you be doing with yourself?" asked Lily.

"I want to become a reporter. I want people to sit up when they read one of my stories. I've spent enough time around Dad's papers to know that editors won't like a woman asking to join a newsroom, let alone the daughter of Walter Norman, but I want to work. I have to."

When Katherine finished, her eyes were sparkling and her cheeks were red, and Lily believed wholeheartedly that her friend would one day see her byline in a newspaper.

"Have you asked your father for a job?" Lily asked.

"Every day since I was twelve. He doesn't want that for me, which is why, at the end of the Season, I'm striking out on my own. I come into some money when I turn twenty-one in June. It won't be a fortune, but it will be enough to buy myself a flat and have a bit to live on."

In the mirror, Katherine leveled a look at her. "What would you be doing?"

"I don't know. Actually"—she stopped herself, clarity coming to her in a flash—"I do. I would have sat my exams for university."

"Where?" Katherine asked.

"Cambridge. It's where my father went."

"Then, when all of this is done, you should go to university," said Katherine as though it was the most natural thing in the world.

Katherine didn't laugh at her or tell her that she couldn't. Instead, Katherine looked upon Lily's confession with blind optimism and hope.

Somehow, Lily felt the old dreams she'd hardly acknowledged herself start to reignite. This is what she needed: a person who would hold her dreams gently in her own heart, next to their own. She wanted to borrow a bit of Katherine's surety, her determination. She wanted to believe that she could do the very things that people seemed to think her incapable of, and most of all she wanted to surprise them all.

Eleven

This has been wonderful, thank you," said Lily as Katherine paid the bill for their meal despite Lily's protests.

"Trust me, it was my pleasure. Thank you for indulging my selfishness and letting me take you out. I think that I needed a lunch away from the Season," said Katherine, snapping her purse closed.

Katherine might think that it had all been for her benefit, but Lily had had a grand time. After leaving Madame Benum's, they'd hopped in the car and tore across town to Soho and found a table at a little restaurant in Chinatown where they'd sat for the past two hours eating everything the owners put in front of them and drinking cup after cup of jasmine tea poured from a clay pot. They'd talked about everything from theater to film, school memories to Katherine's future plans. And not once had either of them brought up a cocktail party or a ball.

"I'm glad you asked me," said Lily.

"I don't suppose you fancy an espresso? It's only that my friend Doris Irving is meeting me at a coffee bar around the corner in a few minutes, and I think you'd like her," said Katherine. She quickly added, "If it's too much, I can tell her you had to hurry home."

"No," said Lily, remembering seeing Katherine's friend in the distance at Vita's party. "I'd very much like to meet her."

"Oh good! She'll be so pleased," said Katherine with a grin.

They left the restaurant on Wardour Street, turning the corner onto Old Compton Street.

"There it is," said Katherine, pointing to a black-and-red sign part of the way down the block that read "2i's Coffee Bar."

"It really was around the corner," said Lily with a laugh.

Lily followed as Katherine pushed open the door of the coffee bar. The scream of an espresso machine met them, and cigarette smoke wafted through the air, mixing with the scent of freshly ground beans.

"I've never been to one of these before," said Lily, gazing around.

"Oh, you'll like it. It's all writers and theater people and students." Katherine waved to a woman with auburn hair whom Lily recognized from the end of Vita's party. She wore a pair of black trousers and a smart green jacket, her long legs capped off by high heels sticking out from under the table. "There she is."

At the table, Katherine dropped into a chair and said, "Doris, this is Lily who I've told you about."

"How do you do?" asked Lily.

"How do you do?" the girl returned in an accent that sounded remarkably like Katharine Hepburn's.

A waitress came to take their order—two espressos for Lily and Katherine—and then Doris eyed Lily and said, "So you're the snob's friend?"

"Doris!" said Katherine sharply.

"I'm sorry. I don't know who the snob is," said Lily, looking from Katherine to Doris.

"She means Leana Hartford," said Katherine. "Doris is not a fan."

"Why should I be? We were in the same class at Madame Vacani's, and she wouldn't even look at me," said Doris, digging into her handbag for a gold cigarette case and matching lighter.

"I'm sorry Leana wasn't friendly. She can be like that sometimes," said Lily.

"Difficult but beautiful," said Doris.

"I think that you need to let this go, Doris," said Katherine. "If you go around hating everyone who is rude to us, you won't have many friends among the debs."

Doris blew a stream of smoke to the ceiling. "Now, isn't that the truth."

"Who's been rude to you?" asked Lily, more than a little taken aback. "And why?"

Doris laughed. "Take your pick! My father's from an American shipping family, which means that every mother who didn't secure an invitation to a presentation party for her daughter is angry that a half American's taking away a spot from a real British girl."

"I can attest to that," said Katherine.

"And then there's Mum," said Doris.

"Doris's mother had a bit of a scandalous divorce before the war," said Katherine.

"And she never met a party she didn't like," said Doris with a grin, making Lily think that perhaps she rather enjoyed being from a notorious family.

"It makes Mrs. Irving very good fun," said Katherine with a laugh. "You'll like her, Lily."

"Since the divorce, Mum's officially persona non grata at court, and I had to be presented by the enterprising Mrs. Kingsley," said Doris as the waitress returned with their drinks.

"Don't forget that you also say absolutely everything that comes to your mind," Katherine teased. "It's very American of you."

"Yes, there is that. My introduction to you being case in point." Doris managed to look contrite. "Sorry about that, Lily."

"Not at all," said Lily.

"Now, Katherine likes to think that I'm far more notorious, but I don't have a nickname like the 'Millionaire Deb,'" said Doris.

"Yet," Katherine reminded her, throwing a napkin across the table and hitting her friend in the face.

Doris whipped the napkin right back before turning her sharp green eyes to Lily. "What's your fatal flaw, Lily Nicholls? You're not allowed at this table without one."

"Oh, let me see," Lily said, crossing her arms and leaning back in her chair as though deep in thought. "My father's dead. People don't like being reminded of that."

"Very uncomfortable," Doris agreed.

"Mummy's been in mourning for so long that she was a veritable recluse until the Season started. People call her 'the Old Vic,'" she said.

"Like the theater?" asked Katherine.

"Queen Victoria because of the mourning and wearing black," said Lily. "I have an estranged sister I've never met who was scandalous enough at sixteen that she was sent to America just before the war, although no one will tell me why. My Season is nearly bankrupting Mummy despite Grandmama's help, so I'm making nearly all of my dresses. Oh, and I live in a house that's *almost* in Fulham."

There was a beat, and then Doris asked in mock horror, "You live in Fulham?" sending the three of them howling with laughter.

A great tapping on the window made them all start up in their chairs. On the other side, Philippa and Ivy stood waving, shopping bags clutched in their hands.

"Oh! They're friends of mine. Do you mind if they come in?" Lily asked.

"They aren't perfect debs, are they?" asked Doris.

"Philippa's Catholic, and Ivy's grandmother's a tyrant who insists she dress like a cream puff," said Lily.

"Perfect! The more the merrier," said Doris with a satisfied nod.

Lily waved the other girls in, and Philippa glided through the coffee bar door with a hesitant Ivy trailing behind. As soon as introductions were done and the other girls had placed their orders, Lily turned to Philippa. "I hadn't expected to see you in Soho."

"I took Ivy shopping. There's a wonderful milliner nearby that had a hat I thought she would love," said Philippa.

"Yes," Ivy breathed, reaching down to touch the hatbox she'd gingerly placed on the floor next to her. "I don't know what Grandmama is going to say about it. It's rather daring."

"Let's see it, then," said Katherine.

"Oh, I couldn't—"

"We'd *love* to see it," cooed Doris.

"Oh, all right then," said Ivy, clearly pleased to have someone to show off to. She pulled out the hat, and placed it on top of the box.

"Oh, it's beautiful," breathed Katherine.

It was. It was a little deep green pillbox with a swath of black netting on the front and a long black feather trained around the brim so that it slanted down and to the back of the hat. It was sophisticated and a bit daring and not at all the sort of thing that Ivy's grandmother would ever dream of letting her debutante granddaughter wear.

"She's going to hate it," said Ivy, as though she could read Lily's thoughts. "I might take it back."

"It's delicious. Put it on," said Doris.

Ivy reached up to unpin her proper cloche and replace it with the green hat. Philippa reached up to tilt it to the perfect angle, sitting back with a satisfied smile.

"Oh, Ivy. You have to keep it. It's perfect," said Lily.

Her friend bit her lip. "I don't know . . ."

"You won't be a deb forever," said Doris.

"Thank goodness for that," said Katherine.

"Don't you like the Season?" Ivy asked, lifting the hat off carefully and putting it back in its box.

Katherine glanced at Lily. "I feel as though I'm biding my time."

"Our friend here has aspirations for greatness—or at least employment. However, I am having a grand time watching the absurdity of it all," said Doris.

"Do you really think it's absurd?" Ivy asked.

"That for the better part of a year we're expected to go to lots of parties all in the hope that we'll meet a nice man? It's positively Victorian," said Doris.

"At least you have most of the pool of nice men to choose from. My family expects me to marry a Catholic. Do you know how many of the deb's delights there are who are Catholic and don't have an unfortunate streak of financial ruin or madness running through their families?" Philippa asked.

"I'm going to guess there aren't many," said Katherine.

"You would be correct." A sparkle came into Philippa's eyes. "But at least there will be dancing."

"I just want to marry someone nice. Only I don't know if that's ever going to happen," said Ivy with a sigh.

"Why not?" asked Lily.

Ivy looked down at her lap. "Men look right through me."

"Well, we shall have to fix that," announced Doris. "Who do we know who would be perfect for Ivy?"

"Oh, no. Don't try to set me up with someone," said Ivy quickly.

"Doris is just teasing," said Katherine, shooting Doris a look.

"I am, although if you ever did want help, I think Lily is the one you should ask," said Doris.

"Me?" said Lily with a laugh.

"Gideon Moore—"

"See, she sees it, too!" cried Ivy, cutting Doris off.

"No, I think Lily's interests lie elsewhere," said Katherine with a sly smile. "Who was the man who fetched you a taxi at the Savoy?"

Lily couldn't help her blush. "I don't know him very well."

"Does he have a name?" asked Doris.

"Ian Bingham," said Lily after taking the last sip of her espresso.

Philippa cocked her head to one side. "Tall, good hair, goes to Cambridge."

"That's the one," said Katherine.

"We've only met once, but I do like speaking to him," she said.

"That is more than I can say of any of the men I've met this spring," said Katherine.

"My mother has a list of eligible men of the Season," said Doris. "She's sorted them into categories. NSIT and DNSIT."

"What does that mean?" asked Ivy.

"Not Safe in Taxis, and Definitely Not Safe in Taxis," Doris replied.

They all burst out laughing.

"Really!" huffed a bearded man in a black jumper hunched over a manuscript a table away, setting them off again.

When finally they'd settled down, the waitress hovered over them, their bill in hand. They paid, a little chastened at having caused an uproar in the coffee bar, but still giddy as they spilled out onto the sidewalk.

"My drinks party is coming up next Wednesday. My mother has hardly let me see the guest list at all, but I'll make sure that you all have invitations," said Philippa.

The other girls promised that they'd come, and Philippa gave a satisfied nod.

"I can take whoever wants a ride home with Lily and me, if you're willing to squeeze into the tiny space in the back," said Katherine.

"Ivy, did you want to drop your hat by my house?" asked Philippa.

Ivy gazed down at the hatbox and sighed. "Yes. That's probably a good idea."

"We'll walk. I'm only in Fitzrovia," said Philippa.

"Doris?" asked Katherine.

"I might need to claim the front seat, Lily. I'm sorry," said Doris, gesturing to her long legs.

"Of course. I'll bunch up in the back," she said.

"Before we all go, I have a proposal. Is everyone going to Christine Faulks's party this Monday? Or Charlotte Damrosch's party tonight?" asked Katherine. There were nods all around. "Good. Then I think at each party where all of us are presented, we should have a toast to imperfectly perfect debutantes."

Lily grinned. "The Imperfects. I like that."

"Good, because it's the best idea I've had all week. Now, let's go before I turn into a pumpkin and have to prepare for Charlotte's party," said Katherine.

Katherine drove them back home, dropping off Doris in Kensington before turning south for Lily's home.

Idling in front of number 17, Katherine turned to Lily. "Do you know, I think this has been the best day of my Season. I have a feeling that with you girls around, I might actually make it through the Scottish balls in September."

"It's been wonderful," Lily agreed. She climbed out of the car and watched Katherine drive off with a wave and a roar of the sports car's engine, thinking just how lucky it was that she'd left Vita's party early.

PART II

Cocktails

"A New Sort of Bluestocking"

I had the pleasure recently of meeting Lillian Nicholls, daughter of the late Lieutenant Michael Nicholls and Mrs. Michael Nicholls of Harley Gardens. Miss Nicholls's name has been on many lips this Season as she has been spotted at parties and dinners in dresses lovely enough to make admiring debs wonder who her dressmaker is. She is a fair, pretty girl and something of a "bluestocking," as comfortable speaking about the novels of Gaskell, Burney, and Thackeray as she is conversing about the latest comings and goings at court. However, Miss Nicholls is proof that the modern bluestocking is no longer a quiet, retiring girl but a merry, cheerful deb who has already been spotted at parties, luncheons, and the theater.

I have further news of Miss Nicholls's cocktail party, to be shared with her cousin Miss Georgina Laningham, the pretty, vibrant daughter of Mr. and Mrs. Elliot Laningham. They will greet their guests at the Hyde Park Hotel on 23rd April.

Twelve

Lily clutched her glass tighter, her eyes darting around the Royal Automobile Club's St. James's Room and catching people as they surreptitiously watched her.

"Stand up and stop looking like a caged animal, Lillian," Grandmama chided her.

"Everyone is watching me," she said.

"You're a debutante and a lovely girl. I would have thought that you would be used to that by now," said Grandmama.

"It's that article in *The Sketch*," she murmured.

"It was a very complimentary article, and your studio portrait was lovely. I only wish they'd chosen a different headline," said Grandmama, smiling at an older woman who approached, a lanky young man in a navy suit at her side.

"Geraldine, how good to see you," said Grandmama, kissing the other woman lightly on her cheek. "Have you met my granddaughter, Lillian?"

"I haven't had the pleasure," said the other woman, her deeply lined face creasing with her smile.

"Lillian, this is Mrs. Spence. Your grandfather was a great friend of Mr. Spence," said Grandmama.

"How do you do, Lillian?" asked Mrs. Spence. Lily dipped her head in deference to the older woman as she gestured to the young man standing next to her. "My grandson, Charles."

"How do you do?" Lily said to the Spences.

"Charles is reading classics at Cambridge," said Mrs. Spence, looking expectantly at her grandson. When Charles didn't say anything, his grandmother gave him a nudge.

"Yes. Yes, I am. Reading classics, that is," Charles stumbled.

Oh dear. A look passed between Lily and Grandmama, and both ladies drew in a breath, preparing themselves for what was sure to be a difficult few minutes of stilted conversation.

"How do you find Cambridge?" Lily asked.

"Very good. Very, very good," murmured Charles.

"I understand that you are an enthusiastic reader yourself," said Mrs. Spence with a tight smile, as though acknowledging that she'd plunged them into this mess but, by God, she was going to soldier on.

"I am, although my taste tends toward more modern literature. I'm afraid my Homer would be rusty," said Lily.

"Yes. Quite," said Charles.

A long pause stretched between them.

"Charles, will you be coming up to London for the Boat Race this year?" asked Grandmama about the traditional regatta that pitted rowers from Oxford and Cambridge against one another in a race along the Thames. With huge marquees pitched along the river bank, the regatta was one of the many events around which the Season was built.

"Oh, I don't know," said Charles.

"I beg your pardon, but I had to stop and say hello."

They all turned, and Lily couldn't help her grin at the sight of Ian Bingham, saving her once again. She hadn't known he'd be at Philippa's drinks, but she sent a little thought of thanks across the room to her friend who was surrounded by a tight group of relatives while the other Imperfects stood a few feet off, giggling away.

She hadn't seen Ian since their first meeting, but she'd looked for him at every party in the days after, even going so far as to ask Leana if he came up to London often.

"I should hope not. Papa insists that he has an invitation to stay at Hartford House whenever he does come up, but fortunately he doesn't use it often," Leana had said.

Charles also seemed brightened by Ian's presence, sticking out a hand to shake his vigorously. "Bingham, if I'd known you would be here, I would have suggested that we drive up together. Grandmother, this is Ian Bingham. We're both at Jesus College."

Charles's grandmother gave Ian a thin smile.

"Grandmama, this is Ian Bingham. Ian, my grandmother, Mrs. Nicholls," Lily said.

Grandmama assessed Ian with interest. "How do you do?"

With the introductions out of the way, Ian gave a smile of apology. "I really didn't want to interrupt, it's just that I saw Spence here, and after seeing Daniel Rutledge earlier—"

"Rutledge is here?" Charles asked. "I'll go and say hello."

Lily, Grandmama, and Ian watched as Charles beat a quick retreat, followed by his grandmother, sighing as she went.

"That was very artfully done, Mr. Bingham," said Grandmama.

Ian fought a smile. "I can't imagine what you might be referring to, Mrs. Nicholls."

The corner of Grandmama's lips lifted a fraction. "I'm sure you can't. And I think that now perhaps it is time that I say hello to a few more people. Lily. Mr. Bingham."

Grandmama nodded and then glided off.

"That's twice you've saved me from an awkward situation," she said.

"I'm afraid the men of our nation's universities aren't acquitting themselves very well," he said.

She laughed. "At least it was not the strangest encounter I've had tonight."

"What is special about tonight?" he asked.

She sighed. "There was a piece about me in one of the society papers. It's rather awkward."

"Was it complimentary?" he asked.

"It was. It's just strange seeing my name in print. It's a bit like having an advertisement placed for everyone to see: 'This girl is a debutante in need of an escort.'"

"Well, I'm sure that no matter what they said, it paled in comparison to meeting the real Lily Nicholls in person," he said.

She blushed. "Now you're teasing me."

He smiled. "Only a little bit. The intention behind the words is true. I realize that this is very presumptuous and that you probably already have plans, but I don't suppose you'd like to have dinner with me after this."

Her heart leaped, but just as quickly she fell back to reality. "I do have plans tonight, actually."

"Oh." He sounded genuinely disappointed. "I should have guessed that Leana would have already invited you, but when I didn't see her here—"

"No, it's not Leana. That is, a few of us are taking Philippa to dinner at Rules before going dancing at the Colony Club to celebrate a successful coming-out party." She hesitated. "Would you like to come with us?"

He looked down, and for a moment she couldn't see his expression. She worried that he'd taken offense to her offer—that she'd been too forward in asking *him* to dinner—but then he lifted his head and smiled. "I can't think of anything I'd like more."

Ian climbed out of the taxi to pay the driver, and Katherine, who had been sitting next to Lily on the back seat, leaned over and in a loud whisper said, "He's very handsome."

Katherine's own date, William Sassoon, snorted a laugh. "I heard that."

"Go help with the fare, William," said Katherine, shooting the son of her father's friend a fond smile.

William heaved a great sigh and then gamely climbed out.

"I like him," said Lily.

"Well yes, I should hope you did if you invited him to dinner," said Katherine.

"No," she said with a laugh. "William."

"He's a dear, promising to be my escort whenever I need him." Katherine brushed off the look that Lily shot her. "He's the closest thing I have to a brother. Now, tell me what happened with Ian."

"I told you everything. He came up and rescued Grandmama and me from an awkward situation. Then he asked me to dinner, so I told him he should come tonight," Lily said.

"You could have gone for dinner with him alone. We would have understood," said Katherine.

She shook her head. "No. I said I would come out tonight to celebrate Philippa, and that's what we're doing. Plus, we're going dancing later."

Katherine gave her a sly smile. "Clever girl."

William stuck his head into the taxi. "Are you done gossiping about us?"

"Why would I ever gossip about you, Will? You never give me anything good to talk about," said Katherine, grabbing his hand to let him help her out of the taxi.

Ian reached for Lily. "Is everything all right?" he asked.

She smiled up at him. "Perfectly."

And perfectly all right it was. All of the Imperfects were there, and Philippa had managed to round up escorts for Ivy and Doris in two trainee solicitors, Shrey Acharya and Max Thompson, who had both proven to be sharp and funny, making them the perfect company. Philippa's escort was Doris's brother, David, who had taken one look at Philippa and seemed to be well on his way to infatuation.

The maître d' sat them around a big table nestled against a red velvet booth at the back of the restaurant, and soon any awkwardness or unfamiliarity had fallen away. Once the first bottle of wine was empty and William had called for a second, they were laughing like old friends.

"Now, have any of you been to Venice?" asked William, mid-story.

"I have," said Doris, raising her hand. "Mummy is mad for Carnival."

"I went one summer," said Shrey from his seat between Doris and Ivy, wineglass in his hand. "I don't think I've ever been so hot before. And it stank."

"Then you two will know that the traffic on the canals can be quite heavy sometimes," said William. "I realized I'd given the gondolier the wrong directions, and he was taking me away from the party I was supposed to be going to, rather than toward it. My Italian is poor at best, so I couldn't tell him that we were going the wrong way."

"Which was entirely your fault," Katherine pointed out.

"Which was entirely my fault. Since we were virtually stationary, I decided that I would just hop from my gondola into another going in the right direction."

"And how much prosecco had you had at this point?" Lily asked with a laugh.

"I resent the implication in that question, young lady," said William, puffing out his chest before grinning. "And, to answer your question, rather a lot."

"Oh, William," laughed Katherine with a shake of her head.

"I stood up, hailed another gondola, and was just making the step from boat to boat when my original gondolier, who understandably hated me at this point, gave a huge push, and straight into the Grand Canal I went."

The table roared with laughter, and William leaned back in his chair with a satisfied smile. "I cannot recommend it."

"You are a ridiculous creature," said Katherine with affection.

He tipped his glass at her. "And so are you, my darling."

"What a charming scene."

The hairs on the back of Lily's neck stood at the sound of Leana's voice, and she turned to see the other deb with Gideon and Raymond Troy flanking her, Cressie, Rupert, and Sophie standing just behind them.

"Hello, Leana," said Lily.

"Lily, you missed a lovely party at Lady Fiona's home tonight. I thought you might be home with your nose in a book, since you are a 'new sort of bluestocking,'" said Leana with narrowed eyes.

Lily's hands balled up into fists in her lap, but she kept her voice steady when she said, "I'm sorry to have missed it, but I'm looking forward to her ball next month."

It had seemed the obvious thing to do: forgo Lady Fiona's drinks for Philippa's, knowing that Lady Fiona would have a second do at the end of May.

"I do hope that you won't be too tired for dinner and dancing after Rebecca's party tomorrow," said Leana.

"I can't imagine I will be," she said.

Leana's eyes narrowed. "Ian, I didn't realize that you were in town."

"Just for the night. Philippa was kind enough to invite me, and this was one of those rare instances where I was able to rearrange things to come up to London," he said.

Lily's cheeks warmed at the thought that he might have made the effort that evening to come up on the chance that he might see her.

"I see," said Leana.

"We're going dancing after dinner if you'd like to come," said Gideon, looking around at their table as though in apology for Leana's blatant ignoring of the rest of them.

"We are, too," said Ivy cheerfully, either not noticing or not caring about the tension snapping over the table.

"Where?" asked Gideon.

"I booked us a table at the Colony Club," said William.

"Maybe we'll see you there, Lily," said Cressie.

Leana looked as though she were about to say something, when Raymond huffed. "Are we going to stand here all night, or are we going to eat?"

"We should take our table," said Rupert softly, his hand on Cressie's elbow.

"It was good to see you, Lily," said Gideon, sending her a small smile before following Raymond and Leana.

As they watched the other party walk away, an unnatural silence fell over Lily's table. They all seemed to sense that something had happened there, although she was sure that most of them couldn't be entirely sure what. For her part, Lily's cheeks burned from embarrassment at Leana's disregard for her friends and for Leana's joke about the bluestocking headline.

That ridiculous article . . .

Well, she was not going to let Leana's jealousy or judgment ruin her night.

"What do you all say to another bottle of wine?" Lily asked.

"I think that's a very good idea," said Katherine.

"Shall I?" William asked, already raising his hand to catch the waiter's attention.

"Champagne again?" Lily asked. "I feel like we should celebrate Philippa's night properly."

"Oh, you don't have to do that," said Philippa.

"We absolutely do," said David, nearly knocking over his water glass into his sister's lap as he tried to flag down the waiter, too.

"David, you won't woo her by soaking me!" Doris called out, the table laughing again.

And just like that, her friends relaxed, the incident with Leana forgotten.

Except for one man.

"Are you okay?" Ian asked, placing his hand on the back of her chair as he leaned down to whisper to her.

"I'm fine," she said. When he raised his brows, she said, "Really, I am."

"We can always go to another nightclub," he offered.

She shook her head. "I think we should do exactly what we planned. Leana doesn't get to dictate who I spend my time with. She isn't my only friend."

"All right then," said Ian, sitting back again. But, she noticed, he didn't take his hand from the back of her chair until their main courses arrived.

A couple hours later, Lily found herself at a table at the edge of the dance floor at the Colony Club. Shrey and Ivy, Philippa and David, and Max and Doris had all paired off. With William and Ian both dutifully dancing with a pair of rather bored-looking debs from the next table, Lily and Katherine were alone at the table, their drinks sweating in tall glasses.

"Philippa looks happy, doesn't she?" Katherine shouted over the band as they watched Philippa's yellow skirts flare out as David pushed her around the floor in a jive.

"I hope she enjoyed tonight," Lily said.

"She has, and I don't think she's looked away from David all night. It was inspired of Doris to bring him along." Katherine looked at her. "And what about you, has it been a good night?"

"It has," she said with a smile.

"In spite of the little incident with Leana earlier? I thought if looks could kill, we all would have been gone in a heartbeat," said Katherine.

Lily rubbed her temple. "I'm sorry about that. I don't know what's wrong with her. She was so nice to me in the beginning, but now she's . . ."

"Being a bit of a brat?" Katherine asked sweetly.

Lily burst out laughing. "I don't know if I'd go that far. I think she's just used to saying 'jump' and watching people jump."

Katherine shot her a look. "That doesn't sound like you."

"Doesn't it?" she asked, thinking about her regret that she'd had to give up school for the Season. How, once she considered the possibility that Grandmama might pull the allowance that she and Mummy lived off of, it had been so easy to turn away from something she loved.

"I know we haven't known each other very long, but I think you'd probably surprise yourself with what you'll do if you give yourself half a chance," said Katherine.

Lily smiled at that. "I could say the same for you, future reporter."

Katherine lifted her drink. "By this time next year, with any luck."

Ian pushed through the crowd with his partner as the band ended the fast song and struck up the first bars of "The Way You Look Tonight." After returning the other girl to her table, he turned to Lily. "Dance with me?"

"Haven't had your fill of dancing?" she asked as he touched a handkerchief to his brow.

He grinned. "Not with you."

She let him lead her out to the middle of the floor and fold her into his arms. Her heart pounded, even as the music slowed into something sweet and swaying she didn't recognize.

"Have you had a good night tonight?" he murmured, his voice reverberating through her chest.

She looked up at him. "I have."

He seemed to hesitate.

"What is it?" she asked.

He shook his head. "No, it's fine."

"Tell me."

"I was just thinking about the first night I met you. I saw you walk in with Gideon," he said, sounding a little sheepish.

"With Gideon?" she asked. That was well before Ian had come to her assistance with the man who thought women at university were a blight on British higher education.

"I've actually known him nearly as long as I've known the Hartfords. My father is the Moore family doctor as well."

"I hadn't realized." She hadn't thought that Ian would have known Gideon, because of where he'd grown up, but it made sense.

"Gideon's one of the few of that crowd who never made me feel like I should be grateful for Mr. Hartford's charity. He's a good one in his own way. You like him, don't you?"

This time it was her turn to choose her words carefully. "I do."

"And if he knew that I was dancing with you?" Ian asked.

"Then I would hope that he would be happy that I had found a partner for this dance, just as I'm sure you would."

He held her gaze for a moment and then nodded before pulling her close.

Thirteen

The day after dancing at the Colony Club, Lily hauled herself out of bed and put on a cream cotton shirt dress and a red cardigan topped with a slim belt with just enough time to walk to her hairdresser on the King's Road. She had learned from her first night of the Season that if she had anything to do the following day, it wouldn't do to drink *too* much champagne—or anything else, for that matter, so she wasn't feeling particularly worse for wear when she sat in the salon chair to have her hair washed and set. However, Celeste, the woman who shampooed her hair at Mr. Gerard's salon, clucked at the dark circles under her eyes.

"Too many late nights out. I see it in all the debutantes that come to me," Celeste admonished her.

Lily smiled tightly, but when she nearly fell asleep under the hood dryer, she had to admit that perhaps she was due a good nap that afternoon in preparation for the night's festivities.

When she left the salon, her blond hair perfectly waved to the nape of her neck, she checked the slim gold watch Grandmama had given her on her sixteenth birthday. It was only just past two o'clock. Plenty of time to relax and then ready herself for the night's cocktail parties. Plenty of time to stop off at her favorite place.

Lily walked up the steps of the redbrick library building, a sense of calm settling over her. She smiled at Miss Kellerman, the librarian who always worked behind the circulation desk on Thursdays, and headed straight for the literature section. Breathing in deep the scent of old books, she decided that, after so many modern novels, today was a day for Anthony Trollope. Heading down the rows until she reached T, she crooked her head to the side and read off the spines until she found the Palliser series. She had begun *Can You Forgive Her?* two years earlier, and she'd been steadily working her way through the series. With a smile, she pulled *The Eustace Diamonds* off the shelf, the green cloth-covered spine crackling slightly as she opened the book to the first chapter.

It was admitted by all her friends, and also by her enemies,—who were in truth the more numerous and active body of the two,—that Lizzie Grey-stock had done very well with herself.

She snorted lightly at that—an unladylike sound that no doubt both Mummy and Grandmama would have chided her for. A debutante knew a thing or two about friends and enemies.

"Good morning, Miss Kellerman," said Lily in a loud whisper as she approached the circulation desk.

"Good morning, Miss Nicholls. Trollope again?" asked the librarian as she reached for the stamp and ink pad with long, elegant hands unencumbered by jewelry. "It has been a while."

"Yes. I thought it was time to return to the Palliser novels," she said, a tinge of guilt that she'd left the series abandoned for some time now.

"We don't see you as often as we used to," Miss Kellerman observed as she stamped the book's card and made note of Lily's selection for the library records.

"No," she said with real regret. "I'm no longer in school."

Miss Kellerman looked up sharply. "Are you not? Miss Lewis and I were positive that you were destined for university."

"So was I," came a voice behind her, louder than was maybe appropriate for a library.

Lily swallowed and braced herself as she turned to greet her former teacher, Miss Hester.

"Good morning, Miss Nicholls," said Miss Hester, her arms wrapped about a pile of books that looked comically large against her small frame.

"Good morning, Miss Hester. I didn't realize that you were a patron of this library," she said.

"I live a very short walk from here," said Miss Hester. "I'm sorry to have overheard that you are no longer in school."

"I'm a debutante," she said.

Miss Hester lifted her chin a fraction of an inch but didn't reply, so Lily hurried to add, "My grandmother and mother thought it best."

"Well, so long as they thought it best," said Miss Hester archly.

Miss Kellerman slid Lily's book across the desk to her, and she murmured her thanks as she stepped aside for her former teacher.

"I'm glad to see that you are still reading," said Miss Hester.

"I can't imagine not," said Lily, although guilt tugged at her when she thought of how many nights she'd gone without picking up a book, as had been her habit when she'd been in school. She tried her best to read in the mornings and on her free afternoons—she'd just finished that Rosamond Lehmann novel, hadn't she?—but what of the mornings she'd slept in and then had to rush off to a luncheon? It suddenly felt, as she stood there in the light-filled center of the library, that she'd lost a part of herself in the last few months.

"Once you are finished with the Palliser series, might I recommend that you turn to our own century?" Miss Hester asked as Miss Kellerman stamped her books.

"What would you recommend?" she asked politely, even though she had been reading more modern novels.

"You might try the American Willa Cather, or perhaps Katherine Mansfield or Rebecca West," said Miss Hester.

"Here you are, Miss Hester," said Miss Kellerman. "We'll see you again next week."

"Thank you," said Miss Hester, carefully placing the books into a canvas bag she then slung over her shoulder. "Miss Nicholls, which direction are you walking in?"

"Down the King's Road, toward Beaufort Street," she said.

"I will walk with you. I'm near Brompton Cemetery," said Miss Hester.

Lily nodded, and they said their goodbyes to Miss Kellerman.

As they left the building, Miss Hester said, "I used to come to this library once a week after teaching. I would alight from the bus early and let myself have an afternoon of browsing the shelves."

"I used to do the same on Wednesdays," said Lily. It had been her treat, a way to reward herself for those slightly terrifying teas with Grandmama each Tuesday.

"I went on Thursdays. That is why we never crossed paths," said Miss Hester in her matter-of-fact way. "Tell me, what do you do as a debutante?"

"Oh, well, I was presented at court, and now there are a number of cocktail parties every week to meet various people. Mine is next week. And once Queen Charlotte's Ball happens in early May, my nights will be taken up by balls. Then there is Ascot, Henley, and the Dublin Horse Show, if I were to go on to Ireland, and then the Scottish balls in September."

"And do you enjoy all of these parties?" asked Miss Hester.

"Some of them are good fun if the right people are there, but there are those that are very dull, and I wonder if it was worth the bother dressing up for them," she said. When Miss Hester didn't speak, she added, "I suppose it all sounds frivolous when I say it out loud."

Miss Hester let out a rare laugh. "No, Miss Nicholls, I was just thinking that it sounds exhausting to an old woman like me. And what will you do after the Season?"

"Oh." What *would* she do? No one had really spoken to her about that. The Season had been the entire focus of every conversation Mummy and Grandmama had about the future. Success was the goal, but what success looked like was more vague. In Grandmama's era, it would have been an engagement—and she supposed that's what it would have been like when Mummy came out as well. The Season was, after all, how Mummy had met and fallen in love with Papa. But now . . . ?

"I suppose that after I'll find a job of some sort," she finally said. No doubt it would be something appropriate like a secretarial position in a "famous department store" as *The Sketch* had reported one former deb had found.

"I do have a friend who wants to be a reporter. And one of the top debs of the Season is going to be going to Oxford to read literature in the autumn," she said.

Miss Hester's keen eyes cut to her. "I had once thought that would be the path that you took, Miss Nicholls."

University. It seemed like such a strange concept. So few women went after finishing at Mrs. Wodely's School. Most were content to take little jobs—if any at all—until they married and became mothers. But to go to university and study simply for the sake of her own edification seemed like an indulgence that belonged to an entirely different girl.

"I hadn't really given it any serious thought. I'd need to take my entrance exams first, and I'm not sure there is enough time to prepare for this year's. Missing the final terms of school, I doubt I'd be ready," she said.

"Yes, it sounds as though you've given it no serious thought at all," said Miss Hester with a smile.

Lily clutched the book to her chest a bit tighter, overwhelmed at the path that had opened up before her. "I don't know where I would even start."

"You could read those books I mentioned." Miss Hester unsnapped the worn metal top of her brown leather handbag and pulled out a card. "And if you ever decide that you do want to engage in serious study for the entrance exams, you can ring me and we can discuss it further."

Lily took the card that had Miss Hester's name and telephone exchange printed on it in a bold, neat font. "You'd offer me guidance?"

Miss Hester nodded. "You were a bright student, Miss Nicholls, and it would be a shame to see that intelligence squandered before it had a real chance to develop. Now, I've just decided that I'm going to have a chop for my dinner tonight, so I think I shall stop at the butcher. I will say goodbye to you here."

"Thank you, Miss Hester," she said, tucking the card into the front cover of *The Eustace Diamonds*. "I'm glad that we happened upon each other today."

Miss Hester smiled. "I am, too, Miss Nicholls. I am, too."

Only silence welcomed Lily as she unlocked the front door of her house and slipped off her handbag and jacket in one practiced move. She hung the jacket on the hook by the door, spotting a piece of Mummy's pale blue notepaper folded up on the silver letter tray on the sideboard as she stepped back. She opened it and read Mummy's message.

> *Poor Angelica is suffering from a wretched migraine, and her maid is visiting her mother today. I have gone to play nursemaid.*
>
> *I've left three new invitations on your desk. Do consider Miss Gorman's ball in particular, as Angelica hears that her cousin Alfred will be there, and he is looking for a sweet-natured girl who will be good company for him.*
>
> *—Mummy*

Lily refolded the note with a laugh and a sigh. She'd never particularly liked Sarah Gorman since Sarah had pushed her into a small stand of flowerpots at Rachel Marlow's eighth birthday party when Lily had refused to share a piece of chocolate cake with her. Although attending two balls on a single night was not unheard of, especially during the busiest weeks of June, she sincerely hoped that she had already given an RSVP to another deb that evening.

"Hannah!" Lily called out. "Hannah!"

Lily wandered through the house, bringing her library book with her as she looked for the housekeeper. In the kitchen, she spotted the empty space where Hannah's coat and hat usually hung. Their absence meant that—for the first time in a very long time—Lily had the house to herself.

The house to herself? A grin broke out over her face. She could do anything she wanted to. She could high-kick down the stairs, sing at the top of her lungs, and do pirouettes on the waxed floors of the entryway. Or she could sprawl out on the sitting room sofa—most unladylike—and read her library book with no one breezing by to tell her to sit up straight.

She hurried through the house to the sitting room, dropped onto one of the green velvet sofas, heeled off her shoes, and opened her book.

Miss Hester's card slid down the front cover to land in her lap.

Lily picked up the card. University. A low tug that had quietly been waiting in her heart since she spoke to Juliet grew a little louder, more insistent. Could she really go to university? What would Mummy and Grandmama think of a girl wanting to dedicate herself to the pursuit of study after her Season was done?

They wouldn't like it, she was almost positive. Or rather, Grandmama wouldn't like it, and that was what mattered.

Grandmama had very specific ideas of what a deb should do and how she should act, and Lily was certain she had opinions about what a former deb should do after her Season was done, too. The likelihood that that included university was slim, and the risk of angering Grandmama rested heavily on her, especially when Grandmama had made the consequences so clear. If Lily and Mummy didn't follow her rules, the money would stop. Mummy would need to sell the house. They would lose this life they had, and it would be Lily's fault.

She couldn't do that to her mother.

Lily didn't fool herself. She knew that Mummy wasn't the warm, caring parent that some of her school friends had had. Mummy could be capricious, frightened, and cold all in the space of the same afternoon. But she was the only parent that Lily had, and she loved Mummy in spite of her flaws. She couldn't leave Mummy unprotected and open to Grandmama's whims.

She tucked the card away in the front of the book again, and opened to the first page.

It was admitted by all her friends, and also by her enemies,—who were in truth the more numerous and active body of the two,—that Lizzie Greystock had done very well—

The bright, jarring sound of the doorbell sent Lily jerking upright on the sofa. A hand pressed to her heart to stop its pounding, she set the book down, hurrying to work her feet back into her ballerina flats.

The doorbell rang again.

"I'm coming," she muttered under her breath.

She passed through the entryway and went to open the front door.

Leana stood on the doorstep in a simple but elegant light-blue-and-white skirt and a white top that was crisply ironed so the collar stood up just slightly in the back. She wore pearls at her throat, white gloves on her hands, a large basket on her arm, and she looked every bit the perfect debutante coming to pay a call.

"Leana," she said, not bothering to hide her surprise. After the way that Leana had regarded her and her friends last night, the last thing she'd expected was a visit.

"I was in Chelsea doing some shopping, so I thought I would drop by," said Leana.

"You were shopping in Chelsea?" Lily asked skeptically. Leana's tastes ran to Hartnell and Dior, not the Bazaar on the King's Road or Kiki Byrne's Sloane Street boutique that appealed to girls in art school.

Leana huffed. "Fine. I wasn't shopping, but I did want to see you. Can I come in?"

"Oh," she said, stepping back. "Of course."

But although her manners meant that she would never leave Leana Hartford waiting on her doorstep or turn her away, an unsettled feeling still fell over Lily as she showed Leana to the sitting room. It wasn't just that Leana had shown a complete disregard for her friends yesterday evening or that Lily felt the immediate urge to pull back for fear that Leana was trying to maneuver her into whatever situation Leana preferred. It was the way that Leana's eyes skimmed over the sitting room, taking in the damask wallpaper twenty years out of date and the heavy hunter-green velvet curtains that showed slight signs of fading if one looked too closely.

"Shall I make us some tea?" Lily asked.

"That would be lovely," said Leana, taking a seat opposite the sofa where Lily's book lay abandoned.

"It won't be a minute," she said.

She hurried to the basement kitchen. During the day, this was Hannah's domain, but with the housekeeper nowhere to be seen, she could move freely about without being shooed away or told she was underfoot.

Lily set the kettle on the stove to boil and then went about fixing the tea tray. The best china kept for visitors went on the tray, along with a plate for a lemon cake that Hannah had left in a tin. Lily spooned out tea leaves into a pot, poured milk from the bottle into a milk jug, and finally filled the teapot with water as soon as it came to the boil. Then she hefted the heavy tray and carefully mounted the stairs.

When she pushed open the sitting room door with her back, she saw Leana was standing at the mantelpiece, a silver-framed photograph of Papa in her hand.

"I thought I'd lost you forever," said Leana.

"Not forever. Just long enough for the water to boil," she said, setting the tea tray down.

"How clever you are. I wouldn't know the first thing about where to find the things to make tea in Hartford House," said Leana.

As though you'd ever want to make your own tea, Lily thought, and then quickly tamped it down. Leana had come to her door in seeming good faith. She would hear what she had to say. It was only fair.

Leana set the photograph back in its place and gracefully sank down again onto the second sofa, her skirt puffing up and settling. "Is that man in the photograph your father?"

Lily set about pouring the tea. "Yes, it is."

"I wondered what he would look like. Papa talks about him sometimes," Leana said.

Her heart twisted as she handed over the cup and saucer to Leana. Having no memories of her own, she wanted so very much to know what Mr. Hartford remembered about Papa, but that didn't change her wariness of this woman in front of her.

"Leana, since we've both established that you weren't browsing the boutiques of Chelsea, may I ask why you are here?" she asked.

Leana trilled a laugh. "How suspicious you sound. Can't I call on a dear friend for a visit?"

When Lily didn't say anything, Leana set her tea aside and reached into her basket. She pulled out a small navy-blue leather box.

"I thought I would bring this by," said Leana.

Lily watched the other deb open the box to reveal a jewelry tray inside. In the late-morning sun, she could see the flash of diamonds, rubies, and sapphires in the shape of rings and earrings.

"You wanted to show me your jewelry?" she asked.

Leana laughed. "No, silly. I thought you could pick something out."

"Pick something out?"

"Not to keep, of course, but I have a few things that I thought might suit you, and you've said such nice things about my jewelry."

She probably had because it was the sort of idle comment that debs made to one another. *Your dress is divine. I wish I had earrings like those. You must tell me who does your hair.*

"Something like this would look beautiful with a white dress for Queen Charlotte's Ball," Leana continued, pulling out one half of a set of earrings with a deep yellow stone in the center surrounded by tiny diamonds and all wrapped up in elegant swoops of gold. "These topazes would look lovely with your hair."

Lily stared at her. "I can't wear your jewelry to Queen Charlotte's."

Leana shrugged one shoulder and pulled the jewelry tray out of the box to reveal another layer—this one full of bracelets and necklaces that sparkled in the sunlight. "Then another ball. I think I have a bracelet that matches the topazes."

"I have my own jewelry," she said, although nothing approaching the variety of what Leana had in front of her.

"Your pearls?" Leana asked with a smile. "You must be bored of them by now. You've worn them to nearly every cocktail party we've been to."

Actually, she'd worn them to every single cocktail party because they were her one good piece of jewelry and she loved them, but she wasn't going to point that out when presented with the bounty of Leana's collection.

"I didn't realize that you took such notice of my jewelry," she said.

Leana dropped her hands, a frown beginning to form on her coral lips. "Lily, you're beginning to sound rather ungrateful. Most girls would be thrilled at the chance to wear some of these things."

Lily folded her hands in her lap, the tea forgotten in front of her because it was beginning to feel as though Leana was trying her best to buy her affection. Yet, if she said that, she knew that Leana would have a fast response that somehow made the accusation more about an insecurity in Lily than anything Leana had done.

When finally the silence had stretched to an awkward length, a flicker of doubt flashed over Leana's beautiful face. "I suppose if you must know, I wanted to apologize."

"For what precisely?" Lily asked.

Leana shifted in Mummy's chair. "For yesterday night. It was rude of me to say those things about the article, and it was rude not to invite your friends out dancing."

"No, it was rude of you not to make any effort to acknowledge my friends," Lily corrected. "Why didn't you?"

"I've never been very good with sharing anything. It's part of my nature, darling. When I was a little girl, I simply couldn't stand it if anyone played with my dolls."

"That must have made it rather difficult when other girls came around to play," she said.

Leana's shoulders sagged a fraction of an inch. "In truth, I had very few friends. Of course, Nanny would arrange with my cousins' nanny for me to see my cousins, and I suppose there was a handful of families that it was acceptable for me to visit. Nanny would put me in party dresses with lace at the collar and tell me not to come back with a spot on me. Not that there were ever many opportunities to dirty my clothes. These were rather staid teas and children's garden parties playing croquet.

"So you see, I've become a little envious of how easy you are with the other debs." Leana smiled ruefully. "The men like me, but I don't think the other women do very much."

"What about all of the girls I met at your luncheon?" she asked.

Leana picked a piece of fluff off her skirt. "A few of them are nice enough, but I think most of them accepted the invitation because of what Jennifer and the other society columnists have written about me."

Lily inclined her head in understanding because it was, after all, exactly the reason she'd given to Mummy to justify going to Leana's luncheon back in March. However, that didn't excuse Leana's behavior.

"We can be friends," she said slowly.

"We *are* friends," said Leana firmly.

"We can be friends," she repeated, "but coming to my house with a box full of jewelry is not an apology."

"I'm not trying to buy your affection, if that's what you mean." When Lily leveled a look at her, Leana huffed. "Fine, I suppose I am in a way, but I also thought it would be a nice thing to do."

"How you act moving forward matters to me more," she said.

Chastised, Leana said, "Tell me what I need to do."

"The jealousy stops. You are not my only friend, just as I'm not yours. You don't get to decide who I see and speak to."

"I understand," said Leana quietly.

"And I do not want to hear anything against the other girls until you actually get to know them. Then you have a right to judge their character, not before," she said.

Leana resisted, but then nodded.

"And finally, you need to stop lashing out at me," she said.

"When have I ever lashed out at you?" Leana asked, sounding genuinely shocked.

"Do you remember the night of Vita Auster's party? You were sour with me the moment I climbed into Gideon's car."

"I didn't do anything," Leana insisted.

"You told me I was treading on your dress, that I was late, and then later that night, when I asked you not to promise dances with me on my behalf, you snapped," she said.

"You were being difficult," Leana defended herself.

"You gave my consent without asking me. I didn't want to dance with those men—whoever they were—and I didn't particularly feel like going to dinner that night, so I didn't."

"I don't want you to waste any time, Lily," said Leana, leaning forward to cover Lily's hand where it rested on the table. "You should be focused on meeting the right sort of men. You seem more interested in making friends with the other girls or speaking to men who are completely unsuitable for you."

"Who is unsuitable?" asked Lily.

"Ian for one," said Leana with a sniff.

She laughed. "How could he be unsuitable? Your father's taken an interest in Ian's education and his career. He's welcome in your home."

"But not really, darling," said Leana as though Lily should know these things. "His father's poor as a church mouse."

"He's a country doctor."

"Which means that he's not one of our kind. Dr. Bingham has virtually no money, and so will his son if Ian doesn't follow Papa's plans for him."

"I like Ian. He's interesting, and he's interested in me," she said.

"What about Gideon?" Leana asked, perking up at the thought.

She did like Gideon—really, she did—except that he fit perhaps too seamlessly into the role of the deb's delight, just as Ian always seemed a little apart. Imperfect in his own way.

"Gideon's offered to drive us from party to party tonight. You are still going, aren't you?" Leana asked, uncertainty in her voice. "I promise I will be on my best behavior."

"Yes, I'm still planning to join you tonight," Lily relented.

"Oh good!" Leana smiled, wide and beautiful.

This is how she captivates people, thought Lily. The open, hopeful look on Leana's face when she was pleased was so seductive. Men fell over themselves to earn it.

"Tell me what you're wearing tonight. You have such beautiful, unique things. Like this jumper. The knitted lace panels are so sweet," said Leana.

And just like that, their visit relaxed into conversation over tea.

Fourteen

"Miss Doris Irving says yes," Mummy read out from the card she held in her right hand.

Lily scanned down her list and ticked off Doris's name.

It was the Saturday before her party with Georgie, and they were sitting at the round morning room table, papers neatly stacked all around them. At Mummy's right hand sat a series of open envelopes that had arrived over the past two weeks. In front of her, a healthy pile of "yes" responses outweighed the "regrets" pile next to it. Methodically, Mummy would pull an envelope off the stack and read out the RSVP. It was Lily's job to make sure that the name matched up with their half of the invitation list—Aunt Angelica and Georgie being the keepers of the other half.

Lily wondered if, across town in Bloomsbury, Georgie was going through the same ritual with Aunt Angelica and whether Aunt Angelica also insisted on commenting on every invitation in turn.

"I thought Angelica said that Doris Irving was brought out by Mrs. Kingsley," said Mummy, looking at Doris's acceptance.

Lily looked up. "She was."

The furrow that seemed permanently etched in Mummy's forehead deepened. "Really, Lily."

"I like Doris. She's fun," she said, thinking about their meeting at the coffee bar, dinner and dancing after Philippa's, and the several other parties where she'd joined her fellow Imperfects since. Just thinking of Doris in her heels, towering over the men of high society and not giving a damn what anyone thought made her smile.

"Her mother is divorced, and her family had to hire her a chaperone. And isn't her father an American?" asked Mummy. "I don't think your grandmother will like that."

"Whether Grandmama likes it or not, the fact is, Doris is a lovely person and a friend." When Mummy gave her a look, she added, "She also has three brothers, all of them unmarried, and she will bring them if we ask."

"Well," said Mummy, reaching for another envelope, "at least she has that to recommend her. Perhaps they know some men who are actually eligible, although I very much doubt it."

Lily tried to stifle a sigh as Mummy pulled free another response and unfolded it. "Miss Katherine Norman says yes. Wonderful. We're to be overrun with Mrs. Kingsley's girls."

"Mummy, you're being unkind. Katherine is also a friend. A very good one," she said, thinking back to dinner last night when she'd joined Katherine, Doris, and Philippa for a meal with David and two of his friends. They'd had a rollicking time, their laughter drawing stares from the other diners and making them laugh harder. It had been so easy—effortless, even—with no one expecting anything of her.

Afterward, they'd snuck into the tennis courts at Regent's Park and played a game, scrambling as best they could in their high-heeled shoes and voluminous petticoats. At one point on their way out of the park, Philippa fell over the hem of her tea-length dress and David scooped her up in his arms, refusing to put her down until he delivered her into a taxi. Lily had never seen her friend smile so openly and without reservation.

"Well, I'm sure that your grandmother will realize I don't want the Norman girl there and will find some reason to side with you. You two always do what you will," said Mummy, picking up another invitation.

Lily clamped her jaw shut. If she did what she wanted, she wouldn't be having a coming-out party at all. She never would have been sent to finishing school in Paris or presented at court. It wasn't that she wasn't grateful for those things, but the more she thought about her encounter with Miss Hester, the more she realized that her life could have taken a different path. Still, what was done was done. She was a debutante, and, she thought, she'd done a rather good job of finding the fun in the entire situation.

"Ginny Douglas and her mother RSVP yes," said Mummy.

Lily picked up her pencil to tick off Ginny's name.

"The Faulkses will all come," said Mummy, reading off another. "I'm not surprised about that. I thought Christine's party looked rather thin."

"There were two other cocktail parties that evening," Lily reminded Mummy, who'd gone with her but refused to admit that it was because of Sir William Faulks's knighthood. "Also, I don't think Christine is particularly popular."

Mummy inclined her head in a way that Lily took for agreement and lifted the next RSVP. "You sent an invitation to the Hartfords?"

Lily glanced at the card, saw that it was a yes, and ticked off Mr. and Mrs. Ethan Hartford and Miss Leana Hartford from her list. "Grandmama insisted, and you know I couldn't very well leave Leana off the list."

After their conversation in the sitting room, Lily had appreciated how much of an effort Leana made to defer to Lily in decisions. Leana had even said hello unprompted to Ivy and Philippa after they arrived at the first party after their conversation, which had made Ivy's eyes widen comically and Philippa look on with an expression of bemusement.

"Leana is one thing, but I do not want Ruth and Ethan at the party. You'll have to uninvite them," said Mummy.

"No."

Mummy pressed her temples as though fighting off a headache.

Lily put down her pencil. "I know you hate the Hartfords, but that was so long ago."

"People do not change," said Mummy.

"They do, though. They have to." If they didn't—well, it would mean that Lily's life was already set, and the thought of that sent a rising feeling up in her throat, as though it choked her. This couldn't be the rest of her life, trying to keep peace between Mummy and Grandmama and going to parties with the same people she'd seen at the last party. There had to be more to her life than this.

Wasn't that what Katherine was always telling her? Was that why her friend was determined to throw it all away and strike out on her own as soon as the Season was finished? She'd admired Katherine for her boldness when Katherine had first told her about her plans, but now she was beginning to see that doing so was vital.

"The Hartfords must have changed—otherwise, why would you have been friends with people who were so cruel to you?" Lily asked.

Mummy sighed. "The friendship wasn't my choice. Michael and Ethan were friends at Harrow, and both played rugby. Michael went into the army, and Ethan began his diplomatic work. He married Ruth just two months before I married Michael, and we were at each other's weddings. You see, Ruth and I both came out in 1921, even though she's a year older than me, because that's when the court presentations resumed after the war."

"But Grandmama said you became good friends."

She half expected her mother to snap at her that Grandmama didn't know anything, but instead Mummy's gaze dropped to her hands, and she began to twist the little sapphire ring she always wore on her left hand.

"We did everything together. Ruth was already a talented hostess and introduced us to the Hartfords' crowd, some of whom she'd gone to finishing school with in Switzerland. You have to understand, after everything that we'd lost during the war, we were all so eager to squeeze as much out of life as we could. There seemed to be a party every night of the week, even when it wasn't the Season. We all went along with it because Ruth wanted us to. Sometimes we would stay up until dawn dancing at a nightclub."

"You went to nightclubs?" Lily asked with a laugh of disbelief.

Mummy cast her a look. "There is a reason I have been remarkably lenient about you sneaking in at dawn when you've been to the Hammersmith Palais de Danse, or wherever young people go dancing these days.

"Things went on like that for a few years, but then I became pregnant with Joanna. I stopped going out every night, and I think Ruth began to resent me for it. I think she was struggling to have a child, and she couldn't understand why I could have this thing that she couldn't. The

Hartfords always thought of themselves as the glittering couple. More beautiful, more mannered, more interesting than anyone else. I cannot tell you how relieved they were when Geoffrey came along. At least they had a son.

"In the years before the war, we still saw one another, of course. Ruth made sure of that. But there were other things to worry about. Michael and I were concerned for Joanna. She was at a difficult age, and we thought it would be a good idea to see her out of London. We sent her to Michael's sister, your aunt Patricia, in Washington, DC, just before war was declared. It was fortuitous, it turned out, because so many parents had to evacuate their children to the countryside. At least Joanna was in another country, safe.

"But then she fell ill with a virus in the spring of 1940. Patricia sent us a telegraph saying the doctors didn't know what she had, and they weren't sure if she was going to live. I traveled over to be with her." Mummy gave her a weak smile. "By the time I arrived in Washington, I found out I was pregnant. I took Joanna to a spa town in North Carolina where she could recover and I could prepare to have you.

"After you were born that November, it became virtually impossible to make the crossing without good reason. The Atlantic crossing was more dangerous than ever with U-boats torpedoing any British ship, even those carrying evacuees. In September, just before you were born, we learned that the SS *City of Benares* had been torpedoed carrying eighty-seven children.

"We stayed and tried to make the best of it, but then we received the telegram that Michael had died." Mummy took a shuddering breath. "He had been assigned to intelligence work in London, and I'd thought nothing of it that he hadn't written as often as he normally would. He was busy. I didn't realize that he'd fallen ill—cancer of the stomach—and deteriorated rapidly. Angelica sent me the telegram."

Mummy pulled a carefully folded handkerchief out of the cuff of her shirt and dabbed under her eyes, careful of her mascara. "I begged the Hartfords to find a way to bring us back home to England. I might have been terrified to do the Atlantic crossing again, but they could have found a way to keep us safe. Ethan refused. He said that his work was too important to risk the scandal of someone finding out he'd used official channels to help a widow and two children.

"We finally made it back after two years when you were old enough to travel, and Joanna was well again. By that time, nearly everything was gone to paying off death duties and Michael's debts. That was all Angelica and Elliott, by the way. Don't let your grandmother pretend otherwise. She didn't lift a finger to help.

"I came back to London, and all I had was the house and a small set of investments from my father, but I did my best to try to return to my old life for your sake. I sent cards telling old friends I was home, and I waited for the telephone to ring. The Hartfords, who had professed to be such great friends, did nothing. They didn't telephone. They didn't visit. They didn't write. As soon as Michael was gone, they dropped me."

"And what happened to Joanna after you returned?" Lily asked quietly, finally broaching the question that had hung heavy and unspoken in their house for years.

Her mother sniffed. "Michael was the one who could manage her when she was young, but even he struggled as she began to grow up. By the time we returned, she was no longer a child, and she chose to leave for the North a month after we returned. It was as far as one could go and still be in civilization, she said. We've not seen each other since. It's better this way."

"I don't remember her," said Lily softly.

"It's best that you were too young," said Mummy firmly. "Joanna could be difficult and bitter at the best of times."

But she was Lily's sister. A family member she'd never met before.

As though reading her thoughts, Mummy said, "I have made mistakes, Lily, but keeping you from meeting Joanna is not one of them."

Lily dropped her gaze to her lap. Everyone seemed to be making decisions for her, but what if she wanted something different?

When she looked up, she found Mummy looking at her with an expression that was almost tender. "I want you to be happy, Lily. I want you to have the very best that you can. Your presentation? The Season? All of it is because I want you to find what I had with Michael and more.

"Pick a man who will take care of you and give you the incredible gift of being a wife and mother. Who will provide for you and make sure you never have to worry about asking for charity from a relative. You shouldn't have to worry about the price of coal or whether you can afford to buy your child new shoes when she needs them. You shouldn't have to watch your daughter make her own clothes out of necessity rather than enjoyment. I want you to have a good life."

Would she find that man? And if she did, would she want those things with him? She knew that everyone around her would expect the answer to come as naturally as breathing, but she wasn't so sure now.

Mummy cleared her throat and straightened. "Now, shall we return to the task at hand?" she asked with false brightness. "Ian Bingham declines with regrets."

"Oh."

"Oh?" her mother asked.

"I had hoped he might come," said Lily, disappointment settling low in her stomach.

"Do I know him?"

She winced. "He is a friend of the Hartfords."

Mummy sighed. "Who are his people?"

"His father is a doctor in Elkenhurst."

"He's the Hartfords' family doctor's son?" asked Mummy.

"Yes," she said.

"What about your friend Gideon?" Mummy asked, toying with the corner of Ian's note of regret. "He's collected you from the house several times, and you've been to dinner with him. Angelica says that he always seems so attentive."

"Has Aunt Angelica been watching me for you?" she asked, a little horrified by the thought.

"Don't make it sound so sinister, Lily. Naturally, Angelica takes an interest in you, especially when I'm not at a party."

"Gideon is a friend," said Lily.

"Then you like him?"

"Of course I like him. I wouldn't be friends with him if I didn't."

"But do you like him enough?" Mummy asked, pulling her little address book across the table toward her. "Shall I invite Mrs. Moore to tea?

I'm certain your grandmother or Angelica could find her address for me if I don't have it here."

"No!" Lily cried. "No, don't do that. It's just that it's too soon."

Her mother closed the address book. "Men like Gideon will not wait around forever for you to make up your mind. I think you would be wise to encourage him." Mummy rose from the table. "I think I shall ask Hannah for tea."

She watched Mummy retreat and then reached across the table and picked up the top note from the "regrets" pile.

Dear Lily,

It is with great regret that I must decline your kind invitation to your drinks party. I have a previous engagement in Cambridge that cannot be broken, although I have tried my best to move it.

I hope that you will forgive me and perhaps save me another dance the next time that I am in London.

Warmest regards,
Ian Bingham

Lily read the note once again. Then she folded it twice and slipped it into her pocket.

Fifteen

Lily didn't know if it was her conversation with Mummy or Ian's regrets, but a cloud hung about her for the rest of the day and into the evening as she went from one cocktail party to another—the hallmark of a busy Saturday evening during the Season. It must have been obvious that she was out of sorts, because she'd allowed herself to be bundled into a taxi with Leana, Gideon, and Raymond to go on to the second event.

Halfway through the drive, Leana abruptly stopped the conversation she was having with Raymond and announced playfully, "Lily, if you don't shake yourself out of this stupor you've been in, I shall have to do something drastic."

Raymond laughed, casually putting his arm around the back of Leana's seat so that his fingers brushed her shoulder. "Something drastic? Is that a promise?"

"Not you." Leana, who was wearing his jacket draped over her shoulders, smacked him gently on the chest while Lily watched, thinking it was the sort of thing an actress would have done in a Hollywood film. She wished that she'd thought to convince Gideon that he should join the couple in the back seat and leave her to ride in the front with the cabbie, unconventional though that might be.

"I'm fine," said Lily.

"You're not telling me something, and I'm going to find out what it is," declared Leana.

"There's nothing to find out," said Lily, edging a little closer to the door to put a bit more distance between Leana and herself.

"You'll tell me by the end of the night," teased Leana.

"Please don't push me, Leana," she said in a low voice.

"Leana, leave her alone," said Gideon from the front seat.

"Oh, Gideon, you're no fun," Leana pouted. "Raymond, where's your flask?"

Raymond put a hand into the jacket Leana wore, but Gideon said, "Don't give her anymore."

"I'll have more if I want," said Leana.

"We're nearly to the Carleton Club. There will be drinks there," said Lily.

"Oh, don't be such a prissy bore," Raymond shot at her as he shoved the flask at Leana, who unscrewed it and tipped back something that smelled like whisky. "Your nagging is worse than my old nanny."

"Excuse me?" Lily asked, stunned.

"That was uncalled for, Troy," said Gideon, twisting harder in his seat.

"I'm just calling her what she is. I don't know why you keep her around, Leana. Sophie and Rebecca are more fun. Christ, even that silly one, Cressie, is," muttered Raymond, taking the flask back from Leana.

Lily looked at Leana, who was rummaging in her evening bag. "Aren't you going to say anything to him?"

Leana pulled out her lipstick and a mirror, not meeting her eyes. "You have been a bit of a sad bore all night. Maybe you would be happier with your *other* friends."

"What other friends?" Raymond scoffed.

"Oh, you know the ones," said Leana as she finished applying lipstick to the bow of her mouth and twisted this way and that to check it.

"You mean flashy, mousy, ugly—"

"Shut up, Raymond," said Gideon sharply.

Lily's blood pounded in her ears as slowly she said, "I will not listen to anyone being rude about my friends."

Raymond shrugged. "Then don't listen."

She waited for the moment Leana would jump in and tell Raymond to stop.

Instead, when Leana finally did look at her, all she asked was, "What?"

"Aren't you going to say anything?" Lily asked.

All Leana did was shrug. "It's his opinion. He has every right to it."

"Driver," said Lily, leaning forward over the gap to the front of the cab.

"Miss?" the driver called over his shoulder.

"Please stop the taxi wherever it is safe," she said.

"Oh please, Lily, you're going to make us late," Leana chided as Gideon asked, "What?" in an urgent tone.

"Please stop the taxi," she repeated, fighting to keep her voice level.

The driver turned off Piccadilly and onto Haymarket, where he pulled up to the curb.

When Lily moved to open the door, Leana said, "She can't leave," and Raymond reached over Leana to stop Lily with a hand on her forearm.

She looked down at his hand on her, her flesh crawling at the thought of this brutish bore of a man touching her. "Let go of me."

"Leave her alone, Troy," insisted Gideon.

"No call for that, sir," said the cabbie, an edge of panic creeping into his voice.

Raymond ignored all of them, squeezing Lily's arm harder. "You've been a miserable drip all evening, and now you're ruining everyone's fun," he growled, his breath reeking of booze.

"If you are attempting to convince me to stay in this cab, you're doing a poor job of it," she said, wrenching her arm away.

When Raymond tried to grab her again, Lily smashed herself against the cab door, the door handle crushing into the bones of her dress so hard she was certain she would bruise.

"Don't touch her!" shouted Gideon, twisting harder in his seat as Lily managed to shift and open the taxi door, stumbling onto the pavement and catching herself on her open palms. The cabbie was out in a flash, helping her back up.

"There you are, miss. Don't want you to fall and ruin your pretty dress," said the man.

Gideon was at her side now, holding her elbow. "Thank you," he said to the cabbie before asking her, "Are you all right?"

Seething, Lily jerked out of his grasp. "He does not touch me, ever again."

Gideon held his hands up, as though calming a startled animal. "He won't. I won't let him."

"*I* won't let him." She glared up at Gideon.

"I'm not Troy, Lily," he said softly.

He wasn't. She knew that. Slowly her breathing began to regulate, but still adrenaline pumped through her veins.

"May I see?" asked Gideon gently after a glance back at the taxi. He pushed down her glove to check over her arm in the light of one of the streetlamps. She didn't miss that her once-clean gloves were now pocked with debris from the pavement.

"You're going to be okay," said Gideon.

"Never again, Gideon. Tell him, or I will." She'd begun shaking so hard that she was on the verge of tears, not of fear but of anger.

"Leana, hand me her wrap," Gideon called over his shoulder, sticking his hand out behind him but not breaking Lily's gaze.

Gently he draped Mummy's mink over her shoulders. She pulled the two ends of the stole around her tight, the soft fur and smooth satin lining a comfort.

"How much did Leana and Raymond have to drink at the last party?" Lily asked.

"I don't care enough about him to have noticed, if I'm being honest. Leana? I think the real question is, how much did she have to drink before she arrived?" asked Gideon.

"She drank beforehand?" she asked.

"Leana always has a drink beforehand. And she's a careless drunk at the best of times, mean at the worst."

Lily lifted her head in acknowledgment. She wasn't going to let Leana have the chance to be mean.

"Give me a moment," said Gideon.

She turned away when Gideon braced himself to lean into the back seat of the taxi. She could hear muffled voices, but she didn't strain to make out the words. She was afraid that what she would hear would only make her angrier.

She couldn't believe that Leana, another woman, had sat there and watched a man berate Lily without a word. Even worse, Leana seemed to *agree* with that oaf.

She thought back to earlier that week in her mother's sitting room when Leana had tried in her high-handed, spoiled way to patch things up between them. She'd really thought that they'd reached an understanding, but the issues between her and Leana went so much deeper than any possessiveness. It wasn't just that Leana didn't want Lily to have other friends. She could see now that Leana was the sort of woman who would choose a man over a friend. That in the hierarchy of Leana's life, so long as there was an eligible man, it didn't matter the situation. That man would come first.

Leana would, no doubt, laugh at her naivete if Lily complained because wasn't that what the Season was for? Meeting a man like Raymond who, on paper, appeared to tick every box: Eldest son set to inherit a barony. Well-off. Respected commission. Handsome. Dashing. But underneath it all, Raymond was a rotter, and Leana had just shown that she was willing to overlook—even accept—that about him.

"Lily," said Gideon softly. She turned as he took a couple steps toward her and led her off a few steps. "They're both sorry."

Lily fixed him with a look. "If you think I believe that . . ."

"Fine, I don't know if they're sorry exactly, but they at least understand that they've upset you." He hesitated. "They want to know if you still want to come with them to the next party."

Lily stared at him.

"I can hail you a separate taxi and I can go with you, or we can go in this one. It's your choice, but I doubt Troy will speak to you again."

A clatter of heels against the pavement announced Leana's arrival.

"Lily." Leana caught up her hand, making a good show of contrition as her eyes sparkled in the streetlights. "Lily, Raymond really is sorry, only he's too stubborn to say. And I'm sorry, too. You know I'm a wretched thing, and I don't mean half the things I say. Come back into the taxi, and we'll go to the next party."

Lily pulled her hand from Leana's. "Do you understand why I'm angry with you?"

"Don't say you're angry with me," pleaded Leana.

"Do you understand why?" she repeated.

Leana's demeanor changed in an instant, the pout and the huffing returning. "Let's just go."

"I'm not climbing back into a taxi with that man," said Lily.

"He didn't mean any of it. That's just Raymond being Raymond," said Leana.

Enough. She stepped around Leana and marched back to the taxi. Without looking at Raymond, she snatched up her evening bag. Out of the corner of her eye, she spotted a taxi rounding the corner onto Haymarket and stuck out her arm to hail it.

"Lily!" Leana cried.

The driver rolled down his window, "Evening, miss. Everything all right?"

"Perfectly. Could you take me to the Carlton Club?" she asked.

The cabbie glanced at Leana and Gideon. "How many?"

"Just myself," she said.

"Hop right in," said the driver.

"Thank you," she said, opening the door for herself.

"Let me come with you," said Gideon.

"I need a moment to myself. I'll see you at the next party," she said.

She slid into the back of the taxi and shut the door behind her.

"How far are we from the Carlton Club?" she asked.

"Less than five minutes to St. James's Street, miss," said the cabbie.

"If you wouldn't mind taking a long way, I'd rather not arrive close to that other taxi," she said.

"How about a scenic drive down the Mall and by Buckingham Palace. It's all my sister's in-laws wanted to see when they came over from America. She was a war bride, you see. Married an American GI."

"That sounds like a perfect distraction. Thank you," she said, and settled back against the leather seat to think.

Lily walked into the Carlton Club, dropped her fur, and made it through the receiving queue to congratulate Deborah O'Malley and Grace Boyne on coming-out. As soon as she was free, she gazed around the room—deep red with polished wood paneling so alike some of the other members clubs she'd been to that Season that she might not have been able to tell it from another. The people were all the same. The same debutantes in one of their five or six cocktail dresses kept in rotation. The same deb's delights in suits—how many they had didn't matter to anyone—fetching drinks, chatting with girls, greeting old schoolmates. Mothers and fathers and aunts and uncles hung around the fringes, supporting Deborah just as the relatives did at every other deb's party.

Would someone just like her walk into Georgie's and her drinks at the Hyde Park Hotel and think to themselves, *Not another of these.*

Probably.

To the far right of the room, next to a large fireplace, Lily saw Gideon watching her. Next to him stood Leana, her head thrown back in laughter, the sheen of her dark hair reflecting the soft light of the room.

She turned away and breathed a sigh of relief when she spotted Katherine by the windows. She hurried over to where her friend stood talking to Max, one of the solicitors from Philippa's dinner.

"Hello, Lily," said Katherine. "I was just telling Max I was wondering where you were."

She smiled at Max and said, "I'm very sorry to do this, but do you mind if I borrow Katherine for a moment?"

"Not at all. I'll find you a drink," he said.

"Thank you," she said.

Katherine watched him go and then immediately asked in a low voice, "What's the matter?"

"Nothing," she said with a shake of her head.

"I thought you were coming over with Leana, but I didn't see you walk in with her," said Katherine.

"I took my own taxi over."

"Are you sure everything's fine?" Katherine asked, searching her expression.

Lily gave a weak smile. "No, but it will be."

Katherine studied her for a moment and then asked, "Are you particularly fond of Deborah or Grace?"

"I hardly know either of them. I met Grace at a luncheon at the beginning of the Season."

"Is there any chance you're hungry?" Katherine asked, mischief playing in her eyes.

Lily laughed. "I'm always hungry at these parties."

"A woman cannot live on passed hors d'oeuvres alone," agreed Katherine. "Come on, then, I'm taking you for dinner."

"Dinner? But we haven't booked in anywhere."

"I'm taking you to a place that is the height of glamour but where you need no reservation," said Katherine.

That was how Lily found herself sneaking past the reception queue, picking up her fur, and bundling herself into another taxi, which Katherine directed to Coventry Street. Katherine kept the conversation light, speaking about the preparations for her ball and asking Lily about her own party that would come up in four days.

When the taxi stopped at their destination and Lily climbed out, she looked up and began to laugh. They were standing in front of a big sign that read "Lyons Corner House" with "The Wimpy" on either side of it.

"Now, you might ask yourself why I've taken you here," said Katherine. "I have it on good authority—my American mother—that a Wimpy Bar is one of the only decent places to find a hamburger in London. And whenever she feels down, a hamburger fixes her right up."

Lily smiled at the sign, pulling her stole closer around her shoulder against the spring night's chill. "I suppose I'll have to have one of these miracle hamburgers to find out, won't I?"

"Wait." Katherine stopped her. "You've never had a hamburger?"

"This will be my first," she said.

Katherine grinned. "Well, I am honored."

Lily followed her friend into the crowded restaurant. It was done up in bold primary colors, red and yellow splashed everywhere. The smell of frying food hung in the air, and the entire place seemed to hum with energy as diners in far more casual clothes than they wore laughed over their meals.

Despite the crowd, they managed to find a table and order a pair of pure beef hamburgers, two Coca-Colas, and a slice of Lyons' square blackcurrant, which Katherine said didn't compare to an American pie but would have to do. When their food came, Lily watched Katherine peel off her gloves and bite into her hamburger. Lily mimicked her friend.

It was messy and juicy and salty and exactly the opposite of what she had expected to be eating that evening. And, she decided as she settled back against her chair feeling content for the first time in hours, it was perfect.

"Thank you," she said.

Katherine shrugged. "We don't have to talk about it, but you looked like you needed to leave."

"I did. I do. I just . . . thank you."

Katherine toasted her with her Coca-Cola, and they settled into a comfortable silence over their meal.

Sixteen

"Come on," Lily muttered under her breath as she tried again to buckle the strap of her right shoe. Her hands were trembling so much that she kept missing the little hole in the leather that would hold the white high heels on her feet.

"Lily!" called Hannah from somewhere down the hall.

"I'm in here!" she shouted back.

A moment later, Hannah bustled through the open door. "What are you doing without your shoes on?"

"I'm trying to put them on," she said, a slight panic creeping into her voice. She was supposed to be a picture of calm and grace on the night of her coming-out drinks—not a trembling mess.

Hannah crouched down and brushed Lily's hands aside. She watched the housekeeper efficiently buckle first the right strap and then the left before sitting back.

"There you are," Hannah said.

"Thank you for staying late tonight," she said.

"Miss you in your dress for your big party? I wouldn't dream of it," said Hannah.

"Hannah!" her mother called out.

"And I think your mother needed the extra set of hands," said Hannah, diplomatically.

Lily gave a little laugh. Mummy had been a ball of nerves all week thanks to at least one telephone call a day from Grandmama and a visit on Sunday after church. The only thing that had helped was when Aunt Angelica came around yesterday, and Hannah set them up in the sitting room with a pot of tea to go over and over every last detail of Lily and Georgie's coming-out drinks.

Lily, for her part, had hidden herself away in her room, reading. She'd gone back to the library to retrieve the titles that Miss Hester had recommended, and she'd already read through *The Garden Party* by Katherine Mansfield and *Mary Olivier* by May Sinclair.

Katherine had been right. She needed a break from it all. Leana's reaction—or lack thereof—to Raymond in the taxi ride over still stung. This odd pulling close and pushing away was too much for her. She didn't know where she stood with Leana, and that layered exhaustion on an already exhausting Season.

"Hannah!" Mummy called out, an edge of desperation creeping into her voice.

Lily stood, brushed down the full lilac satin skirts of her Worth dress with its dark purple embroidery at the top of the bodice—so different from the dress that Madame Benum had envisioned her in—and followed Hannah out of the room only to find Aunt Angelica and Georgie climbing the stairs.

"You're early," said Lily.

"I suspected you might need a little extra help," said Aunt Angelica with a smile nearly as brilliant as her silver lamé dress.

"I didn't even hear the bell," said Lily.

"When no one came to the door, we let ourselves in," said Georgie by way of explanation. "Papa is downstairs, helping himself to a whisky in the sitting room."

"Are you nervous?" Lily asked.

Her cousin's eyes lit up. "Not a bit. It should all be a laugh, don't you think?"

"Angelica, is that you?" called Mummy.

"Yes, darling. I'm here!"

"It's all gone wrong," said Mummy as they piled into her bedroom. "I can't find my earring, and Mrs. Nicholls will be here with the Bentley at any moment."

Lily's aunt rolled her eyes. "That is what all of this fuss is about? For goodness' sake, Josephine, pull yourself together. It's just an earring."

"The sapphires that Michael gave me on our first anniversary. One of them is missing. Hannah, have you seen it?" Mummy asked desperately, hunting in the dishes on her dresser.

"No, ma'am," said Hannah.

"Well, help me look for them!" Mummy cried.

"Josephine!" Aunt Angelica's voice boomed, and Mummy froze. "Take a deep breath and think. When did you last see the pair of them together?"

"I took them out of the safe in Michael's study this afternoon and brought them up to my room," said Mummy.

"Are you certain you brought them up here?" Aunt Angelica asked.

"I—I don't know."

"Lily," said Aunt Angelica, turning her broad body to face Lily, "go downstairs to your father's study and look there."

She glanced at Mummy. "I don't know where the key is kept."

"There's no reason for Lily to go in there," said Mummy, some of the usual cool coming back into her voice.

"Would you prefer that she check your bedroom? Or perhaps we can stand around and think about it until Mrs. Nicholls arrives, and then we'll have to explain to her why her only granddaughter is going to be late to her own coming-out drinks," said Aunt Angelica with an arched brow.

Mummy's lip pursed, but she gave a sharp nod. "Hannah, unlock the study for Lily."

"And I'll help you look in your bedroom," said Angelica brightly. "Georgie, go make sure your father only has one whisky. He can drink as much as he likes after the reception line is over, but I won't have him showing up to the Hyde Park Hotel three sheets to the wind."

Lily moved to follow Hannah and Georgie down the stairs, when Aunt Angelica popped her head out of the bedroom. "Lily, a word."

"Yes?" she asked.

"You know that this is not about an earring, don't you? This is a big night for Josephine. We must keep her calm."

Lily bit her lip and gave her a tiny nod. To Mummy, the party must represent so much more. It was, after a long spell away, the acceptance of the Nicholls family back into the arms of society.

Lily reached the bottom stair just as Hannah was closing a small decorative oak cabinet that hung above the telephone table, key in her hand.

"Come on, then," said Hannah. "If you look in the study, I'll check the sitting room and the corridors."

Lily took the key from the housekeeper but paused before the study door. It wasn't as though she'd never been in it before. Mummy would do the accounts and write correspondence to her solicitor in there because that is where her father's old bankbooks were kept. From time to time, when she was growing up, Hannah had let Lily bring in the tea tray to her mother. However, it still felt like forbidden territory, a heavy, masculine room that had been frozen in time since her father's death.

Lily turned the key in the lock and let herself in and closed the door behind her.

It was quiet in the study, as though it was somehow a different world from the rest of the house. Even though it had been years since any man had been in here except Uncle Elliot as he helped Mummy with some accounting note or other, it still held a distinctly masculine scent, like polished wood and old tobacco smoke. Lily squeezed her eyes shut and breathed deep, imagining what it might be like to have her father standing beside her in the reception queue at her party. To have the luxury of not feeling as though everything relied on her performance that evening to keep Grandmama happy and Mummy in funds.

She let out a breath. No use thinking about things that would never be.

Lily began looking over the Persian rug covering the polished floorboards for the missing earring, moving methodically from one end of the room toward the desk and the window. Under the desk, something gold caught her eye. She stooped to pick it up. A screw that must have worked its way out of the desk or the big leather-and-wood chair over time.

She placed the screw on the desk and hesitated, her hand frozen in the air over the stack of envelopes. The top one was addressed to "Mrs. Michael Nicholls"—unremarkable in itself, but it was the handwriting that gave her pause. It was fine and looping, and she'd seen it before. She flipped over the envelope and read out the return address. "Dovecote Cottage, Hawkshead Hill, Cumberland."

She'd seen a letter like this before when she'd brought Mummy the one that had fallen under the sideboard. And she remembered the way her mother had reacted, stuffing it away and refusing to speak about it when Lily had idly asked who it was from.

Checking that the door was closed, she gingerly pulled the letter free from its envelope and unfolded it, sitting down to read it. It had no salutation or signature, but simply noted the date as "14 April 1958," and ended with a remarkable abruptness.

I will not begin this letter with the usual pleasantries or salutations because I will not pretend that you're ignorant of my motivation for writing it.

You once told me that I should do very well here, where the living is not so dear as London. However, I can assure you that I have needs that cannot be supported without an income. It is a simple matter of mathematics.

I happened to look at a copy of one of those awful society rags this week and found a photograph of a Miss Lillian Nicholls in front of the Savoy. I understand that this means you have brought Lily out. While I am certain you are happy to have brought at least one girl out successfully, I cannot help but wonder at the expense of it all if you are quite so depleted of funds as you say you are. I would ask you to consider whether you will find it prudent, upon reflection, to divert some of those funds to a greater cause that should preserve the very Season you have no doubt spent so much time and effort cultivating.

I shall await your answer.

Lily stared at the letter, her mouth slightly open, for a good long minute. Then, carefully, she placed it on the desk.

Someone wanted money from Mummy. Money they didn't have, if Mummy's requests that she scale back her wardrobe were to be believed.

Lily frowned. It didn't make sense that Grandmama wouldn't have provided for her properly this Season if she was so intent on Lily entering society. She hadn't been there for the discussion of any financial matters, but now that she thought about it, it seemed extraordinary that Grandmama would have left them in the lurch.

Unless Mummy had already sent money to whoever sent this letter. That would mean there had been other letters. Letters that perhaps bore a signature.

Lily reached for one of the desk drawers, her fingers tightening around the pull handle. She tried to pull open the drawer when it stuck. Locked.

The doorbell rang. Lily jerked up, hitting her knee on the underside of the desk. She cried out, clutching at the pain.

"Lily!" Hannah called.

Lily shot out of the chair and tried her best to remember how she'd found the letter. Then she dropped to the floor, careful not to snag her stockings, and began the pantomime of searching for the lost earring.

"Are you still in here?" Hannah asked through the door. "Your grandmother is here."

Lily rose and straightened her dress, trying her best to hide the fact that her knee still throbbed as Hannah opened the door. "I haven't found it."

Hannah's eyes shone as she lifted a white paper box of flowers.

"What are those?" Lily asked.

"I might ask the same thing," came Grandmama's voice from the entryway.

Lily hurried out from behind the desk and past Hannah to greet Grandmama, who wore a very full navy dress with a beautifully sculpted collar that stood up a few inches from her shoulders. A glittering brooch of diamonds sparkled at the center of her neckline. She looked beautiful, and Lily told her grandmother so.

"Don't be ridiculous. I look like an old woman," said Grandmama, but the note of pleasure in her voice was unmistakable. "Let me look at you properly."

Lily took a step back and gave a little spin, her tea-length dress float-ing out around her.

"Very good. Worth always did know what's best for debutantes," said Grandmama with a satisfied smile. "Now, who are these flowers from?"

"There's a note," said Hannah, handing them over.

Lily opened the box, in the middle of which sat a corsage of a white lily and a spray of white orchids that faded to a pale purple that perfectly matched her dress in their centers. She lifted the flowers to her nose. "They're beautiful."

"Crisis averted!" Aunt Angelica's voice rang out.

As Aunt Angelica and Mummy descended, Uncle Elliot and Geor-gie joined them in the entryway, everyone freezing when they spotted Grandmama.

"What crisis?" Grandmama asked, glancing between them.

"A missing earring. But now it's found," Aunt Angelica hurried to say. "Good evening, Mrs. Nicholls."

"Mrs. Nicholls," said Uncle Elliot, clearing his throat and dutifully going to kiss Grandmama on the cheek.

"Hello," said Mummy, reaching the bottom of the stairs.

"The earring had become caught on a silk scarf on your mother's chest of drawers. Who sent you flowers?" said Aunt Angelica, fixating on the box in Lily's hands.

"Flowers?" Mummy asked.

"Oh, how romantic," said Georgie.

"That really depends on the gentleman they're from," said Grand-mama.

"I don't know who sent them," said Lily, holding up the note.

"Well, aren't you going to open it?" asked Georgie.

Lily slid the card out of its small white envelope.

It is my greatest regret that I cannot be there with you tonight. I know you'll shine, and I hope our paths will cross again soon.

—I.B.

"Who is it from?" Mummy asked.

She hesitated. "A friend."

"Is that friend a man?" asked Mummy.

"Do we know him, Lily?" asked Grandmama.

"Yes," she said.

"Who?" Mummy insisted.

"Let the girl have her secrets, Josephine," said Aunt Angelica. "Lily is a good girl. She would never do anything untoward."

Grandmama seemed to contemplate the situation but then nodded in agreement with Aunt Angelica. "If we aren't on our way soon, Georgie and Lily will be late to their own party."

That seemed to snap up Mummy's attention. "Hannah, please bring our wraps, and lock the study door once we're gone. Lily, do you have your lipstick in your evening bag?"

"I do," said Lily.

"Are we all going to fit in the Bentley?" asked Uncle Elliot.

"I think the better question is whether the Bentley will still be here to take all of us. I'm leaving in two minutes. Whoever is not ready may take a taxi," declared Grandmama.

This declaration sent Aunt Angelica and Mummy racing about as Uncle Elliot stood in the corner, looking for the world as though he wished he had a full decanter at hand.

Next to Lily, Georgie whispered, "I think they're more nervous than we are."

When finally they all piled out of the front door and into the huge gray car driven by Grandmama's regular driver, Lily glanced back at the house where Hannah stood in the doorway, waving them off.

A fizz of nerves danced over her skin, even as the Bentley pulled away from the curb. When Mummy went back into the study, she wouldn't be able to tell that Lily had done anything except crouch on the floor in search of the earring. The desk would be undisturbed. The letter untouched. All would be as it had been. As it always was.

Except that now Lily knew where Hannah kept her key.

Once, when she was about sixteen, Lily had been caught in a storm. It had snuck up on her as she walked along the Chelsea Embankment. The gray autumn day had suddenly gone dark, and the misty rain that was the usual accompaniment of an October day had transformed into heavy, piercing raindrops that seemed intent on harm. Along the cement path that lined the Thames, there'd been few places to find shelter, especially as the wind had swept up around her. Instead of running, she'd closed in on herself, pulling her arms in around her books to protect them from the pelting rain. She stood like that, her back to the wind as she shielded herself from the chaos, until finally it subsided into that gentle, reassuring rain of a British autumn.

Standing in the receiving line between Grandmama and Mummy with Georgie, Aunt Angelica, and Uncle Elliot at the end, she wanted to again pull in her arms in protection, except this time it wasn't the weather she needed guarding against. It was the attention.

It came in waves, never really stopping but instead ebbing and flowing as each debutante, mother, father, brother, and deb's delight queued up to thank her and give her their well-wishes. Each time someone stopped in front of her to shake her hand or lightly kiss her cheek, she felt her smile stretch a little wider. She gave the same answers to the same questions, laughed lightly at the same turns of phrase, and said, "Thank you," and "Thank you," and "Thank you," until the words had no meaning.

When finally the receiving line began to thin and the last person was thanked, she let her stiff shoulders drop. She slid a glance over at Georgie, who wore what Lily imagined was the same stunned, exhausted expression on her own face.

"Well, that's that done. I swear I could sleep for days," said Georgie quietly.

"Not yet. Now we're meant to circulate," said Lily.

"Well, at least we're finally out," said Georgie.

At least, Lily thought, there was that.

PART III

Dancing

❧

Seventeen

ily," Mummy called as Lily walked past her open bedroom door with her long white evening gown draped over her arm.

If she and Georgie thought that the pressure of the Season was over with their coming-out drinks, they were quickly realizing how wrong they'd been. Now that their party was done, they could turn their attention to Queen Charlotte's Ball and the upcoming London dances. That, Grandmama had reminded Lily as they drove back from her drinks party, was when the Season really came into its own.

She paused on the threshold of her mother's door. "Yes?"

"Come in, please," said Mummy from her dressing table.

It was rare that her mother would invite her into her bedroom. It was a deeply private place and, like Papa's study, one of some mystery. Lily could remember long stretches of time as a little girl when it seemed as though all Mummy did was sit in this room with a photograph of Papa in her hand, coming down only when Hannah coaxed her to meals in the morning room or Aunt Angelica barged in to demand that Mummy go out and *do* something.

"Why do you have your dress for tonight out?" Mummy asked.

"There was a crease at the back that Hannah thought she might be able to do something about."

"Did she have any luck?" Mummy asked.

She turned the dress to show the smooth fall of pure white crepe de chine.

"Well, it's helpful that you have it. Put the dress down on the bed and come sit," said Mummy, indicating a small chair that was angled to the fireplace.

Lily did as she was told. Then she folded her hands in her lap and waited.

"I've been thinking about my Season and how excited I was before my Queen Charlotte's Ball," Mummy started. "The cocktail parties were nice, but I knew somehow that the dances would be something special. It was at a ball that I met Michael.

"All of you girls are much more sophisticated than I ever was, so I will spare you the speech my mother gave me about the dangers of charming gentlemen." Mummy shot her a look. "I expect at this point if it were to be an issue, I would already be too late."

Lily blushed at the implications. "Mummy . . ." The truth was no one had even tried to steal a kiss from her.

Mummy reached across the gap between them and pressed a hand on her knee. "You're a good girl, Lily. Far better than I probably deserve, given the circumstances of your childhood."

She covered her mother's hand in her own. "I cannot imagine how hard it was to lose Papa when you were so far away."

"We all made sacrifices during the war. Some more than others." Mummy's hand slipped from under hers. "The reason I called you in is that I thought you would like something special to wear tonight."

Lily watched Mummy rise, leather jewelry box in hand, and move toward her dress. Mummy opened the box and set about placing the neatly stacked jewelry trays on the bed. Then she paused and looked over her shoulder at Lily. "Aren't you going to come see?"

Lily rose to her feet and joined Mummy. She'd only seen the contents of her mother's jewelry box once, when Mummy had taken everything out and laid it into velvet cloths on the morning room table while she and Hannah cleaned the pieces. To a little girl's eyes, every stone was enormous and twinkled like starlight. Now, after months of seeing truly impressive jewelry hanging from the necks, ears, and wrists of some debs' mothers, Lily couldn't help noticing that these stones were more modest than her memory. Leana, for one, would not have been impressed.

However, Lily could see how lovingly Mummy picked up pieces and held them to Lily's dress to see the effect against the white fabric.

"What do you think of this?" asked Mummy, holding up a thin bracelet of filigreed gold.

"It's lovely," she said.

"But perhaps not grand enough for Queen Charlotte's Ball."

Mummy put it back, and Lily peered over her shoulder into the jewelry box as her mother lifted up a tray to look at the baubles underneath. It was a strange parallel to Leana's visit only two weeks before and so unlike her mother that she wasn't sure what to do.

Mummy stirred her index finger through the small but beautiful pieces in the bottom of her jewelry box. "I think sapphires would look best with your hair. Michael gave me a sapphire-and-diamond brooch for our tenth wedding anniversary." Mummy shifted a starburst brooch. "Ah, here it is." But it wasn't the brooch that Lily's attention fixated on. It was the slim, long brass key that lay against the jewelry box's velvet lining. A key that looked to be the perfect fit for a desk drawer.

"There," said Mummy, setting the brooch out on the bed next to Lily's dress and covering up the lower portion of the jewelry box with the top tray. "What do you think?"

She shook her head, pulling her attention back to the jewelry. "It's beautiful, but would a brooch really suit the dress?"

Mummy laughed, flipped the brooch over, and unclipped the two sides of it from the mount that held the pin backing. Then she slid each of the dress clips to the point on Lily's dress where the straps met the bodice.

"Oh, it's beautiful," Lily breathed, admiring the way the cool shimmer of platinum seemed to melt into the white of her gown.

"If you like it, it's yours for the night," said Mummy.

She ran her fingers over the clips. "I do very much. I'm so glad I didn't accept any of Leana's things."

"Leana's?" her mother asked sharply.

Lily looked up, her mouth slightly open to protest, but when she saw the look on Mummy's face she stopped herself. "Leana came while you were out the week before my party. She brought her jewelry box with her."

"Did she?"

"She said that she wanted me to pick something to wear tonight. I told her no."

Mummy's expression was difficult to read. "Why didn't you take it?"

She thought for a moment. "She had behaved baldly toward me at a party, and I didn't appreciate what she'd done, so I started to focus on other friends. I think she realized what I was doing, and it felt as though she was trying to buy my forgiveness."

"Buying forgiveness sounds like a Hartford," Mummy muttered before looking up sharply. "But you didn't accept the jewelry?"

She shook her head. "I didn't feel like I should."

"And how are things between you now?" asked Mummy.

Lily thought back to the argument in the taxi. "I haven't seen her except across the room at parties since then."

Mummy let out a sigh of relief. "I can't pretend that I'm not happy about that. That family can be spiteful when they choose to be, and I think the less you see of Leana the better."

"I don't think it's spitefulness that's compelling her. I suspect that Leana is used to having her own way in all things, and she doesn't know how else to behave—even when it comes to someone she thinks of as a friend." Lily paused. "They'll be there tonight at the ball, Leana and Mr. and Mrs. Hartford."

You won't be able to avoid them, she wanted to warn her mother.

"And so will we. This is too important a night to be scared off by the Hartfords," said her mother.

Then Mummy began to reassemble her jewelry box, and Lily knew enough about her mother's moods to understand that she was dismissed.

It took three-quarters of an hour for Grandmama's driver to take the three Nicholls women from Harley Gardens to Mayfair as a jam of taxis and other chauffeured cars filled with debs and their families battled their way to Grosvenor House for the official start of the Season's balls. That was enough time for Lily's nerves to set in. However, when the Bentley stopped and she took a Grosvenor House doorman's offered hand to carefully climb out in front of a line of gawkers who'd stopped to stare at the last season of debs presented to the Queen, she felt strangely calm. She liked the way her white crepe de chine dress fell around her legs, her height an advantage for this style, and the clips Mummy lent her made her feel like a debutante in a way that not even her court presentation had.

She glanced back at Mummy and reached for her gloved hand. "Are you ready?"

That pulled a small smile from her mother's nervous lips. "Aren't I supposed to ask you that? This is your first dance."

"Of course she's ready, Josephine," said Grandmama, the streetlights catching the diamonds of her tiara as she adjusted her arctic fox fur around her shoulders. "She's a natural."

"Thank you, Grandmama," said Lily.

The older woman smiled. "You'll do very well, Lily. Just remember that you've already come this far."

Inside the Great Room at Grosvenor House the air buzzed with the excitement of more than one hundred debs and their families. The massive space, which had once been an ice rink, stretched out before Lily. Dozens of tables covered in white linen cloths and sparkling with silver and crystal with masses of flowers crowning them lined the room. A dance floor with a stage for the band stood on one end, and she knew that every debutante who hadn't yet secured an escort for dinner and the first dance would be sweating through her elbow-length gloves.

"Josephine, what is our table number?" asked Grandmama, gazing out over the crowd, her steel-gray eyes taking everything in.

Mummy fumbled the clasp of her evening clutch. "I have the tickets here."

"We could just look for Philippa's family," Lily suggested.

Queen Charlotte's Ball was, for all intents and purposes, a family affair. Each deb's family would purchase tickets to fill a table of eight or ten. The deb, her mother, and father would attend, as well as any siblings or cousins of the appropriate age. The remaining seats would be filled by deb's delights, vetted and approved by the mothers to make sure that their daughters always had an obliging partner.

Despite Aunt Angelica and Uncle Elliot's usual generosity in including Lily in their plans, they had decided it would be best for Georgie to join up with her school friend whose male cousin seemed to have taken a shine to Georgie. That had put Lily, Mummy, and Grandmama in the rather awkward situation of not having a table until Lily had mentioned it in passing to Philippa. The following day, Philippa's mother had rung and offered them three places at the Groveses' table.

"The girls will have a much better time together, don't you think?" Lily had heard Mrs. Groves's voice bleed through the telephone.

Mummy had agreed and, once Grandmama had consented to the idea, sent a hamper from Fortnum & Mason to the Groveses' house in thanks the following day.

"I think I see Philippa," Lily said, raising a hand to wave.

"Lily, don't make a spectacle of yourself." Mummy slid on her reading glasses and quickly scanned the hand-inked number on their ticket. "Table twenty-six."

"Do you need any assistance finding your table?"

Ian.

Lily couldn't keep the smile from her face as she breathed out and turned to greet him. She'd thought him handsome the handful of times she'd spotted him across a room in a navy suit, but she couldn't have known that the dignified black of evening clothes would bring out the richness of his brown eyes as it did.

"I didn't know you were coming," she said.

His eyes crinkled at the corners. "I wouldn't have missed it. Not another."

A little cough behind her brought her reeling back to reality. She twisted and gestured from Grandmama to Ian. "Grandmama, Mummy, this is Ian Bingham. Ian, you know my grandmother, Mrs. Gerald Nicholls, and this is my mother, Mrs. Michael Nicholls."

Had she not grown up so accustomed to watching her Grandmama's sometimes unreadable face over years of Tuesday teas, she would have missed the slight narrowing of Grandmama's eyes and the way that her lips tightened just slightly before offering Ian a respectful—if reserved—smile. "Mr. Bingham. How do you do?"

"I am all the better for having seen you again, Mrs. Nicholls," he said, clasping Grandmama's delicate hand and half bowing over it before repeating the gesture with Mummy. Grandmama, at least, seemed to soften in the face of good manners, but Mummy retained a bit of chilliness.

Grandmama said, "We didn't have the privilege of hosting you at Lily's coming-out drinks, did we, Mr. Bingham."

"I regret to say that I could not attend. I had business in Cambridge that I couldn't put off," he said.

"Are you a student?" Grandmama asked.

"Under my patronage," boomed a voice from Lily's right. She turned around and saw Mr. and Mrs. Hartford approaching with Leana in tow. Her eyes cut to Mummy, who stood ramrod straight next to her, tension radiating off her, just as she'd been accepting Mrs. Hartford's handshake in their receiving line at Lily's drinks.

"Ian's making a good name for himself, or he will if he manages to stay away from debs," Mr. Hartford continued, letting a heavy hand fall on his protégé's shoulder. He wore a slightly smug smile that, paired with his broad build and light brown hair graying slightly at the temples, gave him the look of a distinguished man assured of his place in the world.

The ruby spikes of Mrs. Hartford's tiara—the Hartford rubies that Leana had spoken so casually about—glinted as she dipped her head gracefully and chided her husband with a soft "Darling."

"Mr. Hartford has been kind enough to underwrite my living as long as I am reading politics," said Ian by way of explanation, his good-natured little laugh not fully explaining away the hint of pink high on his cheeks.

"He has a mind for diplomacy," said Mr. Hartford.

"Are you acquainted with the Nichollses?" Ian asked, clearly wishing to change the subject.

Mummy, who had gone white at the sight of her old friends, simply stared, while Mrs. Hartford looked strangely torn. Only Grandmama and Mr. Hartford seemed just as calm as they had been when the Hartfords had first approached.

"We have known one another for a long time. Ethan was a fast friend of my son's when they were in school," said Grandmama.

"But I haven't had the chance to make Miss Nicholls's acquaintance yet," Mr. Hartford said, turning a smile on Lily that lifted the edges of his carefully groomed mustache.

Mummy's hand shot out to grip Lily's arm. Across from them, Mrs. Hartford reached for her husband, the hand on her husband's forearm squeezing so tightly that the fine wool of his dinner jacket bunched up between her fingers.

"Darling, we must find our table," said Mrs. Hartford brightly.

"I think I saw it by the dance floor," said Leana, who had been uncharacteristically quiet up until that point. "I can check the tickets."

Mrs. Hartford fixed her daughter with an icy stare. "Don't fuss, Leana. Your father will do that. Ethan?"

He glanced down at his wife, his gaze on her fingers. Mrs. Hartford dropped her hand as though she'd been burned, and a cool, detached smile settled over her features.

"Quite right, my dear."

Lily watched Mr. Hartford fit his wife's hand into the crook of his arm before he nodded to Ian. "You're coming, Ian." It was not a question.

Ian gave her an apologetic smile, but then seemed to think better of it. "I do hope you'll save me a dance tonight."

"I would be happy to."

He smiled. "Good. I'll look forward to it."

As she watched him stride off, she became aware that Mummy and Grandmama were both watching her. She closed her eyes, buying herself a moment to collect herself, and then turned.

"It was very rude of Mrs. Hartford not to say hello properly, didn't you think?" she asked as casually as she could.

"Yes, it was. Did you know that Ian Bingham would be here tonight?" Mummy asked.

"No, but I'd hoped he would be."

"And"—Mummy lowered her voice—"are you aware that the Bing-hams have never had—nor will they ever have—money?"

"You've already said as much," she said, glancing around her to make sure that no one was listening.

"Your mother is right, Lillian. It isn't wise to attach yourself to a young man who has to rely on charity in order to see himself through university. At least not until he has established himself. Even if he does have excellent taste in flowers."

Mummy's eyes went wide. "The corsage from your drinks?"

"Grandmama." She glared. "You're jumping too far ahead. I am not attaching myself to anyone. The truth is, I hardly know Ian, but I would like to spend more time getting to know him. He's thoughtful."

"I had hoped that the flowers were from Gideon Moore," murmured Mummy.

"Maybe they could have been," said Lily, flicking her hair behind her shoulders. "Now, we should find our table and join the Groveses."

Eighteen

Lily managed to eat only enough to be polite as waiters whisked away a consommé, sole, chicken, and then a confection of frozen orange and pineapple ice. She couldn't help counting down the courses on the menu, waiting for the moment that she would be signaled to rise.

At half past ten, the signal came. Lily and Philippa exchanged a glance over the table and, with a slight nod of acknowledgment, they began to pull their gloves back over their fingers and into place. All around them, 148 other girls did the same, everyone pretending as though it wasn't extraordinary seeing a mass of young women dressed in white suddenly drift away upstairs to the upper gallery like a stream of ghosts.

Not every debutante in attendance had been chosen to be a handmaiden for this ball—a fact that Lily was acutely aware of as hundreds of envious eyes watched as she and her fellow compatriots lifted hems of ball gowns just enough to climb the carpeted stairs safely.

"It's rather odd, all of the other debs watching us, isn't it?" whispered Philippa out of the corner of her mouth.

"I feel as though half of them wish that I'd trip on my hem, knocking the rest of you down with me," she said.

Philippa laughed lightly. "No, darling, that's what *all* of them are hoping to see."

Lily pressed her lips together, suppressing a smile. It was absurd in some ways. Perhaps Grandmama's influence alone would have seen her selected to be a handmaiden, but it was also possible that her early association with Leana had something to do with it. It was strange to think that it was the first week of May, and she'd met Leana only on the nineteenth of March. That already their friendship had bloomed and died back. Life had been a whirlwind since then, a strange combination of ever changing and always the same.

At the top of the stairs, the girls began to pair up and allow themselves to be directed into a long line. They would descend, two by two, into the ballroom as though appearing for the first time.

"There's Ivy. I promised her that I would walk with her." Philippa glanced at Lily as they approached a breathless-looking Ivy, who stood with Katherine. "Do you know who you're walking with?"

"Me," said Katherine, sliding her arm into Lily's and hugging her close. "If you're brave enough."

"Brave enough?" asked Lily with a laugh.

"To be seen with the Millionaire Deb," Katherine teased.

"I think it's a bit too late to begin worrying about that now. We've eaten Wimpy Burgers together." Lily hugged Katherine to her side. "Nothing could make me happier than to walk with you."

"I'm so excited I could burst!" exclaimed Ivy.

"Tonight everyone's wearing your color, Ivy," said Philippa.

"Oh, I know. My grandmother couldn't be happier about that," said Ivy.

"Marry, and then you can wear whatever you like, but make sure he's a good man," said Philippa with a smile at her friend.

Katherine leaned down and whispered to Lily, "Find a job, and *then* you can wear whatever you like."

"Don't set her off," Lily scolded, swatting at her friend's hand.

"Oh no," Ivy squeaked behind them.

"What's the matter?"

But rather than responding, Ivy simply nodded to something behind Lily's shoulder.

She glanced and saw Leana approaching, Cressie next to her.

She would, she decided, be the generous person tonight and put aside the things that had happened between the two of them, at least for the sake of peace at this ball.

"Leana," she said, pulling herself up to her full height. "You look lovely tonight."

Because Leana did. She wore a gown of chiffon that snaked over a molded sweetheart bodice before cascading from her waist to the floor in a waterfall of white that swayed with her movements. She wore rubies—the junior of her mother's but still magnificent—at her neck and earlobes, and a diamond clip raked back her hair on the right side, leaving her left in soft waves that reminded Lily of Veronica Lake's in an old movie she'd seen at a repertory cinema.

Leana let her eyes skim over the other girls in Lily's group. "So do you, Lily."

It was an unwritten rule that debs traded in compliments like currency, and she felt the sting of the insulting omission targeted at her friends. Before she could say anything, however, Leana tilted her head.

"I thought you were wearing your pearls tonight," Leana said.

Lily lifted a hand to touch one of the clips Mummy had lent her, the points of the setting pressing against her gloves. "I had a change of heart."

Leana's mouth turned down, but she nodded sharply as though receiving some message that Lily didn't understand. "Cressie and I should be going. We are at the front of the procession. The top debs always are."

Which is not you. The implication was loud and clear, but Lily found that she didn't care.

"Who wants to be a top deb when they all look so miserable all the time," Katherine muttered under her breath as Leana walked away.

"Do you think so?" Lily asked.

"Don't you? Juliet looks as though she's bored out of her mind, which is hardly surprising, given that I get the impression she'd rather be reading or at least talking about nineteenth-century American novels. Leana pretends that she has all the confidence of a queen, but you can tell she's on pins and needles all the time. It's as though she's trying her hardest to impress."

"I suppose we all feel some level of pressure. Everyone's family has expectations," Lily said.

Katherine blew out a long breath. "Don't I know it. I don't think Mum and Dad have ever looked prouder than this evening when I came down the stairs."

"You love them very much, don't you?" she asked.

"They're my world, and if I can give them this, at least that's something," said Katherine.

Lily couldn't agree more. The question for her was, would this ever be enough?

"Ladies, ladies," came the half-whispered urging of the woman assigned with the undesirable task of wrangling the debs. A chorus of excited twitters went up.

"Silence please, ladies," the woman pleaded, her expression pained. "We're about to begin."

The gallery settled, and on the stage down below, Bill Savill and His Orchestra began to play. There was a collective intake of breath from the debs as the first girls—the top debs—took their first steps down the stairs.

They shuffled forward, slowly making their way down the gallery until they were nearly to the edge of the steps, when Katherine turned to her. "Thank you."

"For what?" Lily said.

There was a slight panic forming around the edge of Katherine's eyes. "For being my friend. For being brave."

Lily grasped Katherine's hand in her own and pressed it. "It doesn't require any bravery to be your friend."

Katherine inhaled and then nodded. The attendant beckoned to them.

"Are you ready?" Lily asked.

"Yes," said Katherine.

"Don't trip."

Katherine stifled a laugh that earned them a glare from the harried attendant, and together they took the first step off the gallery and down the long stretch back to the ballroom. If hundreds of debs had watched them before, now hundreds more parents and partners followed their progress. She tried to make out Mummy's and Grandmama's faces through the crowd, but the best she could hope for with the light and the distance of the massive ballroom was a glance in the direction of table twenty-six.

When she and Katherine reached the bottom of the steps, they both exhaled gratefully and then fell into place in ranks on the dance floor. Then, as the floor filled, the debutantes wove between one another and split to create an aisle. The ballroom doors were flung open, and the Grosvenor House staff pushed a giant white cake covered in lit candles toward the top of the room. A march by Handel swelled around them as the cake rolled forward. The slow progress of the huge confection stopped at the feet of the Dowager Duchess of Northumberland, the guest of honor who would play the role of Queen Charlotte in this rather odd homage to a birthday party held more than two hundred years before.

The chef who'd created the massive cake stepped forward with a silver sword. Together, he and the Dowager Duchess of Northumberland cut the first piece between the long candles flickering brilliantly in the darkened ballroom. The duchess's jeweled bracelets swayed with her efforts before she relinquished the sword to the chef, her responsibilities done.

All at once, as though feathers thrown into the air and arching gracefully to the ground, the handmaidens sank down into a deep curtsy before the cake. It was done with such seriousness that Lily had to swallow a giggle. Never in her life had she pictured herself curtsying to confectionary.

Next to her, Katherine seemed to wobble a bit, and she wondered if her friend was fighting her own battle against the strange mixture of absurdity and solemnness that they'd somehow found themselves a part of.

When Lily lifted her head, she saw that the duchess had stepped back. Swiftly the waitstaff began to cut the cake, and girls surged forward to retrieve pieces to bring back to their tables.

The London balls had officially begun.

Nineteen

Lily sat in the back of the Norman family's huge Rolls-Royce as it thundered around Sloane Square before turning right onto Cliveden Place. Next to her in the back seat sat a long dress bag that contained her gown for the evening. Her pearls, shoes, stockings, and gloves were packed into a train case that sat on her lap, along with her evening bag filled with lipstick and powder.

She'd told Katherine that it was wholly unnecessary to send the car for her, even though the London bus dispute that had started a few days ago meant she would have had to walk from Harley Gardens to Eaton Square, taxis being increasingly difficult to come by due to the strike. In good shoes, it wouldn't have mattered too much, but Katherine had insisted.

"Let's make an occasion of the entire night. Besides, what is the point of Dad having a car and driver if I can't treat my friends?" Katherine had asked with a laugh on the other end of the telephone.

And so Lily had waited for the massive car to roll up to the front of the house and had tried not to let it bother her that Mummy had taken to her bedroom to stew while up and down the road the neighbors' curtains twitched. Grandmama would likely have risen her eyebrows, as she had when Lily had come to their table at Queen Charlotte's Ball bearing plates of cake.

"I see that you made an interesting choice of companion to walk down with," Grandmama had said.

"I chose a woman of great integrity whom I'm proud to call my friend," she said.

The corners of Grandmama's lips rose, even as Mummy fretted in a low tone, "Katherine Norman, Lily?"

"Sometimes, Josephine, fortune favors the bold," said Grandmama.

After that, Mummy seemed to have given up the fight against Katherine—or anyone else, really—now that the balls were underway. Although some people might still gossip about Katherine and Doris behind their hands at dances, it was undeniable that Mrs. Kingsley's girls leant a certain sparkle to the proceedings. It wasn't just their money; Katherine had an easy way about her, pulling everyone around her into her circle without a care as to who their parents were. Doris had proven to be an incredible dancer, using her height to her advantage, which made her popular with men and—in turn—popular with the girls who wanted to be around those men. But it was the mostly respectable presence of Philippa and Ivy in their little group of five that brought them a hint of refinement and innocence in turn.

Lily looked up as the car glided to a stop outside one of the huge white Eaton Square mansions. The elegant facade was lit up like the West End, the white columns bathed in warm yellow. Society might not approve of the Normans' wealth, but it was undeniable that they had chosen for themselves one of the most desirable addresses in London. Lily wondered how many sought to keep Walter and Kitty Norman out of the upper crust because they occupied an entire Eaton Square house while so many of the old families had been required to sell them off to be broken into flats after the war.

The Normans' driver hopped out and opened Lily's door. As she slid out of the car, a second-floor window burst open, and Doris stuck her head out. "Lily!" her friend called as she waved.

Ivy joined her, and Lily had to suppress a laugh at the thought of Ivy's grandmother's horror if she were to see her granddaughter making a spectacle of herself.

"You're finally here!" shouted Ivy.

"I'll be up in a moment!" she called, wondering with a smile what the neighbors would make of the debs hanging out of the second-story window of the Normans' house.

The front door swung open, and an exasperated housekeeper hurried Lily into the entryway. "Good evening, Miss Nicholls. I'm Mrs. Kent. Miss Katherine asked me to send you right up as soon as you arrived." There was a bang overhead, and Mrs. Kent sucked in a calming breath. "Would you like me to have a maid steam your dress?"

"If you wouldn't mind," she said.

"It would be my pleasure. If you'll follow me," said the housekeeper.

Lily and Mrs. Kent climbed the stairs to the second floor. As soon as they were on the landing, Lily could hear the scream of Little Richard singing "Tutti Frutti" on the record player. A bubble of laughter spilled out from a half-open door.

Mrs. Kent seemed to hesitate, looking askance at the door as though approaching a tiger's cage.

"I'm sure I can find my way from here," Lily said.

The housekeeper shot her a grateful look. "I will send one of the maids up with your dress shortly, Miss Nicholls."

Lily thanked her. As soon as Mrs. Kent beat a fast retreat down the corridor, she pushed open the door.

The room was an explosion of tulle, chiffon, and satin in a rainbow of colors. A large wardrobe stood with its doors hanging open and hangers half-empty. Its contents seemed to have taken over every surface, with Doris holding a teal dress up to her chest and spinning around. Her eyes landed on Lily and she grinned.

"She's here!" Doris called.

The other girls whipped around, and Lily was greeted by a chorus of cheers.

"It took you long enough," teased Katherine, who stood up from the dressing table where she'd been spraying on perfume with an atomizer.

"I told you I could have walked," she protested with a laugh.

Katherine kissed Lily on the cheek. "No, we'll have none of that. Tonight we're going to go in style. Did Mrs. Kent take your dress away to press?"

"Yes, she seemed happy to have an excuse to run away from here," she teased.

"I think I horrify her more than I do the matrons at all of those cocktail parties," said Katherine with a grin.

"Look at all of you, you already look beautiful," said Lily, smiling at the sight of her friends.

"I can't wait for dinner," said Doris. "Mrs. Groves has promised to find us all escorts for tonight."

"Philippa phoned earlier to let us know that all of them are good dancers, but she won't say who they are," said Katherine.

"Then I suppose we'll have to hurry over to hers and find out," she said.

Ivy rushed up, breathless as she held a bright yellow dress with a gold sunburst pattern that fell into contrasting box pleats in the skirt across it up to her chest. "Lily, Katherine wants to lend me this tonight."

"She's unsupervised, so she can wear what she likes," said Doris, grabbing Ivy's shoulders and dropping a kiss on her cheek. "We'll have none of grandmother's white for you, darling."

"It's beautiful. I think you should do it," Lily said definitively.

"Will it fit?" asked Ivy.

"A needle and thread and we'll make it fit like a dream," she said with a firm nod.

Ivy gazed down at the dress longingly, her hand playing over the pleats. "Grandmama will be so angry."

"How will Grandmama ever know?" Doris asked as she dropped onto the tufted stool in front of the mirror and began rummaging through a scattered collection of lipstick on the vanity.

"Oh, she'll know." Ivy grinned brightly. "But I don't care."

"That's the spirit," said Katherine. "Try it on."

Ivy scuttled off behind a screen, and Lily and Katherine exchanged a look.

"You're a terrible influence," said Lily in a low voice.

"I think I'm the best influence. She'll be happier in that dress than yet *another* white frock with bows and frills. You should see what she arrived with," whispered Katherine.

Lily gave a laugh just as Doris turned around and fixed her with a stare.

"Lily Nicholls, we've been wondering about something," said Doris.

"Yes!" cried Ivy from behind the screen.

Katherine smiled slyly. "Do spill."

"Spill what?" she asked as she sat down on the edge of Katherine's high bed.

"Well, I couldn't help but notice at Queen Charlotte's Ball that a certain gentleman seemed to seek you out before we were even seated and then danced with you three times after the cake cutting," said Doris.

"I danced with a lot of men that evening," she said, looking down at Katherine's cream satin duvet and drawing a finger over its quilted pattern.

"Don't play coy," said Katherine.

"Yes, that's usually Philippa's job. She won't tell me a thing about David, even if he is my brother," said Doris.

"That's probably the very reason," said Lily.

"Oh, put them out of their misery," said Katherine with a sigh. "They want to hear about Ian Bingham. He's all they've been able to talk about."

"That's not true," protested Ivy from behind the screen so quickly that Lily knew it probably was true.

"You've been just as bad as Philippa," muttered Doris.

"I resent that on behalf of Philippa, but also agree with the spirit of it," said Ivy, who had emerged from behind the screen.

"Oh, Ivy," Lily breathed. "You look lovely."

"It is a good dress, isn't it?" Ivy asked, spreading her hands over the fabric of the skirt. "The color is so rich."

Lily came up behind her friend, assessing the fit of the dress with an experienced eye. "It needs to come in a little here at the bust. Just a few stitches should do it for tonight, since it's only meant to be temporary. Katherine, is there a sewing basket somewhere in this mess?"

Katherine opened a drawer and began to rummage through it. When she handed over the needle and thread, Lily set to work. "Stand still, Ivy, otherwise I'll skewer you."

"I feel like a Georgian lady being sewn into my dress," Ivy said with a giddy laugh.

As Lily set to work, she said, "I did dance with Ian a few times the other night. I like him, but you already know that."

"But do you like him or *like* him?" Doris asked, cutting straight to the chase as usual.

She laughed. "I don't know yet. I don't know him well enough to tell."

"What do you know?" asked Katherine.

She paused her sewing a moment, running through each of their encounters in her head. "He's intelligent, and he speaks to me as though I actually have something between my ears. He's a little bit serious, but not so much that he isn't fun. He must be observant, because he always seems to know when I'm uncomfortable or uncertain. I think to myself, 'I don't know what to say or who to talk to,' and if he's at a party, he's there."

"And he's good-looking. That can't hurt," said Ivy.

"And tall," said Doris dreamily.

She laughed. "And he's good-looking and tall. But mostly, I like that whenever he speaks to me, I don't feel as though I'm competing with every other woman in the room for his attention. He listens to me, and he seems to really want to know what I have to say."

"I can't even imagine what that must be like. Last Friday at Madeline Cargrew's drinks, Robert Bellingham called me Debbie twice in the space of a single gin and orange," said Doris.

"Why didn't you correct him after the first time?" asked Katherine.

"I did," Doris insisted.

"Do you think Ian likes you?" Ivy asked as Lily tied off a knot and clipped the string before starting to alter the other side.

"He likes her enough that he sent her flowers for her drinks," said Katherine slyly.

"Lily!" shouted a chorus of voices.

"He sent me flowers because he was being polite. He couldn't come," she said.

"Twenty-year-old men at university don't do anything just to be polite. He likes you," said Katherine with a look.

Perhaps a little part of her hoped that was true. Yet she hadn't wanted to examine it too closely for fear that it would all disappear like a wisp of smoke.

"I wonder what Gideon thinks of that," said Doris with a grin before slipping behind the screen herself.

"Who's Gideon?" Katherine asked, pretending to swoon. "There's only Ian now."

"You are being absurd," said Lily.

"And don't you love me for it?" Katherine asked.

"Goodness knows why, but I do," said Lily.

The door opened, and a maid came in carrying Lily's freshly pressed gown. The appearance of another garment distracted the other girls as they cooed over it with even Doris sticking her head out from behind the screen to nod approvingly.

"Thank you," said Lily, and the maid ducked out with a little nod of her head.

"It's lovely," said Ivy, running her hand over the edge of the mint split skirt that showed off an ivory underskirt.

"Did you make this?" Katherine asked, examining the notched detail at the center of the white band that made up the strapless neckline.

"I did," she said. "Audrey Hepburn wore something like it in *Sabrina* and I wanted to try to re-create it."

Katherine threw her head back. "Only you would see Givenchy and think, 'I could make that.'"

"You made this?" Doris asked in disbelief.

Lily nodded.

"Madame Benum, my dressmaker, told me it was a shame that Lily's a debutante. She would hire you on as an assistant in a heartbeat," said Katherine.

"Madame is flattering me," she said.

"Madame flatters no one, and I should know," said Katherine.

"Could you imagine what would happen if I told Mummy that I wanted to give up my Season and become a seamstress? She'd probably lock herself in her bedroom and refuse to leave for a decade," she said.

And Grandmama would disown us all.

"Plenty of debs have opened their own dress shops over the years," said Katherine.

"After their Seasons were done," said Lily.

"Or after their divorces were finalized," said Doris, stepping out and turning to Ivy for help with her zipper.

"Well, that is something that we don't have to worry about tonight," said Katherine. "Lily, you and I should dress."

Lily hurried behind the screen, pulling on her dress over her girdle. She didn't need petticoats for this gown, something that she was sure she would be grateful for after hours of dancing.

When she stepped out to show her friends, Katherine smiled warmly and said, "Perfect."

When Katherine went to change, Lily touched up her carmine-red lipstick and then moved to pull her evening gloves out of her train case.

"Here, let me help you," said Doris, holding out her hand.

Lily handed the gloves over, and her friend helped her ease the right one up her arm and button the small row of buttons at the wrist.

"These are beautiful," said Doris.

"They were my mother's from before the war," she said.

"It's a wonder they're in such perfect condition. All these years and not a stain." Doris looked up in horror. "Oh, Lily. Me and my big mouth. I'm sorry."

"It's fine," she said, but her mood had suddenly deflated a little. Doris was right. The gloves were perfect because they hadn't been used. They were the artifacts of Mummy's old life. Before the war. Before Papa's death. Before everything had changed.

Mummy had loved Papa so powerfully that when he died, she'd nearly broken. Lily had once resented that—and perhaps she still did because her mother had been broken for so long that Lily had been forced to be an adult long before a child should have to worry about such things. But now she found herself wondering at how powerful a love must be to so devastate a woman so bound up by tradition that she refused to engage with a world without that love.

She was afraid of the intensity of that love and its ability to destroy, but she also knew that there was another side. A joyfulness that she didn't know if she would ever experience.

You could if you would let yourself.

Doris stepped back, releasing her left hand. "There, you're all done."

Lily looked down at her left hand all done up in its glove. She hadn't even realized that Doris had finished her right.

"Here, let me help you," she said, returning the favor for Doris as Katherine appeared resplendent in spangled silver, and the room once again descended into the cacophony that was debs in preparation.

Twenty

D inner was a resounding success with even Philippa's taciturn father joining in on the laughter that had begun as soon as Katherine, Doris, Ivy, and Lily arrived. As promised, Mrs. Groves had found escorts for all the girls. Lily had sat next to one of Philippa's brother's friends, an Irish horseman named Brian Walsh with a wicked smile and a shock of blond hair that couldn't quite be contained by pomade, and he spent the dinner teasing her—and the rest of the guests.

It was on Brian's arm that she walked into the ballroom at the Savoy.

"Look at all of these people," Lily said, gazing around at the girls in a wash of hues and the gentlemen in stark white and black.

"And it's only just half past ten. It's bound to become more crowded before the evening's over," said Brian.

"Clearly, this isn't your first debutante ball," she said.

Brian sent her a crooked smile. "Guilty as charged. My twin sister came out last year, although she's serious enough about riding that she put her foot down and declared she'd only do the balls around the Dublin Horse Show. Do you ride?"

"Very poorly," she said. "We went around a rink on a pony a few times at school, but I'm afraid that was years ago." Riding—let alone keeping a pony of her own—was an expense that Mummy would never have indulged. "My cousin Georgie rides, though."

"Well, we'll have to see you on a horse when you come to Dublin. I'll mention to my cousin, Margaret, that we've met. She's out this year as well," he said.

She glanced at him, knowing that a mention to Margaret would likely mean an invitation to Margaret's ball. If she accepted, it would fall to the Walsh family to provide her with a place to stay—often the home of a generous family friend who would no doubt ask for the favor to be returned when their own daughter or niece held her own coming-out ball. However, the way that Brian was looking at her made her wonder if she would perhaps be given the honor of staying with the family in hopes of giving them more time together.

She tried for a moment to imagine what a future as Mrs. Brian Walsh would be. He was a hardy-looking man, a little tanned and ruddy from all his time spent working with horses, but in a pleasant, healthy sort of way. From what she'd gathered at dinner, the Walshes still lived at Glen Dara, the eighteenth-century family seat just outside Dublin. The respectable work of breeding and training horses ruled their lives, and with that would come horse shows, hunts, and hunt balls. She would go from a London girl to a country woman, dressed in tweeds and riding boots. She would no doubt learn to ride properly because it would make Brian happy, and she might even learn to enjoy it herself. She didn't think that she was flattering herself in thinking that they would make a handsome couple, both blond and tall with a healthy red to their cheeks. Grandmama and Mummy probably wouldn't even complain that he was Irish, and her life would move from the familiarity of England to the strangeness of Ireland. Instead, they would be happy to see Lily so efficiently settled.

The only problem was that the thought of her life taking that path left her feeling strangely detached.

"Shall we dance?" Brian asked.

"The song's not over yet," she said as Joe Loss and His Orchestra reached the second chorus of "It Had to Be You."

"Why wait?" he asked, looping his right arm around her back and scooping her free hand up.

With a laugh, they plunged into the fray, Brian expertly spinning her away from a couple who came careening from their right, the deb's delight diligently counting steps while his partner squealed with glee at every spin.

"That was close," he said, pulling her into him.

She tried to relax into his embrace, closing her eyes and letting the light citrus-and-wood scent of his Floris No. 89 cologne wrap around them. He was a nice man. Most of the deb's delights were, at least when they were in female company.

She thought back to earlier that evening when her friends had interrogated her about Gideon and Ian. Gideon was undoubtedly the prize that Mummy wanted her to pursue—and likely he would be Grandmama's choice as well. If her life with Brian would be one of horses and country pursuits, a life as Mrs. Gideon Moore would be filled with society. That was Gideon to a T—a man with an easy laugh who was always game for dinner or dancing, a bottle of champagne close at hand. Yet there was a depth there. She'd seen it herself in the moments he'd stepped up to help her.

Ian, on the other hand, felt utterly decent, deeply reliable. He held himself at a little bit of a remove, as though he was assessing the situation and trying to understand how all of it fit together. He may not have had the flash and dash of a soldier with a sports car, but there was weight to him, and she couldn't help but feel as though every moment he spent with her was fully her own. He was a serious man who took her seriously, and she enjoyed the novelty and comfort of that.

Almost as though her thoughts had summoned him, Gideon stepped into her view. She started when he tapped Brian on the shoulder. She and Brian stopped swaying, and he tucked her protectively under his arm.

Gideon offered an apologetic smile. "Sorry, old boy, but do you mind terribly if I borrow your partner? There's a bit of a situation, and I suspect that Lily's the only sensible one in this entire room."

There was that word again. *Sensible.*

"A situation?" she asked.

His expression turned grim. "Leana."

"But she's barely spoken to me since Queen Charlotte's. Why would she need me?" she asked.

Gideon dropped his voice. "Leana's rather jolly this evening."

Which, for Leana, could only mean one thing. She was drunk at half past ten at one of the first balls of the Season.

A resentment she wasn't particularly proud of sparked up in her. She wondered if Leana had intentionally drunk too much so that she could send people scurrying after her. But then she remembered the eagerness with which Leana had adopted her, the near desperation to make Lily *her* friend. Perhaps there was manipulation in her former friend's acting, but there was unhappiness, too. Lily knew it.

Lily turned to Brian. "I should go see to her."

Brian stepped back and took a gallant bow. "Of course. Perhaps we'll have another dance later."

"An entire one," she promised.

Gideon grabbed her elbow gently and began to lead her away. She turned back and saw that Brian had already stepped off the dance floor, his eyes fixed on a group of debs all giggling as he approached.

"I'm sorry, but you're the only one I've ever seen her really listen to when she's like this," said Gideon.

"Like what exactly?" she asked, not wanting to argue that Leana didn't listen to anyone if it didn't suit her.

"Just as you might expect, given that she had three martinis before dinner," he said in a voice pitched low.

"Three?" she asked, aghast.

"And then there was a decent white and a very nice claret followed by port," he said.

"Did everyone drink like that?" she asked.

"No one is quite like Leana. She makes sure of that," he said.

Lily sighed.

"Nice one?" Gideon asked.

"Nice one what?" she asked.

He nodded back in the direction of Brian.

"I think so." She glanced over her shoulder and found Brian speaking with a petite brunette on the side of the dance floor. "Then again, maybe not nice enough."

"It isn't personal. I have it on good authority that the senior Walsh is ill. Cancer of the lungs, by the sound of it. Young Brian may be inheriting sooner than he hopes," said Gideon.

"That's horrible," she said.

Gideon slid her a look. "We're all motivated by something, Lily. Walsh needs a wife to help him manage Glen Dara and, I suspect, pay for the running of it. My father's been badgering me to settle down, although God knows why I'd want to when I'm just twenty-six. And then there's Leana." He stopped abruptly in front of a panel in the ballroom's wall and pushed it open to reveal a disguised door leading to an antechamber of some sort. A high-pitched laugh rose above the sound of the orchestra to meet them as Lily stepped inside.

"Look who I found," Gideon announced to Leana, who lay half-sprawled over a pink velvet sofa with her light blue net skirts pooling on the ground, her weight leaned heavily on Raymond while she cradled a cocktail glass in one hand. In the corner, Cressie and Rupert were arguing, and Cecil, who sat with a pale-faced girl Lily had never seen before, gave Lily a small smile, but then his face fell again.

Leana's swimming eyes fixed momentarily on Lily, and then the Deb of the Year's head reared back in an exaggerated manner. "Found your friends a bit too common for you, so you've come crawling back?"

Lily stiffened. "Speak to me like that again and I'll leave."

"Leana, play nice," Gideon warned.

"You spend all of your time with *those* girls now," Leana continued, gesturing wildly in the direction of the now-closed door and sloshing her drink over the side of her glass and onto her ivory elbow-length gloves. "It isn't fair."

"No one's better than you, darling. Everyone with a shred of taste knows that," Raymond boomed, his red face a clear indication that he was just as tight as Leana.

"Troy, let's give the ladies a chance to catch up. Repair the tiff they're in and all that," said Gideon with forced jocularity.

Cecil shot to his feet, dragging his date with him, while it took Raymond quite a bit of grouching before he finally staggered to his feet and out the door that Gideon held ajar. Cressie started to move as soon as Rupert stood, but Lily pointed to her.

"No. You stay," Lily ordered. She was not going to spend the entirety of her first ball looking after Leana. Not when she knew that all she'd likely receive in return was abuse.

Cressie pouted, but she sank back down into her seat and began picking at the folds of her rose-and-white skirts.

Thank you, mouthed Gideon as he closed the door.

You owe me, she glared.

When the door was shut, Lily sank down on her heels so that she was eye level with Leana. Bracing her arms against her knees, she said, "You're drunk."

Leana threw back her dark hair and let out a howling laugh. "A keen deduction from the bluestocking among us."

"Lily, don't . . ." Cressie started, but Lily stopped her with a shake of her head.

"No. Leana needs to hear this," she said. "You're drunk, and you risking exposing yourself to ridicule if you drink anything more."

Leana laughed. "Ridicule? Who would ridicule me? I'm the Deb of the Year. The magazines have as much as decided it."

"And as Deb of the Year, you're held to a higher standard," she said, playing into Leana's vanity.

Leana's gaze dropped to her drink, but her fingers still remained firmly wrapped around it.

"Now, you are going to give me your glass. Then you are going to drink a pot of coffee and sit here until you are sober enough that you can make it out to a taxi without disgracing yourself," said Lily.

Leana's face scrunched up as though she'd eaten something distasteful. "No wonder Mummy warned me away from you. I thought it was just because you're poor and from a thoroughly middle-of-the-road family, but it turns out you're as much fun as your mother. The Old Vic," Leana cackled before aiming her drink at her lips and managing to get most of it down her mouth.

Lily drew in a steadying breath. Logic told her that Leana lashed out for the same reason that anyone did: she was vulnerable, hurting, afraid. Yet that didn't take any of the sting out when it came time to be the one in the way of those barbs.

"Perhaps your mother was right, but *I'm* also right and you know that, otherwise you wouldn't be acting this way," she said.

"And what way is that?" Leana asked with a sneer.

"Like a child who is hopping up and down, desperate for her mother's attention." She should know. For years she'd been like that child, only her way of earning Mummy's or Grandmama's love had been to squash herself into the perfect little girl until all she could think about was how to break free. The longer she spent around people like Leana, the more she was beginning to realize that society—the world that the most important women in her life wanted her to fit into so badly—might not be for her.

When Leana didn't respond, Lily rose and shook out her skirts. "I'm going to arrange for coffee and water to be sent here."

For a moment she thought that Leana would protest, but instead Leana held the dregs of her drink up, allowing Lily to prize it from her hand.

"I am done," Leana announced, trying to stand up but dropping back to the sofa when her feet slowly slid from under her.

"You are done, but you are not to leave this room," she said.

"What am I supposed to do?" squeaked Cressie from her corner of the room.

"You're going to sit here and make sure that she does all of those things I just said. It's what top debs do for one another," she said.

When she slipped out the door and glanced back, Cressie's mouth was still hanging wide open.

Twenty-One

Lily left the anteroom feeling lighter than she had in a long time. Before, she hadn't been able to help the guilt that weighed on her, even as things had begun to sour with Leana. Now there was a line in the sand, and she knew on which side she firmly stood, even if a part of her couldn't help but mourn what could have been.

Lily had seen flashes of Leana as she really was, when the polish that carried the deb through the Season slipped. Lonely and angry, Leana clung to the bit of power she was allowed in a world that thought so little of women that they were rarely afforded that privilege. But those moments were too often smothered by the layers of judgment and bitterness that Leana wore draped around her shoulders like her mink stole, enjoying the sight of people twisting themselves to please her. To bolster her. It was in the backhanded compliments that Leana meted out as she kept her group of acolytes in line and the way she always had to glitter brightest. Lily had seen the streak of meanness that lived under the perfect deb, the anxious daughter, the angry woman, and she'd decided she didn't want to be a part of it any longer.

However, she knew what it would mean to a deb like Leana if news of her drunkenness spread. Gossip like that would rip through the drawing rooms and sitting rooms of London society by the following evening. Some of the shine would come off one of the jewels of the Season, and so many would be happy for it, because if there was one thing high society loved more than a perfect deb, it was the revelation that a society page darling might be disappointingly human.

Lily shook her head and hugged the edge of the ballroom wall, smiling tightly at the wallflower debs seated on gold chairs to watch the dance floor with suspicious, anxious gazes. When she reached an exit, she let herself out, the sounds of the ball muffling behind her. She inhaled deeply enough that the boning of her bodice pressed painfully against her girdle and exhaled a slow, steadying breath. All she had to do was this one task, and then her evening would be her own again.

Lily was halfway down the richly carpeted corridor when, from around the far corner, Ian appeared.

"Hello," she said, stopping short, her wide split overskirt gracefully settling around her silver heels. "I didn't know that you'd be here."

"University has been keeping me busy, but I asked for an invitation and a ride up to London when I found out that my friend Ralph is a cousin of Miss Simmonds," he said, smiling cheekily as he named their hostess for the night.

"Oh, I see," she said.

His eyes softened as he approached her carefully, as though giving her time to pull away before he placed a hand on the gap of skin between her shoulder and the top of her long gloves. When he touched her, she shivered, and when he leaned in to kiss her on the cheek, her breath caught in her throat. He hesitated a moment, as though arrested by a realization.

"It's good to see you, Lily," he said, his tone low and intimate.

Her lips parted, but by the time she thought to speak he'd stepped back, and the tension strung taut between them slackened.

"Taking a moment for a bit of fresh air?" he asked.

"No. That is . . ." She hesitated. "I was actually trying to find a member of staff."

He frowned. "Are you well?"

"It's an acquaintance. It seems that she's had a little too much champagne with dinner. I wanted to find her some coffee," she said.

"Your acquaintance wouldn't happen to be the daughter of my patron, would she?"

When she didn't respond, he rocked back on his heels, his hands clasped behind his back. "No, quite right not to say. That would be indiscreet."

"I'm sorry," she said.

"Not at all. It shows a good character not to gossip about others behind their backs," he said.

"Don't give me too much credit. The Season seems to be fueled by gossip. I'm just tired of talking about this particular deb," she said.

"Well, shall we find someone to help with that coffee?" he asked, holding out the crook of his arm.

Arm in arm they went, stopping the first Savoy staff member that they could find. It was simple enough to arrange for coffee to be sent to Leana and to ask for the staff's discretion. Leana, Lily knew, would not be the first drunken ball guest the Savoy had ever had to attend to.

"Well, that's done," Ian said as they watched the staff member hurry away with his orders.

"Thank you. I appreciated the company," she said.

"Have you had the chance to dance yet?" he asked, jerking his head back toward the ballroom.

"I've danced once, with my escort for the evening."

She caught the tick in his jaw, as though he'd weighed the thought that she might have come to the ball accompanied, found that he didn't like it, but held himself back from saying anything because what right did he have? Finally, he cleared his throat. "An escort?"

"You have heard of escorts, haven't you?" she teased as they approached the ballroom's white-and-gilt doors and the muffled sound of the music and laughing partygoers drifted out once again. "They're the most fashionable accessory a deb can have this time of year. And, of course, they're useful for other things, too, like securing taxis, fetching drinks, and chasing down coats."

"And filling out dance cards," he said.

"Some do that job better than others."

"And why is your escort not here with you, helping you find coffee?" he asked.

She shrugged. "The last I saw him he was asking a pretty girl four inches shorter than me to dance."

"That's not very gallant," Ian said.

"I've been told that he's determined to make something of this Season as well—if gossip is to be believed."

"There is that gossip again," Ian said.

They stopped in front of the ballroom door, but neither of them moved to open it. Instead, Ian grabbed her hand. "Come with me."

He pulled her gently along the corridor, the carpet muffling the sound of their shoes. Tucked around the corner, it was quiet, but when Ian inched a door open, the sound of the orchestra playing in the River Room spilled out. Then he held out his hand.

A flush of delicious heat swooped low in her stomach as she placed her hand in his. Although she still wore her gloves, the warmth of his skin bled through the soft fabric, and she sucked in a breath when his other hand covered her bare shoulder blade.

"I'm not a very good dancer. I know the basics, but I haven't had many opportunities to practice in the last few years," he confessed as "The Way You Look Tonight" drifted out to them.

She smiled. It was the song they'd danced to at the Colony Club.

"I don't mind," she said as they began to sway.

"Good. I should hate to disappoint you."

She swallowed and chanced a look at him. "How could you disappoint me?"

His chuckle was low. "In so many ways. You're lovely, Lily."

She dipped her chin. "I'm not."

"You're beautiful, but you're much more than that. You're intelligent, you're principled, and I think you are far bolder than you give yourself credit for."

"I'm not sure many people appreciate boldness in a debutante," she said.

"And what is a debutante meant to be?" he asked.

"A lady first, and I suppose a wife and mother later. She should know how to enter every social situation and support her husband's career in any way she can."

It was what Grandmama and Mummy had done. It was what was expected of her. So why did the thought of doing the same feel so cloyingly claustrophobic?

It hadn't always been like this. She'd gone along with Grandmama's plans because she hadn't had another choice, but once she'd overcome the disappointment of leaving school early she'd settled into the idea of being a deb. But what about next year and the year after that and twenty years from then? Would she still be seeing the same people? If the Season continued on despite the abolition of the court presentations, would she be one of the young matrons standing on the edges of the ballroom watching her own daughter dance at a ball?

Ian spun her, pulling her a little closer so that her cheek could almost rest against the soft wool of his jacket. The thought was tempting, but she held back.

"You're quiet," he said.

"I'm thinking about what my life would look like if no one expected me to become a deb," she said.

"What would you have done?" he asked.

"I would be studying for my university entrance exams. I had a teacher who encouraged me and I saw her at the library last month, just by chance. When I told her I was doing the Season, I could tell she was disappointed. I suppose I'm a little disappointed, too."

"Then why did you agree to do the Season?" he asked.

"There was only really one choice. Mummy and I are able to live the way we do because of the good will of Grandmama. Neither of them have said as much, but I've gathered over the years that Papa was a good soldier but a poor manager of money. The house was the only real asset left after Mummy paid the death duties. Mummy had some investments, but by the time I turned twelve those were virtually gone. We didn't have enough to even send me to school, so Grandmama stepped in." She gave a little laugh. "I shouldn't be telling you any of this."

"Why not?" he asked.

"Because it isn't done to speak about money," she said.

"What would happen if you quit the Season right now and decided to dedicate yourself to studying?" he asked.

A longing tugged at her, but still she shook her head. "I would never do that." It wasn't just the shame that it would bring upon Grandmama and Mummy; it was the very real possibility that Grandmama would stop Mummy's allowance. They were stretched enough as it was with Lily's Season, and being cut off would crush Mummy.

And then there was the letter from Dovecote Cottage. The veiled threats, the hints at money . . . it didn't make sense. Anyone who knew anything about their family knew that Grandmama was the wealthy doyenne. Not Mummy.

"I know something about feeling obligated to others," said Ian softly, pulling her attention back to him, to the dance. "For a long time, I didn't understand why Dad humbled himself to accept Mr. Hartford's offer. Dad's a very good doctor, but he was the newcomer in Elkenhurst when he started. It took him a good twenty-five years until the other doctor retired. It's only now that his patient load has grown to a level that can sustain him.

"When Mr. Hartford offered to take me out of the local grammar school and pay my fees, Dad couldn't say no. Mr. Hartford has funded my education all the way to university, but there are restrictions that come with that."

"What kind of restrictions?" she asked.

"I'll take my degree and become a public servant."

"Just like he did," she said.

"I'll work as his aide, learning under him until there is a posting that might be appropriate. No hopes of being an academic, I'm afraid," he said with a rueful smile.

"That's what you would want to do?" she asked.

"Yes. The musty economics professor in ancient tweed with elbow patches. I might even have taken up a pipe to complete the look," he said with a laugh.

"But what about Geoffrey, Leana's brother? Wouldn't Mr. Hartford have those sorts of ambitions for him?" she asked.

"It was obvious from an early age that Geoffrey isn't well suited for diplomatic work. He's temperamentally too unpredictable. I suspect that may be one of the things that helped him say no," said Ian.

"And what would happen if you said no to Mr. Hartford?" she asked.

His jaw twitched. "He has invested in me, and I think he wants to see a return on his investment."

Understanding dawned on her. "You think that if you don't do as he says, he'll ask you to pay everything back."

"Not me. My father. It's not something I could risk. Calling in that debt would cripple my family," he said.

"I'm so sorry."

"I sometimes wonder what life would be like if I was braver," he said.

"Is that why you don't stay with the Hartfords when you come to London?" she asked.

"How do you know that?" he asked.

She blushed. "Leana mentioned it once."

A grin split his expression. "Have you been asking about me?"

"No! Well, not really."

He laughed. "Yes, that's one of the reasons that I don't stay at Hartford House. The other is that I can't help but feel like the doctor's son, invited up to the big house so long as he doesn't touch anything or make a fuss."

"I don't seem to be in any of the Hartfords' good graces these days. Not that it should matter." She found more and more that maybe there had been some truth to Mummy's warnings.

"Would you care for another dance?" he asked, not letting her go even as applause filled the ballroom next to them and voices overtook the music for a moment.

"Yes," she said. "I would."

He hesitated. "When can I see you again?"

Her heart beat a little faster. "When will you be in London again?"

He grimaced. "Not until the end of the month."

An idea popped into her head that at first had her shrinking back but then, what had he called her? Bold?

"In that case, perhaps you would be willing to act as my escort to Katherine Norman's ball at her family's home in Surrey on the twenty-ninth of May. I'm sure that Katherine and Mrs. Norman won't mind me asking you," she said.

"Will your friends be there?" he asked.

"The Imperfects?"

He laughed. "Is that what you call yourselves?"

"It seems fitting, doesn't it?"

"How?" he asked.

"Because none of us are quite the ideal debutante."

"The Imperfects," he mused. "I like it."

"I do, too. But why do you ask whether they'll be there?" she asked.

"Because they're your friends, and there's nothing I'd like to do more than know you and them better, Lily Nicholls."

This time, when he spun her around and then pulled her in close, she rested her cheek on his chest and closed her eyes as they moved together.

After the song ended, Lily and Ian begrudgingly returned to the ballroom, but rather than slip away, he stayed by her side, drawing a significant look from Katherine even as he asked Katherine to dance.

"I'd be happy to, if Lily can spare you," said Katherine.

Ian laughed, while Lily blushed.

As the band began to play "Lovely to Look At," William Sassoon slid up next to Lily. "Your friend's taken my date."

"It hardly seems fair, does it?" she asked, tilting her head.

He crossed his arms as though studying Ian and Katherine. "I think we can do better than that, don't you?"

She laughed. "I should hope so!"

"Let's show them, then," he said, and neatly swept her onto the floor.

As soon as her dance with William was done, she danced with Beatrice Sanders's boyfriend, Simon, and then Shrey, Max, Ian again, a man she'd never met who—like so many other deb's delights—was named Charles, and on and on until she was breathless, her head spinning. But whenever there was a break in the music, she found Ian by her side.

When at last the band broke for breakfast around two o'clock, Ian placed a light hand on the small of her back, but Katherine grabbed her arm.

"We shall join you gentlemen in a moment," Katherine announced.

In a giggling rush, the Imperfects hurried to the powder room and cornered Lily.

"What is going on with Ian?" Katherine asked as soon as the door was shut.

"Has he kissed you yet?" Doris demanded.

"What? No! We've only danced," said Lily, blushing.

"He looks like he wants to kiss you," said Ivy dreamily.

"She looks like she'd be happy to let him," said Philippa with a raised brow.

"We've danced and we've talked. That's all," she said.

"But you want to kiss him?" asked Doris, looking up from the mirror where she was reapplying her crimson lipstick.

"Oh, leave her alone," said Katherine, swiping playfully at her friend.

Doris pouted at the mirror to examine her lipstick. "You started it."

"Mum is putting together the birthday dinner for my coming-out ball. Bring Ian," said Katherine.

"Are we invited to dinner?" asked Lily with a laugh.

"Of course you are! You all are. How could I want anyone else to come? And, if your grandmother can stand the thought of you staying with someone so scandalous as me," Katherine added, looking at Ivy, "I'd like you all to stay the night as well. Then you won't need to find your way back to London in the early hours of the morning."

"I'll make my grandmother say yes," said Ivy with a look of determination that Lily couldn't have imagined on her friend's face even a couple of months before.

"What do you think?" asked Philippa. "Have we let the men stew long enough?"

"I think so," said Katherine.

The friends all gathered up their things, with Lily falling into line beside Katherine as they left the powder room.

"I have a confession to make," said Lily.

"Do you?" Katherine asked.

"I may already have asked Ian to your ball."

"How cheeky," said Katherine with an appreciative smile. "And did he say yes?"

"He did," she said with a grin.

Katherine slipped an arm around her waist. "Well, aren't you a clever one?"

"Thank you," said Lily with a grin, her eyes meeting Ian's as she walked into the room where they were to have breakfast. "I'm feeling rather clever at the moment."

Twenty-Two

Lily pushed the heavy door to Harley Gardens open at five o'clock the morning after Cora Simmonds's ball, squinting in the faint light of dawn that was already beginning to break. Her silver shoes dangled from her fingers because she'd taken them off in the taxi home to ease the pain from dancing most of the night. The ball had gone on for hours, with things only breaking up after the band had stopped playing. Doris, Max, and a few others had tried to persuade her to go to London Airport for a second breakfast amid the novelty and glamour of air travel. Ian had looked at her in question, but Lily had shaken her head and let him drop her in a taxi. She knew how many late nights the next few months would hold.

"A marathon, not a sprint," she murmured to herself as she let Mummy's mink stole slip down her shoulders.

She would have to pick up her things from Katherine's house later that day, but for now all she wanted was to fall into bed and sleep for hours.

But she would see Ian again. She was sure of it now.

Lily was halfway to the stairs before she noticed it. The door to Papa's study was cracked open, a faint light struggling through the door and into the dimmed entryway. All at once, her fatigue was gone. There was no reason for that door to be open.

Carefully Lily placed her shoes and her evening bag on the carpet and crept over to the door. With a light touch, she eased it open a little and peered inside. Sprawled out over Papa's desk on top of a series of papers lay Mummy, a half-full decanter of scotch close at hand and a finger of liquor still left in a single crystal glass.

Lily stood there, staring. Mummy, who never touched a drop of alcohol, even at the cocktail parties, had been drinking—heavily it would seem. But then she looked at Mummy's face more closely, saw the telltale black smudges of tear-streaked mascara under her eyes, and realized that she couldn't just leave her there. She would take Mummy to bed.

Lily pushed open the door fully and made her way to Papa's desk. It was covered in papers, a ledger, the black leather checkbook. Her heart broke a little knowing that she was out at a ball and Mummy was back home doing the accounts, likely worrying over how to stretch Grandmama's money. Wondering how she could continue to give Lily a proper Season and afford their lives.

Lily lifted a hand to shake Mummy gently awake when something underneath the open ledger caught her eye.

Carefully she moved the account book. It was a letter written in the same looping hand as the one that had come from Dovecote Cottage, but this letter was dated two days ago.

I will not begin this letter with the usual pleasantries or salutations because I will not pretend that you do not understand my motivation for writing it.

I fear that you may not have taken my last letters seriously. That you don't trust that I will do the things that I promise. I should have thought that you learned a long time ago what a danger it is not to take me at my word.

The £75 you have sent is not enough. You will send me the full £150 I am due for my part in keeping this secret each month, or I will tell Lily all of it, from the affair to the circumstances of her birth. She will understand the truth about her father and what you did.

Lily dropped the letter, her eyes darting to her mother, so weak and vulnerable lying with her head pillowed on the desk. Her mother, who was so frightened of Grandmama that she could not enter that big house on Cadogan Place without a slight tremor in her hands. Ever since Grandmama had bestowed an allowance on them and saved them from genteel poverty, Lily had assumed it was fear of upsetting the balance that had made her mother meek. Now she knew that there was another fear that must lurk in the back of her mother's mind: the fear that one day Grandmama might find out the truth.

Lily was not Michael Nicholls's daughter.

Lily reached her hand out to steady herself against the man she'd always called Papa's desk.

The man who she'd never met, who had died long before she could remember but whose memory she'd been taught to worship, was not her papa.

Tears stung Lily's eyes, but they weren't from sadness. Anger filled her, red and raging. She was not legitimate. Her mother had lied to her about everything, building a life around the myth of losing her husband when they were separated by an ocean. Her mother had retreated into herself, letting herself be ridiculed and scorned behind her back because everyone thought she so loved her husband that she'd all but shunned society until she needed to bring her daughter out.

Suddenly it made sense why her mother had hidden from society. It was easier to keep a secret when you spoke to almost no one. She'd kept Lily's life small, discouraging Lily from making the lasting sort of friends who might become a fuller part of their lives because it would have meant inviting the parents of those girls into their circle as well.

Lily understood why her mother had presented her and attended some of the more important parties. She was making a good show of it even as she must live in fear because every conversation with her mother, every glance at Lily was a chance that someone might realize what had happened in the past. Every party and ball could undo everything her mother had tried to preserve in amber in this house.

And what of Lily's father—her true father? Was he out there, a proud father of a deb? Had he been a part of her mother's life or a passing fling? Had he been the first? The only? Had her mother loved him?

An estranged daughter. An illegitimate daughter. A weeping widow. A dead husband.

The overwhelming urge to laugh bubbled up in Lily at the absurdity of her family—the mess of it all—and she had to clamp her hand down on her mouth to keep the sound from escaping and waking her mother. She breathed heavily through her nose, tears stinging her eyes as she tried to control herself. She needed to pull her world back together, but like a vase that's fallen from a high shelf, she couldn't be put back together again.

It was all too much. As quickly as she dared, she replaced the letter where she'd found it. She began to back away slowly, careful not to touch Mummy, when she caught sight of the half-drunk scotch. Snatching the glass up, she knocked back the dregs, pressing a hand to her mouth to cover the coughs that tried to escape. But she liked the burn of the alcohol—welcomed it, even—and for one tiny moment she could understand why some people were tempted to drink their lives away.

Lily tried her best to avoid her mother for the rest of the day. It wasn't difficult to do because the morning of Lily's discovery in Michael Nicholls's study, her mother had retired to her room and asked Hannah not to disturb her. All day that Saturday, Lily stared at the pages of a book Miss Hester had recommended, not reading but wondering. Did her mother know? Had she replaced the letter correctly? Had the glass of scotch she'd rashly drank given away her presence in the forbidden study early that morning?

But that evening, she and her mother had both dressed for Lucia Clare's ball because her mother had come out with Lucia's aunt and deemed that a close enough connection that she was obligated to go. But this time, instead of the jives around the ballroom and private dances in hallways, Lily hung back.

"What's wrong?" Katherine had asked after Lily had gripped her arm and once again pretended to be in incredibly deep conversation when a deb's delight approached and looked as though he intended to ask one of them to dance.

"I'm not feeling like myself," she'd said.

"Is that because a certain gentleman is not in attendance?" Katherine teased.

But when Lily didn't respond to her friend's teasing about Ian and the romantic dance she'd shared the details of the previous evening, Katherine frowned. "You really aren't feeling like yourself tonight, are you? Are you certain that you don't want to go home early?"

"And risk my mother asking why? No thank you. I'll be fine. I promise," she'd said, squeezing out a smile and silently vowing that the next time she was asked to dance she would do it, if only to reassure her friends that everything was fine.

But everything isn't fine, and saying so makes you as much of a liar as your mother.

No, she'd told herself firmly. Lying to your daughter about her father for nearly two decades was something entirely different.

On Sunday, when they received a telephone call from Grandmama summoning them to Cadogan Place, she reluctantly put on a light pink silk day dress she'd just finished and climbed into a taxi with her mother.

"That's a pretty dress," said her mother halfway through the otherwise silent ride over to Belgravia.

"Thank you," she said.

"Did you make it?" her mother asked.

"I reworked one of Georgie's old ones." She picked at a piece of fluff on the fabric. "And I thought you would appreciate me saving the expense of a new dress. You did say that you needed the extra money."

"Yes," said her mother shortly.

"Why is that?"

Her mother looked a little taken aback. "I told you, the Season is very expensive."

"But Grandmama has taken care of all of the expenses."

"There are things your grandmother doesn't know about," said her mother.

But Lily knew about those things. She knew that her mother was skimming money to pay a blackmailer. She knew that her mother had been lying to her all her life.

The taxi pulled up to the curb, and her mother fumbled with her handbag to pay the man. Lily watched her closely as she counted out the correct coins and then took a breath.

"Let's see what it is she wants," her mother muttered.

In the grand house, they were greeted by Mrs. Parker and shown up to the usual drawing room. As always, Grandmama was immaculate in champagne-colored silk, but this time there was no pretense of tea. Instead, she sat behind a small table, her diary open in front of her.

"Josephine, Lillian, sit down. We have a great deal to discuss," said Grandmama, turning her still-smooth cheek to accept a kiss from Lily.

"Do we?" asked Lily.

Grandmama shot her a look. "Now that dances have started, you will have a number of choices to make. The London balls are easy enough to handle. Even if they fall on the same night, you can choose to go to two in an evening. However, when it comes to the country balls, the distance between homes makes that more difficult."

Lily already felt exhausted thinking about the months of late parties that would stretch before her.

"Things become even more complicated when it comes to the Dublin Horse Show," said Grandmama.

"I expect an invitation from Brian Walsh's cousin, Margaret, any day now. Brian was my escort at Philippa's dinner on Friday," she said.

Grandmama slid on a thin pair of spectacles to make a mark in her diary. "Very good."

"But should I really think about going to Dublin? Surely the expense—"

"Don't worry yourself about expense," said Grandmama. "A debutante only has one Season to make an impact. You should go to Dublin for at least a week."

"What about the country balls in June?" her mother asked.

"Who has invited you?" asked Grandmama.

"We said yes to the Honorable Sarah Bragg's ball and Beryl Marcombe. They're both in East Sussex on the same weekend," said Mummy.

"And there is Katherine Norman's ball in two weeks. She's invited me and the rest of our friends to come up early and stay that night," Lily said.

"Staying at the Normans' home?" Grandmama asked, tipping her nose down to peer over her spectacles.

"Is that the best idea?" her mother asked.

"I've already told her that I'll go," she said.

"Attending the Norman girl's ball is one thing, but staying with the family is another entirely," said Grandmama.

"Why?" she asked.

"They aren't our kind of people," said Grandmama.

"I don't care. Katherine is a good friend. It's her ball—and her birthday, for that matter—and I'm going to stay with her," she said.

"Lily! What has come over you speaking to your grandmother in such a way?" asked her mother.

Grandmama held up a hand. "Have you already told people that you will be staying at Balcombe Manor?"

"Yes," Lily lied. The only people who knew were the Imperfects and Ian.

"That makes it awkward to extract Lily from the acceptance. Has Katherine's mother arranged for an escort for you?" Grandmama asked.

"Yes, she's already asked Ian Bingham," she said.

Her mother sighed. "I had hoped that when your friendship with Leana had cooled you'd seen sense that mixing with the Hartfords would bring you no good."

"Ian isn't a Hartford," she said.

"He is taking money from one," said Grandmama.

"Is there anything wrong with taking money from someone who gives it willingly?" Lily asked, her voice sharp.

Her mother's eyes widened, but Grandmama's expression remained cool.

"You seem to have particularly strong feelings on this matter, Lillian," said Grandmama.

Lily held her grandmother's gaze. "I was only making a point. Now, what other balls are there to consider?"

As soon as they were in the taxi home, her mother turned to Lily. "I do not understand you, Lily. What were you thinking speaking to your grandmother like that?"

"Like what?" she asked, keeping her expression passive.

"You know that Grandmama is the reason that we have the life we do. If it weren't for her, we would have nothing."

"Then why is Ian taking money from the Hartfords any worse than us allowing Grandmama to pay for everything?" she asked.

"Money always comes with strings attached," said her mother.

Lily turned to the window, watching the traffic rush by down Sloane Street.

After a moment, her mother said, "I've seen more of the world than you have. I know how difficult life can be."

"Difficult?" Lily snapped. "Do you think I don't know how difficult you find this? All my life I've tiptoed around the house, not wanting to make things more difficult for you than they needed to be. I worked hard at school because I didn't want you to worry. I've never had real friends until now because I worried that if I did, they might want to come and see where I lived and that would upset you."

"You didn't have to do any of those things," said her mother tightly, glancing at the cabbie, who was doing a very good job of pretending not to listen.

Lily didn't care. They were finally talking, and she wasn't going to let this go. "I did all of those things because I wanted you to be happy. That was all I wanted."

"Lily." Her mother's tone was low and warning, but Lily was not done yet.

"I am doing the Season because Grandmama told me to."

"We both are," said her mother.

"Would you have wanted me to be a deb without her pushing?" she asked.

Her mother pursed her lips, as though trying to keep the words in, but they came out nonetheless. "I don't know. Society can be cruel, and bringing you out exposes you to that."

"You could have told Grandmama no," she said.

"No, I couldn't. We both know that," said her mother.

But her mother could have. She could have done what so many other women had been forced to do and sell the house, find a job, live a less comfortable life. Her mother presented things as though there were no options, but there are always options, they just might not be palatable.

"Your grandmother just wants what's best for you. We might not agree about many things, but we can agree on that," said her mother. "Ian Bingham, a student whose fortunes are tied to someone else's charity, isn't the best man for you."

"You brought me out and told me that I'm a woman now, and that makes you terrified that you're losing control over me because I'm meeting people on my own and making my own decisions," Lily said, the anger that had seethed in her since she'd read the letter yesterday morning surging again.

"You're naive if you think that it doesn't matter who you spend your time with. I can help you keep from making a mistake," her mother said.

"Like the mistake you made befriending the Hartfords? Or perhaps the mistake you made when you went to America to care for Joanna—a child who you blame for ruining your life?"

Just like you must blame me.

"She was old enough to—" But then her mother stopped herself. "I will not talk about Joanna."

Lily crossed her arms over her chest. "Because you're afraid."

"Because it's too painful!" her mother shouted, slapping her hand down on the taxi's seat.

Shock sent adrenaline rushing through Lily. Her mother had never yelled at her. Not once. She'd never cared enough to bother.

"Joanna changed. She is not a good person," said her mother, clearly struggling to control herself. "You have to understand that."

"Then explain it to me," she challenged. "Tell me about her—*anything* about her."

Her mother's lips wobbled and her eyes filled with sorrow.

"You never speak about her," said Lily quietly.

Her mother remained silent.

Lily sighed. "I am going to Katherine's ball. Ian will be my escort. My world isn't just our house any longer, Mother, and I'm not going to sit alone, waiting for you to be happy."

"You were never alone. I was always here," her mother whispered.

Lily held her chin up, her eyes never wavering from her mother's. They both knew that living under the same roof was not the same thing as trusting one another. As being a family.

In the end, it was Mummy who broke her gaze first to stare out the window until they returned to Harley Gardens.

Twenty-Three

Laughter rippled across the dinner table as William dipped his head, caught the pineapple that had been perched atop it neatly in his right hand, and dropped into his seat, feigning exhaustion with a grin. This wasn't the strained, polite chuckle of society, but the rollicking, contented laughter of a group of people who truly enjoyed one another's company.

They were a bit of a ragtag band, Lily thought as she looked around the birthday dinner before Katherine's ball. She was surrounded by her friends and their invited escorts for the evening. Ivy, Philippa, Doris, and Katherine all were rosy cheeked already from wine and amusement, and the men at each of their right hands were handsome in their dinner jackets. Interspersed throughout the group were the older adults—friends and business associates of Mr. Norman's, each wearing an indulgent look that hinted at their own memories of when they were young themselves.

It was not nearly as intimate as some of the dinners she'd been to since coming out, but from the moment she walked into the Louis XIV–inspired entryway of Balcombe Manor that was gilded within an inch of its life, she'd known that no party Katherine's parents ever threw would be intimate. It was clear that the Normans liked everything on a grand scale, including their dinners, and the people who could overlook or—better yet—accept the fact that the Normans' money was new and their ambitions legion seemed happy to settle in for an evening of excellent food, exquisite wine, and entertaining company.

And most importantly of all, Ian sat to Lily's right. She'd caught him sneaking glances at her throughout the evening, each time earning a little smile from her as though they were enjoying a joke of their own. He'd driven up in time for cocktails in the gold drawing room. He'd greeted his host and hostess first, and then gone straight to her and remained by her side the entire evening.

"I don't think I've ever seen a man dance quite like Carmen Miranda before," said Mr. Norman, sweeping up his glass of wine in one of his dinner-plate-size hands to toast William.

"That's what makes it a talent, Dad," said Katherine with a smile for her father.

"How you did that all with a pineapple on your head . . ." said Ivy in wonder.

"And where on earth in this house the butler managed to find a pineapple, I'll never know," said Mrs. Norman, dabbing at her eyes with a lace-edged handkerchief between the laughs that sent the storm-gray bugle beads covering her entire skin-tight dress shivering. "Quite ingenious of you, Bertram."

"Thank you, madam," said Bertram from his spot quietly near the wine, where he could silently observe the diners and anticipate their needs.

"I think I can safely say that this is the most amusing deb's dinner I'll be at this Season," said Mrs. Norman, her American accent softened by years of living in Britain.

"Because you're throwing it, darling," said Mr. Norman down his end of the table, the affection for his wife plain on his ruddy face.

"I think, perhaps, we had better adjourn," said Mrs. Norman, sending her fellow ladies a knowing smile.

Dutifully, the gentlemen rose, a few of the older men who were there more out of duty to their daughters and the Norman family eager to be left to their port. When Lily stood and collected her evening bag, Ian stayed her with a gentle hand to her wrist right where she'd folded back and buttoned her gloves for dinner.

"Will you do me the honor of giving me the first dance?" he asked, his voice pitched low.

She smiled. "If you can find me."

He chuckled. "And then perhaps the one after that, and the one after that as well."

"Don't be ridiculous," she said with a laugh.

"No, you're right. I suppose I do have to let the others dance with you, too. Just know that I won't like it one bit."

His fingers lifted from her wrist, the skin he'd touched tingling. She looked up. There was a tenderness in his eyes, but this time it felt different than all of the other times she'd seen him look at her before. Something swelled in her chest just as powerfully as the dread of the secret she now carried with her soured her stomach.

She should have said something—what, she didn't know—but instead she followed the other ladies out of the room.

In the corridor, Katherine slung her arm through Lily's and pulled Lily into her side as they walked.

"Are you going to thank me for the very great favor I did you tonight?" her friend asked.

"What favor was that?" she asked as they walked through the open double doors of the blue drawing room done in deep navy and white trim.

"Seating you next to Ian. I told Mum that was the only condition of this dinner: my friend Lily had to sit next to the man who makes her eyes sparkle," said Katherine.

Despite her hesitation in the dining room, Lily leaned into her friend's side, letting the jasmine and vanilla of Katherine's perfume wrap around her. "You're becoming positively poetic. Is it the wine?"

"Probably," said Katherine with a grin.

"Well, thank you."

Katherine nudged her. "And?"

"And what?" she asked.

"Do you still like him, or has he done something horrible to discredit himself since he arrived?" Katherine asked.

She did. Oh, she did more than she should.

She was a fraud. She didn't belong here among those doing the Season. A bastard from a modest family, she should never had been presented at court. The Nicholls weren't nobility. They couldn't hide their scandals in plain sight by applying a veneer of acceptability with the right clothes, the right schools, the right manners taught from birth. She didn't have any of the resources around her that would protect her if word of her parentage ever got out. If she even could figure out who her father was.

She wondered about the letter writer and who they were, why they had her mother's secret. The Cumberland address should have reassured her, but train travel made it too easy for a determined, disgruntled person to slip down to London and take matters into their own hands. Not knowing who sent the letter meant that every new person she met could be the one threatening to expose her family's secret.

Lily sighed. "I still like Ian. Immensely."

Katherine's brows shot up. "Immensely? Well, that is something. But why so glum? Are you worried that he doesn't feel the same way? Because anyone who was just at that dinner could disabuse you of that notion."

"No. No, it's nothing like that," she said softly. "Let's not talk about it now. This is your birthday and your coming-out ball. This night is meant to be about *you*."

Katherine tugged at the top of one of her long gloves as her gaze darted around the room. "This night is about Mum and Dad. They're the ones who want to be at the center of this circus."

This, she realized, was the first time she'd ever seen Katherine nervous. It was odd. Katherine was usually so assured, it felt unsettling to see her shaken.

"This party matters very much to your parents," she said.

"It does. They think it will unlock doors that have never been open to them before. I think they're trying to grab at something that will always be just out of reach, but I'll smile and dance and even enjoy myself because it's important that I try," said Katherine.

"And then, when this Season is over, you'll be your own woman," Lily said as they approached the door.

As they accepted coupes of champagne from a pair of waiting footmen bearing trays, Katherine said, "I think I can drink to that."

Lily lifted her champagne coupe and pinged her glass gently against Katherine's. "To the most determined debutante I know."

"Thank you," said Katherine, taking a large swallow of her drink before muttering, "Christ, I'm glad you're here."

The guests who had not been invited to dinner began to arrive for the ball at half past ten on the dot, some spilling out of cars driven down from London in twos and fours. Others came from dinners the Normans had arranged for guests with other Surrey families roped into hosting on the understanding that they too would return a similar favor for a debutante or hunt ball in the future.

As Lily and the dinner party—now once again mixed company after the men had rejoined them smelling faintly of port and cigars—moved through the house to the veranda, she could hear laughter filling the entryway of Balcombe Manor as guests handed off wraps. There was a crackle in the air, a sense of fun and slightly manic excitement that only the promise of a truly extravagant night could bring.

There would be no royal dukes in attendance at this ball, and certain very old-fashioned families would have chosen to stay at home rather than be caught gawking at the opulence of the party the Normans were bound to throw for their only daughter. However, most of society was too fueled by curiosity to miss this evening, and they dutifully poured out of cars in their satins and silks, family jewels sparkling on the heads and necks of those who owned them.

When the dinner party reached the French doors open to the veranda, even Lily, who had seen the preparations underway when she'd arrived at the house earlier that afternoon, gasped. Katherine's dance was outside with a huge white marquee set up off to the side in case of rain. It wouldn't be necessary, though, as the warm May evening greeted them with open arms and not even the faintest whisper of rain. Down the steps dozens of candles in lanterns flickered, creating a pathway to a huge parquet dance floor. The band was already playing something soft and sweet on a stage swathed in yellow and white flowers. But the floral displays weren't contained only to the stage. There were huge bouquets anchoring the four corners of the dance floor, while others spilled out over the white tablecloths that covered dozens of tables dotting the lawn. Lampposts with flickering gaslights stood among them, assisting the moon that hung heavy and nearly full in the sky. The effect was beautiful, as though walking among a jungle of blooms and moonlight.

Beyond the main area, there was another path of lanterns leading down to the edge of a lake with a sand beach created a century ago by some earl or another, according to Mr. Norman, who'd taken pride in showing the Imperfects around that afternoon. On the beach, torches flickered, illuminating a fleet of rowboats watched over by a man dressed as a gondolier who stood on the lake's dock, waiting no doubt to scold tipsy debs and their escorts as they took the boats out. In the middle of the lake, an island was also illuminated, so that partygoers would be able to escape the excitement of the ball in full swing back onshore.

"Katherine," squealed Ivy at the bottom of the stairs, clapping her hands in delight and sending the tulle of her ivory-colored skirts shaking.

"It is beautiful," said Philippa, casting an appreciative glance around.

"And so elegant. I could almost hate you for it," said Doris, looking suitably impressed.

Lily laughed. "Except we like you too much for that."

Katherine inhaled and nodded. "I just want to make it through this evening."

A few minutes later, when the lawn around the dance floor had begun to fill up with people clutching glasses of champagne, the band called for the floor to be cleared. Everyone edged to the grass. Mr. Norman stepped out onto the floor with his daughter, beaming as he led her in the first dance to "They Can't Take That Away from Me." When he spun her, the copper spangles Madame Benum had scattered across her tulle dress of the same color flashed like fire in the light.

Lily watched her friend dancing arm in arm with her father, and a sense of sadness slipped through her. She'd long ago reconciled herself to being the girl without the father, but at least she had the idea of a father in the man whose photographs were scattered around the house. But now that she knew that Michael Nicholls was just a lie, the emptiness that was always there grew. Her father was a faceless, nameless man. A partner in an ill-fated love affair or a regretful fling, she didn't know.

When the song ended, everyone clapped, and Katherine kissed her father on the cheek before he barked a laugh and swept her up in a hug, Katherine's gold shoes leaving the ground as her father spun her around. All of this—the dinner, the ball, the gowns, the Season—it was all so clearly because they loved their daughter and were determined to give her the best life she could have. For the Normans that meant moving in these circles, meeting these men with an eye to one day marry one of them. This life had a brand of security that was always just out of reach for all but a select few, but once they were accepted, they became a part of those ranks that would close up and protect their own.

Katherine, she knew, saw life differently. She cared for her parents—even respected their social ambitions—but she didn't share their need for this life. This was a hurdle to be leaped over with as much grace and dignity as possible. Then she would begin her own life on her own terms.

And what am I doing?

As the song transitioned to "All of You," Lily saw Ian approach from out of the corner of her eye. She turned with a smile, but he was frowning.

"Is all well?" he asked.

"Of course," she said, making a show of smiling a little wider.

He hesitated, studying her, and she almost flinched under the scrutiny, believing that he more than most might know if something was not. But he nodded. "Then shall we dance?"

This dance never could have held in it the intimacy of the hallway at the Savoy when it was just the two of them, but he led her out onto the floor and she settled easily into his arms.

"You look beautiful tonight. I haven't told you that yet, and I should have," he said.

"You don't have to," she protested gently, even though she liked the way it sounded when he said it.

"But I want to. The problem is, every time we begin to speak, I find myself caught up." He pulled her close enough that Grandmama would have objected if she had been there. "I like speaking with you, Lily Nicholls."

"I like speaking with you, too, Ian Bingham," she said.

"Then do you want to tell me why you looked so sad just now?" he asked.

She did—badly—but confiding in him would only open her up to risk. She doubted that a man of his kindness would ever pull away from her in disgust, but there were other ways of being let down. There would be no more dinners, no more invitations to dance except out of obligation when it was too awkward to avoid the situation. Even if he did like her as much as Katherine and her friends seemed to think, it wouldn't be enough to satisfy the path that had been laid out for him. He was destined to be a diplomat. The woman he married would become a diplomat's wife, no doubt vetted and scrutinized so that she wouldn't offend at official functions. She would need to be a pillar of respectability—not fundamentally flawed by the very nature of her birth.

"I was thinking about fathers and daughters," she finally said.

"I see. Anything in particular?"

"They're sad thoughts for another day," she said.

"Then I hope one day you'll let me hear them. I'd very much like to."

She squeezed her eyes shut and tried not to think about the fact that, if life had been different, perhaps she could have let him.

The song ended all too quickly, and couples began to break up around them. Ian looked as though he might ask her to dance again, but another man she vaguely recognized from some cocktail party or ball stepped up to her, his hand outstretched.

"Would you care to dance?" the newcomer asked.

Lily sent Ian a regretful smile and took the other man's hand for a waltz.

After that dance, she danced with Brian and talked about his Irish horses. William danced a jive with her and teased her about keeping up with the music, and Peter Wharton had her for a cha-cha. She was just catching her breath after coming off the dance floor when Cecil stepped up to her in full mess dress.

"Cecil!" she exclaimed, kissing him on the cheek and standing back to take in his red jacket with gold buttons. "You look very handsome in your uniform. I feel as though I haven't seen you in ages."

"That's because you haven't. You've been hiding from us," he teased her.

"Not hiding," she hedged.

"Wherever you've been, you've missed all the fun tonight," he said with a snort.

"Why does it sound like it wasn't fun at all?"

"Gideon and Leana spent the entire drive down bickering at each other. But that's always the way it is with them, isn't it?"

She shook her head. "I never did understand why they sniped at each other so often."

Cecil sent her an odd look. "But surely you see it, too?"

"See what?" she asked.

"Gideon's been in love with Leana for years, but she doesn't see him as anything other than an escort at the best of times and a glorified coatrack at the worst."

She reared back with a strangled laugh. "In love?"

Cecil frowned. "Didn't you know?"

"No." No she hadn't, but now so much made sense. She'd liked Gideon from the beginning, but she'd never felt drawn to him the way that she had with Ian. Perhaps she'd sensed without realizing it that Gideon's heart was already given.

"You weren't . . . ?"

She looked up at Cecil, who wore an expression of such concern that she patted his hand. "No. I'm not madly in love with Gideon and now jealous of Leana."

"I had wondered, especially in the beginning. He seemed to take a shine to you," said Cecil.

"That was friendship. Nothing more," she said, realizing how obvious those words were now. "You don't think Leana knows about Gideon, do you?"

"I think that's why Leana tries so hard to parade Raymond around in front of him," said Cecil with a sniff.

"You don't like Raymond."

"What's to like? Look at him." Cecil nodded through the crowd to where Raymond and Leana were laughing, each red-cheeked with a glass of champagne clenched tightly in their hands. They were beautiful together—him in his inky evening clothes and her in a strapless satin dress of deep emerald with white trim. To someone who didn't know them, they might appear the perfect couple.

"Do you want to say hello?" Cecil asked, a hint of doubt in his voice.

"I don't think so," she said.

But as she spoke, Leana angled her chin in Lily's direction, and their eyes locked. The moment stretched out, seeming to go on for an age. Then, Leana threw her head back and laughed, snapping the connection between them.

"Lily!" Leana called out. "Come join us."

"I don't think there's any avoiding her now," said Cecil.

"I don't suppose there is," she said through gritted teeth.

Cecil had the good graces to look a little sheepish. "My apologies."

She sighed and gave a shake of her head. "It's no fault of yours."

Dutifully, Cecil led her over to Leana and her inevitable cluster of admirers ruled at the top by Raymond.

"I made it to your friend's party, as you can see. Isn't that good of me?" Leana asked, a bit of champagne spilling over the edge of her glass and onto her fine gloves.

Lily itched to grab a cloth and dab at the spot, trying to save the expensive leather from ruin. Instead, she laced her fingers together in front of her.

"I'm sure Katherine appreciates you being here," she said.

"She should. It was a bloody long drive down from London," grumbled Raymond, although Lily knew that it couldn't have taken them more than an hour and a half.

"That's a forfeit," announced Leana as Raymond groaned.

"A forfeit?" Lily asked.

"We've decided to make a game of tonight. There are certain rules that each of us must follow, and if we don't, it's a forfeit and the other decides on the punishment. Raymond is forbidden from complaining about the drive," said Leana.

"Especially since I was the one who was behind the wheel," said Gideon, gliding into the group with a diminutive brunette in tiered pale yellow tulle who was gazing up at him adoringly. His arm still linked with his date's, he leaned down to kiss Lily on the cheek. "Hello, darling Lily. It's been so long."

"It has," she said, meaning every word of it.

"We'll dance later and you can tell me all about having friends who don't drive you crazy," he whispered in her ear before pulling back.

"I know what your next forfeit should be," Leana announced, drawing everyone's attention back to her.

"What is that?" Raymond asked with a smirk.

"You have to do the most outrageous thing you can think of in the next ten seconds," said Leana. "One . . . two . . ."

"Fascinating as this is, I'm going to fetch Lucy here a drink. Would anyone else want one?" Gideon asked.

"I would," Leana interrupted herself before continuing. "Five . . . six . . ."

Raymond suddenly dropped to the floor. The women around them gasped and instinctively took a step back. It took a moment for Lily to realize that Raymond hadn't fallen to the ground. He'd fallen to one knee.

"Marry me," he said, his booming voice ringing out over the crowd.

"What?" Leana gawked.

He grasped her hand. "Marry me."

All around them, the dancers on the floor had stopped. The band played on, but more and more people stilled to look at what was attracting so much attention, some going up on tiptoe for a better view.

"Troy, be serious," said Cecil, looking a little pale.

"Marry me," he repeated for a third time, shaking Leana's hand a little.

It was, truly, the most outrageous thing he could do within the space of ten seconds. A proposal already? To Leana Hartford, the Deb of the Year? If Leana accepted, she would be the first deb to be engaged that

Season. That was a triumph in and of itself, but to be engaged to Lieutenant Raymond Troy? On paper he was ideal: he came from a good family, he had a commission in a distinguished regiment, he had his own wealth if the rumors were true, and one day he would become a baron. But he was also brash, unpleasant, and well on his way to being a nasty drunk. Surely, Lily couldn't be the only one to see that.

Finally, after what felt like an eternity of bated breath and pounding hearts, Leana eyed him up and down and said, "All right then. Yes."

A cheer rose up that rippled out over the ball followed fast by the chatter of nearly every gossip in society. This ball was no longer about Katherine's debut. It was about Miss Leana Hartford and Lieutenant Raymond Troy's engagement, and years from now people would still recall the night of the engagement at the ball.

Raymond rose to his feet to sweep Leana up and kiss her, but Lily was already turning away. She had to find Katherine.

Twenty-Four

Lily pushed through the crowd until she spotted Katherine. Although her friend was surrounded by people on all sides, she seemed somehow apart, as though this crowd had forgotten that the reason they were all there was her.

"Katherine," she said, gasping for breath.

"Did you hear? There's been a proposal at my ball," said Katherine with a strangled little laugh. "Who is it?"

She swallowed. "Leana and Raymond Troy."

Katherine nodded absently, her dark blond curls bouncing across her shoulders. "I should have guessed."

"Would you like to step away for a moment to talk?" Lily asked.

Katherine looked around as though just noticing for the first time that several people had started to watch them with interest. "I think that's probably a good idea."

Lily followed her friend up the veranda steps and through the house to a sitting room painted in pale pink that had been converted into a space for ladies who needed a moment's rest from the dancing outside. Given that it was still early in the evening, no one was making use of the low-set ivory sofas yet.

As soon as they were alone, Lily said, "I'm sorry."

"For what?" asked Katherine as she sank down onto a gold-and-ivory upholstered chair, slumped against the back, her beaded tulle skirts spread wide.

Lily took the chair across from her. "That Leana has stolen away your evening from you."

Katherine took a deep breath. "I don't think she's stolen it. Maybe borrowed it for a while until the fireworks at midnight."

"No one should be 'borrowing' attention from you at your own coming-out ball," she said. "And it's your birthday."

"I can't imagine that Mum and Dad are very happy about having the event they've been planning for upward of a year taken over by another girl, but I don't suppose there's anything that can be done about that." Katherine gave a half laugh. "Do you know, I actually feel a little sorry for Leana."

"Why?" she said.

"I just think that some women are destined to collect proposals like they collect dresses. Acquiring them and discarding them just as easily."

"You don't think that this engagement will last?" Lily asked.

"Maybe I'm wrong, but even if they make it to a wedding day, I doubt it will be very blissful," said Katherine, shooting her a significant look. "It doesn't seem as though they have very much in common."

Little except a taste for alcohol and dancing and a belief that they were the best society had to offer. Both Leana and Raymond moved through the world with the confidence of two people who believed that everyone around them should bend to their will. So far they might have been in concert, but how long could that last once the Season and all of the parties were over?

"I suppose you're right. At the rate that things are going, they might drink each other to an early grave if they actually married," Lily said. "But are you sure you aren't upset?"

Katherine reached over the gap between them to pat her friend's arm. "Don't worry so much, darling. Go out, dance, drink, and flirt with Ian. I meant what I said earlier. He adores you."

Lily hesitated, weighing her next words carefully. "Do you ever feel as though there are two ways forward and you don't know which to take?"

Katherine let her head drop to the back of the sofa. "Torn in two? Every day so far this Season. Oh, don't look so surprised. It is all well and good to make grand plans like mine, but actually executing them is another matter. I've written out what I want to do every which way I can think. I've made budgets for myself, looked at listings for flats, even tried to make a few discreet inquiries about jobs with newspapers. But none of that is actually packing my bags and telling my parents that I'm determined to give this all up."

"Grandmama and Mummy want me to go to the Dublin Horse Show and then on to Scotland after the country balls. But what happens next?" she asked. What if everything that she'd been told she should want had started to feel like a dress she'd grown out of?

Katherine smiled. "I suspect you already know, you're just afraid to say it. But when you do, I think that whatever you decide will be extraordinary."

There was a screech of laughter in the hall, and a woman's voice said, "Can you believe how gauche it all is? The entire house is gold. I mean, look at this room."

The door burst open, and Lady Fiona Summerton, Sophie Cartwright, and Cressie spilled giggling into the room as Sophie said, "And the mother's dress? She looks like a chorus girl from thirty years ago—"

The three debs stopped short with a collective gasp when they saw Katherine.

"Oh! We thought that this room would be free," said Sophie, her hand held to her mouth and her gaze flicking between Lily and Katherine. Whether it was regret over being unkind or regret over being caught that filled her eyes, Lily didn't know.

Lily lifted her chin. "Please do go on, Sophie. Exactly what do you think of your hostess's dress?" Katherine cleared her throat, but Lily pressed on. "And while you're doing that, perhaps you can tell us exactly what you find so gauche about the party that you have been quite generously invited to."

"Lily," said Katherine, her tone soft but urgent.

Cressie began, "We didn't mean to—"

"I'm certain that if you felt you could no longer stay, the Normans would very generously arrange for transportation back to wherever you came from, Cressie," she said.

"It was only a joke," said Lady Fiona.

"Then why am I not laughing?" Lily asked, her hands pressed hard against her thighs as she tried to control the anger bubbling up in her. Damn these girls, and damn all of these people here to gawk at Katherine and her parents, who had been nothing but good and kind to her and the other Imperfects.

"I'm sorry," said Sophie. Lily opened her mouth to reply, but then Sophie threw back her shoulders. "However, I only say what I see."

Lily raked her eyes up and down the trio's dresses, all variations on the same style that nearly every deb wore. Strapless, satin, pale in color, full skirts. Safe, boring, unoriginal, milquetoast.

"I'm sure that you're all equipped to be arbiters of fashion," Lily said.

"We'll find another room," said Cressie meekly.

"No. Take this one, if you can stand to be in it," said Lily. "Come on, Katherine."

The three debs stepped to the side, faces burning tomato red, as Lily swept by them, Katherine close behind. When the door shut behind them, however, Lily began to deflate.

"I can't believe I just told off Lady Fiona. Grandmama would be horrified," she murmured.

Katherine began to laugh, a manic, desperate sort of laugh that went on until tears began to leak from her eyes. When Katherine covered her face with her hands, her shoulders shaking, Lily pulled her around the corner. Then she wrapped her friend in a hug until Katherine's crying jags began to slow.

Finally, Katherine pulled back, her gloves sodden with mascara. "I try not to let them bother me, but sometimes the bloody wretches are too much," she muttered, dabbing under her eyes to try to repair the damage done by her tears.

"They are ignorant and wrong and—"

"Badly dressed?" Katherine asked with a little half laugh. "They deserved to hear every word of that. Let them feel what it's like to have someone else's scorn for a change."

"I'm sorry, Katherine. I know better than most that people can be horrible about your family when they think that your back is turned.

You can bear it up until a point, but hearing it said in front of you is different."

Katherine shook her head. "What hurts is seeing Mum and Dad so happy, choosing to stay ignorant while everyone talks about them. This is what they wanted. Balcombe Manor. Everyone happy. They feel as though they're a part of this world that they've been kept out of for so long."

Except they never would be. The Normans would always be outsiders, just as Lily now understood she was. If there was even a hint of a rumor that she might be illegitimate, the fragile world that Mummy had tried to build around her would shatter. She was a woman with one foot in and one foot out of this rarefied world, and she wondered how long she could last knowing the truth.

"Come on," she said, taking her friend's hand and tucking it into her elbow. "Let's go clean your makeup up."

"Is it horrible?" Katherine asked, examining her stained gloves.

She smiled. "It's nothing that a little time and care can't fix."

Lily sat with Katherine as her friend removed and then reapplied her makeup in her sumptuous bedroom that could have doubled as a starlet's room in a 1930s screwball comedy, with its tufted satin headboard and gauze curtains everywhere. She watched Katherine compose herself and begin the process that every girl at this ball would know well, building up thin layers of makeup as slowly her unadorned self receded from view and the debutante emerged.

They found Katherine new gloves and headed downstairs, plunging back into the fray. All it had taken was a whispered sentence—"She needs us tonight"—and the Imperfects surrounded Katherine, keeping her cocooned in a protective barrier of love and loyalty.

When the dancing gave way to fireworks and then a dinner at midnight, she looked for Ian, but she couldn't find him and was led into the marquee by a perfectly pleasant man named Victor Penn who told her faintly amusing stories about the horses that he kept on his family estate in the next county. When the band struck up again after the meal, Victor politely asked her to dance, but when the dance was finished, she gently turned down his offer of a drink.

Alone again, she doubled back down the steps of the veranda, intending to make for the torchlit man-made beach. The dancing was in full swing, and there were only a few people in the clusters of chairs and sofas that had been dragged out onto the sand from the house for the comfort of the guests.

She was almost around the far edge of the dance floor when Gideon stumbled into her path. "Lily, darling. There you are!"

"Gideon." She squinted at him in the half light, noting the way his collar was rucked up on one side. And was he missing one of his mother-of-pearl shirt studs? "Are you quite well?"

He shook his head emphatically and then grinned goofily. "Never better."

"Are you certain? You seem . . ."

"In my cups? Blotto? Tipsy? Squiffy?" He laughed, a lock of his usually immaculate dark hair falling over his brow.

"Well, yes," she said.

"That, my darling, Lily, is because I am. I am drunk."

"Why don't we sit down for a moment?" she said, laying a hand on his arm.

He stared down at her hand and then looked up at her, his eyes wide. "No. No we have to dance. We're at a ball!"

Without warning, he picked her up by the waist, whirling her around, sending her watercolor silk skirts billowing out. She gave a yelp as a couple jumped out of the way just in time to avoid the heel of her shoe as her feet flew up from the ground.

"Gideon! Gideon, stop!" she yelled.

He lowered her enough that she was on the grass again, but he didn't let her go. Instead, he pressed his face to her temple, shimmying her around in a mockery of a waltz.

"I'm an idiot, did you know that?" he murmured to her.

"You're not an idiot, but you are tight."

"No, I *am*. If I was a smarter man, I would have fallen in love with someone like you, but it was always her. Bloody spoiled brat."

She pulled back as far as she could, fixing him with a stare. "Leana's engagement has upset you."

"She doesn't even love him. I don't know if she loves anyone except for herself," he said bitterly.

"I understand why you're upset, but you can't behave like this," she said as gently as she could.

"She's going to marry that bastard Troy. That bloody bastard," he spat.

"Lower your voice," she said sharply.

"I don't care who knows what I think," he said.

"You might not right now, but you will tomorrow," she said, noting the people who were edging closer, trying to hear every word.

He fell silent, his lip stuck out like a little boy.

"Did you tell Leana how you felt about her?" she asked.

"I told her I loved her two weeks ago, actually. Do you know what she did? She laughed in my face. Told me that I was good enough to be an escort, but that she is looking for a title. Troy has one of those. Or he will when his father, the baron, dies. Bloody bastard."

"Oh, Gideon."

"Damn her," he muttered. Then louder, "Damn her! I'm finding a drink."

"I'm not sure that's such a good—"

"Are you coming?"

He was a mess and was only going to become worse if he kept drinking, but she couldn't begrudge him that. Not tonight.

Still, she gave it one last try. "I think it might be a good idea for you to rest for a moment. Come down to the beach with me."

Gideon shoved a hand through his dark hair, gripping the ends of it as though he was going to pull a clump of it out, and then stalked off.

She looked around, noticing how quickly the people at her edge of the party whipped around in the other direction, and she sighed before resuming her trip to the beach.

When she reached the sand, she nodded to a cluster of debs she recognized from one of the spring's countless cocktail parties, and then she settled down onto a chesterfield that sat with its legs half-sunk in the sand.

There she sat, her eyes fixed on the black water of the lake, thinking about the absurdity of the situation she found herself in. She was one of the final few women who had been selected to be presented at court—a privilege that so many couldn't even begin to aspire to—and yet she'd never felt more outside of society than she did in that moment. It wasn't just learning the truth about her birth. She didn't feel as though she *belonged*. Not in any sense of the word.

She'd always flirted with the fringes of this world. The invitations to birthdays and tea parties had been a courtesy—she could see that now. She'd never had true friends until she met Katherine and the Imperfects. They had fallen in with one another so naturally because each of them was an outsider in her own way. She could see these friendships stretching out before them throughout the years, at weddings and christenings, holidays and garden parties, triumphs and tragedies. She could not see the same future for herself among the rest of the people at this party.

She lifted her head and, through the flickering torchlight, caught a glimpse of a tall figure moving toward her.

Her heart warmed at the sight of Ian, even as her stomach dropped. He always seemed to know when she needed him, even when she shouldn't want him there as badly as she did.

He stopped in front of her, a champagne glass bubbling merrily in each of his hands. "Would it be terribly cliché to say penny for your thoughts?"

She laughed softly. "Perhaps, but I don't mind the cliché."

He handed her a glass. "I thought you looked like you needed this. I actually thought that about two hours ago, but every time I looked, you were swept away dancing with someone else or clustered around your friends. Katherine seemed a little shaky earlier."

"She was, but I think she'll be all right. You could have found me for the midnight meal," she said, before taking a sip and letting the bubbles burst on her tongue.

"Again, I was too slow. I lost out to . . ."

"Victor Penn," she supplied.

"Victor Penn," he said, as though weighing the name. "He must have known that I always came in second at footraces at school. May I sit?" he asked, gesturing to the seat next to her.

She nodded and watched as he settled himself down on the other end of the chesterfield, his legs angled to her and crossed at the ankles. She'd kicked off her silver shoes as soon as she sat, glad for relief from the ache of dancing. Now her stockinged feet were tucked up under her, curling into the froth of her skirts.

They sat there for a moment in companionable silence, looking out at the lake. The laughter of the other couples on the beach drifted over to them, mixing with the light laps of waves from the boats guests had begun to row out to the island against the dock.

"You seem subdued," Ian said after a moment.

She took another sip of champagne. "I suppose I am."

"Is something the matter?" he asked.

She rolled the stem of her glass between her fingers. "Do you ever have the feeling that you've made a mistake, even though you've done everything that everyone has told you just as you should?"

He let out a long breath. "If I'm being truthful? More often than I would like to admit."

She shivered in the cooling air, and immediately he was up. He wedged his glass in the sand and peeled his dinner jacket down his arms, draping it neatly around her shoulders. She smiled her thanks and then pulled the lapels closer around her.

"There are good moments, too," Ian said after he'd settled down again. "Moments when I think that I've done exactly the right thing at the right time."

"Like what?" she asked.

"Asking you to dance at the Savoy was one of them," he said.

"Is that so?" she asked softly.

He studied her a moment and then shifted forward a few inches on the chesterfield, the leather creaking under his weight. "Even before that, there was the evening I met you. I saw you through the crowd, and I thought, 'I'd like to know what that woman is thinking.'"

"I was trying and failing to shake that horrid man who thought that women shouldn't be allowed at universities. Thank you again for saving me," she said.

He inched forward again so that his knee touched hers through the fall of her skirts. "As I recall, you were doing a very nice job of putting him in his place all on your own. I merely hurried things along so that I could meet you."

"Oh," she breathed.

"Lily"—his voice shook as though he was trying to hold a vital part of himself back—"I would very much like to kiss you right now."

Everything seemed to slow, stretching out like a film that had been run through its reel once too many times. But this moment with Ian was all new.

She reached for his hand, entwining her fingers in his. He lifted the back of her hand to his lips and pressed a kiss to the top of her glove. She shivered, and when she didn't pull back, he turned her hand over to kiss the pulse of her wrist, just to the side of the tiny buttons that marched up the side of it. He slid his hand until his fingertips played over bare skin under the dinner jacket he'd draped over her shoulders. His fingers skirted her collarbone, caressing that sensitive line until he let them slide up her neck to cup her face.

"Ian?" she asked, her voice shaking.

"Hmmm?"

"Please kiss me."

He pulled her forward to meet him halfway, his lips touching hers in a test. A tease. Then he angled his head a little to the right and kissed her deeper. Her lips parted, and he moved again to take her lower lip between his, tugging just a bit and sending warmth coursing through her body.

Her hand went to his hair, gripping at the short strands at the base of his neck. She wanted to rip off her gloves, to feel the silkiness with her bare skin, but that would require letting go of him, and no longer kissing him was not an option.

Somewhere in the back of her mind, a voice told her she shouldn't be doing this for all of those reasons she'd pored over again and again since learning her family's secret. But she wanted this moment more, so she spread her free hand against the fabric of his shirt and tried to drink in every moment of this kiss.

It took an outburst to break them apart. Two men shouting at each other. A woman beginning to yell.

She broke their kiss by pulling back just a fraction to murmur, "What is that?" against his lips.

With a frustrated growl, Ian looked over her shoulder. "It looks like there's an argument of some sort on the dock."

She twisted, aware that his left hand was still under his jacket and around her waist, stroking at the satin of her bodice.

"Oh no, that's Gideon," she said.

"The boatman seems not to want to let him row out," Ian said.

She turned her gaze back to him. "I can imagine why. I crossed paths with Gideon while walking down here. He's very drunk."

"He shouldn't be going out on the water," said Ian, even as, when she looked back, she saw Gideon climbing into a rowboat followed by the girl she'd met earlier, Lucy, and another couple. "It's strange, he doesn't usually strike me as the type to be this drunk at a ball."

"He isn't. He usually saves the worst of the drinking for the nightclub afterward." She hesitated. "He's in love with Leana."

Ian's eyes widened in understanding. "So tonight has not been Gideon's night."

She shook her head. "He's taken the news badly. Apparently, Leana was somewhat cruel when he told her he loved her a couple weeks ago, and I suspect a public proposal was a slap in the face."

"That doesn't surprise me one bit," said Ian with a sigh.

"I wish someone would take him home."

"You care for Gideon very much, don't you?" he asked.

"I do. He's been a good friend in his way. Truth be told, Mummy pushed for me to pursue Gideon."

There was a little hitch in the smooth stroke of his thumb over her bodice. "And what would you say to that now?"

She smiled. "That my attention's focused on another man."

His hand splayed across her waist, and he leaned in to kiss her again. Before their mouths could touch, there was a great splash and twin screams that sliced through the night air.

Twenty-Five

Lily and Ian shot up from the chesterfield, both stumbling for their footing in the soft sand.

"What was that?" she asked, scanning the lake.

"There," said Ian, pointing to a gray shape on the water. It was the boat that had been carrying Gideon and his party, only now it was upside down.

She gripped Ian's arm. "Oh my God. They've capsized."

Almost simultaneously, three heads broke the surface on the far side of the boat. It was the other man, one arm around each of the debs who sputtered and splashed.

"Stop struggling!" Lily could hear him shout to the girls across the water.

"Ian, I don't see Gideon," she said, craning her neck to search the water.

By now several people had crowded at the edge of the dock.

"Why aren't they helping him?" she asked, growing desperate.

"Right," said Ian, and he was off, sand kicking up in his wake as he ran for the dock. She followed him, forgetting all about her heels that lay abandoned next to the chesterfield.

Ian pushed through the crowd to the boatman. "Have you seen him?" Lily heard him demand as he tugged off his tie and ripped at the laces of his shoes.

"He stood up. I told him not to get in the boat, but he took it anyway, and he stood up," said the boatman, wringing his hands.

"How deep is this water at the dock?" Ian demanded to the crowd. "Does anyone know?"

"At least six feet this time of year," said a man in his early thirties who wore a light blue bow tie. "I'm a friend of the family that used to own Balcombe. I swam here as a boy."

Ian kicked off his shoes and dove in, striking out with long strokes in the direction of the overturned boat.

"Aren't you going to help him?" Lily asked, grabbing the boatman's arm.

The man shrugged, his hands spread in front of him. "I can't swim."

"Bloody hell." The man in the bow tie yanked it off and tossed his jacket to Lily.

She watched as the man dove in after Ian, matching Ian's pace. She held her breath, not daring to move as she watched them swim up to the boat. Ian dove under, breaking the surface again just as the other man caught up to him. They exchanged a hurried word that was lost on the wind and both dove down again.

Murmurs began to rise up around her on the dock as seconds ticked by. All she could do was stand there, her fingers knitted into the stranger's jacket while Ian's own enveloped her in his fresh, woodsy scent, offering a little comfort as she waited.

After what seemed like an eternity, the two men broke the surface, gasping for air. Between them bobbed Gideon, his head lolling forward.

A gasp rose up from the dock, but all Lily could whisper was "No."

Gideon didn't struggle or even look up as Ian and the other man swam back to shore with him braced between them.

"Do you think he's all right?" asked a girl behind her in a squeak.

"Look at him," muttered a man.

Lily wanted to whip around and shout at them to shut up, just shut up until they knew, but she couldn't look away, as though it was her gaze that was keeping the three of them afloat.

When she realized they would be taking him to the beach rather than trying to lift Gideon up to the dock, Lily shouted, "Let me through! Move!"

People parted, and she raced off the dock and down to the beach to meet them. Ian and the other man were panting heavily as they reached the shore. Without a word, she flung both jackets aside, plunging her feet into the water to take Gideon under his right arm. With Ian on his left and the stranger grasping his feet, they dragged Gideon high up onto the sand.

Lily dropped to her friend's side, hardly noticing the way her cold, soaked skirts clung to her legs. She grasped Gideon's hand. It was freezing and his nails were already beginning to turn blue.

"Get a doctor," Ian ordered his fellow rescuer.

The other man nodded, splattering them with water as he sprinted away. Ian began to press on Gideon's chest in a rhythmic pattern. Then he pinched Gideon's nose and breathed into Gideon's mouth a few times.

He glanced up at her when he went back to pressing on Gideon's chest. "I have a friend who's studying to be a cardiologist. He tells me that the Americans are using this method now in the military to revive unresponsive people."

"Do whatever you can. Please," she said, her tears beginning to fall. She couldn't remember the last time she'd prayed outside of the obligatory family visits to Grandmama's church for Easter and Christmas services, but she pressed her hands to her chest and silently begged for Gideon's life.

"He was trapped under the boat," said Ian, his tone grim. "I think his jacket caught on one of the oarlocks, and that's what kept him down there."

"Oh, Gideon," she murmured.

She watched on the edge of fear as Ian continued to try to breathe life into Gideon. It was only when the rescuer came back, a man with graying hair and a slightly bowlegged gait following behind him, that Ian sat back on his heels.

"You've done very well," said the older man, placing a hand on Ian's shoulder and hinging himself down onto the sand next to Gideon. "I'll do what I can from here."

Clearly exhausted, Ian rose stiffly and came around to her, looping an arm around her shoulders. The wetness of his shirt drenched the part of her dress that hadn't become soaked when she'd waded in, but she didn't care. All that mattered was that he was there with her, waiting and worrying together.

The doctor pressed his fingers to Gideon's neck, testing for a pulse. He did the same with his wrists and then looked up at Lily and then Ian. "You may wish to take the young lady away."

"I'm not leaving him," she whispered.

The doctor sighed and shook his head. "I'm afraid he's gone. I'm very sorry."

Lily crumpled into the sand. Ian sank with her, wrapping his arms around her and pulling her close so that she could bury her face in his chest and cry. But no amount of comfort would bring Gideon back.

"Come on," Ian murmured in her ear after a moment. "Let's get you up to the house so that you can change into something dry."

She lifted her tearstained face to him. "Thank you. Thank you for trying to save him."

"This way, Lily. Come on."

She let him pull her up gently. Someone in the somber crowd that had spread to the beach now held out Ian's jacket. Ian pulled it over her shoulders, as though he could wrap her up in armor and keep her safe from what had just happened. The partygoers parted, letting them through.

All along the path back up to the house, people stared. There was no music now. No one danced. Instead, the air filled with the sound of hushed murmurs and crickets chirping.

Katherine stepped out of the crowd. Lily looked up at her friend, searching for . . . comfort? An explanation? She didn't know.

"I'm so sorry, darling," said Katherine, her own eyes brimming with tears.

"I'm going to take her up to make sure that she doesn't catch cold," said Ian.

Katherine nodded, pulling her shoulders back as she resumed the mantle of host. "Any one of the staff can help find clothes for both of you. Ask them to take her to my bedroom. No one will disturb you there."

"Thank you," said Ian.

Katherine put out a hand to stop him. "Thank you for trying to help."

Lily saw him pause, as though unsure whether he should take the praise. Moving a little closer to him, she slipped her fingers into his. He looked at her, his eyes hollow.

"I'll let you go," said Katherine, backing away quietly.

Lily managed to hold her head up high until they reached the house. At the top of the veranda steps, Bertram, the butler, intercepted them and gently hurried them upstairs. Somehow the staff had gotten wind of the incident, and two rooms had been swiftly prepared.

"Miss Nicholls, you will find Miss Katherine's personal maid is waiting to help you," said Bertram gently, indicating a polished wood door. "Mr. Bingham, you are one down the hallway. I can ring for Mr. Norman's valet, if you wish."

"Thank you. That won't be necessary," said Ian.

The butler gave a brief bow and retreated down the corridor the way they'd come.

As soon as he was out of sight, Lily's shoulders slumped. She pressed a hand to her forehead, hot tears coursing down her face once again. But unlike her tears of fear shed on the shore while kneeling next to Gideon's body, these were tears of sorrow. He was her friend, and she would never again hear him tease her or dance with him. He would no longer smile and roll his eyes when he thought someone was being particularly absurd. His joy and his kindness were gone.

Lily felt the strength of Ian's arms circle around her. She let him pull her into his chest, resting his cheek on the top of her head. He didn't try to console her or persuade her to stop crying. Instead, he simply stood with her, waiting to weather out her storm of grief.

Twenty-Six

"You're certain that you will be fine being alone?" asked Ian, easing the car he'd borrowed from a friend from Cambridge around the corner of Harley Gardens.

Lily looked up from the window she'd been staring out of. She was still wrapped in Katherine's clothes—not a gown as the maid had suggested she wear, but a navy cardigan, starched white blouse, and a pair of fawn trousers with butter-soft tan loafers pulled straight from Katherine's wardrobe.

As soon as she'd left Ian's embrace, she'd known that she couldn't stay at the ball. She couldn't stand the thought of being around all those people, seeing them eye her with curiosity as they pointed out the girl who'd tried to save Second Lieutenant Gideon Moore—or even worse, watching those who could witness tragedy one moment and then laugh as though nothing had happened the next go back to their merry evening.

She needn't have worried. By the time that she'd dressed in Katherine's borrowed clothes and found Ian waiting for her in the hall, the ball had been called off. Debs and their escorts were piling into cars, yelling back and forth about whose country house or which London nightclub they would reconvene at since their evening had been cut short. Most of the older partygoers had the good graces to look saddened by what had happened that evening, but even they couldn't hide the relief on their faces at the thought of turning in earlier than expected.

Ian had taken one look at her and told her he was taking her home. She'd been quiet as they said goodbye to Katherine and the other Imperfects, hardly uttering a word. The drive back in the borrowed car had passed in virtual silence. It hadn't been until Harley Gardens that Ian had nudged her into consciousness.

"Do you want me to come in?" he asked.

"I'll be fine," she finally said.

He killed the idling engine and shifted in his seat to face her. Worry etched his brow, and he leaned a little to catch a proper look at her face under the streetlights. "You're certain?"

No. She wasn't certain of anything any longer. All that she knew was that she was upset and angry and tired. So very, very tired.

"Thank you for driving me home," she said, collecting her evening bag and the small case she'd taken to Katherine's for what was supposed to have been an overnight stay.

He stopped her with a hand on her arm just as she reached for the door handle. "I know that now isn't the time to say this, but I need you to know that you were the best part of tonight. The best part of everything these past few months."

Her heart squeezed, but somehow she knew that she couldn't trust any emotion right now. Not painted as they were against the backdrop of Gideon's death. Instead of answering, she offered Ian a tight smile and pushed the door open to the light mist that filled the night air.

Lily let herself into the house as she had done so many times that Season. She dropped her key into her clutch, and her clutch onto the sideboard. She was about to toe off her shoes as she normally would, but then she caught sight of herself in the entryway mirror. Slowly she straightened. Her shoulder-length hair was lopsided and slightly wavy from where she'd swiped at it with wet hands. Her brilliant red lipstick had worn off hours ago, and much of her foundation must have befallen the same fate because the circles under her eyes had grown deep and purple as bruises.

She smoothed her hands over her light blond hair, pushing it off her forehead. She looked wretched, and it wasn't because of the late hour or the fact that she'd woken early to finish her dress before heading to Paddington Station to board the train that morning. It was because standing before her was a woman—hardened and a little too world-wise—whom she hardly recognized. Where was the girl, fresh out of school, who had been cautiously excited about being one of the last debutantes to curtsy for the Queen? How had she become this stranger who crashed from ball to ball, pretending she cared that she was admired by men and befriended by women who—except for a handful—would barely have spoken to her if they were in school? How had this become her life in two short months?

The grandfather clock chimed two o'clock, snapping her gaze away. This was her fault. She had allowed this to happen to her. She'd bent so far trying to make Grandmama and her mother happy that she'd broken. But what right did they have to ask that of her, especially when her mother hadn't even given her the respect of telling her who her father really was?

"Who is he?" she murmured.

With a sigh, she picked up her evening bag, intending to go upstairs to bed as she normally would, but when she passed by the locked door of the study that belonged to the man she'd thought for so long was her father, she hesitated a moment.

Who is he?

She climbed the steps to the landing where a small table held a Moorcroft vase done in a poppy motif.

Who is he?

She climbed to the top of the stairs, but instead of turning right to her bedroom, she turned left.

Who is he? The question compelled her forward, dragging her closer and closer to her mother's bedroom until she stood in front of the door. A thin slice of light spilled out from the gap between the door and the carpet. Before she could snap herself out it, she lifted a hand and knocked.

"Lily?" came her mother's muffled call through the door.

She twisted the doorknob and let herself in through the small sitting room attached to her mother's bedroom.

Her mother was seated in bed, a book in her lap. She wore a white nightgown trimmed with a scrap of lace at the collar. Her hair was done up in pin curls and tied with a pink silk scarf, even though Lily was certain that no one would see her mother until Monday when Aunt Angelica would join them for tea and a gossip about the weekend's events. How strange, she thought, that the only time she saw her mother in color was in the privacy of her bedroom.

"You're home early," said her mother, closing her book. "And what are you doing wearing those clothes? What happened to your hair? You only just had it done."

"Something happened at the party," she said.

"What do you mean?"

"There was an accident. Gideon drowned."

"Drowned? What do you mean?"

"I was there when they pulled him out of the water. I was by his side on the beach."

"Oh, Lily."

Her mother started to rise from bed, but Lily stopped her with a raised hand. "Why did you and Grandmama want me to be a debutante so badly?"

"What a strange question. I was a debutante, as was your aunt and your grandmothers on both sides. You know that it's tradition," her mother said.

"But why does that matter?" she demanded, her voice rising a notch.

"There is stability in tradition. Responsibility. Honor," said her mother. "You are a debutante because of who you are. A Nicholls."

"But I'm not, am I?"

The question hung in the air, heavy and choking, until her mother whispered, "I beg your pardon?"

"I'm not a Nicholls. Not by blood."

"I don't know what you're saying," said her mother, even as the color drained from her face.

"Yes, you do!" she shouted, the dam breaking. She strode over to her mother's jewelry box and tore it open while her mother yelped and pushed back the covers. However, Lily was faster than a woman half-tangled in bedsheets. As soon as her fingers wrapped around the brass desk key, Lily wrenched it free.

"Lily! What are you doing?" her mother shouted behind her as Lily marched from the room, her feet pounding against the stairs. She paid her mother no mind. Instead, she snatched up the study key from Hannah's hiding spot and unlocked the study door just as her mother reached the bottom of the stairs. Flinging the door open, she made for the desk, jammed the drawer key in the lock, and turned it.

"Lily, no!" her mother shouted from the study doorway, her hands braced on either side as though she was holding herself up.

Lily pulled the drawer clean off its track and upended the contents onto the desk. The ledger slid off and hit the carpet with a muffled smack, and a stack of envelopes spilled out in front of her. She half expected her mother to pounce on her as she sifted through the papers until she found the one she was looking for.

"What is this?" she demanded, pulling the letter free from its envelope.

"I don't know what you're talking about," said her mother, swallowing hard.

"'You *will* send me the full one hundred and fifty pounds I am due for my part in keeping this secret each month, or I will tell Lily all of it, from the affair to the circumstances of her birth. She will understand the truth about her father and what *you* did.'" She looked up from the paper. "Who is my father?"

All the fear and horror seemed to drain from her mother, leaving behind only exhaustion. She watched as her mother staggered into the room and lowered herself into one of the club chairs.

"You were never supposed to know," her mother murmured.

"That the man you let me call Papa, who we've been living in this odd half mourning over my entire life, isn't my father? I have a right to know that!" She was shouting now, but she didn't care. All of the anger she'd been holding crammed down inside of her was bubbling up. It would not be put back.

"You don't understand," her mother started.

"Then *make* me understand!"

"If I tell you this story, it will change everything," said her mother weakly.

Lily grabbed a handful of letters and shook them at her mother. "*These* changed everything. There's nothing you can tell me that will hurt more than happening on the truth by chance. Who is my father?"

Her mother cradled her forehead in her hand, shielding her eyes. "Ethan Hartford."

Lily froze. "Ethan Hartford? Leana's father?"

"Now do you see why I didn't want you to have anything to do with the Hartfords?"

"They knew," she murmured as she sank down into the desk chair. "They knew this entire time, and they invited me into their home." Except they hadn't. It had been Leana who pursued their friendship, issuing her the invitation to her luncheon that had seemed all the more exciting because Lily's mother had forbidden it.

Her mother slowly shook her head. "I tried to warn you. I tried to tell you that you should stay away from that family."

Her stomach soured. "Do you think Leana knew?" she asked quietly.

"I don't know. Ruth and Ethan were two of my very dearest friends at one time, but as soon as that changed, I realized that I didn't really know them at all. They gave me only what they wanted me to see—the perfect couple with the perfect life."

They sat there in silence, the tick of the grandfather clock in the corridor filling the room as the time stretched out between mother and disappointed daughter.

"Why did you do it?" she asked.

Her mother lifted her head. "What?"

"Why did you do it? Why did you have an affair with Mr. Hartford?"

A bitter laugh burst out from her mother's lips. "*That's* what you think happened? Oh, you foolish girl."

"Why else would someone blackmail you?" she asked, holding up the letter. "That's why you asked me to economize despite Grandmama's allowance, wasn't it? That's why you pushed me so hard to become a debutante. The Season was a way for you to pay this person off."

"No. Becoming a debutante meant legitimacy, Lily. It was supposed to help you. Protect you," said her mother.

"What would have helped is if you never had an affair with that horrid man," she bit out.

Her mother shot up out of her seat and strode to the desk, slamming her hands down on top of it. "Don't you dare accuse me of that! You should know more than anyone that I never would have done that to Michael. I loved—I loved him."

"You can't have it both ways, Mother," said Lily in disgust. "You had an affair. You became pregnant with me. You betrayed your husband. It's as simple as that."

"You naive girl."

"Then explain it to me. Help me understand why you lied to me," she said, half pleading.

Slowly her mother straightened her shoulders, seeming to grow from her diminutive height until she filled the room, bolstered by her indignation.

"I never had an affair with Ethan Hartford. Joanna did."

"Joanna? My sister?" she whispered.

"Joanna, your mother."

"That's not possible," Lily gasped out.

It couldn't be true. If it was, that meant—

"Why not? She was sixteen and determined to ruin her life," said her mother.

"But you sent her away to America. She was a child," she said, desperate to cling to what she knew to be real, because if what her mother told her was true—if her sister was her mother and her mother was her grandmother—the lies could not grow any bigger.

"By the time Joanna turned thirteen she was climbing out of her bedroom window to meet the son of our greengrocer," her mother continued. "We thought we could control her by sending her off to board, but that didn't stop her during breaks in term. She was beginning to make a reputation for herself, so we sent her to your aunt Patricia and uncle Howard in Washington, DC. When the war broke out, Ethan Hartford told me that he would look in on her when he was sent there for work. As a friend. I didn't realize that he would have his sights on my daughter.

"Your aunt sent a telegraph in spring of 1940, telling me that she'd discovered the affair. When she was found out, Joanna confessed that she'd been suffering the signs of morning sickness for a few weeks. I telephoned Ethan and demanded he bring me over on the first ship he could, telling everyone before I left that I was taking Joanna away to a spa town for her health. I also let it slip to Angelica I was unexpectedly pregnant but my doctor warned me about saying anything too early because it had been such a long time since I'd had a child. It wasn't a difficult story to believe. There were other pregnancies after Joanna, but none of them lasted more than a few months."

Her mother swallowed as though trying to push past a rising emotion in her throat. "I knew that I could rely on Angelica to spread the news. She can't help herself, really. By the end of my first week in Washington, I already had letters from friends back in London, sympathizing that I had to risk my safety with a crossing in my condition. I wrote back, telling everyone how unwell Joanna had become after a virus that even the best doctors couldn't identify and how long her recovery would be. We spent months in a wretched house on the edges of Hot Springs, North Carolina, waiting for *you*.

"By the time you were born that November, there was no reason for anyone in England to believe anything other than what Angelica and I had told them. But we couldn't return. Not before Joanna had recovered. By the time that I was ready to make the arrangements that January, I received a cable from your grandmother. My husband was dead."

Lily's fingers had dug into the padded leather of the chair's arms. *My husband*. Not *your father*. She realized now that she couldn't remember a time when her mother—Josephine—had referred to him as Lily's father. Papa had been a name Lily had assigned to the man she'd never met. Josephine had simply never corrected her.

"Why did you not go back after that?" Lily asked.

Josephine waved her hand in front of her. "It wasn't like it is now, where you can simply book passage on a ship. Special arrangements needed to be made. You may not believe that I cared, but with the U-boats patrolling the Atlantic, I couldn't risk the crossing with a newborn and a daughter who had just given birth.

"I wrote to Ethan before you were born and told him that Joanna would need money to support you. We used that money to stay in Hot Springs."

"Did he . . . ?" She couldn't bring herself to finish the question.

"Ever want anything to do with you? Don't take it to heart, Lily. He never really had anything to do with his own children. Neither did Ruth, for that matter. Once Ethan had what he wanted from Joanna, he was done with all of us. Michael's death only made it easier to sever the connection," said Josephine.

The sharp pain that had pierced her heart when she'd found the blackmail letter on the study desk a few weeks ago caught her again, but it was the shame—rolling waves of shame—that made her cover her face and turn away.

"Every bit of communication came through Ethan's solicitors," Josephine continued, either not noticing or not caring about Lily's distress. "He had been our friend for decades, but he'd used our daughter and then went about making arrangements like she was a common tart. I suppose she was, in a way.

"She received one hundred and fifty pounds a month from his solicitors until you turned eighteen. We were not to contact him in any way. If I saw Ethan in public, I was supposed to leave wherever I was with no explanation. If either Joanna or I deviated from this agreement, there would be no money."

"Joanna sent the letters," Lily managed.

"Of course she did. She spent one night here after we disembarked in Southampton, and then she took herself off to a place called Hawkshead Hill. I didn't hear a word from her until November."

"When I turned eighteen," Lily murmured.

"She wrote demanding that I pay the money that Ethan was no longer giving her. She said that if I didn't, she would expose everything. That is how little this family meant to her," said Josephine.

"Why didn't she take me? Why did you raise me?" Lily asked.

Josephine lifted her head. "If I had you, at least I knew that your grandmother would never let her son's daughter suffer for lack of funds. You ruined my life, Lily. The very least you could do was be of some use."

Lily's stomach contracted, and she lunged for the wastepaper basket that sat under the desk. Her stomach heaved, and she vomited again and again until her body felt empty.

When, sweat covering her brow, she put the basket down, she saw that Josephine had risen and was holding out a handkerchief at arm's length.

"Thank you," Lily murmured miserably, taking the cloth. She dabbed at her mouth, trying to steady herself.

Finally, she asked, "Why didn't you tell me that you're my grand-mother and not my mother?"

Josephine shrugged. "One wrong word and people would begin to ask questions. It was easier to lie to you than to worry that you might say something you shouldn't because you were too young to understand."

"Is that why you discouraged me from having friends?" she asked.

"Intimacy brings about questions. Not just from children but from their parents," said Josephine.

In her desperation to preserve their income from Mr. Hartford, Jo-sephine had doomed Lily to a childhood of isolation and loneliness. Lily had grown up in a home that was cold and lacking in affection, allowed to think that she was the reason her mother seemed to care so little for her. Instead, it was Josephine who had harbored such resentment for Lily that she'd starved her of affection and deprived her of a relationship with her birth mother.

Lily pushed up from the desk. She had heard enough. She grabbed the envelope she'd brandished at Josephine.

"What are you doing?" Josephine asked.

She held up the envelope. "I'm taking this with me."

She was halfway to the door when she heard Josephine call out, "Lily, you cannot write to her."

Lily glanced over her shoulder. "I'm not going to write to her."

No, writing would never do. A letter was too easy to ignore, and she needed answers.

"Lily?" Josephine followed her into the corridor. "What are you doing? You should go upstairs to bed. We can talk more in the morning."

But Lily made straight for the front door, pausing only to pick up the case she'd taken to Katherine's and her mackintosh off the hook in the hallway. Then she let herself out of the house and into the pouring rain.

Lily squinted through the rain, looking for a sign in the reluctant dawn. There it was. In the window, a solitary light.

She hurried up to the front door of the huge white house, her feet aching in the soaked loafers that she'd borrowed from Katherine what seemed like an age ago. She hadn't wanted to take a taxi to Eaton Square. It had seemed like a waste of money, and she'd craved the walk through the rain. It was healing somehow, all of that water running down the gap between her neck and her mackintosh. Now, however, she was cold and ready to be somewhere warm.

That won't change Josephine's lies.

That won't bring Gideon back.

No, it wouldn't change anything. Yet she had to try.

She leaned on the buzzer and then pushed her wet hair back from her face as best she could. It took a few moments, but the door opened.

"Miss Nicholls," said Mrs. Kent.

"Good morning. I'm sorry to intrude, but do you suppose I could use your telephone?"

The Normans' London housekeeper, to her credit, didn't hesitate. Instead, she let Lily in and quickly took her wet jacket. "I'll find you some dry clothes. This way."

When the housekeeper led her to a sitting room with a telephone extension, Lily thanked her and asked, "Do you know the exchange for Balcombe Manor?"

Mrs. Kent gave her the number for the Normans' country house, adding, "It's a terrible business what happened there this evening."

Tears pricked at Lily's eyes as she nodded.

"I'll find you those clothes," said Mrs. Kent softly.

"Thank you."

When the door closed, Lily picked up the telephone and gave the operator the exchange for Balcombe Manor. Bertram picked up after two rings.

"Bertram, I'm very sorry to telephone this early, but could you please find Miss Norman, for me?" she asked.

"Yes, Miss Nicholls," said the butler.

When Katherine picked up the telephone, she sounded breathless. "Lily, is everything all right?"

"No. No, it's not. I need to go to Cumberland as soon as I can."

"Why?" Katherine asked.

"Because that's where my mother lives."

There was a long pause on the line until finally Katherine asked, "What?"

"I just found out that my mother's not my mother, and my father's not my father," she said, giving a hollow laugh at the absurdity of it.

"But how—"

"My sister became pregnant when she had an affair with a married man. My mother—Josephine—pretended I was her daughter," she said.

"Bloody hell," murmured Katherine.

"I think I've heard you swear more tonight than I ever have before," she said, beginning to shiver in her wet clothes.

"There's been a lot to swear about. So you're going to go up there to find your sister? I mean your mother?"

"Joanna," she said firmly. "Yes."

"Do you have a plan?" Katherine asked.

Lily fell silent. She hadn't thought that far ahead. "I don't know how I'm going to make my way up there," she finally said.

"Do you know what you'll say when you do?" asked Katherine.

"No."

"Where are you?"

"I'm at your London house," she said.

"Good. Tell Mrs. Kent to give you whatever it is you need. Don't move. I'll be there in an hour," Katherine promised.

"It's an hour-and-a-half drive," Lily said absently.

"Not the way I drive," said Katherine. "Promise me that you won't leave the house."

"I promise," she said.

"Good. Lily, you don't have to do any of this alone if you don't want to," said Katherine.

"Thank you," she whispered, her voice cracking.

Then she put down the phone and began to cry.

PART IV

Carriages

DEATH AT DEB'S BALL
Grenadier Guard Drowned in Boating Accident

DEB'S DANCE TURNS DEADLY
*Debauchery Leads to Drowning Death in
Newspaper Mogul's Lake*

HAS DEBAUCHERY OF
TODAY'S YOUTH GONE TOO FAR?

Twenty-Seven

Y ou're certain you have your ticket?" Katherine fussed at Lily over the din of King's Cross Station.

"I have it here," she said, patting her borrowed handbag. It was one of the things Katherine pulled out for her after driving up to London as soon as they had hung up the telephone the morning before. Of course, Lily had insisted that all she needed was to borrow the essentials, but Katherine herself had packed her a suitcase full of clothes while listening to her friend's plan.

"You promise that you'll telephone when you arrive?" asked Katherine, searching Lily's expression.

"I promise. You really didn't have to come along," she said.

"Of course I wanted to see you off," said Katherine as though Lily's trip north was a perfectly normal jaunt. But they both knew that the cheeriness was forced. Lily had told Katherine everything over a cup of tea as soon as her friend had arrived, even if she felt guilty afterward for adding to Katherine's own problems. Back at Balcombe Manor, the police were making routine inquiries into Gideon's death, and Katherine had told her that the sadness and strain of it all had sent her mother into fits of sobbing.

Lily pressed a hand to her friend's arm. "Thank you again for everything you've done."

"It's nothing," said Katherine.

"It's everything." Everything had changed, and Lily didn't know who to trust any longer except for her friends.

"Please don't tell the other Imperfects what's happened. Not yet," she said.

"They're going to be worried about you," warned Katherine.

"I know. Tell them I just need a little time on my own. I'll be back," she promised.

"What shall I tell Ian if he calls trying to find you?" Katherine asked.

Lily hesitated. She'd thought about Ian so often in the long hours since she'd left Harley Gardens. She wanted to go back to that moment on the beach before everything had changed. She wanted to kiss him again, wrapped up in the warmth of his jacket and the comforting scent of his soap. Even then, she'd been worried about what he might think if people found out that Michael Nicholls wasn't her father, but that felt laughable compared to what she knew now.

She couldn't go back to that time. Her life had changed, and she needed answers if she was ever going to move forward. Answers to questions only she could ask.

She finally settled on "I don't know."

"Then neither of us have to say anything to him until you figure that out for yourself," said Katherine with a firm nod. "Now, you need to go or you'll miss your train."

Lily pulled Katherine into a tight hug.

"Take care of yourself, Lily," Katherine whispered.

"I will," she promised.

Katherine gave her one last squeeze and then stepped back. Lily stooped to pick up her borrowed suitcase. It should have felt strange to be taking the journey with another woman's clothes on her back, but somehow it was fitting. She didn't know what her trip would bring, but she did know that she was going to come back different.

"Right. I'd better go," she said.

She gave one last little wave to Katherine, took a deep breath, and then headed for her platform and the long trip north to the truth.

Lily's train wound its way through the picturesque Cotswolds to the farmland of the Midlands and into the industrial towns of the North of England. She changed trains at Wolverhampton, taking a moment to buy herself a packaged sandwich of what would prove to be slightly soggy bread, waxy cheese, and limp cress. When she opened her coin purse and saw that, when she wasn't looking, Katherine had slipped into it a tightly folded envelope with ten new five-pound banknotes, a handful of shillings, and a note that read *Don't worry about money. Just find the answers you need,* Lily added a cup of tea and a copy of the *Birmingham Times* as well.

The pages of the paper were spread out before her now, the head-line "6,000 Troops Ready to Deliver Petrol: Action if London Bus Strike Spreads" reminding her in heavy black ink of her life back in London, but she'd long abandoned reading it. Instead, she fixed her gaze on the countryside that grew ever greener as her train crossed into Cumberland.

You ruined my life, Lily. The very least you could do was be of some use.

The words, tipped with bitterness and tossed like spears, reverber-ated through every bit of her. Lily had never fooled herself into thinking that Josephine had any particularly warm feeling toward her. Now she understood that it wasn't just because Josephine blamed her for stealing her last moments with her husband. It was because, to Josephine, Lily was just an obligation.

The conductor stopped in the aisle, drawing Lily's attention with a light cough. "Change to the train at platform one in two minutes, miss."

She thanked him and began to gather up her things. One more train, a bus, and then she would be at Hawkshead Hill and one step closer to the answers that she sought.

The driver heaved his weight into the lever that opened the bus doors, and Lily carefully let herself down the stairs to the muddy ground. She was glad now that Katherine had insisted that she take her green utilitarian Wellies, arguing that the North was always so much wetter than London. If nothing else, Lily's feet would remain dry.

With Katherine's suitcase rapping gently against her right leg and her handbag swinging off her left wrist, she made her way across the village's main road to a shop with a cheery red sign and pots of begonias on either side of the porch. She pushed open the door, the bell above it announcing her arrival with a jangle. At the counter, a young woman looked up from the magazine she was reading and adjusted her wire-rimmed spectacles.

"Good afternoon," said the shopgirl with a curious glance.

"Good afternoon. I was wondering if you might help me. You wouldn't happen to know a Miss Joanna Nicholls who lives in Hawkshead Hill or thereabouts, would you?"

The shopgirl tilted her head. "There's no one of that name here."

"Oh," said Lily, her heart falling.

"There is a Mrs. Bute who lives out that way, though. Her Christian name's Joanna."

Lily's chin jerked up. Bute was her mother's maiden name. "Yes, that will be her. I hadn't realized she was married."

"Widowed. Has been as long as I've known her. Are you a friend of hers?" the young woman asked.

"I've never met her before, but I need to speak with her. It's urgent," she said.

The girl leaned over the wooden shop counter, a conspiratorial smile creeping across her lips. "My mum reckons that Mrs. Bute isn't a widow at all. Of course, no way to know that, and she does wear a ring and all."

Lily's stomach soured, wondering what Josephine would think knowing that, even in exile, Joanna hadn't escaped the rumors Josephine had feared.

"Can you tell me where I might find her?" she asked.

"Dovecote Cottage," said the shopgirl, clearly losing interest when Lily was unwilling to add to her gossip.

"Is that far?" she asked.

That earned her a shrug. "It's about a half hour's walk. Just take Main Street out to where it becomes Loanthwaite Lane and make a left. Follow the road to the village. It isn't big, so you won't miss the cottage."

Lily thanked the young woman and then headed back outside. She looked up at the sky as a delivery man drove by in his truck. On the corner, a couple holding an Ordnance Survey map of the Lake District peered at the markings. Across the way at the pub, two men sat smoking in the window. None of these people knew that, standing there on the threshold of this shop in a village she'd never heard of before, she was preparing herself to do the most frightening thing of her life.

The walk did little to calm her. The repetition of her suitcase rapping against her leg gave it all a sense of methodical rhythm, perfect for rolling over each and every possible scenario that could go wrong in her head.

Joanna could slam the door in her face.

Joanna could be out of the house for the day.

Joanna could reject her.

Joanna could be happy to see her.

Each of these scenarios terrified her in their own way, but she was determined with each step to find the woman who'd given birth to her.

Her feet began to ache about a half mile into her walk in the same places where she'd rubbed them raw walking to the Normans' in the rain. She hadn't known that was where she was going when she left Harley Gardens. She'd simply turned out of the front door of the only house she'd ever known and set to walking. However, now she was beginning to understand. Katherine had challenged her to think about what she wanted. Not Grandmama, not Josephine. Lily. All of that talk about working and creating a life for herself made Lily wonder if it might be possible for her.

She knew now that there had always been two paths before her: one, the path of marriage and family amid high society that was predictable, and the other one unknown and untrodden by most. She'd thought she wanted what others told her was best for her. Now she didn't know where she would end up, but she couldn't stand the thought of stuffing everything she'd learned down and retreating into the supposed safety of society. She knew too much.

She reached the outskirts of Hawkshead Hill as pastures with sheep gave way to cottages that poked out between stone walls and little stands of conifer. She thought about knocking on the door to the first white-washed cottage she came to at the junction in the road to ask where Dovecote Cottage was, but this wasn't London. The place was small enough that she could find it on her own.

Dovecote Cottage, it turned out, was a few hundred feet down the road. The neat house was white like its neighbor, with an iron gate covering a gap between a low hedge. But unlike the other cottages she'd passed, an exuberant garden burst forth from behind the stone wall that separated the yard from the road. Lily retrieved her handkerchief from her jacket pocket and dabbed at her forehead and the top of her lip as she gazed up the garden path bordered in rows of lavender. It led to a pale yellow front door—a cheery, welcoming color that she hoped would reflect the disposition of the woman who lived within—that was framed in climbing roses just starting to bloom for the summer.

She wished for a moment that she'd spent at least some of the long train journey rehearsing what it was she wanted to say to the stranger who was her mother. But something had held her back, as though she was protecting herself from the possibility of disappointment if she couldn't find Joanna.

She squared her shoulders, pushed back the wisps of her hair that escaped the twist she'd pulled it back into, and placed a hand on the garden gate. However, before she could open it, a woman dressed in an old tweed skirt and a faded green jumper with a white collar sticking out of the neck of it rounded the corner of the house, holding a plant in a clay pot in one hand and a shovel in the other. The woman's eyes fell on Lily, and she stopped short, the plant and shovel falling to the grass with dull thuds. The pot split in two at her feet.

"What are you doing here?" the woman asked.

"I-I'm sorry. I'm Lily Nicholls," she managed to get out around her dry tongue.

The woman pressed a hand to her forehead. "I know who you are. You look just like I did when I was your age."

Tears sprung at the corners of Lily's eyes.

"Did Josephine tell you where I live?" the woman, who she had no doubt now was Joanna, asked.

Lily shook her head. "I found the letters you wrote her."

Joanna pressed her lips together, just the same way that Josephine did when she was perturbed. "Then you know who I am?"

"You're my—"

"No. Not here," said Joanna, glancing each way down the road. "You'd best come inside."

With a nod, Lily lifted the latch on the gate and followed her mother into the cottage.

Twenty-Eight

The interior of Dovecote Cottage bore little resemblance to the neatness of the garden. In the entryway that seemed more like a mudroom, Wellies and walking boots lay strewn about, left wherever they'd been tossed after coming off tired feet. A waxed jacket hung askew from a hook so that one of the arms almost reached the ground, and an olive felt hat had fallen onto a scuffed and scarred wooden bench where Joanna obviously pulled on and off her boots, if the patches of mud on the legs could be trusted.

As soon as Joanna closed the door, there was a scrambling on the floor, and a brown-and-white spaniel burst through a door off the entryway. Lily watched as the dog danced at his mistress's feet with delight.

"Jorey, down," said Joanna sharply. The dog plopped its bottom down, his tail still wagging in a sweeping brush across the slate floor.

"He's a beautiful dog," Lily said, watching awkwardly as Joanna stooped to unlace and then heel off her gardening boots.

"He's a bloody nuisance, but he's a good companion in the winter. Not a half-bad gun dog, either, when he's put to it." Joanna glanced at her. "You can put your case down where you're standing and your jacket on the peg."

Lily did as she was told. When she turned back, she found Joanna studying her.

"Come on, then," said Joanna briskly with a nod to a door.

Lily followed her through to a small sitting room.

"I hope you don't mind the chill," Joanna called over her shoulder. "It never becomes as warm up here as it does in London, but I prefer to keep the electric fire off once we're out of the winter. Much more sensible than running up bills."

"I don't mind," said Lily.

"You can sit there, right in the light so I can look at you," said Joanna, pointing to a well-worn plaid sofa across from two armchairs, one of which she unceremoniously dropped into.

As Lily took her seat, Jorey came up to her and put his head on her knee. She scratched the dog's ears, the feeling of his silky fur providing her with a little grounding in this strange situation.

"Yes, you do look very much like me when I was eighteen. Of course, I cared a great deal more about what I looked like then than I do now," said Joanna, touching the fine lines that formed a crinkle on her weatherworn forehead. "Even after, it took me some time to learn."

"To learn what?" she asked.

"How did you find out about me? I can't imagine Josephine let you see those letters," said Joanna, ignoring her question with the brusqueness of a country woman used to spending time among dogs and horses, which didn't need pleasantries to smooth over wounded feelings.

"No. She fell asleep in the study, and I saw them when I went to try to put her to bed."

"How sweet," said Joanna, her eyes narrowing. "What sort of job did she make of it? Was she the warm, loving mother of the women's magazines and women's pictures?"

"Not particularly," said Lily.

"No," said Joanna, a rueful smile stretching over her unlipsticked lips. "That isn't Josephine at all, is it? Do you know, she had little interest in me when I came around. I would be carted out to show off to guests and told that I had to do and say all of the right things, but that was the extent of it."

It was the story that Josephine had told her about Ruth Hartford treating her son, Geoffrey, like he was a plaything to be taken out on occasion rather than a boy.

"Nanny saw to the raising of me until they sacked her when I was ten," Joanna continued, digging out a crumpled packet of cigarettes from her skirt pocket and touching a lighter to the tip of one. "The money dried up, you see. I don't suppose Josephine hired Nanny back when you came around, did she?"

"I never had a nanny," said Lily.

"What a shame. I'm surprised that the dragon lady—Papa's mother—didn't have anything to say about that."

"Grandmama wasn't in our lives very much until I was older," she said. "Hannah, our housekeeper, helped raise me."

Joanna's lips quirked. "Oh, Hannah. She's better than any of us deserve."

Lily felt a pang of guilt that Hannah was likely at home, wondering what had happened to her.

"So, what is it that you want?" Joanna asked abruptly.

Lily leaned forward, finally catching on to the threads of this strange conversation. "I want to know what happened. What *really* happened."

Joanna leveled a look at her. "And you think that I'll be the one to give it to you?"

"Everyone's been lying to me my entire life. As far as I know, you've never tried to come see me. You never wrote. You never telephoned. In a way, you're the only one who hasn't lied to me."

"In a way," said Joanna.

"So why would you start now?" she asked.

Joanna looked thoughtful as she picked a flake of tobacco from her tongue. "I don't suppose it matters now. Not if you already know the worst of it."

She watched Joanna settle back into the armchair, her pale blond hair resting on the back cushion and her hand holding the cigarette draped over the arm. It was incredible to see the comfort and ease this woman wore about her even when confronted with what must be the greatest secret of her life.

"I suppose Josephine told you I was rather wild as a child?" Joanna asked.

She nodded.

"She isn't wrong, but it isn't precisely right, either. I was spirited—I will admit to that—but I suspect I would have done rather well with someone who understood how to channel that into something useful. Instead, I had a long string of rather hapless young women taking care of me, all milquetoast and so pale that they looked as though they might melt away with the first drop of rain. It wasn't until Nanny arrived when I was seven that they finally hired someone sensible, but I suspect that by that point there was no putting my independence back in the proverbial bottle.

"Maybe the war's shown everyone that girls can be worth something. But when I was growing up, nothing was expected of me except to sit down, be quiet, and not make an embarrassment of the family." Joanna grinned. "I did make rather a hash of that, didn't I?"

"What happened?" Lily asked, refusing to be pulled in by Joanna's cynical joviality.

Joanna laughed through another cloud of smoke and stretched forward to tap the ash off her cigarette into the saucer of an abandoned teacup. "Exactly what you would expect from a girl who'd been given too much free rein. I was a terror—I will admit that fully. It started with simple things like refusing to go to church or dance lessons. All I was really interested in was horses. But then the money for riding ran out, and I was told that was no longer going to be on offer. Not that it mattered. I turned thirteen that year, and suddenly all I could think about was boys. I suppose that shocks you."

"I doubt that many things would shock me any longer," said Lily.

Joanna snorted. "That may very well be true." She leaned across the gap between them. "Tell me, did you give Josephine hell, as our American friends would say?"

Lily frowned. "I don't know what you mean."

Joanna sat back heavily, almost disappointed. "No, I don't suppose you'd be the type. No matter. I gave her and Papa more than a lifetime of worry. I took a fancy to our butcher's boy in Fulham when I was fourteen."

"I heard that it was the greengrocer's son when you were thirteen," said Lily.

Joanna laughed. "I was precocious, but not that precocious. A police constable caught the butcher's boy and me kissing in Bishops Park. He marched me right up to that dreadful house in Harley Gardens and announced that I was up to no good. Josephine wailed a bit, and Papa paced around as though figuring out what to do was the greatest dilemma facing man. In the end, do you know what they did?" Joanna paused. "They told me to be a good girl and sent me off to bed with a tray for my dinner.

"The next time I was caught, it wasn't quite so innocent. The boy, Gerry, was seventeen, and I was sixteen. He was the brother of a girl I went to school with before Josephine and Papa sent me off to board, claiming it was for my own good. Hannah had her day off, and Josephine and Papa were both out. Josephine came back from volunteering at the Women's Institute and found us half-dressed in my bed."

Lily's brows jumped, and Joanna laughed. "Have I finally shocked you?"

"Yes. You have."

Joanna looked satisfied. "I saw a photograph of you in one of the society papers. It said you were presented and that you had a coming-out do. I suppose Josephine got what she wanted in the end. The debutante daughter. That's what she'd hoped for me, you know. Papa, too, I suppose, but he never would have mentioned that. The Season was all the mothers' doing in those days."

"It still is, except for a few girls whose mothers have died. Their fathers try to do their best," Lily said.

Joanna snubbed out her cigarette and reached for another. "After Josephine caught me with Gerry, there was hardly any discussion. They packed me off to Papa's sister in Washington, DC. They sent me with a respectable family they knew who was traveling over who saw me through from New York to Washington on the train. Aunt Patricia and Uncle Howard collected me from the train station in their huge black Oldsmobile, and we drove off to their house in Georgetown. They stuck me up in a room and practically locked the door and threw away the key.

The only places I was allowed to go were school and church. Anywhere else and I had to have a chaperone. And then Ethan came."

Up until that moment, Joanna's voice had had an ironic, wry tone to it. At the mention of Mr. Hartford, however, it had become strained, as though the memory itself was almost too painful to revisit.

"Josephine will have told you that Ethan was a friend of the family. He came to Washington at the end of autumn after the war broke out. Without his wife, although I'm certain he preferred it that way. He called on Aunt Patricia and told her that he'd promised my parents he would look in on me. He asked if he could take me to lunch. Show me a bit of fun. He said that it would be good for him, too, after all of the meetings he was having about America's decision to stay out of the war.

"The first time he took me to lunch, I put on my best dress. It was my first properly grown-up one—shimmering mint-green silk with little cloth-covered buttons going up the front and gathers under my bust. I had shoes with heels, and Aunt Patricia even let me put on a bit of lipstick. At lunch, Ethan ordered a bottle of champagne and caviar with toast points, and afterward we strolled around the Mall. It felt an entire world away from Gerry and the butcher's boy.

"Ethan began to collect me once a week. Often it would be lunch, but sometimes he would take me to the cinema. He spent Christmas with us because Aunt Patricia felt sorry that he should be away from his family for the holiday.

"In January, he asked for permission to take me to the National Symphony Orchestra at Constitution Hall, and I sat there pretending to listen to one of Chopin's piano concertos but really all I wanted was for him to take my hand." Joanna's eyes had become a little dreamy. "I was in love with him by then. How couldn't I be? He was an older man, and I was a girl who thought she was wiser than she was. I'd been shipped off as a punishment and locked up in a big house and told I was very naughty. He sprung me out of that house every week and told me I was brilliant. That I was pretty. Only I understood how difficult his work was.

"I would tell you that he seduced me, but a seduction implies that one of the parties enters into the affair without wanting the exact same thing from the start. I wanted him just as badly as he told me he wanted me. I didn't realize that no man of forty-one should want anything to do with a sixteen-year-old girl."

Joanna's expression darkened. "I started to sneak out at night, shinnying down the trellis that ran up to my back bedroom and then through the garden gate to his car that would be parked down the road. It was fun doing something so incredibly wrong right under everyone's noses, but that only lasted a few weeks. By the middle of March, I was sick as a dog. I knew what that likely meant, especially when I missed my monthlies.

"I wrote him a letter, but naive as I was, I didn't think anything of leaving it unsealed in an envelope in my desk drawer. The next day, my aunt was waiting for me in the parlor when I came home from school, the letter on the table in front of her. A maid had found it. Before I could try to explain, Aunt Patricia had telephoned my mother long-distance, and Josephine was there in Washington two weeks later. I suppose you know the rest."

"Josephine told me that she pretended that you'd fallen ill and she rushed off to Washington to nurse you back to health," said Lily.

Joanna scoffed. "I'm sure that fit her picture of herself nicely. Always the perfect wife and mother. She was smart about it, though, I will give her that. She told Aunt Angelica—who never could keep her mouth shut—that she was pregnant before she left. It bought her time. Meanwhile, Aunt Patricia put it around that I had fallen horribly ill—I can't remember what disease she chose—and locked me in my room until Josephine arrived.

"I'll never forget what Josephine said when she walked into my bedroom for the first time. She hadn't seen me in months, and I was miserable and heartbroken, but she took one look and said, 'I suppose you're very pleased with yourself.' I told her I was, even though I was scared out of my wits.

"She took me down to Hot Springs, and we waited in a poky little house on the edge of the town. The only person I saw was the doctor and the maid." Joanna pointed her cigarette at Lily. "You caused me fourteen hours of pain in the end."

Lily took a deep breath. "Why did you let her keep me? Why pass me off as your sister?"

For the first time since Lily had entered that messy little cottage, Joanna looked uncertain. "I didn't have any other choice. I stole writing paper once, before Josephine thought to take it away from me, and I wrote to that man. I told him what was happening. That I was going to have his baby. I got the letter back unopened with 'Addressee unknown' scrawled across the front of it in blue ink. I was sixteen, and the man who I loved and who had told me that he loved me had just abandoned me in a foreign country. What was I supposed to do?"

"That doesn't answer my questions," Lily said, her voice cracking.

Pain seemed to pull at the edges of Joanna's mouth even as she took a long draw on her cigarette. She blew the smoke out, as though steadying herself, and then asked, "Do you know where you are staying the night?"

Lily jerked at the abrupt change in the conversation. "No, I hadn't thought that far ahead."

"The bus to the train station won't be running much past six, so my guess is you'll have to find a room in a guesthouse. I suppose you do have money," Joanna said.

"Yes," said Lily.

"I'll call ahead to Mrs. Roberts in Hawkshead and let her know you're coming. She'll probably try to read you the scriptures, but she runs a good, clean establishment."

A moment later, Lily found herself being hustled into her coat while Jorey watched at his mistress's feet. Joanna held out her suitcase to her. When their fingers brushed on the handle, Lily turned quickly for the door, hoping that it would hide the tears that were beginning to collect in the corners of her eyes.

She was halfway down the path when Joanna called out, "Lily!"

She half turned to her mother.

"There's more to the story, but I can't face it today. Come back tomorrow around ten o'clock. I'll tell you the rest."

Lily swallowed around the lump in her throat. "I will."

"I'll make tea," Joanna added weakly.

She nodded and hurried to the edge of the garden. It wasn't until she was on the outskirts of the village that she realized that Joanna, who had an entire cottage to herself, hadn't offered her a place to stay.

Twenty-Nine

J oanna had been true to her word and telephoned ahead, so when Lily found Mrs. Roberts's guesthouse with the help of instructions from the girl at the shop in Hawkshead, a room was ready and waiting for her as promised. However, Joanna hadn't prepared her for the inquisitiveness of her hostess.

"And will you be staying long?" Mrs. Roberts asked after she'd shown Lily the bathroom down the hall from her room.

"I don't know," she said, still holding her suitcase.

"There are not many people who come to see Mrs. Bute," Mrs. Roberts tried.

"No, I don't suppose there are."

"And how is it that you said you know her?" asked the landlady.

"If you'll excuse me, I'm rather tired, Mrs. Roberts," she said, indicating the open door of her room.

Mrs. Roberts folded her hands in front of her, her expression suddenly frosty. "I don't know what you were planning for your tea. I didn't know you were coming until it was too late. What I have for the other guests might not stretch."

The thought of being forced to sit around a dinner table with other guests made Lily's skin itch.

"If you could spare some bread and cheese and a little tea, I'll make do with that," said Lily.

"It'll cost you extra," said Mrs. Roberts.

"That's fine. I don't suppose that I could use your telephone?"

"Where will you be calling?" Mrs. Roberts asked.

"London and Cambridge." When she saw the landlady's brows pop, she quickly added, "Naturally, I'll pay the extra expense."

"I suppose you can use the telephone. Note down the time and I'll add it to your bill," said Mrs. Roberts.

She thanked the landlady and made for her room. She shut the door and sagged against it, letting her suitcase hit the carpet with a dull thud.

She was exhausted—a bone-deep tiredness that could only come from being wrung out over the course of an afternoon. She hadn't known what kind of greeting to expect from Joanna, but it certainly wasn't what she'd received. Perhaps if Joanna hadn't played a part in perpetuating a lie that had shaped everything about who Lily thought she was, she might have admired her carefree attitude. It couldn't be easy to be a still-young woman playing at being a widow in a remote village where even the shopkeepers commented on your business. It looked, at least from the outside, like a lonely life with only Jorey to keep Joanna company.

But for all of Joanna's bravado, Lily hadn't missed the way that Joanna's face had crumpled when she'd spoken about feeling abandoned by Ethan Hartford. He'd used her and then cast her aside.

A pulsing ball of rage that had been building over days rose up in Lily's throat. Ethan Hartford had taken advantage of Joanna. When he heard that Lily was going to be born, he'd paid to keep them all away, quiet and shoved into obscurity, while he went on with his own life with no consequence except for the loss of £150 a month. His abuse of a girl too young to understand what he was doing to her went unpunished.

Lily snatched a lace-trimmed pillow off the bed, pressed it against her face, and screamed into it. She screamed her rage and her disappointment and her sorrow with all of her might until her muffled voice became raw and every muscle in her body went limp. Then she dropped onto the bed, her limbs limp, and fell asleep.

Lily awoke with a start. Disoriented in a strange room done up in dusky pink with valances, frills, and bows everywhere, it took her a moment to remember where she was. Mrs. Roberts's guesthouse. Hawkshead. The next village over from Joanna.

She rolled off the twin bed with a groan and went to the little mirror hanging over the sink in the corner of the room. She had creases on her face, and her hair—already wrecked from its beauty parlor set—was all pushed up on one side.

She splashed some water on her face and opened her suitcase to retrieve her comb. A few minutes later she was looking at least somewhat presentable. Her stomach growled, and she checked the time on her watch. It was half past nine.

Carefully, she opened the door. The lights in the hall were low, but she could see enough to find a tray with a few bits and bobs laid out on a plate for her and a pot of tea covered in a cozy. She eased the tray into her room, sending up a little silent thank-you to Mrs. Roberts, when she saw a note tucked between a piece of cheese and a few slices of bread.

The telephone is in the room off the ground floor hall.

Lily took a bite of the sharp, sour cheddar as she rummaged through her luggage for her address book and diary. It seemed preposterous to her now that two slim pale blue leather books had ruled her life so completely this year. In her address book, the information for every one of her fellow debs and their escorts was scribbled down. In the diary, she'd written the details of every party, tea, luncheon, and ball in pencil. She opened the diary to the ribbon marker for the following week, reading off the names of all of the different parties she was meant to be going to in London and the home counties. Thomasina Beckett's ball at the Dorchester tonight, Alice Macaulay's ball Monday at the Hyde Park Hotel, Lucy Cannadine's ball at her family's home on Tuesday, up to Eton for the Fourth of June picnic and the regatta, then down to East Sussex with Philippa and Ivy for the Honorable Sarah Bragg's ball on Friday. It seemed so strange, this world where her greatest worries were what she would wear, whether or not she would have an escort for a dance, and if she would be seated with one of the Imperfects at dinner.

Lily set aside the diary and took the address book with her downstairs, along with a cup of tea, moving quietly so as not to disturb any of the other guests. She wasn't sure if any of them would still be about at this hour, but she didn't want to cross paths with any of them.

In the hall, she found the telephone room. It was more of a booth than a room, with a tiny table and a chair squeezed into it. There was a pad of paper and a pencil for notes sitting on the table next to a small desk lamp. If she kept her knees tucked under the table, she could just close the glass-fronted door to give her a small bit of privacy.

She had two calls to make that evening, one infinitely easier than the other. She thought about taking the easy road, but silently shook her head. She wasn't a coward. Still, her fingers trembled when she paged through the diary until she found the first number.

She picked up the receiver and gave the switchboard operator the exchange. A few moments passed while she waited to be connected. Then the line jumped to life, and on the other end she heard Ian say, "Hello?"

"It's Lily."

"Lily." The relief in his voice made her heart ache. "I tried to call you earlier, but your mother said you weren't feeling well enough to come to the phone."

She cradled the phone to her ear. "I'm fine. Well, I'm as fine as I can be. The truth is I'm not in London right now."

"What's happened? Where are you?" he asked in a rush.

She squeezed her eyes shut. It hurt to hear him so concerned and to know what she was about to do. "Maybe I'm not fine after all. I'm upset and sad and a little lost."

"I'm sorry about Gideon," he said quietly. "I know that you two were close."

"Thank you," she whispered. She did miss Gideon and the way he laughed as he danced her around the floor at countless nightclubs. But she also missed the way worry would etch his brow and he'd pull her aside for a quiet word. He'd been a rare thing among the deb's delights: a friend.

"I found something out about my family right after you dropped me at the house the night it happened," she continued.

"Do you want to talk about it?" he asked.

The tears that had been threatening all day finally began to spill. "I'm afraid."

"Afraid of what?"

"Afraid that if I tell you, everything will change," she said. *That you won't look at me the same way any longer.*

"Lily," he said softly, "I can't imagine that there's anything in this world that would change how I feel about you."

She pressed a hand to her heart, willing it to stop beating quite so quickly. All her life she'd been surrounded by lies—so many that she hadn't even realized that they were right there in front of her. The last thing she wanted to do was to lie to this man and try to pretend that everything she'd learned hadn't happened. She owed him the truth, even if it might break her own heart.

"It's my father. I found out . . . That is, I thought my mother had had an affair and my father . . ." She swallowed around the lump rising in her throat. "My father wasn't actually my father. But when you dropped me off, I learned that my mother isn't who I thought she was, either."

There was a slight hesitation, and then he asked, "You were adopted?"

"No. That is, not in the way you think. The woman who I thought was my mother is my grandmother."

There was a long pause on the line.

"You learned this all on the night Gideon died?" he finally asked.

"Some of it. I read a letter I wasn't meant to see a few weeks ago, and I thought that my mother had had an affair. I thought that was the worst betrayal I'd learn about, but I was wrong." She gave a hollow laugh. "Naive of me, really."

"I'm sorry, Lily." His voice sounded tight and strained.

She leaned her forehead against her palm, wishing that she could take the words back, but she knew she had to push forward. To finish what she'd started, because if she didn't tell him, she would be no better than everyone who'd spent the last eighteen years lying to her, because that kiss they'd shared on the beach was a promise that perhaps there could be more between them. She *wanted* there to be more.

"I'm in the Lake District now, trying to find out more about my mother. I . . . I met her today," she said.

"Who is she?" he asked.

If I tell you, I won't ever be able to take it back.

"I knew her as my estranged sister, Joanna," she said.

Another silence.

"I understand if you don't want to speak to me anymore," she began, dashing away a tear.

"Why would I do that?" he asked sharply before softening his tone to say, "I would never want that."

"But I've just told you I'm illegitimate. That my family lied about everything—to me, to everyone. Everything you know about me is untrue. My father is a man who turned his back on me before I was even born. And my mother—the woman who gave birth to me—left me behind to be raised by my grandmother. Everything I know about myself is *wrong*. I'm wrong."

She was crying now, deep jagging sobs that shook her body at that little telephone table. She clung to the phone as a lifeline, even as she dreaded the next words out of Ian's mouth. They would, she had no doubt, be final.

When her sobs finally eased into hiccuping breaths, Ian said, "I'm so sorry that you've gone through all of this, Lily. I'm so sorry that you're hurt. I cannot imagine how difficult this must be."

She nodded miserably, even though he couldn't see her. "Then you understand."

"I understand that you might need time. That now is not the moment to push you for answers or promises," he said.

"I don't know what I'm going to do," she whispered into the receiver.

"You do. You just don't realize it. Think about what it is that you want. Not your grandmother or your mother or your friends. Don't think about what's expected of you and what people want you to do. Think about what *you* want."

She used the edge of her soft wool cardigan to swipe at her wet cheeks. "That sounds like very good advice."

He gave a low chuckle. "It's advice I should follow myself from time to time. How long are you going to stay up north?"

"I don't really know. I haven't thought of anything beyond making my way here. I didn't have much of a plan," she admitted, although thanks to Katherine's generosity, she was well funded.

"I have no doubt you'll come up with a very good one. Perhaps, when you're back in London, we'll see each other again, and you can tell me what you've decided," he said, a forced cheeriness in his voice.

Her shoulders sagged. He was just being kind. She had unloaded a lifetime's worth of family secrets on him, and he'd listened to her, but that was all he was obligated to do. They weren't married—they had seen each other only a handful of times, danced, and shared one kiss—and he was under no obligation to listen to her. It was only his goodness that was keeping him from hanging up the phone and deciding to spend his time on a girl who came with fewer complications.

It was better this way, she tried to tell herself. Ethan Hartford was his benefactor and associating with her could only complicate things. She needed to let Ian go.

"It's late," she said with a shaky breath. "I should probably say goodbye before the landlady objects."

"Take care of yourself, Lily. Promise me that you will," he said.

She murmured in agreement and then hung up the telephone. She took a deep breath, trying to shake off the raw sadness that hung about her. If none of this had happened, she would have just been piling into a taxi after a long dinner—hopefully with people she enjoyed the company of. She would be on her way to Thomasina's ball, looking forward to her night and hoping to see Ian.

That was all over now. He was right that she needed time to think about herself and what she wanted. Grandmama might have been able to control her with money, but the threat of cutting Josephine off seemed so inconsequential now when Josephine had betrayed her trust so thoroughly.

Lily had set aside Leana and her manipulation in favor of friends who cared for her. She knew it was now time to draw the same boundaries with her family. She didn't know what that looked like, but her old obligations were gone.

One thing Lily knew in her bones was that her time as a debutante was over. She could see now the way that the Season bound her up in silk ribbons until all she could do was flit from cocktail party to dance to luncheon, so exhausted by it all that some days she hardly knew where she was going until she reached the receiving line and saw which debutante was standing, slightly wide-eyed, next to her family to greet their guests. Everything was the same. The people, the parties—only the hosts changed.

The world was larger than those allowed into high society. She wanted to live in that world.

She reached for the telephone again. There was no need for her address book for this number. She rattled off the exchange to the switchboard from memory, and then waited for the connection to be put through.

"Norman household."

"Hello, Mrs. Kent. It's Lily Nicholls. Is Katherine available?"

"Yes, miss. If you will wait one moment," said the housekeeper.

There was a pause on the line, and then a breathless Katherine picked up. "Lily, how are you?"

"I wasn't sure I would get through. I thought you were due at Thomasina's ball this evening."

"I wanted to be here when you called. Besides, everyone's up in arms right now over Gideon's death. All of the talk has been about whether or not it would be appropriate for balls to go forward this week," said Katherine.

She pressed a hand to her forehead, hating that she hadn't even thought of that. "Of course, there hasn't even been a funeral yet."

"My thinking precisely, but some of the mothers are more worried about their daughters missing out on their coming-out balls. They're saying it isn't fair that a drunk young man died and ruined their girls' fun. It's all predictably awful. But anyway, you're not ringing to talk about all of these horrid people. Tell me, did you meet her?"

Lily let out a breath. "I did."

"And what did she say? Was she shocked?" asked Katherine

"Yes, I think she was, but she invited me inside. She wasn't what I was expecting," she said.

"No?"

"She has a way about her, as though she doesn't care what the world thinks. She enjoys being shocking, but there's a brittleness, too. A bit of bitterness as well."

"Did you ask her why she . . . ?"

"Gave me up?" Lily filled in for her friend.

"Lily . . ."

"You can say it. That's exactly what it is." She sighed. "No. Most of the story came tumbling out, but when I asked her why she agreed to give me to Josephine, she told me to come back tomorrow."

"Come back? You mean you aren't there now?" Katherine asked.

She snorted. "I'm at a guesthouse the next village over. I suppose it was ridiculous to think that she might welcome me with open arms."

"Of course it wasn't ridiculous. You're her daughter. Oh, Lily, are you okay?" Katherine asked.

"I feel as though nothing makes sense any longer," she confessed.

"Perhaps tomorrow will help. I assume you will go back," said Katherine.

"Joanna is expecting me at ten o'clock," she said.

"Will you ring me and let me know what happens?" Katherine asked.

"I will."

"And, Lily? No matter what happens with Joanna, don't forget that you don't have to hurry back. You can take all of the time that you need."

She shook her head. "I can't go back to Harley Gardens. Or Grandmama's, for that matter."

"You don't have to. You know that Mum and Dad would always welcome you as a guest, but I might have another idea."

"What is that?" she asked.

"I don't want to say until I can be certain. Just give me some time, and I promise everything will work out in the end," said Katherine.

Lily wanted to ask how Katherine could make a promise like that in the face of everything she knew. Lily had no money of her own. She had no home or place to stay. She was an unmarried woman with no independent wealth, so no bank would extend her a line of credit. She was entirely dependent upon Grandmama, even needing to rely on Katherine's generosity for the money that had purchased her train ticket and was paying for her room in Mrs. Roberts's guesthouse.

But she trusted her friend more than she trusted anyone else, and so she pushed down her doubts.

"I'll telephone you tomorrow after I see Joanna," she promised, and said her goodbyes.

Thirty

Lily hardly slept and gave up trying around five in the morning. Instead, she read a romantic novel that Katherine had pressed on her before she left for the train station. It was light and fun and a welcome change from the serious, ponderous works that Miss Hester had recommended. She devoured nearly a third of the book by the time her stomach started growling.

At half past seven, she headed downstairs for breakfast, eating in silence along with the other guests who seemed to consist of a couple on their honeymoon, a traveling salesman, and an older gentleman whose olive tweeds were a bit battered but clearly had been well-made.

The summer sun shone through the lace curtains of her room that morning, so after breakfast she pulled on the saddle shoes she'd borrowed from Katherine, took up her handbag, and let herself out of the house. It was too early to call on Joanna, but she wanted to walk.

It was a beautiful day, with the sun shining on the rolling hills, making everything glow with the lush green of an English summer. She breathed deep, the freshness of the air so unlike the smoke of London.

As she walked, her mind began to clear. Instead, her focus was on the burn in her legs as she took to the hills and the way that the sun felt on her face. She found a public footpath that mirrored the road and climbed up over the stile, crushing long grass underfoot and releasing the sweet smell of summer as she walked past sheep who placidly watched her from their fields. For a woman who'd let herself wake up later and later as her evenings stretched out during the Season, it felt good to be in the morning air, exercising her body in a way she hadn't since she was at school and was made to play netball by her games mistress.

However, all the while, she was aware of her appointment that morning, and with a half hour to go, she set out backtracking along her path to Hawkshead Hill.

When she arrived at Dovecote Cottage, she let herself in through the garden gate and rang the bell. The yellow cottage door whipped open a few seconds later, as though Joanna had been watching for her at the sitting room window.

"Come in," said Joanna, gesturing her inside.

Lily frowned, but stepped over the threshold. Jorey ran up to her and stuck his head under her hand for a scratch. Joanna didn't move, but instead crossed her arms over her chest.

"This was a mistake," Joanna announced.

Lily's stomach fell. "A mistake?"

"You shouldn't be here. I have a life here as a widow. People are already asking who you are," Joanna said.

"But I didn't meet anyone on the road."

Joanna laughed. "You clearly haven't lived in a village. Everyone knows everyone's business around here. How am I supposed to answer when they ask me why a girl who looks remarkably like me shows up at my door? Did you ever think of that?"

Lily stared until Joanna flinched and looked away. Suddenly she understood.

"You spoke to Josephine," Lily said.

Joanna opened her mouth, but then snapped it shut.

"Yesterday you said you would tell me why you gave me up. What did Josephine say that made you change your mind?" she asked.

Joanna's arms fell to her sides, and she had the good graces to look defeated. "She agreed to send two hundred pounds a month."

"Two hundred pounds? But Josephine doesn't have two hundred pounds to spare," she said.

"She's gone to your great-grandmother," said Joanna.

Lily stared at her in disbelief. "Grandmama knows?"

"I don't know what Josephine said, but whatever it was, your great-grandmother offered to pay if I would send you back to London and go back to the way that things were before. No visits, no letters, no telephone calls. No contact at all."

"Why?" she asked.

"Because they want things to go back to the way they were," said Joanna.

Because neither Grandmama nor Josephine could let go of the life they wanted for her. The life that they'd known, where debutantes were presented at court and there was a Season and those two facts ruled their lives for much of the year. To them, there was safety in even a dying tradition. To Lily, there was suffocation.

She couldn't stuff what she knew back into a box to be locked up and shoved to a far corner of her mind and forgotten, just as she didn't know if she could forgive Grandmama or Josephine for how they'd lied to her.

"You should know that Josephine hates both of us," Lily said quietly. "She hates you for your affair and for keeping her from being with your father at the end, and she hates me because I couldn't let her pretend that everything could go back to the way it was again. I doubt Grandmama feels very different if she knows the truth."

Joanna fished out her cigarettes from a battered brown leather handbag that hung off a hook in the entryway, lit one, and dragged on it as though it was a life preserver. With a steadying breath, Josephine said, "It's more complicated than that. They both care for you in their own way, even if they have a bloody hard time admitting it."

Lily dashed at a tear that had escaped the corner of one of her eyes. "I doubt that very much."

"But I don't. The first thing Josephine did when I telephoned yesterday was demand to know how you seemed. I told her that you were surprisingly self-possessed for a woman who had just been told that everything she's known about her family was wrong because she'd been lied to by the woman she thought was her mother. And do you know what Josephine said?" Joanna paused before pushing on. "She said, 'That's Lily. She's made of steel.'"

"I don't feel as though I am," she whispered, sinking down onto the boot bench in Joanna's entryway.

Jorey whimpered, staring up at her.

Joanna sighed. "Do those questions you asked yesterday really matter to you?"

Why did you let her keep me? Why pass me off as your sister?

"Yes. Answer them, and I'll walk away. I understand that you're not my mother—not in the ways that matter—and I won't pretend that you want to be after all of these years. You've made that clear enough. But you could be the first person who tells me the truth because it's the right thing to do," she said.

"I suppose there's no harm in you knowing. Not now that everything has happened," said Joanna, pushing her chin-length blond hair behind her ear. "Ask your questions."

"Why did you let her keep me?" Lily asked.

"Because I didn't have a choice. I was a frightened sixteen-year-old girl in a foreign country. I had no money, and not a useful bone in my body. I knew that I needed Josephine's help, and her condition was that I agree to give you up by pretending that you were hers."

"But why? Why not send me out for adoption? Why do something so cruel?" Lily asked.

Joanna's lips formed a grim line. "I don't think we realized how awful it would be for you if you ever found out. If we'd stopped for a moment to think about it, perhaps we would have reconsidered."

"Then *why?*" Lily pushed.

"Money."

The single word hung in the air, heavy and rotten. It was the same reason Josephine had given her just packaged up and presented differently.

"I agreed to it because I knew that I could make one of my conditions that I receive the money Ethan sent as an allowance for you," said Joanna. "All I had to do was give up my right to you, and promise never to contact you. Josephine had already planted the seeds that you were hers. Everything was in place. All I had to do was say yes. And so I became the sister who ran away."

"You traded me for money," Lily murmured.

"I traded you for a *life*." Joanna gestured around the entryway, her lit cigarette flaring orange between her fingers. "It may not look like much to you, but everything here is my own. I choose how to live my life. I choose when I eat and who I socialize with. I work in my garden and ride my horse. No one tells me what to do. No one judges me simply for being."

The defensiveness dropped from Joanna's voice. "I can't give you whatever it is that you came here looking for. I'm sorry that I can't be a mother. I don't know how to do those things."

Lily looked at the woman who stood before her, furiously smoking a cigarette as though that would somehow chase away the feelings that Lily had brought with her to this little northern village. Joanna had seemed so sure of herself yesterday, but now she could see that what she'd told Katherine was true. The blasé exterior hid something far more damaged underneath.

"I didn't come here because I needed a mother. I came here because I needed answers. You've given those to me, and I thank you for that. I didn't make any agreement with Josephine, but I understand that you did. I won't make this any more difficult for you than it needs to be. I won't write to you, and I won't contact you again," she said.

Joanna hesitated and then nodded. "That's for the best."

Lily lifted her chin. "I think so as well."

"Will you go back to London?" Joanna asked.

"No, not yet. I have some things that I need to sort out for myself."

"The Season will still be underway. Won't you be missed?"

Lily raised a brow.

"I grew up in that world, remember? I was supposed to be a debutante, although I suppose the war would have put a stop to that anyway. I doubt I'll ever forget things like that," said Joanna quietly.

"No, I don't think I'll be going back for the Season. I've a great deal to think about," she said.

"What will you do instead?" Joanna asked, fascination tinging her voice.

"That is something I need to figure out for myself," said Lily.

She stood and gathered her handbag from the bench next to her. As she straightened her skirt, she could see Joanna hovering out of the corner of her eye, as though Joanna didn't know what to do. However, when Lily looked up again, she found that Joanna had crossed to the front door, her hand on the knob.

"Can I ask you one more thing?" Lily asked before Joanna could open the door.

"Anything."

"Was it worth it?"

Joanna hung her head. "Will you hate me if I say yes?"

"No," said Lily.

"The truth is, I don't know. It's a decision I made, and I can't look back and scrutinize it too closely."

"If you did that, you might find that you regret it," she said.

Joanna pressed her fingers to her lips and murmured, "I did what I had to do."

As she walked past Joanna, Lily paused. "You're wrong, you know. You might have traded me for a life, but the foundation of all of it is built on guilt. You and Josephine. And how will either of you ever live with yourselves knowing that?"

Then she walked out the door and down the garden path without a glance back.

Thirty-One

Lily went straight from Joanna's cottage to Mrs. Roberts's guesthouse, packed her bag, gave up her room, and paid her bill plus extra for her two telephone calls and her dinner. Then she boarded the bus to Windermere and checked herself into a proper hotel near the shore of the lake. The hotel in town was more anonymous than the guesthouse, and no one seemed to care that a young woman was traveling alone. It was the start of the summer season, after all, and the lakeside town seemed to be waking up and shaking off its cold winter sleep.

Lily called Katherine from a telephone box down the road from her hotel as soon as she was settled in.

"What are you going to do?" Katherine asked after Lily told her everything that had happened that morning at Dovecote Cottage.

"I'm going to stay here for a while and think. I can't do that back in London, where everything is familiar. I need some time to myself."

"I'll help you however I can no matter what you decide." Katherine hesitated, and then added, "Is there still time for you to study for a university entrance exam?"

"I'm completely unprepared for this year, and even with a few months, I don't know if I could."

But I will. If not this year, then next.

"Well, whatever you decide, I hope you do come back to London eventually, because I have some news of my own," said Katherine, her excitement clear over the crackling line.

"News?"

"I told Mum and Dad that I'm not going back to being a deb."

"Oh, Katherine, what did they say?" she asked, shifting the receiver so she could hear better.

"They weren't the happiest, but they said they understood. I'm twenty-one now, and I have my own money. And how could they not agree to it after everything that happened at my coming-out ball?"

"None of that was your fault," said Lily.

"No, it wasn't," agreed Katherine, "but it did make me think about what an absolute waste so much of this has been. For Gideon to die in such a senseless way, and for all of those guests to simply go on to another house or another nightclub. It's ghastly."

"I know," said Lily, swallowing back her rising tears. She'd cried enough these last few days. There would be plenty of time to mourn, but she also wanted to be able to lift her head and look forward.

"What will you do now that you're not doing the Season any longer?" she asked.

"I told Mum and Dad about my plan to buy my own flat. I told them that I want a job. Dad's not very pleased to find out that his only child wants to become a reporter. He said reporters spend most of their lives digging through society's scraps and being paid accordingly. He tried to convince me to consider becoming a secretary in his office."

"I can't imagine you as a secretary," said Lily.

"I'd be terrible at it. I'm far too nosy and not discreet at all. Plus, I doubt that Dad and I would last the year before we killed each other," said Katherine with a laugh.

"I'm glad you've told them."

"I was a terrible debutante," said Katherine.

"No, you weren't."

"Well, I would have been in the end. I didn't care about it for the right reasons. I was only doing it for Mum and Dad's sake. I probably would have abandoned the entire thing if it hadn't been for you and the Imperfects," said Katherine.

"How are they?" asked Lily, missing the constant chatter and teasing of her friends.

"They're worried about you. I haven't told them anything except that you needed to leave London for a few days. I think they're all quite jealous, especially Philippa. Her parents found out about David, and they aren't happy about him at all. They keep trying to foist some Catholic boy on her. Victor Longford?"

"He's three inches shorter than Philippa and has the intellect of a potato," she said, rattling off the man's vital statistics just like her aunt Angelica would.

Katherine burst out laughing. "I'll tell her you're on her side."

"Always. Let them all know I'll be back soon," she promised, looking out the phone box and down the road to the sliver of blue lake she could see in the distance. "I just have to figure a few things out first."

"Whenever you're ready, give me a ring and let me know your train. I'll pick you up from the station," said Katherine.

"You don't have to do that," said Lily.

"I know, but I want to," said Katherine. "Oh, and, Lily, there's something else you should know. Ian Bingham telephoned me early this morning."

"He did?" she asked.

"He said you'd spoken and wanted to see if I'd heard from you. He told me that he didn't want to be intrusive, but he was worried about you. He thought you could use a friend."

She closed her eyes and leaned her head against the cool windowpane of the phone box. "That's good of him."

"Does he know?" Katherine asked.

"He knows. I told him yesterday just before you and I spoke."

"He seems like a good man," said Katherine.

"He is a good man." *Far too good.*

"He likes you," Katherine pushed.

"It's complicated right now."

"Everything's complicated," said Katherine.

"His benefactor is Ethan Hartford," Lily said.

"So?"

"Ethan Hartford is the man that Joanna had the affair with."

There was a silence on the other end of the line that stretched so long she wondered if they'd been disconnected. "Oh my God," Katherine finally whispered. "That dirty old man."

Lily barked a laugh in surprise. "Dirty old man?"

"Well, it's what he is, isn't it?" asked Katherine indignantly.

Lily couldn't stop laughing, buckling over at the waist as she laughed and laughed. There was nothing funny about Mr. Hartford taking advantage of Joanna, but the idea of the intimidating diplomat with an imposing house in Mayfair and an estate in the country being reduced to a figure of mockery struck her as hysterical. He would be so angry if anyone thought of him that way. His *daughter* would be livid.

The operator came on the line, and Lily hurried to feed a few more coins into the phone as her laughs subsided.

"Thank you. I needed that," she said with a chuckle.

"You know, if Ethan Hartford's your father . . ."

"That means that Leana and I are half sisters," she finished for Katherine.

"Can you imagine Leana's face if she knew?" asked Katherine.

"She would be appalled," she agreed.

"You're well rid of them," said Katherine.

"Maybe," said Lily, but she couldn't help thinking that there was unfinished business that awaited her whenever she did decide to return to London.

Thirty-Two

After a week in Windermere, haunting bookshops and walking in the hills during the day and reading in her room at night, Lily decided it was time to stop hiding and face the rest of her life. She'd had enough time to think, and although she had hardly any answers, she knew how she wanted to take the first step toward a new life.

That afternoon, she packed up her suitcase, checked out of the hotel, and bought a ticket on the night train before telephoning Katherine.

"I'm coming home. I'm due to arrive on the train from Wolverhampton at 9:04 tomorrow morning," she'd shouted down a crackling connection.

"I'll be there with bells on," Katherine promised.

And sure enough, when Lily stepped off the train at King's Cross Station the following morning and looked about the platform, there her friend was. Katherine was hard to miss in a black pair of cigarette trousers, a crisp white shirt, and a cherry-red cardigan, waving so hard her handbag swung back and forth in a huge arc. Lily laughed before hurrying up the platform to sweep her friend into a big hug.

"I'm so glad you're here! I've been waiting for an hour," said Katherine.

"The train's on time," she said with a laugh.

"I know, but I was so worried that I'd miss you that I came early. Even the porters are starting to stare at me as though I'm suspicious. I have our driver, Benjamin, waiting with the car. Dad wouldn't hear of me coming to pick you up without him," she said with an indulgent smile.

"How is the new flat?" Lily asked.

"Somehow both a mess and completely empty at the same time," said Katherine cheerfully.

On one of their daily calls from the phone box down the road from the hotel, Lily had learned that Katherine had decided to let a flat on Greville Place in Maida Vale. Katherine had moved out of her parents' home five days before. The moment Lily had mentioned she was heading back to London, Katherine had offered her a room rent-free until she could find a job.

"I've never lived alone. You'll be keeping me from going mad rattling around the place on my own," Katherine had said.

Now, standing in the middle of King's Cross Station, facing the prospect of putting together a life for herself, Lily was glad she'd let herself be talked into it.

"Come on," said Katherine, taking her arm and leading her across the station floor. "Benjamin is parked right out this exit."

Lily said hello to the balding driver with the kind smile as he took her suitcase from her and stowed it in the boot of the Rolls-Royce. As soon as she and Katherine climbed in the back, her friend said, "Shall we go home? Find you a bite to eat?"

"I'd like to go to Harley Gardens," said Lily.

Katherine shot her a look. "Are you certain?"

"Yes," she said with a firm nod. She'd used her time away to make up her mind about several things, but she knew that she wouldn't be able to move on with her life until she closed the door on some of her past.

"All right then." Katherine leaned forward a little in her seat. "Benjamin, could you please take us to number seventeen Harley Gardens? We have some business to attend to."

Lily looked up at the front of her childhood home from the back seat of the Normans' Rolls-Royce.

"Are you certain that you want to do this?" Katherine asked.

She kept her gaze on the house. "As certain as I've ever been about anything. If I don't do it now, I don't think I'll ever be able to."

"I could go. You could send me with a list of things to pack," Katherine offered.

She shook her head and gave her friend a smile. "No. There are things I need to say, too. It needs to be me."

She pulled the front door key out of her handbag and waved off Benjamin as he moved to climb out of the car to open her door, instead letting herself out onto the sidewalk. Then she walked up to the steps of the house at Harley Gardens, but before she could put the key in the lock, the door flew open and Hannah rushed out onto the front step to bundle her into a hug.

"Oh, there you are! I've been so worried about you!" cried the housekeeper.

Lily squeezed the older woman tightly. "I'm fine, Hannah. I promise."

Hannah set her at an arm's length. "Don't you ever do that to me again. I was close to telephoning Scotland Yard, but Mrs. Nicholls wouldn't hear of it. Only, she wouldn't tell me where you were."

"I'm sorry that I worried you," she said as Hannah ushered her into the house. "Hannah, there are some things I need to discuss with Josephine. Do know where she is?"

"That's a funny thing, calling your mother by her Christian name. She's in the sitting room with your grandmother." Hannah dropped her voice. "The first Mrs. Nicholls has been visiting every day, arriving just after breakfast and staying until just before supper."

They were waiting for her to come back, knowing that at some point she would have to reckon with her old life.

"Thank you," said Lily, giving Hannah another quick hug.

Before she could lose her nerve, she went to the sitting room and knocked.

"Come in," Josephine called.

Lily rolled her shoulders back, touched her hair to check that none of it had escaped from the short ponytail she'd taken to wearing during her time in the Lake District, and twisted the knob.

Inside the sitting room, she found Josephine in her customary black, pearls at her neck. However, everything from her skirt to her black silk blouse seemed to hang off her, and there were dark smudges under her eyes.

Grandmama sat ramrod straight on the green brocade chair Josephine usually occupied, not a crease in her prim plum suit or a hair out of place from her chignon. However, her face was pale, and she wore a frown that pulled at the thin skin at the edges of her lips.

"I thought I heard a noise down in the entryway," said Josephine.

"Lillian," Grandmama said, "you've had your mother worried sick about you."

"Grandmama, I'm glad you're here. There's a serious matter I need to discuss with both of you," she said.

"This *is* a serious matter, young lady. If you think that you can simply go off to heaven knows where on your own and leave all of your obligations behind—do you know how many excuses your mother and I have made for you this past week and a half? Everyone is asking where you are."

"I'm sorry that you felt that you needed to explain my absence," she said.

"Where have you been, and what have you have been doing with yourself?" asked Josephine before Grandmama could reply.

"You know where I've been. You spoke to Joanna," said Lily, still standing before them.

"That was days ago. I made it clear to her that you were to come back to London," said Josephine.

Lily raised a brow. "Strangely, that message was lost in the midst of learning more about the circumstances of my birth."

"Don't believe anything that woman tells you," Grandmama huffed.

"She's nothing more than a grasping, selfish woman intent on destroying this family," agreed Josephine.

"She is selfish, but she's not entirely to blame. She found herself in an impossible situation. Have you told her the truth?" Lily asked, nodding toward Grandmama.

Josephine shifted in her seat. "It became necessary to explain things."

"And?" Lily looked at her grandmother.

"What do you expect me to say?" Grandmama asked, looking away for the first time.

Lily's eyes narrowed. "Perhaps we could start with an apology."

No one said anything.

"Well then, this should make some things easier," she murmured before clearing her throat. "There are a few things I want to tell you. First, I won't be going back to the Season."

"Lillian, be reasonable," said Grandmama. "You only have one chance to be a debutante."

"I've already heard that the Season will continue next year, even if the court presentations are over. Maybe Lily can participate next year—or do the Scottish balls and the London parties in the autumn," said Josephine.

"I won't be doing any of it, no matter whether there's a Season next year or not. I'm leaving," she said.

"Don't be so ungrateful," said Grandmama.

"What should I be grateful for?" she shouted.

"Lillian, lower your voice," said Grandmama.

"No! I've gone along with everything you've wanted, from years of Tuesday teas to leaving school early because *you* thought it was best. But it's over. I'm eighteen, and you don't have the right to tell me what I should do any longer," she said.

"Are you going to let your daughter yell at her grandmother in your house?" Grandmama snapped at Josephine.

Lily jabbed a finger at Grandmama. "This is not your house! You do not set the rules. You are a guest here."

"Josephine," Grandmama warned.

Lily turned on Josephine. "Why do you let her speak to you like that?"

"Lily, you know our circumstances," Josephine said, shrinking into her seat.

"Then change your circumstances! You are so frightened of Grandmama taking her money away that you let her run everything in our lives," she said.

"It isn't that easy," said Josephine.

"No one said it was going to be easy! I'm sure it would be incredibly hard to sell this house and admit that you might need to find a job, but at least you'd be making choices about your own life," she said.

"I'm not strong," Josephine whispered.

Frustrated as she was by Josephine's weakness, she raked a hand through her hair, loosening her ponytail. "You should have been. For both of us. If you had, you wouldn't have had to live this lie. Instead, you let Grandmama manipulate both of us into doing what she wanted."

"If you feel that way, why did you come back?" Grandmama asked.

"Because I thought it would be cruel to use a letter to tell the woman who raised me that I'm leaving," said Lily.

"Leaving?" both women asked.

"I'm going to go live with Katherine Norman. She's decided to leave the Season as well and has taken a flat on her own. She's asked me to join her. It'll give me a place to stay while I look for work."

"Don't be ridiculous, Lily," scoffed Grandmama. "You don't need to work."

If you fold yourself back into your little, old life and do as you're told, I'll take care of you.

"I think you'll find that I'm quite serious. Katherine is waiting in the car outside. I'm going to pack a few things as well as my books. I'll give Hannah instructions about where to send the rest," she said.

Color had begun to rise on Grandmama's cheeks. "You're throwing everything that we've worked so hard for away."

"Did Joanna put you up to this?" Josephine asked. "This is exactly the sort of thing she would do to try to hurt this family."

Lily sighed, her head beginning to hurt at the rise and fall of anger and disappointment rushing through her. "Joanna sent me away, just like you wanted her to."

"At least that girl did one good thing in her life," said Grandmama with a sniff.

Lily was done, but there was one final thing she needed to know. She turned to Josephine and asked, "Did you ever love me?"

"I clothed you. I fed you. I sent you to school. I gave you everything I could to set you on the right path in the world," said Josephine.

"That isn't the same thing as love," said Lily.

Josephine's eyes flashed, and for the first time since she'd returned, Lily saw some spark there.

"Every time I look at you, I see her, and all she could think about was herself," seethed Josephine.

"She was a child. She was taken advantage of when she should have been protected," Lily managed between gritted teeth.

"She's the reason that Michael died alone in this house when I was thousands of miles away. If I had been here, I could have done something." Josephine's voice cracked, and she buried her head in her hands.

Lily watched as Grandmama awkwardly reached for Josephine and patted her on the back while she sobbed. It was, Lily realized in that moment, possible to feel sorry for Josephine and the loss that she'd suffered and to hate the damage she'd wreaked at the same time.

"Your husband had cancer. There was nothing you could have done," Lily said softly.

"I could have been here," Josephine managed. "I miss him so much."

"I do, too," Grandmama murmured.

"I'm sorry for that," said Lily, pulling a handkerchief out of the sleeve of her cardigan and handing it to Josephine. Josephine took it and swiped at her eyes, tilting her head back to try to stem the tears.

"I don't expect you to understand why I did the things that I did. Just know that I did what I thought was best for my family. For you," said Josephine.

"I don't forgive you for that, and I don't know if I ever will. You lied to me, but it's more than that. You both took away my choices from me," she said.

"There's never a choice. Not for girls like you, Lillian," said Grandmama.

"I had to do everything I could to make sure that you and your reputation were unbreakable. That's what our kind of people do with their daughters," said Josephine.

These women would never understand. They were too much a product of their own little worlds. They would never venture out. Never change from what was comfortable.

"The world is changing. Girls are doing things other than getting married. The Season might continue next year, but I'll wager that with the presentations over, it will die out soon enough. I want to see what all of those changes bring. The Season was fun for a while, and it brought me my best friends, but I want more than it can give me," she said.

"You think that you're too good to be a wife and mother?" asked Grandmama.

"I think I deserve to have more than one choice about what the rest of my life looks like. I want to go to university. I'm going to earn my place. I'm going to work, and when I'm not working, I'm going to study. Then"—she spread her hands wide—"I don't know."

"You're throwing everything away," said Grandmama.

"That's just it. I'm not throwing anything away," she said.

When neither woman protested, Lily made for the door.

"If you leave this house today, do not come back," called out Grandmama.

She stopped and turned. "As this is not your house, that is not your decision."

They both looked to Josephine.

"Don't make this any harder than it needs to be, Lily. You know I don't have a choice," said Josephine.

Lily waited for the disappointment, but she found it absent. She'd already reconciled herself to who Josephine was.

"I hope that one day, you'll realize that you do. I'll be gone as soon as I collect my things."

Thirty-Three

Packing took the better part of an hour. She'd thought that maybe Josephine or Grandmama might come up to her bedroom, but only Hannah appeared, Katherine in tow.

"I thought we could help," said Hannah.

Katherine's eyes widened as she looked around at the room strewn with clothes, shoes, and books. "You could start a library."

Lily laughed. "That is the hazard of being a reader."

"No. It's the hazard of being a future English literature student at a university," said Katherine.

For the first time since she entered Harley Gardens that day, Lily smiled.

Once the suitcases and the box of books Lily decided were vital were packed, Benjamin discarded the newspaper he was reading and jumped out of the car to help them load things in.

"I'll take it from here, miss," he said, and Lily gratefully handed him the heaviest of her suitcases.

In the back seat, Lily leaned heavily against the headrest and closed her eyes.

"It's done," she said with a sigh.

"Are you okay?" asked Katherine.

Lily opened her eyes and tilted her head to look at her friend. "I will be."

"Tomorrow will be easier, and then the next day, and the next," said Katherine.

"Yes. Yes, I think it will."

Katherine gave her a smile, and Benjamin climbed behind the wheel to take them to their new home.

The flat in Maida Vale, it turned out, was part of a larger house that had been chopped up into different units after the war. On the pavement in front of it, Lily studied the tall white building as Benjamin unloaded the car. This would be her home, at least until she knew whether she'd been accepted into university or not. If she was, she would be off to school in a little more than a year. If she wasn't . . . Lily would figure it out. She had veered off the path that she'd been on and into the unbroken tall grass. She would have to find her own way now, and she wanted to relish every moment that she could.

"Come on," said Katherine, excitedly pulling her key out of her handbag. "I have something exciting to show you."

Lily laughed. "More exciting than moving into a new flat in a new neighborhood?"

"More exciting than that," said Katherine, eyes shining.

Katherine led their procession through the front door and up the stairs to the second floor. Benjamin huffed and puffed behind Lily, having insisted on carrying the box of books. He set it down with a great whooshing breath of relief.

"Is this all, miss?" he asked Lily.

"Yes, it is. And thank you," she said.

"Yes, thank you, Benjamin. And please tell my father that we were grateful for the use of the car," said Katherine.

He tipped his hat to them both and made for the stairs. Katherine spun around and jammed her key into the lock of the door, rattling it about until it gave.

"Here we are!" Katherine sang out, dropping one of Lily's suitcases in the entryway.

The flat was beautiful, with clean white walls that gave way to ornate cornices and a plaster ceiling that rose in the sitting room. Boxes sat scattered across the warm blond wood floors, and in the small kitchen there was already a collection of newspapers neatly piled up on the table.

"I'm an atrocious cook, but I'm determined to learn," said Katherine, facing off against the cooker with hands on her hips as though she was staring down an enemy.

"I can teach you," said Lily with a laugh. "And I can also do up some curtains and things to make it more homey. I'll ask Hannah to send my sewing machine, if Josephine will let it out of the house."

"That will save us money, too. We'll *economize*," said Katherine, rolling the word around in her mouth with delight.

"I'll teach you how to do that, too," said Lily, knowing that her friend had never wanted for a thing in her life.

"I'm happy to learn," said Katherine. "But I haven't shown you my surprise yet!"

Lily followed as Katherine practically dashed down the corridor that led to the flat's two bedrooms. At one of the doors, Katherine paused and gave her a grin. "Are you ready?"

Lily nodded, and Katherine threw open the door.

Lily stepped inside, taking it all in. There was a double bed neatly made with an ivory duvet. A tall wardrobe was pushed up against one of the walls with a dresser set with a mirror next to it. A chair upholstered in deep blue velvet sat next to the window, a little table close at hand that would be perfect for mugs of tea. But what made her stop was the desk.

It was wide and modern, with long, slim, unadorned legs. On top of its polished wooden top sat a stack of writing paper, a cup of pencils, and a fountain pen laid out just so. There was a shelf fitted above it, a dictionary already waiting for her.

"I thought you needed your own space to study," said Katherine. "I spoke to Ian and asked him what might be useful. He wasn't certain whether you would want a typewriter or not. I have a typewriter in my room, so you can always use that if you need—"

"Thank you," Lily said softly, putting an arm around her friend's waist and pulling her into a side hug. "It's perfect just the way it is."

"I want you to be happy," said Katherine, resting her head on Lily's shoulder.

"I am. I really, really am," she said, meaning every word of it.

"What do you want to do first?" asked Katherine.

"First, I'm going to unpack. I'll help you with some of those boxes in the corridor if you like. Then I'm going to call my old teacher and ask her if she'll take me on as a student to help me prepare for the entrance exams."

"Have you decided on a university?" asked Katherine.

The corner of her mouth edged up. "I thought Cambridge."

Katherine grinned. "Would that be because of a certain politics student?"

"I don't know what you mean to imply," she said primly. Then she shook her head. "I can't think about him yet."

"You need time and space," said Katherine.

"Yes." Not only had she been hurt, everything she'd known about herself had been turned upside down. She needed to find out who she was again above all else, and so she resolved to put Ian aside. For now.

"What will you do after you call your old teacher?" Katherine asked, settling down onto the bed.

"I'll go to Madame Benum and ask her if she'll take me on as an assistant."

"Oh, I'm sure she will. She has to," said Katherine.

"Then I think we should throw a party, but our sort of party. We'll invite the Imperfects if they can stand to take a day off from Royal Ascot this week."

"They're dying to come see the place," said Katherine.

"Good. I'll teach you how to roast a chicken just for the occasion," she said.

"And I'll take care of the cocktails. It'll be such fun," said Katherine with a laugh.

Lily looked around at her new home and smiled. "I think it really will be."

The party *was* fun. Katherine mixed the drinks far too strong, and they nearly forgot about the food, only saving the chicken from disaster at the last minute. The Imperfects celebrated the first proper dinner in the

Greville Place flat with two bottles of champagne that Doris had lifted from her father's wine cellar, and everyone woke up the next morning with a sore head.

That didn't stop Lily from launching into her first week of freedom with more enthusiasm that she'd felt in months. She made arrangements with Miss Hester for her lessons—future payments to be made upon Lily finding a job—and then marched over to Madame Benum's shop to ask for such employment. Madame asked her one question—"Are you a debutante any longer?"—and hired her on the spot.

Most of her time not spent at the shop, Lily was at her desk, but one afternoon a week and a half after settling in at the flat, she set aside her books early. She pulled on her best cotton summer dress printed all over with yellow and blue flowers on a white background and a full petticoat, and carefully did her makeup in her dresser mirror. Slipping on the light blue high heels she'd worn as a deb, she took a look at herself in the long mirror Katherine had hung on the back of the bathroom door.

"Perfect," she murmured.

Then she boarded the bus, thankful that the strike action was over, and headed to Mayfair.

She walked up to Hartford House, remembering the first time that she'd approached it. It had seemed so grand, such a symbol of the prestigious Hartford name. Now she understood that all of that gentility hid secrets just like any other family.

Lily rang the doorbell and waited. After a moment, the housekeeper, Mrs. Hastings, opened the door.

"Hello, is Mr. Hartford home?" she asked.

"He is not, Miss Nicholls," said Mrs. Hastings, moving to close the door.

"Are you certain? It's past five o'clock," she said.

"He hasn't arrived home yet," said Mrs. Hastings.

"Could I leave a message?" asked Lily.

The housekeeper's eyes flickered behind her, and Lily looked over her shoulder as a black sedan pulled up to the curb. A driver in uniform jumped out and opened the door. Mr. Hartford climbed out, briefcase in one hand and umbrella in the other. He looked every inch respectable, from his conservative gray suit to the gray hair brushed back from his temples. When he looked up and locked eyes with Lily, he froze.

She set her chin, refusing to look away. She would not be intimidated by this man who had bought eighteen years of her family's silence with his money. She had confronted Joanna, Josephine, and Grandmama. She had taken control of her life, and now she was deciding the shape it would take.

Ethan Hartford could not take any of that away from her.

She watched as her father slowly approached his own doorstep. He came to a stop a few feet from her.

"Mrs. Hastings, what is the meaning of this?" he snapped as Mrs. Hastings stammered an apology.

"I would like to speak with you," Lily said, moving her body between Mr. Hartford and the door.

"I'm a very busy man," he said.

"I would be happy to have this conversation here in the street if that would be more convenient for you," she said sweetly.

Mr. Hartford narrowed his eyes for a moment but then lifted his chin. "You can have five minutes."

"That's more than you've ever given me before," she said, stepping through the doorway and past the horrified Mrs. Hastings.

Mr. Hartford stormed past her, shoving his umbrella and briefcase at Mrs. Hastings. Lily followed, folding her hands in front of her to hide their trembling.

Mr. Hartford yanked open a door and stepped inside. It was a small sitting room that clearly was not in use in the summer, because the curtains were drawn tightly against the sunlight.

"How dare you come here," he raged as he turned around.

"How dare you rape a sixteen-year-old girl and then buy her silence," she said as calmly as she could.

His mouth gaped open like a fish yanked out of the water. "How dare you—"

"I have the letters from your solicitor to Josephine, as well as a letter from you," she lied, not knowing whether or not Joanna or Josephine had kept any correspondence over the years, but not caring.

The threat of it was good enough to terrify a man who cleaned up his messes with money. "I've spoken to Josephine and Joanna. I know what happened.

"You made a mistake, you know, in cutting Josephine off when I turned eighteen. She'd been sending money to Joanna for years, and Joanna was content and happy with the idea of staying quiet so long as it continued. But then the money was gone and she became desperate. Now I know as well."

Mr. Hartford's eyes widened, and for the first time she saw fear. "How much do you want?"

She jerked back in disgust. "I don't want your money."

"I won't acknowledge you," he warned.

"I cannot imagine anything more embarrassing than the entire world knowing that *you* are my father."

"Then why are you here?" he asked, worry starting to creep into his eyes.

Slowly she walked up to him until they were standing only a half a foot apart. Even with her height, she had to tilt her head back to look him square in the face, but that didn't matter. He smelled like fear.

"I don't know how many girls you did this to and how many children like me you've left behind, paying their families for their silence, but you'll never do this again because if I hear even the faintest rumor that you have, I'll release all of it to the papers. I have a close personal relationship with the Norman family—a family you and your friends no doubt have snubbed many times over, which is unwise, considering the number of papers Mr. Norman owns," she said.

"That would ruin me," he whimpered.

"It would ruin your family, too, but why would I care what happens to you and your family when you cared so little about mine?"

He backed up a step, his legs hitting a chair behind him so that he sat down hard in it. "I'm sorry," he whispered.

"No, you're not. You're sorry you were caught. But I'm sorry for you, a pathetic old man who is going to live for the rest of his life in fear of his own daughter."

He dropped his head into his hands. She took a moment to take in the sight of that—the great man brought low in his own home.

The door opened, Leana pushing through it while looking down at an invitation. "Papa, do you know a Mr.— You," she said, stopping at the sight of Lily.

"Leana, leave us alone," ordered her father, panic rising in his voice.

"What are you doing here?" Leana asked.

"I just came to settle some business that I had with Mr. Hartford. I'll show myself out." She hesitated. "Oh, Mr. Hartford, what we discussed earlier? It applies to the Bingham family as well. You would do well to remember that."

She walked around the father and daughter, her skirts swaying as she did. She was glad she came. She felt lighter, unburdened knowing that Mr. Hartford was frightened. It would have been satisfying to release the story to the papers immediately and bring him down for what he'd done to her family and any number of other families, but there would have been too much collateral damage. Leana, difficult as she was, didn't deserve to suffer for what her father had done.

The muffled fall of heels behind her slowed her progress, and when Leana cried, "Wait!" Lily stopped.

"What is all of this about? What business do you have with my father?" Leana asked.

"That's something you should ask him," she said.

Leana stared at her, as though searching her face for an answer. Lily could see the telltale smudges under her eyes that heralded the sleepless nights of a debutante that no amount of pancake could completely cover. She was glad for many reasons that she'd left that world behind.

"You never congratulated me on my engagement," said Leana.

"I will if that's what you want," she said.

"I have it all now. Jennifer called me Deb of the Year in the *Tatler*. I'm engaged. My ball is coming up this week," said Leana, but there was a distinct hint of misery in her voice.

"Are you happy?" she asked.

Leana looked away. "The Season isn't about being happy."

Lily took a step forward to press her hand on Leana's forearm. "I hope that one day you will be."

When Leana didn't say anything, she gave a final nod.

At the front door, she didn't wait for Mrs. Hastings. Instead, she twisted the knob herself and walked out into the sunshine of a late-summer afternoon feeling lighter than she had in weeks.

Epilogue

AUTUMN 1959

That's the last of them," said Lily, folding the box away and stacking it on top of the others.

Katherine looked up from the books she was alphabetizing. "That took less time than I thought."

"We were motivated. My lectures start soon, and you have to get back to London," she said.

"The magazine can wait," said Katherine.

"No, it can't," said Lily with a grin, knowing how much her friend loved the job she'd held for the last eight months as a writer for a small but growing magazine focused on current affairs. "I know how much you hate being away from it."

Katherine matched her smile. "I'd live there if they'd let me."

"Do not tell them that if you want any hope of a promotion in the future. You should leave them wondering at least a little bit about your loyalties."

Katherine laughed. "I won't."

"And you have to promise me that you'll go back to the flat to sleep. And that you'll have at least one decent meal a day," she said.

"The few that I can actually cook without burning them," Katherine muttered.

It was true that cooking lessons hadn't been a resounding success, but as soon as Lily had word that she'd won her place at Cambridge, she'd insisted that Katherine really try to master at least a half dozen recipes so that she wouldn't live solely on food eaten out in restaurants.

"Speaking of meals, should we have those sandwiches I packed?" she asked.

"Lily Nicholls, you cannot celebrate your first day at Cambridge with a sad, squashed sandwich you packed hours ago. I'm taking you out for a celebratory meal," said Katherine.

"You really don't have to do that," said Lily.

"I insist." Katherine checked her wristwatch. "Find your coat. We're going now."

After more than a year of living together, Lily had learned that there were times when it was impossible to argue with her friend, so she dutifully pulled on her navy jacket and picked up her handbag.

"Where should we go?" Lily asked as she locked up.

"A friend suggested a place by Newnham College."

She shot her friend a look. "You have friends at Cambridge?"

Katherine waved a hand about. "I have friends all over England. You just don't ask about them."

"You're better at keeping in touch with people than I am," Lily said. It was true, too. Other than the Imperfects, she'd seen very little of the debutante crowd since she'd left the Season. Katherine, however, was proving to be a champion at absorbing gossip and maintaining relationships. All traits that helped her be good at her job, Katherine insisted when Lily teased her about simply being nosy.

"Did you see that Leana Hartford was married to that awful Raymond Troy last week? *The Times* had the announcement, and *The Sketch* and the *Tatler* ran the photographs," said Katherine.

"No, I hadn't," she said.

"I still can't believe they were engaged at my coming-out party. It seems a world away. Does it bother you that you weren't invited to the wedding? I know you were close to her once," said Katherine.

"Actually, I was invited," said Lily as they made their way through the corridor past other girls moving into halls. "I declined, but I sent a gift."

Over the past months, with the distance of time, she'd come to pity Leana rather than resent her. The drinking, the possessiveness, the loneliness—it all now seemed sadder than she'd ever realized during the brief time that she'd known Leana.

"You were invited? I had no idea," said Katherine.

"I don't tell you everything," she said with a laugh.

"I know, and it's very distressing," said Katherine as they walked out into the courtyard.

"Lily!" a man's voice called out.

Lily frowned and turned toward the sound. Ian Bingham was leaning against the wall of the courtyard, hands in the pockets of a pair of gray trousers and a wide grin on his face. Her chest contracted at the sight of him. She hadn't seen him since the night of Katherine's party, but she'd thought of him. How could she not when a part of her had wanted every day to pick up the telephone and call him? But she hadn't let herself because there had been things she needed to do first. Decisions she had to make free from anyone else.

But to see him now . . .

"Ian," she breathed as he stepped in front of her. "What are you doing here?"

"I heard that you'd be coming up this autumn," he said.

"How?" she asked.

He nodded to Katherine. "I had a little bit of help."

"Katherine!"

Katherine shrugged. "It's obvious that you still care about him. I understand why you wanted to give yourself time, but now that you're here in Cambridge, why wouldn't you want to see him? It's been ages."

Katherine was right. She did want to see him, more than she could say.

"It's more complicated than that," she said, taking a step back. "If we were to become involved, it could be difficult for you. The Hartfords and I are not on good terms."

He stepped forward, reaching for her hand. "That doesn't matter."

"It does matter, Ian," she insisted, even though she couldn't let go of his hand.

"No, it doesn't, because I cut ties with Mr. Hartford. After Katherine told me that you'd decided to strike out on your own, I thought about what it was that I wanted. I realized that I want to be a scholar more than I want a comfortable life. I told him, and he cut me off," he said.

She stiffened. "And your family? I know you were worried—"

"Nothing. He didn't call in the debt or even try to stop me. I think Mr. Hartford was glad to see the back of me." He rocked on his heels with a grin. "You are now looking at a poor graduate student who is taking tutoring jobs to pay for his meals. I hope you don't mind."

"If you're happy, then I don't mind at all," she said.

"Good, because I don't plan to be a poor graduate student forever," he said. "I don't know what my life is going to look like, but I—"

Lily stopped him by going up on tiptoe and kissing him. She could feel him stiffen in shock for a moment, and then his hands were around her waist, pulling her to him and angling his mouth to deepen the kiss. She fell into it happily, wanting nothing more than this moment with this man.

When finally he broke away, his forehead against hers, she whispered, "Why don't we take things one step at a time and worry about what might happen in the future when we come to it?"

He stole another kiss. "I think that sounds like a grand idea. I want to take you to dinner tomorrow."

"If you asked, I would say yes," she said.

"Good. Then I'll come collect you at seven, but first . . ." He edged away from her slightly. "Katherine, I believe I owe *you* dinner."

Katherine looked up from the newspaper she'd produced from somewhere and folded it in half. "I should think you do. It's hungry work playing matchmaker."

Lily looped her right arm through Ian's and her left through Katherine's. "Lead the way."

Author's Note

I came to write *The Last Dance of the Debutante* because of my mother. In February 2020, just before the coronavirus pandemic sent Britain and so much of the rest of the world into lockdown, my friends Beatrice, Mary, and I took our mothers out for what would turn out to be a rollicking afternoon tea at Flemings hotel in Mayfair. Given that Mum had to travel up to London for the afternoon, it seemed only logical to have a bit of a browse beforehand at our favorite bookstore, Hatchards.

Laden with books, we stopped in a coffee shop to chat and kill some time before heading to tea. This was when Mum said the words every historical novelist likes to hear, "I think there's a book you should read. It might make a good novel."

It turned out the book was *Last Curtsey: The End of the Debutantes* by Fiona MacCarthy. One of Britain's great modern biographers, Mac-Carthy had been among the last debutantes presented to the Queen in 1958. The book was a wonderful record of a world that truly is no more, with rich, often wry descriptions of the preparations for the Season, the cocktail parties, balls, teas, luncheons, and more. MacCarthy writes lovingly about this time, even as she acknowledges what an old-fashioned thing it was in 1958 to still be presenting girls to society in hopes of them marrying well.

The Britain of the late 1950s was a country on the brink of change. It had come out of austerity after the war in the middle of the decade, and, as historian Dominic Sandbrook writes in his excellent look at Britain from 1956 to 1964, *Never Had It So Good: A History of Britain from Suez to the Beatles,* change was afoot:

> *It was in the mid-fifties . . . that rationing and austerity came to an end, consumer activity began rapidly escalating, the first commercial television channel was established, and a retreat from empire began in earnest.*

In 1958, there were signals of the approaching "Swinging Sixties" and the social changes that would come. More and more women began to enter the workforce, the youth culture that would dominate everything from fashion to music to film was beginning to blossom, and the shift of political power from the Conservative governments of Harold Macmillan and Alec Douglas-Home to the Labour government of Harold Wilson in 1964 was edging closer.

As I wrote in *The Last Dance of the Debutante,* the death of the Season was not immediate. Jennifer, the *Tatler's* venerated society columnist who is mentioned several times in this book, writes:

> *I want to say how heartily sick I am of reading . . . such statements such as the "Death of the débutante"—"No more débutantes"—"The end of the débutantes' seasons." This is rubbish. There are just as many débutantes coming out in 1959 as in any previous year.*

She was right, of course. Legend has it that Princess Margaret later said the presentation parties stopped because "every tart in London was getting in," but the definitive end of that tradition didn't stop the Season outright. While researching this book, I was lucky enough to speak to several former debs from 1958 and the early 1960s and learned not only that the Seasons endured for a time, but also that different debs had vastly different experiences. Vivacious, outgoing girls—and they were girls of their late teens and very early twenties—did well, even if they were not the prettiest, most well-off, or from the very best families. Those who were shyer struggled no matter where they fell in the stratified world of high society. Some made friends for life; others left their Season behind and never looked back.

How the Season looked for these girls also could vary wildly. One woman I spoke to had both a coming-out drinks party at a private members club and a ball at the Ritz. Another spoke of the many parties she attended, hopping into taxis to career around London from event to event and then on to a nightclub after. The one former deb I spoke to who curtsied to the Queen in 1958 was presented at court but did no other parts of the Season.

However, MacCarthy writes that by the late 1960s and certainly by the mid-1970s, the Season was, for all intents and purposes, done. In 1975, Jennifer, writing for *Queen*, had stopped listing debutante dances. Queen Charlotte's Ball ended in 1976, and although it has seen a very modest revival in modern London, it has never again approached the importance to high society that it once had.

I find the debs of 1958 and the Seasons after them fascinating because they sit at a junction of social change. Many of the debutantes from 1958 went on to become wives and mothers, as tradition dictated, but not all of them took conventional paths. Sally Croker-Poole married the Aga Khan in 1969, and Jennifer Murray (née Jennifer Mather) became the first woman to pilot a helicopter around the world. There are fashion models for Mary Quant and women who devoted themselves to saving Britain's historic manor houses—usually by finding enterprising ways to make the houses pay their way. Some women, like Lily, went to university and received their degrees. MacCarthy herself left her husband and became a writer for *The Guardian* before establishing herself as one of Britain's great biographers with her works about Eric Gill and William Morris.

In writing this book, I relied heavily on MacCarthy's history for a framework, but all of the debutantes are fictional. The only parties that were real events were the markers of the Season's calendar: the presentation parties, the Berkeley Dress Show, Queen Charlotte's Ball, the Boat Race, Royal Ascot, Henley, the Dublin Horse Show, and on and on.

However, the real debutante balls and cocktail parties that I read about provided the basis for the events of this book.

I've been asked several times while writing *The Last Dance of the Debutante* whether I was a deb. Being born and raised in an affluent part of Los Angeles, I had the opportunity. Although not socially significant to life in Los Angeles the way the Season was to British high society in 1958, the Junior League in my area did sponsor debutantes and hold a coming-out ball. I have a vague memory of a photograph of a half dozen or so girls in white dresses in our local paper. Years later, I mentioned to Mum that I would have liked to have been presented, mostly for the party and the big dress, as I suspect I would have found the preparations tiresome.* It turned out that a family friend who was a former Junior League deb had offered to sponsor me, but Mum had thought I would have balked at the idea. A missed opportunity, but perhaps for the best.

My closest encounter with a deb-like tradition was in the Pasadena Tournament of Roses Royal Court selections. Every year, approximately one thousand girls from all over the Pasadena area apply to be the queen and her court, who sit on top of a rose-covered float during the New Year's Day Rose Parade. This tradition is so pervasive that, nearly two decades later while standing in a queue at Christ Church in Oxford with visiting friends, I was describing the Royal Court selection, and a woman behind me said, "You must be from Pasadena. I did that."

All of my friends tried out for the Tournament of Roses Royal Court because when you were a high school senior in and around Pasadena, that's what you did. We were particularly excited because the reigning queen from the previous year had been from our high school. The deal was sweetened by the promise of a big party for all of the applicants and their dates, which meant the chance to meet boys from other schools in the area—a completely exotic, but exciting concept to us.

I made it past the initial round of interviews to the quarterfinals, but washed out. Two years later, my sister, Justine, made it to the semi-

---

* While I am good at following rules, I often bristle at being told directly what to do. Years after high school, I found out I had been demoted from homecoming queen to princess because I had chosen to go to a play rather than attend my high school's coronation dance, a story my best friend tells me sums up my priorities well.

finals. My mother still displays the photographs from our Royal Court tryouts in the house, which my brother-in-law finds hilarious, since neither of us have ever showed an interest in beauty pageants before or after.

I've always been drawn to writing about women, especially during times of major social change. Some, such as my last book, *The Last Garden in England*, have focused on women during times of war and all of the opportunities—positive and negative—that have come with that. Although the story of Lily, Katherine, and the other Imperfects is set in more glamorous surrounds than a World War II convalescent hospital, I hope it highlights one piece of the changing story of women in Britain during the twentieth century.

Acknowledgments

Many people worked incredibly hard to bring this book to readers. In particular, I would like to thank my agent, Emily Sylvan Kim, and my editors, Hannah Braaten and Kate Dresser, who both shaped this book. I would also like to thank Jennifer Bergstrom, Aimée Bell, Michelle Podberezniak, Abby Zidle, Andrew Nguyen, Molly Gregory, Caroline Pallotta, Allison Green, Iris Chen, Christine Masters, Jamie Putorti, Kaitlyn Snowden, Sally Marvin, Sammi Sontag, Paul O'Halloran, Cordia Leung, Fiona Sharp, Athena Reekers, Gregory Tilney, and the entire team at Gallery Books and Simon & Schuster Canada. I would also be remiss in not mentioning Danielle Noe.

Several former debutantes were kind enough to give me a bit of their time and share their memories with me. Thank you, Anthea St. Aubin d'Ancey, Sue, and Iones. And a special thank-you to Sophie (and Lettuce!) for all your help in the early stages of research.

Thank you to Alexis Anne, Lindsay Emory, Mary Chris Escobar, Laura von Holt, Alexandra Haughton, Kristin Harmel, Mary Shannon, Beatrice Bazell, Jemima Lovett, Sonia Moghe, Katherine Ingram, Christy Cloninger, and Sean Warlick. A particular thank-you to Ian Stephens and Shrey Agarwal, who lent me their names for this book.

Thank you to my incredible family: Mum, Dad, Justine, and Mark.

(But mostly Nora.) Your support and encouragement mean the world to me and I could not write without it.

Thank you to all of the reviewers, bloggers, Bookstagrammers, and BookTubers who have read and spread the word about my books. I cannot express my appreciation enough.

And finally—and most importantly—thank you to all of my readers. Whether this is the first of my books you've read or you're a dedicated member of the Ask an Author crew, it is a joy and a privilege to be able to write stories for you.